Newcastle
City Council

Newcastle Libraries and Information Service

 0845 002 0336

Due for return	Due for return	Due for return

Please return this item to any of Newcastle's Libraries by the last date shown above. If not requested by another customer the loan can be renewed, you can do this by phone, post or in person.
Charges may be made for late returns.

How I Became a Holy Mother

Works by Ruth Prawer Jhabvala

NOVELS
To Whom She Will *(published in the USA as* Amrita*)*
The Nature of Passion
Esmond in India
The Householder
Get Ready for Battle
A Backward Place
A New Dominion *(published in the USA as* Travelers*)*
Heat and Dust
In Search of Love and Beauty
Out of India
Three Continents
Poet and Dancer
Shards of Memory
My Nine Lives

SHORT STORIES
Like Birds, Like Fishes
A Stronger Climate
An Experience of India
East Into Upper East: Plain Tales from New York and
New Delhi
How I Became a Holy Mother and other stories

How I Became A Holy Mother

Ruth Prawer Jhabvala

FOREWORD BY FRANCIS KING

CAPUCHIN CLASSICS

CAPUCHIN CLASSICS
LONDON

How I Became a Holy Mother
First published in 1976
This edition published by Capuchin Classics 2008

© Ruth Prawer Jhabvala 1976

Capuchin Classics
128 Kensington Church Street, London W8 4BH
Telephone: +44 (0)20 7221 7166
Fax: +44 (0)20 7792 9288
E-mail: info@capuchin-classics.co.uk
www.capuchin-classics.co.uk

Châtelaine of Capuchin Classics: Emma Howard

ISBN: 978-0-9557312-3-5

Contents

Foreword

At a literary party in the 1950s I found myself standing next to a small, olive-skinned woman in an elegant sari. Earlier I had heard her speaking to our hostess in what had seemed to be a faintly Indian accent. Since on both sides of my family I have connections with India going back for generations, my conversational opening was: 'What part of India do you come from?' With a small smile, the woman replied 'I don't *come* from any part of India. I merely live there. In Delhi,' she added. She smiled again, head uptilted, clearly enjoying my amazement. 'What took you there?' She replied that what had motivated her had not been a romantic impulse or a deliberate desire to learn about a different culture, but merely the chance that, as a student at Queen Mary College, London, she had met and fallen in love with an Indian student, Cyrus Jhabvala, later to become a distinguished architect, and so had married him. Gradually, in the ensuing conversation, I realised that this woman was Ruth Prawer Jhabvala, a writer whom, even then when she was far less famous than now, I had already come to admire.

Mine has always been the perhaps now old-fashioned view that one of the essential gifts for a novelist is the ability to know precisely what it is like to be someone other than oneself. Ruth Prawer Jhabvala possesses not merely that ability but also the rarer ability to *become* someone else. She was born into a well-to-do cultivated, happy German-Jewish family in Cologne in 1927. But in 1939 an inevitable decision had to be taken: to survive, father, mother, Ruth and a brother who eventually became an Oxford Professor of German Language and Literature, must seek refuge from the Nazis in England. With the adaptability of a child, Ruth was soon indistinguishable from any other Jewish girl in North London.

These two transformations from German into English and

English into Indian, were to be followed by a third. When, in the early Seventies I met her at another literary party, she spoke of her decision, soon to be implemented, to quit India for the States. Having just myself returned from India, I had been speaking to her of the conflicting emotions that the vast country had aroused in me: on the one hand an intense pleasure in its scenic beauty and on the other a horror at the suffering insistently visible all around me. I remember that I told her that, in order to stifle that horror, I made a deliberate decision to take only an aesthetic view of everything that I saw. At that she demanded almost angrily: 'But can you? *Can* you?' She went on to tell me how she found herself more and more unwilling to go out from her comfortable Delhi flat into streets teeming with human misery. We agreed that the most terrible aspect of this misery was the realisation that to attempt to alleviate it was like attempting to bail out a sinking boat with a teaspoon. Children and dogs besieged one. If one gave a scrap of bread to one of the former or a small coin to one of the latter, then all the rest pursued one in a pack. At least the dogs kept their distance. But the desperate hands of the children plucked at one's sleeve or clawed at one's shoulder.

After she had moved to the States, she produced more remarkable books and, having become friend and confidante of the highly successful film partnership of James Ivory and Ismail Merchant, also wonderfully professional scripts for such features as *Shakespeare Wallah, Autobiography of a Princess,* and *The Europeans.* But I think that, despite the high artistic quality of everything that she has written, she will, like Kipling, be above all remembered for her Indian tales. Some critics have seen her essentially as an outsider looking in on the exotic world to which her marriage transported her. But for me she seems miraculously to have become an insider from the first moment when she arrived in so dauntingly alien a civilisation.

Certain types constantly recur in her stories. Of these, among her Indian men there is, first and foremost, the swami, powerful both in physique and personality, who dominates his followers and drains them of psychological and physical energy in order to charge his rampant egotism. Her attitude to such men is complex – is their authority truly supernatural or is it merely derived from their overweening personalities? In contrast her Indian women, whether wives treated as mere chattels by their husbands or mistresses treated with capricious generosity by their elderly patrons, are pathetically vulnerable. Her English males tend to be conventional, complacent, even feeble creatures, whose wives abandon them either for Indian lovers or for an itinerant life of seeking in vain for spiritual enlightenment.

Jhabvala has recorded that in writing about India she is 'always attempting to present India to myself, in the hope of so giving myself some kind of foothold... I describe the Indian scene not for its own sake but for mine.' As a result of this, she rarely refers explicitly to a multitude of political, social and moral problems. But just as a diagnosis of an illness can be reached by examination of a drop of blood or of a tiny area of tissue, so a page or even merely a paragraph of one of her stories can provide a diagnosis of what is amiss with the beautiful but often frightening world that is her subject.

Having reread these stories – so observant, so humane, so elegantly told and so beautifully crafted – I came to the conclusion that, if I had been on the jury that decided to give the Nobel Prize to an octogenarian woman novelist who in her youth settled in England from abroad, then my vote would unhesitatingly have gone not to Doris Lessing, fine novelist though she is, but to an even finer one, Ruth Prawer Jhabvala.

Francis King
London, May 2008

Introduction: Myself in India

I have lived in India for most of my adult life. My husband is Indian and so are my children. I am not, and less so every year.

India reacts very strongly on people. Some loathe it, some love it, most do both. There is a special problem of adjustment for the sort of people who come today, who tend to be liberal in outlook and have been educated to be sensitive and receptive to other cultures. But it is not always easy to be sensitive and receptive to India: there comes a point where you have to close up in order to protect yourself. The place is very strong and often proves too strong for European nerves. There is a cycle that Europeans – by Europeans I mean all Westerners, including Americans – tend to pass through. It goes like this: first stage, tremendous enthusiasm – everything Indian is marvellous; second stage, everything Indian not so marvellous; third stage, everything Indian abominable. For some people it ends there, for others the cycle renews itself and goes on. I have been through it so many times that now I think of myself as strapped to a wheel that goes round and round and sometimes I'm up and sometimes I'm down. When I meet other Europeans, I can usually tell after a few moments' conversation at what stage of the cycle they happen to be. Everyone likes to talk about India, whether they happen to be loving or loathing it. It is a topic on which a lot of things can be said, and on a variety of aspects – social, economic, political, philosophical: it makes fascinating viewing from every side.

However, I must admit that I am no longer interested in India. What I am interested in now is myself in India – which sometimes, in moments of despondency, I tend to think of as my survival in India. I had better say straightaway that the reason why I live in India is because my strongest human ties are here. If I hadn't married an Indian, I don't think I would ever have come here for I am not attracted – or used not to be attracted – to the things that usually bring people to India. I know I am the wrong type of person to live here. To stay and endure, one should have a mission and a cause, to be patient, cheerful, unselfish, strong. I am a central European with an English education and a deplorable tendency to constant self-analysis. I am irritable and have weak nerves.

The most salient fact about India is that it is very poor and very backward. There are so many other things to be said about it but this must remain the basis of all of them. We may praise Indian democracy, go into raptures over Indian music, admire Indian intellectuals – but whatever we say, not for one moment should we lose sight of the fact that a very great number of Indians never get enough to eat. Literally that: from birth to death they never for one day cease to suffer from hunger. *Can* one lose sight of that fact? God knows, I've tried. But after seeing what one has to see here every day, it is not really possible to go on living one's life the way one is used to. People dying of starvation in the streets, children kidnapped and maimed to be sent out as beggars – but there is no point in making a catalogue of the horrors with which one lives, *on* which one lives, as on the back of an animal. Obviously, there has to be some adjustment.

There are several ways. The first and best is to be a strong person who plunges in and does what he can as a doctor or social worker. I often think that perhaps this is the only condition under which Europeans have any right to be here. I know several people like that. They are usually attached to some mission. They work very hard and stay very cheerful. Every few years they are sent on home leave. Once I met such a person – a woman doctor – who had just returned from her first home leave after being out here for twelve years. I asked her: but what does it feel like to go back after such a long time? How do you manage to adapt yourself? She didn't understand. This question which was of such tremendous import to me – how to adapt oneself to the differences between Europe and India – didn't mean a thing to her. It simply didn't matter. And she was right, for in view of the things she sees and does every day, the delicate nuances of one's own sensibilities are best forgotten.

Another approach to India's basic conditions is to accept them. This seems to be the approach favoured by most Indians. Perhaps it has something to do with their belief in reincarnation. If things are not to your liking in this life, there is always the chance that in your next life everything will be different. It appears to be a consoling thought for both rich and poor. The rich man stuffing himself on pilao can do so with an easy conscience because he knows he has earned this privilege by his good conduct in previous lives; and the poor man can watch him with some degree of equanimity for he knows that next time round it may well be *he* who will be digging into that pilao while the other will be crouching outside the door with an empty stomach. However, this path of acceptance is not open to you if you don't have a belief in reincarnation ingrained within you. And if you don't accept, then what can you do? Sometimes one wants just to run away and go to a place where everyone has enough to eat and clothes to wear and a home fit to live in. But even when you get there, can you ever forget? Having once seen the sights in India, and the way it has been ordained that people must live out their lives, nowhere in the world can ever be all that good to be in again.

None of this is what I wanted to say. I wanted to concentrate only on myself in India. But I could not do so before indicating the basis on which everyone who comes here has to live. I have a nice house, I do my best to live in an agreeable way. I shut all my windows, I let down the blinds, I turn on the air-conditioner;

I read a lot of books, with a special preference for the great masters of the novel. All the time I know myself to be on the back of this great animal of poverty and backwardness. It is not possible to pretend otherwise. Or rather, one does pretend, but retribution follows. Even if one never rolls up the blinds and never turns off the air-conditioner, something is bound to go wrong. People are not meant to shut themselves up in rooms and pretend there is nothing outside.

Now I think I am drawing nearer to what I want to be my subject. Yes, something is wrong: I am not happy this way. I feel lonely, shut in, shut off. It is my own fault. I should go out more and meet people and learn what is going on. All right, so I am not a doctor nor a social worker nor a saint nor at all a good person; then the only thing to do is to try and push that aspect of India out of sight and turn to others. There are many others. I live in the capital where so much is going on. The winter is one round of parties, art exhibitions, plays, music and dance recitals, visiting European artistes: there need never be a dull moment. Yet all my moments are dull. Why? It is my own fault, I know. I can't quite explain it to myself but somehow I have no heart for these things here. Is it because all the time underneath I feel the animal moving? But I have decided to ignore the animal. I wish to concentrate only on modern, Westernized India, and on modern, well-off, cultured Westernized Indians.

Let me try and describe a Westernized Indian woman with whom I ought to have a lot in common and whose company I ought to enjoy. She has been to Oxford or Cambridge or some smart American college. She speaks flawless, easy, colloquial English with a charming lilt of an accent. She has a degree in economics or political science or English literature. She comes from a good family. Her father may have been an ICS officer or some other high-ranking government official; he too was at Oxford or Cambridge, and he and her mother travelled in Europe in pre-war days. They have always lived a Western-style life, with Western food and an admiration for Western culture. The daughter now tends rather to frown on this. She feels one should be more deeply Indian, and with this end in view, she wears handloom saris and traditional jewellery and has painted an abnormally large vermilion mark on her forehead. She is interested in Indian classical music and dance. If she is rich enough – she may have married into one of the big Indian business houses – she will become a patroness of the arts and hold delicious parties on her lawn on summer nights. All her friends are there – and she has so many, both Indian and European, all interesting people – and trays of iced drinks are carried round by servants in uniform and there is intelligent conversation and then there is a superbly arranged buffet supper and more intelligent conversation, and then the crown of the evening: a famous Indian maestro performing on the sitar. The guests recline on carpets and cushions on the lawn. The sky sparkles with stars and the languid summer air is fragrant with jasmine. There are many pretty girls reclining against bolsters; their faces are melancholy for the music is stirring their hearts, and sometimes they sigh with yearning and happiness and look down at their pretty toes (adorned with a tiny silver toe-ring) peeping out from under the sari. Here is Indian life and culture at its highest and best. Yet, with all that, it need not be thought that our hostess has forgotten her Western education. Not at all. In her one may see the best of East and West combined. She is interested in a great variety of topics and can hold her own in any discussion. She loves to exercise her emancipated mind, and whatever the subject of conversation – economics, or politics, or literature, or film – she has a well-formulated opinion on it and knows how to express herself. How lucky for me if I could have such a person for a friend! What enjoyable, lively times we two could have together!

In fact, my teeth are set on edge if I have to listen to her for more than five minutes – yes, even though everything she says is so true and in line with the most advanced opinions of today. But when she says it, somehow, even though I know the words to be true, they ring completely false. It is merely lips moving and sounds coming out: it doesn't mean anything, nothing of what she says (though she says it with such conviction, skill, and charm) is of the least importance to her. She is only making conversation in the way she knows educated women have to make conversation. And so it is with all of them. Everything they say, all that lively conversation round the buffet table, is not prompted by anything they really feel strongly about but by what they think they ought to feel strongly about. This applies not only to subjects which are naturally alien to them – for instance, when they talk oh so solemnly! and with such profound intelligence! of Godard and Beckett and ecology – but when they talk about themselves too. They know Modern India to be an important subject and they have a lot to say about it: but though they themselves *are* Modern India, they don't look at themselves, they are not conditioned to look at themselves except with the eyes of foreign experts whom they have been taught to respect. And while they are fully aware of India's problems and are up on all the statistics and all the arguments for and against nationalization and a socialistic pattern of society, all the time it is as if they were talking about some *other* place – as if it were a subject for debate – an abstract subject – and not a live animal actually moving under their feet.

But if I have no taste for the company of these Westernized Indians, then what else is there? Other Indians don't really have a social life, not in our terms; the whole conception of such a life is imported. It is true that Indians are gregarious in so far as they hate to be alone and always like to sit together in groups; but these groups are clan-units – it is the family, or clan-members, who gather together and enjoy each other's company. And again, their conception of enjoying each other's company is different from ours. For them it is enough just to *be* together; there are long stretches of silence in which everyone stares into space. From time to time there is a little spurt of conversation, usually on some commonplace everyday subject such as rising prices, a forthcoming marriage, or a troublesome neighbour. There is no attempt at exercising the mind or testing one's wits against those of others: the pleasure lies only in having other familiar people around and enjoying the air together and looking forward to the next meal. There is actually something very restful about this mode of social intercourse and certainly holds more pleasure than the synthetic social life led by Westernized Indians. It is also more adapted to the Indian climate which invites one to be absolutely relaxed in mind and body, to do nothing, to think nothing, just to feel, to *be*. I have in fact enjoyed sitting around like that for hours on end. But there is something in me that after some time revolts against such lassitude. I can't just *be*! Suddenly I jump up and rush away out of that contented circle. I want to do something terribly difficult like climbing a mountain or reading the *Critique of Pure Reason*. I feel tempted to bang my head against the wall as if to wake myself up. Anything to prevent myself from being sucked down into that bog of passive, intuitive being. I feel I cannot, I must not allow myself to live this way.

Of course there are other Europeans more or less in the same situation as myself. For instance, other women married to Indians. But I hesitate to seek them out. People suffering from the same disease do not usually make good company for one another. Who is to listen to whose complaints? On the other hand, with what enthusiasm I welcome visitors from abroad. Their physical presence alone is a pleasure to me. I love to see their fresh complexions, their red cheeks that speak of wind and rain; and I like to see their clothes and their shoes, to admire the texture of these solid European materials and the industrial skills that have gone into making them. I also like to hear the way in which these people speak. In some strange way their accents, their intonations are redolent to me of the places from which they have come, so that as voices rise and fall I hear in them the wind stirring in English trees or a mild brook murmuring through a summer wood. And apart from these sensuous pleasures, there is also the pleasure of hearing what they have to say. I listen avidly to what is said about people I know or have heard of and about new plays and restaurants and changes and fashions. However, neither the subject nor my interest in it is inexhaustible; and after that, it is my turn. What about India? Now they want to hear, but I don't want to say. I feel myself growing sullen. I don't want to talk about India. There is nothing I can tell them. There is nothing they would understand. However, I do begin to talk, and after a time even to talk with passion. But everything I say is wrong. I listen to myself with horror; they too listen with horror. I want to stop and reverse, but I can't. I want to cry out, this is not what I mean! You are listening to me in entirely the wrong context! But there is no way of explaining the context. It would take too long, and anyway what is the point? It's such a small, personal thing. I fall silent. I have nothing more to say. I turn my face and want them to go away.

So I am back again alone in my room with the blinds drawn and the air-conditioner on. Sometimes, when I think of my life, it seems to have contracted to this one point and to be concentrated in this one room, and it is always a very hot, very long afternoon when the air-conditioner has failed. I cannot describe the *oppression* of such afternoons. It is a physical oppression – heat pressing down on me and pressing in the walls and the ceiling and congealing together with time which has stood still and will never move again. And it is not only those two – heat and time – that are laying their weight on me but behind them, or held within them, there is something more which I can only describe as the whole of India. This is hyperbole, but I need hyperbole to express my feelings about those countless afternoons spent over what now seem to me countless years in a country for which I was not born. India swallows me up and now it seems to me that I am no longer in my room but in the white-hot city streets under a white-hot sky; people cannot live in such heat so everything is deserted – no, not quite, for here comes a smiling leper in a cart being pushed by another leper; there is also the carcase of a dog and vultures have swooped down on it. The river has dried up and stretches in miles of flat cracked earth; it is not possible to make out where the river ceases and the land begins for this too is as flat, as cracked, as dry as the river-bed and stretches on for ever. Until we come to a jungle in which wild beasts live, and then there are ravines and here live outlaws with the hearts of wild beasts. Sometimes they make raids into the villages and they rob and burn and mutilate and kill for sport. More mountains and these are very, very high and now it is no longer hot but terribly cold, we are in snow and ice and here is Mount Kailash on which sits Siva the Destroyer wearing a necklace of human skulls. Down in the plains they are worshipping him. I can see them from here – they are doing something strange – what is it? I draw nearer. Now I can see. They are killing a boy. They hack him to pieces and now they bury the pieces into the foundations dug for a new bridge. There is a priest with them who is quite naked except for ash smeared all over him; he is reciting some holy verses over the foundations, to bless and propitiate.

I am using these exaggerated images in order to give some idea of how intolerable India – the idea, the sensation of it – can become. A point is reached where one must escape, and if one can't do so physically, then some other way must be found. And I think it is not only Europeans but Indians too who feel themselves compelled to seek refuge from their often unbearable environment. Here perhaps less than anywhere else is it possible to believe that this world, this life, is all there is for us, and the temptation to write it off and substitute something more satisfying becomes overwhelming. This brings up the question whether religion is such a potent force in India because life is so terrible, or is it the other way round – is life so terrible because, with the eyes of the spirit turned elsewhere, there is no incentive to improve its quality? Whichever it is, the fact remains that the eyes of the spirit *are* turned elsewhere, and it really is true that God seems more present in India than in other places. Every morning I wake up at 3 a.m. to the sound of someone pouring out his spirit in devotional song; and then at dawn the temple bells ring, and again at dusk, and conch-shells are blown, and there is the smell of incense and of the slightly overblown flowers that are placed at the feet of smiling, pink-cheeked idols. I read in the papers that the Lord Krishna has been reborn as the son of a weaver woman in a village somewhere in Madhya Pradesh. On the banks of the river there are figures in meditation and one of them may turn out to be the teller in your bank who cashed your cheque just a few days ago; now he is in the lotus pose and his eyes are turned up and he is in ecstasy. There are ashrams full of little old half-starved widows who skip and dance about, they giggle and play hide and seek because they are Krishna's milkmaids. And over all this there is a sky of enormous proportions – so much larger than the earth on which you live, and often so incredibly-beautiful, an unflawed unearthly blue by day, all shining with stars at night, that it is difficult to believe that something grand and wonderful beyond the bounds of human comprehension does not emanate from there.

I love listening to Indian devotional songs. They seem pure like water drawn from a well; and the emotions they express are both beautiful and easy to understand because the imagery employed is so human. The soul crying out for God is always shown as the beloved yearning for the lover in an easily recognizable way ('I wait for Him. Do you hear His step? He has come'). I feel soothed when I hear such songs and all my discontentment falls away. I see that everything I have been fretting about is of no importance at all because all that matters is this promise of eternal bliss in the

Lover's arms. I become patient and good and feel that everything is good. Unfortunately this tranquil state does not last for long, and after a time it again seems to me that nothing is good and neither am I. Once somebody said to me: 'Just see, how sweet is the Indian soul that can see God in a cow!' But when I try to assume this sweetness, it turns sour: for, however much I may try and fool myself, whatever veils I may try, for the sake of peace of mind, to draw over my eyes, it is soon enough clear to me that the cow *is* a cow, and a very scrawny, underfed, diseased one at that And then I feel that I want to keep this knowledge, however painful it is, and not exchange it for some other that may be true for an Indian but can never quite become that for me.

And here, it seems to me, I come to the heart of my problem. To live in India and be at peace one must to a very considerable extent become Indian and adopt Indian attitudes, habits, beliefs, assume if possible an Indian personality. But how is this possible? And even if it were possible – without cheating oneself – would it be desirable? Should one want to try and become something other than what one is? I don't always say no to this question. Sometimes it seems to me how pleasant it would be to say yes and give in and wear a sari and be meek and accepting and see God in a cow. Other times it seems worthwhile to be defiant and European and – all right, be crushed by one's environment, but all the same have made some attempt to remain standing. Of course, this can't go on indefinitely and in the end I'm bound to lose – if only at the point where my ashes are immersed in the Ganges to the accompaniment of Vedic hymns, and then who will say that I have not truly merged with India?

I do sometimes go back to Europe. But after a time I get bored there and want to come back here. I also find it hard now to stand the European climate. I have got used to intense heat and seem to need it.

A Bad Woman

It was a tiny house in an outer suburb of Bombay. There was a tiny garden in front and then a porch leading to a passage from which opened two rooms, one on the left and one on the right; the passage ended in a tiny courtyard and the courtyard in a tiny kitchen; that was all. Chameli had been enchanted with the place when he had first brought her there. She thought she would be very happy there (actually, she could be happy anywhere, she had that sort of temperament). She kept everything bright and clean, grew flowers, kept a nightingale in a cage, sewed curtains on a little sewing-machine Sethji had brought for her, and sang all the time. That was during the first few weeks; after that she became a little melancholy.

It was being so alone. She didn't mind being by herself in the house when Sethji had gone back to Delhi; she wasn't afraid, not even in the nights. But it was having no one at all to talk to – no friendly faces around her, no friendly neighbours – that was so depressing. Even during the worst time of her life (the two years of her marriage), she had always had friends and neighbours to gossip and giggle with, so that she had managed to snatch some lighthearted moments in the midst of all her sufferings. But here the people living around her were very unfriendly. Sometimes, true, one or two of the women might drop in on her, and although she was always pleased when they did so, she noticed that they did not come in a nice neighbourly spirit; she couldn't quite explain it to herself, but somehow it was almost as if they had come to spy on her, they looked round them so carefully and asked her pointed questions and exchanged looks with one another. And if she invited them to sit down and have something, they either refused or, if they accepted, sat on the very edge of the chair as if they were afraid of getting themselves dirty and tasted anything she gave them in a slow, experimental way, taking tiny sips or bites and then looking up into the air as if they were waiting for something bad to happen to them.

But even if they had been willing to be friendly with her, she would never have been able to gossip with them the way she had done with her Delhi neighbours. There, in Delhi, they had all spoken the same kind of Hindi: courtly, often oblique, shot through with little coquetries and pleasantries which were implicit in the language itself. But here they spoke mainly Gujerati or Marathi, neither of which Chameli could understand, and whatever Hindi they knew was so crude, so lacking in all those refinements which in Delhi came natural as the movements of the tongue, that it made her wince to have to listen to it. Her servant, a sour skinny middle-aged woman called Gangubai, did not speak any Hindi – or, if she did, pretended not to, so that there was no communication between them at all, apart from the contemptuous grunts Gangubai let out in her mistress's direction from time to time during the course of her work and unfailingly when it was finished and she was ready to go home, thrusting her feet back into the cast-off shoes which had been waiting for her outside the kitchen door.

Chameli wrote letters to Sethji in Delhi: 'When will you come to me? I look out of the window and wait for you. The hours pass slowly. Please bring some Delhi halwa. Please come.' There was no answer, so she wrote more letters and the reply came: 'Business is urgent here, when it is less pressing I will start. The heat is great and the mango crop has failed, price of mangoes Rs.4 a dozen, no one can afford. It is better if you don't write any more. I am well and happy.' So she stopped writing and waited. She paced around the tiny house, and sometimes she rocked herself on the rocking-chair on the porch and looked out with sad eyes at the people passing who often did not greet her, even those who had been to visit her. Three times a day she turned on the radio to listen to her favourite programme of music from the files, and she poked her finger through the bars of her nightingale's cage and talked to it because there was no one else.

Then Sethji came, and she talked and talked and talked and didn't stop, and she ran backwards and forwards serving him, cooking for him, massaging him, doing everything she possibly could think of for him, talking all the time even though she knew he wasn't listening much, till he fell asleep and then she sat by him and fanned her hand over him to keep the flies away. He took his teeth out when he slept, his mouth was open, snores came out of it, and his big jowls quivered. She looked at him and, in spite of herself, she sighed. A tear came out of her eye and splashed on to his cheek; she wiped it away with her hand and when she did so, her fingers lingering over his soft loose flesh, more tears came, more and more, raining out of her eyes.

But when he left her to go home to Delhi, she thought her heart would break. She wanted to cry out to him, take me with you! to fall at his feet and implore him. But she didn't. Instead she kept quite still, didn't say one word, held her face averted so that he wouldn't be able to see the expression on it. She knew how impossible it was for him to take her back to Delhi, where all his family was and everyone knew him and he was a big man; and how grateful she ought to be to him for bringing her here to Bombay, keeping her and hiring this pretty house for her and a servant to go with it. And she *was* grateful – without him where would she be? How would she eat? That was why she kept silent and didn't utter one word of complaint as she watched him leave. He was very cheerful, hummed a little tune and pinched her breast behind the door before waddling down the garden path in his clean white dhoti, his umbrella in one hand and the little bundle of provisions she had prepared for his journey in the other. She watched his taxi drive away, and it was only when it was quite out of sight and for a few minutes afterwards to make sure he hadn't forgotten something and wasn't coming back, that she left the porch and went into her bedroom, there to lie across her bed and give vent to her feelings.

She could no longer bear to stay all day in the house and began to go out for walks by herself. It was something at least to get ready for these walks, wear a pretty sari, powder on her face, flowers in her hair, and walk daintily down the road holding a parasol over herself to shield her against the sun. She walked down to the sea. The sand got into her sandals and she took them off and walked with them in her hand, up and down the beach. But she didn't enjoy it. It wasn't like walking by the river in Delhi where there was always something interesting going on, even if it was only the buffaloes wallowing in the water or the holy men doing yoga on the bank. The sea was very boring: nothing but waves rolling, one after another, all the time without stop, wave after foolish wave. What for? Nevertheless she came back the next day, and the next, and walked up and down, watching the waves. It was better than sitting in the house, having to hear Gangubai's snorts of contempt and look out at the women passing by on the street and wish they would come in and talk to her, or at least greet her.

It was on the beach that she first met Ravi. It seemed he came there every day; she saw him sitting there for hours and hours on the same spot on the beach, all by himself. He had some books and sometimes he read them, but most of the time he simply stared out at the sea or lay on his stomach and idly combed mounds of sand together. He seemed as bored as she was. She began to look out for him and, after some time, realized that he had begun to look out for her too, or at least to be aware of her. From then on it was only a matter of time before they came together. That it took as long as it did was more his fault than hers. She had been ready to smile at him for some time, but whenever their eyes had been about to meet, he would at the last moment look away and scowl.

That scowl of his was his most characteristic expression. He looked on everyone, on everything, on the whole world with displeasure. It took about a week before he stopped scowling at Chameli, another week before he smiled. But then, what radiance there was in that smile, what depths of pleasure and of love. And she smiled back in the same way. Never had she had such feelings for anyone. She was fond of Sethji, true, but he was thirty years older than she was; whereas Ravi was of her own age and when they were not lovers together then they were friends, or brother and sister, or simply accomplices against all the other people in the world who were all old and knew nothing of the feelings that lived in Chameli and Ravi.

Now the house was as it should always have been, alive and gay. The flowers she grew in pots began to bloom, the nightingale to sing; she washed the curtains, polished the furniture, tried out new recipes, rocked herself on the veranda and smiled at all the women who walked by and didn't greet her. She showered presents of cloth on Gangubai who examined them carefully, holding them up to the light and then folding them away for herself with her usual grunt of contempt. Chameli just laughed at her and, when she left at the end of the day, locked the door behind her with a final laugh and then danced back into the house to bathe and dress and scent herself. When it was dark, Ravi came. They rolled around on the bed and played like children before becoming serious like lovers, and then they slept and then they ate and then it was dawn and time for Ravi to creep out of the house and run home to his. After he had gone, she stood by the window and smiled to herself, slowly braiding her hair; she felt heavy and tired though postponing the delicious moment before she would sink on to the bed and drop instantly like a stone into a dreamless sleep from which she would only wake when it was afternoon and not so long to wait before he came again.

Ravi was a student, but after he met Chameli, he did no more studying. Not that he had done very much before. The hours she had seen him lounging on the beach were hours in which he was supposed to have been at his classes; but he found them very tedious, and moreover regarded them as useless. He was not interested in passing any examinations, although his family had high hopes for him and wanted him to become something distinguished like a lawyer or a gazetted government officer. Ravi saw nothing pleasing in such a prospect; on the contrary, it disgusted him, both for its own sake and because it was his family who wanted it. It was a principle with him that anything his family might want, he would want the opposite; they for him stood for everything that was bad in a world which, in any case, was rotten to the core. Chameli was shocked by this attitude of his towards his family. She had always been very fond of her own family, her mother and her father and everyone, and still often shed tears because she could no longer go to them. He laughed at her – 'what have they ever done for you?' he asked her. This seemed a strange question to her because the answer to it was so obvious: they had brought her into this world, had looked after her and fed her when she was small and helpless and could not fend for herself. She loved and honoured them for that. What came after was not their fault – who was to know that her husband would turn out the way he did? Her mother too had cried bitterly over her daughter's misfortune, but what could she do? What could anyone do? It was fate. 'And now?' Ravi asked her, fiercely. 'Where are they now?' She stroked his angry face. How childish he was, how little he knew of life and the world. He pushed her hand away and demanded an answer: as if there was an answer anyone could give outright like that in words. He gripped her arms and shook her: 'Now you're a bad woman, so they're too good to know you, is that it? Is it? Is it?' His fingers dug deep into her flesh so that tears sprang into her eyes and she cried out in pain. The moment she did so, he gathered her close into his arms, as close as he could, muttering through clenched teeth, 'You're mine, mine, mine,' and now there were tears in his eyes too.

But though she avoided the subject of her own family, she often returned to talking to him about his. She felt she would have failed in her duty if she did not try to inspire him with some affection for those who had given him birth and to whom subsequently he owed everything. But it was a hopeless task. The moment his family was mentioned, his usual scowl spread over his handsome face, he became bitter, and said, 'You don't know them.' If she continued to urge him, then he would burst out into such words of hatred that she had to cover his mouth with her hand fearing that something bad might happen to him for speaking in this way. Afterwards he would feel slightly ashamed, he would turn his face away and mutter, 'Well they are like that, what can I do,' in sulky self-defence.

But from what she pieced together about his family, she couldn't see what it was about them that made him so dislike them. His father was a very rich man, a textile manufacturer with a cloth mill in Bombay and another one in Ahmedabad, whose time and thoughts were concentrated solely – as Ravi said contemptuously – on making more money. But why not? There was nothing to be contemptuous about. It was like that in business, one had to make money, otherwise what was the use of being in business. Chameli thought wistfully of her own father, who had not been in business, but had only a small salary from his job as railway inspector on which they had all had to live. But Ravi said he hated money because it made people greedy and unscrupulous the way his father was and all his uncles. As for his mother and his aunts and all his other female relations, they thought of nothing but the jewellery with which their safes were crammed and which were taken out on big occasions and hung about their persons to dazzle and awe those less well endowed; and in between conferring with their jewellers, or ordering new saris to be embroidered for them, or haggling with the Kashmiri shawl-seller, they spent their time planning advantageous marriages for their children – marriages in which not the happiness of the main protagonists was considered, oh no, that was of no account whatever, but only the question of how much money would be coming into the family, what status they would enjoy in the community, and how grand the wedding festivities were going to be.

Chameli laughed: everything he was saying, with such disgust, was so natural, more, even beautiful and right, it was what everyone cared for. Everyone liked to be rich, everyone wanted grand marriages in the family; and every woman loved jewellery and costly saris, what did he know about it. Would you like me, she challenged him, if I didn't wear pretty clothes and took good care of myself and put on my gold earrings and bangles? Yes, he said, best of all I like you with nothing on at all. Oh be quiet, keep your silly mouth shut, will you – and she gave him a playful slap which he returned, and after that they were too busy with one another to talk any more on that subject.

But she came back to it, quite often, even at the risk of making him scowl. She wanted to educate him in the ways of the world, of which he was as ignorant as a child. His notions were, it seemed to her, completely divorced from anything real. She asked him – all right, so you don't like money, you don't like your studies, you don't want to be a lawyer or a gazetted officer, you don't want to marry a rich girl whom your family will find for you, all right: but what do you want, what is it? He had no answer, only some vague ideas which he couldn't put properly into words, and some lines of poetry about the stars, and the sea, and the soul. It made her smile. Yes, she too loved poetry, she loved music, every day she listened with rapture to songs on the radio that spoke of moonlight and the scent of flowers. But that wasn't life as one had to live it. It was only the moments snatched in between, in the teeth of reality, gaiety plucked with desperate courage out of one's surrounding circumstances. When her husband had turned out to be cruel, had beaten her and forbidden her to visit or write to her family, and finally had turned out to have another wife and three children all of whom he brought to live in the house: at that time whatsoever smiles she could muster, the flashes of happiness that came and went, were just a moment's light relief, a sudden spatter of cool raindrops scorched up almost at once in the surrounding waste of heat. But what could he know about that? He had suffered so little that he thought it was these flashes that were real and could be for ever. She tousled his hair, she kissed his neck; she loved his innocence, but she feared for him too, for his awakening.

She feared most at present what would happen when Sethji came again. She had worked out a signal for Ravi: when Sethji came, she would replace the usual light bulb on the porch with a green one, and as long as the green bulb was there, Ravi must stay away. She kept impressing this on him, and he made no comment beyond a gloomy assent. 'It won't be for long,' she comforted him. 'He never stays long.' She scanned his face anxiously – his young, young beautiful face – but he turned it away from her, rolled over on to his stomach, buried his head under a pillow and, it seemed, went to sleep.

Unexpected, unannounced, so that she was glad she had the green bulb all ready, Sethji came. It was not difficult for her to pretend she was happy to see him. In a way, she *was* happy: she liked Sethji, she was grateful to him, she knew how much she owed him. And of course he brought news from home – not of her family, true, he had no contact with them, but at least of the streets, the shops, the weather. She plied him with questions – Is the new cinema in Patel Nagar ready yet? Were there many dust storms? Did the rains come on time? – so many, that he threw up his hands and laughed and begged for time to answer. Then she asked, looking away from him, ashamed, drawing circles with her forefinger, how is Bibiji and all of them? And Sethji too turned his face away and said yes, they were well, all well. Bibiji and all of them were his wife and family, to whom Chameli was truly attached and who had been so kind to her. It was they who had taken her in when she had run away from her husband, and her own father and mother had not allowed her to come home again. In her desperation she had run to Bibiji's house – who had been kind to her in the past, had bought some of her embroideries and commissioned more – and Bibiji had taken her in, had allowed her to live with them and do sewing work and other tasks around the house. If it had not been for Bibiji, what would have happened to Chameli? That was why she was ashamed when she thought of her, because she owed her so much. Probably Bibiji hated her now and had very bad thoughts about her, and of course she was right. But if it had not been Chameli, it might have been someone else, someone who would have demanded a lot of money and made trouble and not been content, like Chameli, to be taken hundreds of miles away to Bombay and left there.

She cooked for Sethji with the same care as she did for Ravi, and tendered to all his needs with true devotion. He was pleased with her – patted her in various places and pinched her and said with approval that she was getting fat, Bombay seemed to suit her. And Chameli laughed out loud with pleasure, because she felt that yes, Bombay did suit her. Her body had attained a sort of joyful ripeness, and she liked passing her hands downwards from her breasts over her stomach and hips to feel herself burgeoning, her young flesh swelling. Her arms in particular were very plump and shapely, and how graceful they looked coming out of the short sleeves and adorned with many bangles. She was, moreover, bubbling over with good spirits, ran here and there to lavish a hundred little attentions on Sethji, light on her feet in spite of her heavy burden of breasts and hips, and exquisite as a courtesan in all her movements; when he had finished eating, she sat on the floor in front of him and, pressing his calves and ankles with skilful fingers, she sang a tender love-song which, even though her voice was untrained, was full of sweet, true feeling. Sethji sighed with contentment and soon he was asleep on the bed, with his head sunk deep in the soft pillows.

She stayed lying beside him for a while, and then she got up and quietly, on naked feet, crept outside on to the porch. She stood under the green bulb and peered out into the street. But it was silent and empty; there was no one there. The night was warm and very still, and the houses opposite, usually full of noise and activity, looked frozen in moonlight. She waited under the green bulb, full of longing, her heart so strained with yearning that surely he must feel it. But he did not come, and at last, after waiting for a long time, she gave up, went back inside, and lay down next to Sethji.

This was repeated every night. As soon as Sethji was asleep, she would creep out and wait on the porch. And wait, night after night, in vain. She looked forward impatiently to Sethji's departure and, when the day finally came, she joyfully watched him walking off down the little garden path, carrying his umbrella and his food parcel tied up in a cloth. She could hardly wait for the taxi to turn the corner, and at once went inside to fetch a chair. She stood on it, on tiptoe, and stretched up to unscrew the green bulb. Gangubai watched her suspiciously. Chameli gave her the bulb as a present, and then she took a beautiful piece of sky-blue satin out of her trunk and gave her that as well.

Later that night, when Gangubai had gone home, Chameli sat by the window, bathed, powdered, scented, wearing her prettiest sari of all, every nail brightly polished, henna on the soles of her feet and the palms of her hands and in the parting of her hair. A rich jasmine scent rose from her body and from sticks of incense which she had lighted all round the house. Everything was ready for him and she sat and waited and looked impatiently at the clock. But that night too he did not come. She went out and paced impatiently on the porch. The sleep and silence all around her nearly drove her mad. She wanted to shout out loud, 'Where are you?' It was as if she was alone in the world. She went back into the house and suddenly began to claw at her hair which she had taken so much trouble to arrange. One earring came undone and rolled under the bed and she crawled along the floor to look for it. But she gave up quite soon and simply stayed lying on the floor. Once she raised her head and gave out one long, loud cry. She thought perhaps she would never see him again and she could not bear it.

But she did see him again, the very next day. She went out to look for him and found him on the beach, in the same spot as she had seen him in the beginning, and in the same way, his books disregarded by his side, lying on his stomach and idly combing sand together. She sat down beside him and, without looking up, he said at once, 'Go away.' She took no notice but moved a little closer: to see him again, be near him, was all she wanted. She didn't want to reproach him even for causing her such suffering. That was finished now and they were together again.

'Don't come near me,' he said.

She smiled and put out her hand to touch his hair; even when he jerked away from her, she still continued to smile. He looked so charming when he was being sulky: his eyes were lowered and his long lashes quivered on his cheeks. He was as beautiful as a girl, and yet already there was such manliness in him, a promise of such strength.

'Listen,' she said. 'It's not my fault. What can I do? I have to live, and he's kind to me. That's all. Like a father.'

He groaned and buried his face in his arms, lying flat on his stomach in the sand.

'When you are older it will be different. Then you will take care of me.' She spoke to him soothingly in words that didn't mean much. She couldn't think of him as older, and certainly it had never occurred to her that he would take care of her, the way Sethji did now. And anyway, the future was not important to her, and she spoke only to make him feel better.

He sat up, but he still didn't look at her. He scooped up fistfuls of sand from between his feet and watched it trickling from out of his fingers. He appeared not to be listening to her, but she knew that he was. She had moved closer to him and was speaking to him very intimately, in a low voice. They were almost alone on the whole wide beach. People did not come here in the mornings, and there were only one or two coconut-sellers who had nowhere else to go, and a few boys, a long way off at the sea's edge, picking up jelly-fish and shells. Chameli no longer spoke of the future but of the past. She recalled to him all the things they had done together, and the account was thrilling, and thrilling the way she told it. 'Remember?' she kept saying, close to his ear, and gently touched him with one finger, and though he didn't answer, she saw his mouth-corner twitch. And at last, with one particularly telling little occurrence she recalled to his memory, she won him over completely, so that he left off sifting sand and, flinging himself down in abandon, burst into a loud roar of laughter. She too laughed, but in a refined, coy manner, turning her head aside and covering her mouth with her hand; and she wished that they were at home now, the two of them, in the dark room on the bed on which they did all the things of which she had spoken, instead of out here in the glaring light of day amid dull, empty wastes of sand and sea.

He began to come again night after night. But something had changed, they were no longer as happy as they had been. Chameli did her best – made herself pretty, cooked lovely meals – but the old times did not come back again. It was almost as if Ravi didn't want them back again. He was abrupt with her, often rude, rejecting all her little tendernesses. Nor did he now confide his feelings to her the way he had done before when he had talked about the stars, and the sky, and the soul, and if she mentioned his family, he replied with a shrug as if they no longer bothered him. Nothing any longer bothered him. He seemed vacant and like one who did not care what happened to him. He often smelled of drink, and she began to suspect that he visited the little huts in the creeks where illicit liquor was distilled and which were frequented by bad characters. But when she asked him, he made no reply and, if she insisted, he turned on her so fiercely that she was afraid and had to keep quiet.

There was something reckless and violent about him now which had hot been there before. He often hurt her and, if she cried out, he laughed and did it again. He had become skilled and self-confident, and all that boyish awkwardness which she had so adored had gone. And after he had finished making love, he no longer sank into an innocent sleep as he used to do, but he would get up, wearing only a lungi, his chest naked, and swagger restlessly around the house. He was ravenously hungry, and though she always served him a meal soon after he came, towards midnight or the early hours of the morning he would ask for more food and, when she gave it to him, he sat on the floor and gulped it down greedily. Once, as she watched him eating thus, he suddenly reminded her of her husband, who had always eaten in the same greedy way: so that she cried out 'Don't!' and Ravi looked up and his eyes stared straight into hers, and at that moment they too reminded her of her husband, for they were no longer the brooding, dreaming eyes that she had known but, as if a veil had been torn from them, stark, bold, manly, cruel.

Often he didn't want to leave. He might be lying on the bed when it was time to go, heavily asleep after the big meal he had eaten, and when she tried to shake him awake, he would grunt and mutter to be left alone. She begged, she pleaded, finally in her desperation she threw cold water over him, drenching him and the bed. He sat up, cursed her, shook himself like a dog, while she hurriedly helped him to dress and, almost dragging him off the bed, thrust him towards the door and out into the street. By that time it was almost dawn, and she was terrified that he would be seen, by the milkman and the newspaper boys and the first early morning walkers, as he made his way to his own house, still wet, still half asleep, and staggering like a drunkard.

He had become so reckless that once he even came in the day, when Gangubai was still there. Chameli was sewing herself a new blouse on her little sewing-machine, and she was just inserting the cloth under the needle when she heard his voice calling her from outside. She gave a start and the needle went deep into her finger so that the blood came spurting out. Thrusting it into her month to suck up the blood, she went running out and found him standing right there on the veranda for all the world to see. She pulled him inside, into the little passage, and then pushed him into the bedroom and bolted the door. He smelled strongly of liquor and was swaying a bit.

'Why have you come?' she whispered.

'To sleep,' he replied and sank promptly on to the bed. She shook him to make him get up again: 'Go away, go quickly,' she said in a low voice, hoping Gangubai would not hear. But already Gangubai was pounding on the door, shouting: 'Did you call me?'

'No no!' Chameli shouted back. 'Let me alone! I'm resting!'

'Who is that?' Ravi asked, and Gangubai demanded from outside the door: 'Has anyone come?'

'No one!' Chameli cried in agony. She put her hand over Ravi's mouth and called to Gangubai, 'Go away! Do your work!' as peremptorily as she could. She heard the servant muttering to herself and waited to hear her move away, out into the courtyard. Only then did she take her hand from Ravi's mouth.

'What's the matter?' he asked; he was already half asleep. Suddenly she noticed that his face was smeared with blood. She wondered whether he had been in a fight, but a moment later realized that the blood came from her own finger, which was still bleeding. She tore two strips from the end of her sari; one of them she tied impatiently round her finger, the other she dipped into water and began to wash her blood from Ravi's face. She did this tenderly, lovingly, like a mother to her child, kneeling on the floor by the bed and gazing down into his sleeping face. But what she saw there frightened her. She recalled his face as she had first known it – sulky but soft, rounded, misty, full of boyish innocence; now all that had gone. What had happened? What had changed him so quickly? She felt bewildered and sad.

From that day on the stream of presents given to Gangubai never stopped: now it was not only lengths of cloth, but money too, and once or twice pieces of jewellery. Gangubai received everything without comment, without change of expression; she had even given up her previous snorts of contempt but was now only a silent, passive figure around the house, arriving punctually at the same hour every morning, leaving punctually at the same hour every evening. She was clean and scrupulous in her work and beyond reproach. But Gangubai was not Chameli's only worry. The neighbouring women had begun to interest themselves in her again, and sometimes when she looked out of the window she saw a little group of them gathered outside, their heads close together, whispering excitedly and every now and again throwing looks over their shoulders towards the house. If she sat on the porch, some of them would stop to greet her and even linger a bit as if they wanted to say something more or hoped to be asked in. One or two of the bolder ones did come in, without being asked, they sat in her house and looked around them with glittering eyes, and once she even caught them bending down to peer under the sofa as if they suspected she was hiding someone there.

She lived, day and night, in fear. Fear of Ravi himself, of what he would do next, the violence that seemed to be smouldering in him, the recklessness; and of the consequences of that recklessness, which already had awakened suspicion and hostility all around her. Any day now she feared his family would take action against her, and she had visions of them in their big white house (the men weighty and rich, the women in gorgeous saris and bedecked with jewellery) deciding to call in the police to have her turned out of her house and thrown into jail or confined in one of those homes for fallen women where she would have to wear thick white cotton saris and be taught to spin. She started at every noise – thinking, they have come, they are here – and no longer dared to sit in the porch and indeed, after a while, to leave her bedroom. She kept herself locked in there, wouldn't let Gangubai come in to clean, no longer bothered to bathe and dress herself. Her nightingale, left alone in its cage, ceased to sing, her flowers, which she neglected to water, withered and died. She sat all day, played patience with herself, peered from behind the curtain, and cried from fear and despair.

Ravi continued, night after night, to visit her. He never missed, though often she longed for him not to come. But if he was even a little late, she began to pace up and down the room wondering what had happened, whether his family had locked him up or whether he had got into trouble in one of those little huts in which he now spent so much of his time drinking illicit liquor. When at last he came, her relief was always tempered with annoyance, and she frequently thought to herself, if only he would leave me alone, just for one night. Sometimes she begged him to do so – she said she wasn't well, needed rest – but he never heeded her and came all the same. She no longer bothered to take any trouble for him – often she didn't even change her sari or comb her hair, and the food she served him was badly cooked and mostly stale. He appeared not to care, or even to notice. Sometimes he hardly talked to or looked at her at all, he simply ate and went to sleep, and later woke her up to give him something more to eat. But once, just once, it was as it had been before and they loved each other with the same fervour as at the beginning. That night all that had happened in between, all the changes they had undergone, dropped away and they slept in each other's arms like children and both cried with relief and happiness and then they laughed and, drop by drop, kissed each other's tears away. So the next night she waited for him eagerly, all spruced up again in a pink silk sari with little silver stars on it, but when he came, he was drunk and, in answer to her remonstrances, hit her on the face and made her nose bleed.

After all that how great was her relief when, one fine day, Sethji came back again! She gaily climbed on to a chair and put a new green bulb in and, that done, danced back into the house to devote herself entirely to him. She could hardly bear to take her eyes away from him: she loved to see him sitting there in her house, comfortable, solid, round all over from the round little bald patch on his head down to his round belly and his short round feet. He laughed at the fuss she made of him, but laughed with pleasure, and soon he took his teeth out, as always when he felt very comfortable, so that his face fell into kind old lines and when he laughed he showed his empty gums like a sweet harmless old baby. She sat at his feet and massaged his legs slowly and tenderly and, while she was doing this, she looked up at him with adoring eyes. He patted her cheek and said, 'What's the matter? You look pulled down'; she said, 'That's because I've been waiting for you so long'; she shut her eyes passionately, murmuring, 'Waiting and waiting and waiting and waiting,' and then, though he tried to prevent her, she crouched down to lay her head in a gesture of submission and devotion on his feet.

But later at night, when he was asleep, she got up again from his side and crept out on to the porch. She was afraid of whom she would find there: yet, though she had been half expecting him, she could not suppress a little cry when she actually saw him. Lit up by the green bulb, he was leaning against the balustrade of the porch, looking silently towards the house. He didn't say anything to her, neither did he move.

She clutched him by both arms and whispered, 'Please go.'

'What harm am I doing?'

'No,' she kept saying; 'no.' She pulled at his arms and he allowed himself to be dragged out into the street, quite docilely; he seemed sad rather than anything else. And seeing him like that, she too became sad. She pleaded with him, 'What can I do? Is it my fault.' Suddenly they embraced and clung to each other, in the middle of the empty street in front of all those silent, sleeping houses. They didn't say anything to each other, but they stayed like that for some time. At last she freed herself from him and said, 'You go first,' and she watched him walking away, and then she went back indoors to lie again by Sethji's side.

Later she woke up with a start. She sat up in bed and listened, but there was no sound; she tiptoed quietly out on to the porch but it was empty. Nevertheless her heart continued to pound with fear – till at last she could stand it no longer. She shook Sethji by the shoulder and said into his sleeping ear, 'Please take me away from here.'

He did not wake up easily, and even when he did, partly heaving himself out of the depths of middle-aged sleep, he thought she was talking in her dreams and made clucking noises at her. But she shook him again by the shoulder and said, 'Put me anywhere you like, only take me away from here.'

He was bewildered, not understanding what it was all about in the middle of the night, so she began to make up reasons for him: the Bombay climate did not suit her, she was lonely, she had no friends, she didn't care for the food, her servant stole from her – desperately she made up one thing after another, and at last burst into sobs and beat her hands against his chest, crying like a child, 'Take me away, take me away!'

He attempted to soothe her, promised that they would talk about it in the morning, he would see to everything, make it all well, till at last she lay down again and allowed him to go back to sleep. She herself continued to be awake, lying on her back, her eyes wide open, listening, waiting.

She did not have to wait long. She heard his footsteps running along the road, then up the path to her house, and next moment he was pounding on the outer door. She ran to open it before the noise could waken Sethji. Ravi pushed past her without even looking at her. He strode into the bedroom and turned on the light and looked at Sethji lying there. Sethji sat up in bed; his hand went to his heart, he cried, 'Who is it? What?' He looked old and afraid and his toothless mouth had dropped open.

Chameli tried to hold on to Ravi, but Ravi was a big strong man now. He advanced towards the bed and he pushed Sethji down. Chameli heard bleating sounds from Sethji, and she saw Ravi's face swelling and turning dark with fury and effort as he strained and strained, with his hands round Sethji's neck. Chameli ran away. Right out of the house, along all the streets, till she got to the beach and to the sea and could get no further. She sank down at the edge of the sea where the waves rolled as endlessly, as boringly as ever. But she didn't mind them now – on the contrary, she asked for nothing better than to be allowed to sit here in peace and watch them.

A Star and Two Girls

No one knew who had brought the two English girls to the party. It was the usual kind of film star's party, with a lot of illicit liquor and heavy Indian food; and the usual kind of people were there, like directors and playback singers and actors and lots of hangers-on. It was the hangers-on who got drunk the quickest, and one of them had to be carried out quite early. There were also some well-known actresses, and they all wore plain white saris and no jewellery and sat very demurely with their eyes cast down so that it was evident at one glance that they were virtuous. The two English girls, on the other hand, were not a bit demure but looked around them with bright eyes and were ready to talk to anyone who talked to them. Their names were Gwen and Maggie.

Suraj, who gave the party in honour of his own birthday, had good reason to be satisfied with it. It went on till four o'clock in the morning, most people were drunk and some so drunk that they got sick; a lot of jokes were told which the actresses had to pretend not to understand. At the height of good spirits several men broke into a rough, spontaneous dance, while the others stood round in a circle and rhythmically clapped and cheered them on to dance more and more wildly till they collapsed in exhaustion on the floor, and then everyone laughed and helped them to their feet again. An excellent party in every way, and next day, lying in bed at noon, Suraj thought back on it with satisfaction. However, he found that what he thought most about was the two English girls, and here his satisfaction was not entirely unmixed. Although friendly, there had been something aloof about them, and Suraj even had a hazy memory – all memories of the party were hazy for he had drunk a good deal – of some kind of a rebuff. What had happened? What was it? He couldn't remember, he only had a vague idea that his advances – not even advances, his friendliness – were not met with the same eager gratitude that he was used to. And then quite suddenly, quite early too, the two girls had left. One minute they were there, and the next, just as he turned round to look for them again, they had gone. He frowned, then laughed. He was going to find them again; for nothing in particular, only for his own amusement. It was something to look forward to.

Gwen and Maggie were pleased to see him when he turned up at their hotel. Indeed, anyone would have been pleased to see Suraj: he was tremendously handsome and wore beautiful clothes and walked in the way people do who know everyone is looking at them. He had real star quality. Gwen and Maggie were not, however, absolutely bowled over by this; they kept their heads and this pleased Suraj and at the same time put him on his mettle. He wanted very much to have them like and admire him and found himself eager to do a great deal for them. He wanted to introduce them to the film world, to show them Bombay, to throw everything open for them. He escorted them to expensive restaurants and took them for long drives in his car. He invited them to his shooting sessions and showed them round the studios and introduced them to many famous stars. He was eager for them to pronounce an impossible wish so that he might be able to fulfil it. But all their wishes were quite possible and the most he could do was to fulfil them to the brim, doing everything on as large and grand a scale as possible. He took them to the races, and a polo match, and a wrestling bout, and a cricket match, and everywhere they had front seats and were made much of because they were with him. They accepted all this gladly and were always profuse in words of appreciation and gratitude. 'It was quite perfect,' they would say. 'Thank you so much for taking us.' 'Tremendous . . . fabulous . . . thanks most awfully . . . absolutely marvellous': but he sensed that it was only their words that were so profuse, and that actually they were not as overwhelmed as they pretended to be. On the contrary, he felt there was something detached and amused in their attitude, and indeed they took everything so much in their stride that he became quite frantic in trying to think up more and more, better and better treats for them. Sometimes he was annoyed at their level-headedness, and then annoyed at himself that he – he, Suraj! – should care to impress them.

He always thought of them together: Gwen and Maggie, as if they were one person. Yet they were very different. Maggie was large, pretty, ash-blonde, with a radiant smile and dimples in her healthy cheeks; Gwen, on the other hand, didn't look a bit healthy – in fact, she looked rather consumptive or at least as if she had a weak chest, very thin and with a deathly pale, transparent skin and light red hair. They had been at school together and had all sorts of jokes from that time which Suraj didn't understand; now they were on a world trip which their parents had given them as a present on their eighteenth birthdays. When they got back, Maggie hoped to start work on a fashion magazine, Gwen had been promised a job in an art gallery. Neither of them was in a hurry to return home, though, and start on this new life.

What they liked to do best was to lie for hours and hours on the beach. Gwen would shelter herself under a parasol because her skin was so delicate, but Maggie would lie in full sunshine wearing a tight, bright yellow swimming-costume and smeared with suntan oil, lying now on her back and now on her stomach so that both sides should get done equally. Suraj would get restless and ask, 'What shall we do now?' but they wouldn't even answer him, they were so drowsy and content. Sometimes Maggie went off into the sea with him, and there she shrieked and kicked her arms and legs and fought with him among the waves, while Gwen watched them from under her parasol, looking composed and rather elegant in some sort of flowing, flowered shift. When they came back again, Suraj rubbed a towel vigorously to and fro across his back but Maggie simply flopped down on the sand and let the sun dry the drops of water from her skin.

'Aren't you hungry?' Suraj asked hopefully. He himself was starving – he always needed a lot of food at regular times and his swim in the sea combined with the idle morning had left him hungrier than ever. But those two, if they bothered to answer him at all, only shook their heads; it wasn't as if they didn't have hearty appetites – they did, whenever they settled down to a meal, he was amazed at the quantities they put away with unabashed relish – but only that they couldn't be bothered to move. 'It's restful here,' Gwen murmured, and Maggie, lying face down on the sand, said 'Hmm' in luxurious assent. Suraj was afraid they would drop off to sleep, and then he would patiently have to wait till they woke up before he could get anything to eat, so he began to talk rather desperately, using a loud, wide-awake, voice to rouse them:

'Yesterday we saw my new rushes. Everyone said they are wonderful, this is going to be a big hit. Everyone said.'

'What fun.'

'They said it is my best role yet. I play a poor rickshaw-wallah and one day my sister is abducted by a rich man. The scene in which I realize what has happened is very emotional. There is no dialogue, only the expression on my face. It was a great strain playing this scene – ooph, afterwards I felt exhausted, terrible. You don't know what it is like for an actor: you see, we, really *feel* what we are acting and it is, oh I can't explain, but a great burden here, here on the heart.' He clutched it.

'I know exactly what you mean,' Gwen said. 'I was in the school play once – you remember, Mag? It was only a small part but it was agony. Of course I muffed the whole thing and was never taken again in any other school play which was disappointing but also a tremendous relief because I honestly don't think I could ever have lived through such moments of fearful dread again.'

'Don't be an ass,' said Maggie and made amused sounds from out of the sand.

'I'm completely serious,' Gwen insisted, and then she looked at Suraj with wide, green eyes: 'She doesn't understand. But you do, don't you? You know what I mean.'

He felt uncomfortable. Was she laughing at him? But her eyes, as she looked at him unblinkingly, were clear and frank. He dared not answer but instead laughed to show that he understood the joke (if it was a joke). Then he shouted: 'But aren't you hungry yet? Aren't you starving?'

He enjoyed looking at them and beyond that he enjoyed the fact that they liked to be looked at. It was not so with pretty Indian girls – or if it was, they did their best to hide it, putting on a proud, injured air, giving little tosses of the head and twitching at their saris. But Gwen and Maggie bathed in admiration as if it were sunshine, they smiled and basked themselves like cats. When they were on the beach together, Suraj loved feasting his eyes on Maggie's naked thighs as they came bursting – so firm, golden and healthy, brushed with a down of blonde hair and grains of sand – from out of her tight yellow swimming-costume; and far from discouraging him, Maggie kept shifting them from here to there so that he could see them better, and sometimes she looked at them herself, likewise with admiration and approval, and tenderly brushed the sand off them. On the other hand, Suraj got very annoyed if anyone else looked at the two girls. Unfortunately most people did, not only because the two were young and pretty but also because they were foreign and different. Sometimes Suraj made scenes on this score – in restaurants, in cinema foyers, suddenly he would seize someone by the shirt-front and thrust his face forward and say rude, challenging things in Hindi. The two girls would try and calm him down and get him away as quickly as possible, almost hustling him off while he continued to throw furious glances at the offender and his big strong shoulders twitched inside the silk shirt, impatient for a fight.

But the worst scene was with one of his own friends. Suraj had many friends. They liked to be with him wherever he went, and he liked to have them there: they gave each other confidence, he to move in the middle of a crowd who applauded and, where possible, imitated his every word and action, they to be seen and known in the company of a celebrity. They sat in his house from early morning, eating his food and drinking his liquor and smoking his cigarettes, they accompanied him on the set and loudly applauded every shot of his, they thronged to his parties, they begged for passes to his premières, they accompanied him on his travels at his expense. When he wished them to go away – which was not very often, though more often than usual now that he had met Gwen and Maggie – he told them so quite without ceremony; and indeed they did not expect ceremony from him. He would not allow them to see much of the two English girls. He knew only too well what thoughts they would have, what ribald comments they would pass about them to each other – he had often enough made the same kind of comments himself. But now the idea made him angry. The girls were his friends, they were under his protection. His companions realized his feelings, so that when they did meet the girls, which was sometimes unavoidable, they were on their guard and were careful to throw nothing but covert glances in that direction and to pass their comments well out of their patron's earshot.

Once, however, one of them spoke too loudly. It was a very hot and trying day, on the set of one of Suraj's films. An excellent scene, full of dramatic and emotional content, had been planned for that day, and Suraj had invited the two English girls to be present. However, everything went wrong. The electricians could not fix the lights to the cameraman's satisfaction and everyone had to sit around and wait, and then the leading lady's make-up had to be done again. It was the sort of frustrating day that happened often enough in Suraj's professional career; but today it infuriated him because of his two guests whom he had specially invited to witness one of his great scenes. He sat and smoked cigarette after cigarette, frowning and not speaking much, and feeling very hot in his costume which consisted of silk leggings, a cloth of gold coat, and a huge silk turban with a jewel and a feather in it. Everyone was in a bad mood. The director and the cameraman shouted at each other, and the assistant director had an argument with the sound recordist, and the leading lady got angry with the tailor who kneeled on the floor sewing spangles on to her Moghul princess dress. Suraj's friends yawned and were restless and called for many bottles of Coca Cola. Only Gwen and Maggie were not bored. They sat on the two chairs allotted to them, one in a raspberry pink dress and the other in a lemon yellow one, sucking cold drinks through a straw and looking very happy to be there and grateful that they had been invited.

The heat, the boredom, the fact that Suraj seemed to be preoccupied made his friends more careless than usual. They began to point out certain characteristics of the two English girls to each other – for instance, that they happened to be showing a great deal of long leg – and they tittered together and one of them volunteered a remark which was certainly funny but was unfortunately overheard by Suraj. Quick as a flash he jumped up (his chair fell over) and the next thing that was heard was a resounding slap. Those that had been quarrelling or arguing stopped doing so and it was suddenly very quiet in that noisy place so that the next slap sounded even louder than the first. The leading lady let out a little cry of terror. After the second slap, Suraj's victim hid his head in his arms; otherwise he made no attempt to defend himself, nor did he offer to run away but stood as if awaiting any further chastisement his patron might wish to inflict. Suraj began to belabour him with his fists, the feather in his turban shook and trembled furiously as he rained blows on the young man's head and shoulders; since no resistance was offered, he continued to do so until others begged him to desist and hung on to his arms. The leading lady cried 'Oh, oh' as she watched, and from time to time she flung her hands before her face as if she could not bear to see any more. Gwen and Maggie averted their eyes from the scene of violence, and when it was over, they sat very quiet, no longer bright and interested and happy to be there but, on the contrary, as if they were uncomfortable and wished to be away.

When next he saw them, Suraj had forgotten about this incident and was surprised when they brought it up. 'It's all right,' he said, waving his hand to wave it all away. 'He apologized to me.'

'*He* apologized to *you!*'

'Yes,' Suraj said and stared at them and they stared back at him. There was a brief silence. Then Suraj said, 'Hurry up, aren't you ready yet?' He had come to the hotel to fetch them and take them out to witness a gala beauty contest.

Gwen said, 'You know, I think I don't feel like it.'

'Me neither,' Maggie said. They both took off their shoes and lay down on their twin beds.

'Are you ill?'

'Not ill exactly,' Gwen said.

'Our table is booked! Everyone is expecting us!'

'You go, Suraj. Who cares if we're there or not. You're the big attraction.'

He paced the room in agitation. He ran his hand through his hair. 'What is this? Good heavens. First you say yes, we are coming, and now –'

'I know. We're awful.'

He stood by the window. The room, on the third floor of the hotel, overlooked the sea and the curtains were drawn right back, giving a clear view out. Dusk had fallen and the sea looked silver and so did the sky and the ships that lay out on the water. Suraj looked out, and it was so peaceful that his agitation subsided, leaving him instead sad, melancholy. He said, 'Something is wrong.' He turned back into the room and looked at them.

'It's what you did yesterday,' Gwen said at once, and Maggie too came in with 'It made us feel dreadful.' Both seemed relieved to be able to talk about it to him, and they went on in a rush: 'It was so unfair, Suraj. That poor boy, after all, what had he done? Nothing.'

'Wait,' Suraj said.

'To humiliate him like that in front of everyone – how could you? It was so shaming. Unbearable. Oh God, Suraj.' And they blushed, their faces red with someone else's shame.

'Wait,' Suraj said again. But strangely enough, he was grateful to them for being so frank with him. He remembered the differences he had had with Indian women of his acquaintance – not only with girlfriends but with relatives too, with his own mother or sisters. If for some reason they were offended with him, they would be haughty, toss their head, shrug one shoulder, push out their underlip, be eloquent in injured silence; and it was not until he had done a hundred little acts of propitiation that they would at last consent to tell him what he had done to offend them. Gwen and Maggie's directness surprised and pleased him. His feelings towards them grew very warm, and while of course he wanted to acquit himself, he was also at the same time eager to meet their frankness with an even greater one of his own, to explain and to describe his life, his whole world, and make them understand him utterly.

He told them about his own earlier years when he had run away from home and come to Bombay to become a film star. He had been very poor and dependent on other people's goodwill even for food and shelter. Fortunately, he had acquired a patron, a successful film star who had allowed him to join his retinue and follow him around wherever he went. How grateful Suraj had been for this privilege! It had enabled him to penetrate straightaway into that world which he had come to conquer, to pass freely in and out of studios, be present at story conferences, see the newest rushes, go to film-world parties, drink the whisky and smoke the cigarettes which he would never have been able to afford on his own. In return, all that his patron required was perfect obedience and perfect allegiance, to be there when he was feeling bored or lonely, to laugh at his jokes, to praise him and run down his rival. All this Suraj and the star's other friends did gladly, vying with each other as to who could do it the best; and not only because the star was who he was, no, but because they genuinely loved and admired and looked up to him. 'He was like a god to me!' Suraj exclaimed, and his whole face shone with this past adoration.

Gwen and Maggie, still lying on their beds, smiled at his fervour. They appreciated it very much. Maggie said, 'I wish I could feel like that about someone.'

Gwen said, 'Did you know that in the fourth I was mad about Miss Kemp? Except I couldn't stand the way she spat when she spoke.'

'Even today,' Suraj said, 'well – he is not so great any more, I will tell you, he doesn't get half the amount, not one quarter, for a film that I get, and everyone knows he drinks too much and other vices also. Well, he is old now. But even today, when I meet him – he can say, Suraj, run out and get me a packet of cigarettes, and I would run if he ordered me like that, yes today! Once, years ago, he humiliated me in front of everyone because he was angry with me. I felt bad, of course, I went away and cried and wanted to be dead; but not for one moment did I feel angry with him – only with myself because I had offended him. Next day I went back and touched his feet and begged his pardon and he forgave me. How I loved him at that moment, how grateful I was to him. He was my father, my guide, my guru. I owed everything to him.'

'I'm starving,' Maggie suddenly said.

Suraj jumped up and said, 'Let's go out! Let me take you to –' He racked his brains for somewhere glorious and wonderful enough where he could spend a lot of money and make them happy.

But they preferred to stay in the hotel. They rang the bell and a lot of food was ordered and brought up. They all three ate heartily and sent for several more dishes so that the room became cluttered with used plates and silver dishcovers. Afterwards they leaned out of the window and looked at the sea and the strings of light on the shore and those on the ships far out on the water, and they threw out breadcrumbs for the seagulls though these were all asleep. They competed as to who could throw them the furthest, and Suraj won hands down and that made him happier than ever – he loved winning games; and he thought, leaning out of the window between them both, that never in all his life had he enjoyed such a grand friendship, such jolly times as he had with these two English girls.

Yet there were occasions when he was annoyed with them. Suddenly he would suspect that they didn't take him seriously enough; that they didn't realize quite who he was. Then he felt compelled to tell them. Last year he had been voted Actor of the Year by the All India Critics Association; he had more than five hundred fan letters every day; all over the country there were Suraj Fan Clubs who wore badges and celebrated his birthday and organized teas at which to meet each other and talk about him. Gwen and Maggie listened to him politely and made their usual appreciative remarks of 'How fascinating' or 'How lovely' or 'What fun'. It wasn't enough: he couldn't quite say what more it was he wanted from them but only that he wanted more, much more, he wanted them to get excited and look at him the way other girls did. And because they didn't do that, they didn't lose their heads, he went and lost his: he became very boastful and told them not only of the grand things he had done and was doing but the even grander ones that lay waiting for him in the future. They continued to listen politely though they no longer commented, and their silence made him talk louder and bigger, his claims became exaggerated and ridiculous, and the worst of it was that he himself was aware of this and was ashamed of it: but instead of keeping quiet, he felt compelled to talk more and more, even thrusting out his chest and beating the flat of his hand against it, at the same time hating himself, and hating them for bringing him to this pass.

On the next day he lay in bed and thought resentful thoughts about them. They were really nothing more than two very ordinary English girls of whom he himself had seen plenty; there was absolutely no reason why they should have so high an opinion of themselves. He decided that he hated people who had a high opinion of themselves. He also decided that he would not see them any more. He stayed in bed and had his breakfast and then his friends came and sat round the bed and they all played cards and had a lot of jokes. It was good fun. Later in the day he sent them away and got dressed very nicely and went to visit an actress friend. He was pleased with the reception he got there. She fussed over him and so did her mother and they pampered him with a rich tea of fritters and sweetmeats. He sat with them in their drawing-room which was rather dark but had lots of furniture and ornaments and red velvet curtains. There was teasing and tittering and the actress sat with her hands demurely in her lap and her eyelids lowered except sometimes when she raised them a tiny bit to dart a look of fire at him. A crumb of sweetmeat had got enticingly stuck to her lip and, when her mother left the room for a moment, he darted forward to kiss it away while she tried to ward him off with her soft, weak arms. Then some photographers came to take her publicity pictures, and although Suraj wanted her to send them away, she wouldn't but posed for them in various attitudes in her drawing-room. Now she looked reflective by a vase of flowers and holding one flower in her hand, now she stuck her finger through the bars of her parrot's cage and tenderly puckered her mouth at him, now she was gay and threw back her head and laughed with spontaneous laughter into the cameras. All the time she was very sweet with the photographers, dazzling them with charm, while Suraj watched and got more and more cross. When they had gone, he began to pick a quarrel with her to which she was not slow to respond, and soon they were taunting each other with their shortcomings in both their personal and professional lives. The mother, after attempting to soothe them down, joined in on the daughter's side, but before the quarrel could reach its climax, Suraj got up in disgust and left them. Surprised and disappointed, they called after him, 'What's the matter? Why are you going?' but he didn't bother to answer. When he got home, there was a telephone message from the actress, and she kept trying to ring him the whole evening till in the end he took the receiver off the hook.

He felt terrible. His whole life seemed to him empty and futile. He sat all alone in his large, modern drawing-room which had been done up by an interior decorator and contained several modern paintings which Suraj secretly disliked; indeed, the whole room was only pleasant to him when it was full of his friends or had a big party going. He drank one whisky after the other. He perspired, he wept a little, his mind became soaked and soft. He heard the doorbell ring but he didn't take any notice and it rang again and he still didn't take any notice. Then Gwen and Maggie came in and said they'd been trying to phone and phone, and where had he been all the time and what was the matter? All his misery disappeared like a flash and he tried to rise to his feet but he was very unsteady and they said he had better sit down again. They sat down with him, one on each side. He tried to tell them a lot of things but his tongue was too big and furry. Finally he only waved his hand at them to express everything he wanted to but couldn't say and he cried a bit more but now it was with contentment. They suggested he should go to bed and he let them help him into his pyjamas, and when they had settled him and made him comfortable, he fell asleep at once with a smile of satisfaction on his face.

This incident drew them, if anything, closer together. The girls did not speak about it much but neither did they try to avoid the subject, and whenever they referred to it, it was in a light, amused way. Suraj even became quite proud of it and felt it was a manly thing to get drunk and have to be put to bed. And now that they had seen him in this state, he felt there was nothing he need hide from them; he trusted them completely and wanted them to know everything about him, not only the things of which he was very proud but others also. He told them more and more about his early days, his childhood in a town in the North, his family who expected him to go to college and from whom in the end he had had to run away because they could never sympathize with his higher ambitions. He also told them a lot about his early days of hardship in Bombay, before he met his patron and began to do well: how he had attached himself to groups of people on the outskirts of the film industry and had followed them around and sat with them in cheap restaurants, hoping that someone would buy him a meal and yet so shy to accept it that often he had walked away the moment the menu was brought. He had lived with anyone who was ready to put him up, and there were always people who didn't mind if he unrolled his bedding on their veranda or, during the monsoon, in whatever space he could find inside; on hot nights he often slept out on the beach. His greatest fear was always that his family would find him before he had achieved what he wanted and had become rich and famous (he never had any doubts that he would). He missed them and wanted to he with them, but he dared not even write to them. Sometimes he did write to them but he never sent the letters, he crumpled them up and threw them away. He also wrote some poetry. He was often alone at that time and went for long walks and had many strange thoughts and feelings. Sometimes these thoughts were very happy and then he wouldn't walk but run on the empty beach and even cry out and jump into the air; but sometimes they were sad, and then he would lie down on the sand and bury his head in his arms and fall asleep like one falling into a heavy, unpleasant stupor. He spent his eighteenth birthday like that, alone and asleep.

Gwen and Maggie were eager to tell him about their lives too. Only they did not have very much to tell. Their present world tour was their first big adventure; before that they had simply been at boarding school and the holidays they had spent at home with their families or gone to stay on the Continent with family friends. They looked forward, however, to a lot of things happening to them in the future.

'What things?' Suraj asked them.

They smiled and looked thoughtful. They were on a deserted, beach several miles out of town. Suraj had brought them here in his car, and he had also carried lunch along in a big picnic basket. There were chickens and fried pancakes stuffed with potatoes, and he had gone to a lot of trouble and managed to procure a bottle of champagne which he twirled lovingly in its ice bucket. He had wanted to bring a servant along to serve the food and make everything comfortable for them, but they said they preferred to manage on their own. Indeed, it was surprising how well they did manage. Whereas Suraj was inclined rather roughly to pull things out of the basket, throw away the paper and begin to eat, they first spread a scarf (he had forgotten, or rather, never thought of a tablecloth) and set everything out very nicely, and Gwen even took a few steps away to see what it looked like and then came back and touched up the arrangement with her long, pale hands.

They told him about what they hoped to do in London. They were both trying to persuade their families to let them take a flat together instead of living at home. They even described how they would furnish the flat with a Victorian chest-of-drawers and commercial posters on the walls. Gwen would keep a Siamese cat and Maggie a bull-terrier. They would probably go out a lot – they both liked dancing and good food in good restaurants – but they also expected to be at home quite often for Maggie wanted to learn Spanish and Gwen to do a lot of reading. They loved cooking and looked forward to making all sorts of delicious, unusual little dishes and entertaining their friends.

'What friends?' Suraj said with a knowing smile.

They shrugged and smiled back: 'Just friends.'

'Boyfriends?'

'Those too, I expect,' Maggie said with cheerful pleasure.

'Ah-ha!' said Suraj and winked; and when they didn't take him up on it, he said, 'I think in England all the girls have a lot of boy friends and they have a very good time together. Isn't it? Tell me. The truth now.' He became quite roguish and even shook a finger at them, so that they both burst out laughing and said, 'Get along with you,' in nasal cockney accents.

'Please don't try to put me off the scent,' he said. 'I know all about it. The, parties where you switch the lights off and petting in cars and all that pre-marital sex. I think it's a very good thing. I believe in a free society, and I think it is a sign of backwardness when society is not free in this respect.'

Maggie rolled around in the sand, from her stomach to her back, covering herself with tiny golden grains in the process. She said, 'Gwen didn't sleep with anyone till last year, but I was only fifteen. I developed early.'

The expression on Suraj's face changed suddenly, utterly. Perhaps Maggie noticed, perhaps she didn't, but in any case she went on: 'My first time wasn't terribly successful. It was at the end of the hols and I was feeling awful and wondering would school never stop, would nothing ever happen, and then I met this man in Kensington Gardens. You know how at that age one is absolutely panting for new experiences. But it didn't come up to expectations really. In fact, it was such a disappointment that it put me off sex for more than a year.'

'Who is coming for a swim!' Suraj shouted with unnatural brightness and jumped up and dashed towards the sea. He was glad when they did not follow. He swam strongly, taking pleasure in battling against the waves. When he was tired, he lay on his back and floated, letting himself be carried out a little further than was quite wise. His mind and feelings were in turmoil. He found he could not bear the idea of the two girls with other men. Not because he was personally jealous but because it was outrageous to think of them that way: Maggie so wholesome, untouched, firm-fleshed, and Gwen who was frail and pale and grown too tall like a girl who's been ill and lying in bed for a long time. They were not women, they were friends, his friends. He felt it was his duty to protect them, and it made him furious to think of them going back to England where he would no longer be able to do so and they would be prey to anyone who came along, to all those people who believed in pre-marital sex and other loose practices.

One day he decided to take them to his mother's house. They were surprised – they hadn't realized his mother was in Bombay, they thought she was still far away in the place from which he had run away. Now they learned that, after his father's death a few years ago, he had brought her and the rest of the family to Bombay and had bought a house for them and kept them there. He seemed shy to speak of all this and was indeed quite irritable, as if he resented having broken his silence on the subject. The two girls dressed up carefully in silk frocks and stockings and high-heeled shoes, so that they looked as if they were going to church. Suraj was rather silent and even a little surly all the way he drove them there, and his mood did not improve when they reached their destination. The house was large and full of women. There was not only his mother but also various unmarried sisters and a lot of old aunts and other dependants. They crowded round and touched and patted Suraj and said he was looking weak. A lot of food was brought, and the girls were urged to eat which they did – even the strangest and most outrageous pickles – with their usual grateful enthusiasm. Everyone looked at them from top to toe and smiled at them to show goodwill, and the girls smiled back; only Suraj was frowning.

'Are you married?' one of the sisters asked the girls in English. 'Any children?'

'I'm afraid not,' Gwen said. She stretched her hand out for another fritter and murmured, 'Delicious,' as she popped it, piping hot, into her mouth.

'Look at that one,' said an aunt in Hindi. 'Thin as a fish-bone, but how she eats.'

They all laughed, and the girls too laughed though they hadn't understood what was said. Suraj suddenly shouted, 'Be quiet!' and hit his fist on the table. The girls looked at him in surprise, but the relatives composed their faces and were quiet at once.

'Rest, son,' said his mother. 'Don't upset yourself.' She stroked his hair and his cheeks soothingly; an aunt kneeled on the floor and began to press his ankles but he drew them away ungraciously. 'Listen,' said his mother; she put her hand secretively to the side of her mouth and began to whisper in his ear. He did not seem to like what he heard. Other relatives came and whispered in his other ear. Suddenly he stood up; he told the girls, 'Come on, we are going.'

They held a glass of sherbet in one hand, a coloured sweetmeat in the other. 'What, already?'

'Come on.'

He did not look like a person with whom one could argue. They took a last gulp of their sherbet and hastily ate up the remains of their sweetmeats. They got up, still chewing, and dusting crumbs from their hands.

'But you have eaten nothing!' cried the relatives. They snatched up the platters of food and followed the departing guests with them. 'One little piece of barfi,' they pleaded. 'Only to taste.' Gwen and Maggie lingered and looked willing enough, but Suraj hustled them out of the house and into the car and slammed the car-door after them decisively. He did not speak to them much on the way home and left them at their hotel with a curt, half-angry goodbye.

Next day he said to them aggressively, 'You don't know anything about our Indian way of life.'

'You didn't give us much time to find out,' Gwen said.

They were in the girls' hotel room, and Gwen was lying on the bed with a book and Maggie sat in an armchair with one foot drawn up and painting her toenails silver.

'I could see you were very bored there,' he said after a while.

'Bored!'

'Yes.' Then he said again: 'You don't know anything about the way we live.'

'We were having a simply marvellous time. Everyone was so kind, and those fabulous sweets! Only you were cross and disagreeable.'

Suddenly he roared: 'Because I was bored! Yes, it was I! I was bored! Very bored!' He turned from the window and glared at his two friends as if he hated them. Embarrassed by so much strong feeling, Maggie blushed and bent her head closer over her toenails. Gwen too avoided looking at Suraj.

'Our Indian families are like that,' he said. 'What do you know of it. Yes, I love them but – they want so much! They eat me up! You know nothing.'

He wandered to their dressing-table and absentmindedly sprayed himself from one of the bottles. A dewy English flower-smell enveloped him and he liked it and sprayed himself some more. This seemed to calm him.

'How did you like the house?' he said. 'I bought it for them for six lakhs of rupees. And the furniture? Do you think it is in good taste?'

'It looked awfully comfortable.'

'They want a silver tea-set.' He laughed. 'And another car. They say they need two. Supposing someone wants to go shopping and another person wants to go to the temple, then what? They quarrel a lot about the car. Do your families also have many quarrels?'

The two girls looked at each other and began to laugh. Gwen said, 'They have differences of opinion. It's very subtle.'

'First thing when I go there I have to hear about all the quarrels. Next thing I have to hear is the girls they have found for me to marry. Ooph! It's always the same: after half an hour I want to run away and then they begin to cry and then I stay. What sort of people we are! I think you must be having a good laugh at us.'

He sprayed himself again from the atomizer, he worked the lever up and down vigorously so that a lot of scent came out and enveloped him in a cool, fragrant mist. Maggie, whose bottle it was, cried 'Hey!'

'I like it.' He took out some more and shut his eyes with pleasure. 'Yesterday they again had a girl for me. Very good family, very pretty, sixteen years old. I wanted to say: But I'm going to marry these two! Only to see the fun. And why not?' he said suddenly. 'Why shouldn't I marry you two? I can do what I like. We can all stay together in my apartment, there are many rooms I never use. Or I will build a new house for us – yes, I'll do that, a brand-new house to most modern design!' He became enthusiastic. He imagined himself always enveloped in an atmosphere of English floral scent. He would buy English clothes for them. They would have a cook who knew how to prepare all English dishes. 'Will you like it?' he asked them. 'Do you think it will be nice?' But although they said it would be wonderful, he frowned and said, 'No, you wouldn't like it. You don't want to stay here. You think our poor India is very backward.'

He was often dissatisfied nowadays. He had always enjoyed being surrounded by his friends and talking and laughing with them and having them run little errands for him. Now he tired of them quickly, and in the middle of a friendly session – drinking, joking, having fun – he would tell them to go away. They were surprised, and he was surprised himself; and when they had gone, he wandered round the big, empty apartment by himself and wished for them back again. He had become used to having many people laugh when he made a joke and hearing from them what a big actor he was and how much better than all his rivals. He wanted to hear that, he needed it. Yet, all the same, when they said it now, he became irritated with them. Their jokes too no longer amused him, and the whole tenor of their conversation – which he had lived on and thrived on, which had been *his* – now often filled him with boredom and even disgust. It was the same not only with his friends but with his mistresses too. Everything that had once excited him about them now had the opposite effect. Their intensely feminine being – their soft, fat bodies, their long oiled hair, the heavy, heady Indian perfumes they used, the transparent sari drawn coyly over the enticing cleft that emerged from their low-cut blouses, the little jingle that rang out from bracelets and anklets and golden chains as they moved, their demure, clinging, giggling ways, their little sulks and tantrums – all this, which had once spelled everything feminine and desirable to him, now affected him unpleasantly. As a result, he was tough with his girls, sometimes brutal, and deliberately picked quarrels with them.

But he also quarrelled with Gwen and Maggie. He felt obscurely that they were the cause of his dissatisfaction with what had up till now been a satisfying or, at any rate, an enviable life. Although they never uttered a critical word, he thought of them as critical, as setting themselves up as superior, and it angered him. He defended things against them that they had never attacked and had no thoughts of attacking. These ranged from his family to the Bombay film industry to the whole of India which he admitted was not very advanced in the material sense but which amply made up for this shortcoming by the richness of its spiritual heritage. The two girls did not deny it, in fact they even agreed with him – politely rather than enthusiastically: they had not come here on any higher quest but were ready to concede that such a quest was possible, indeed they knew that many people came on it. Yet their agreement far from soothing only exasperated him further for it made him feel as if they were humouring him. Then he would turn right round and say that no, India *was* poor and backward, he felt ashamed when he thought of how far behind it lagged other countries like England and America and also when he thought of the starving people in the streets and the fact that after so many years of Independence no further progress had been made but of course, he said, they wouldn't understand that, they were only foreigners and could have no conception of the deep feelings that an Indian had for his country. The girls took these changes of mood very well although sometimes, if he carried on for too long a time or at too high a pitch, they said, 'Oh do shut up, Suraj,' but so calmly, even patiently, that there was no offence in it. Indeed, when they said that, he at once stopped talking that Way and became instead extremely attentive and proposed all sorts of outings and other amusements for them and did everything he could to make amends and show them how much he cared for them. But one thing he could not bear and that was when they talked of going away. He had already made them cancel a visit to Isphahan they had planned on their way back, and now he kept persuading them to postpone going home to England, even though their parents and their jobs were waiting for them there and anxious letters were already beginning to arrive.

He wanted them with him everywhere nowadays. Even when they would have much preferred to stay doing nothing on the beach, he made them come and watch him shooting or took them along to some film-world function that he had to attend. But he did not like to see them enjoying themselves too much there. If he noticed them talking too long to any one person, he would come and take them away to meet someone else; and afterwards he would ask them, 'What were you talking so much to him?' and while they were trying to recollect what had been said (which was rarely interesting enough to remember), he went on to suggest, 'It is best not to know such people very well.'

'But, Suraj, he was charming!'

'Yes, yes, for you he must have put on a very nice face.'

'Oh dear. What's he done then? What's the matter with him?'

But Suraj would not tell them. He became indeed rather prim and said it was not necessary for them to know such things, and all their entreaties could not unseal his lips any further. Then they became exasperated, furious with him, but he enjoyed that and laughed with pleasure at the names they called him.

A producer gave a party in the banquet-room of a big hotel. Everyone was there. Long buffet tables had been laid out with huge platters of pilao, lobster and prawn curries, mountains of kebabs heaped with sliced raw onions. The less important guests jostled and pushed each other in piling up their plates as if they had never eaten before and would perhaps never eat again. Streamers and paper lanterns festooned the ceiling, and everything was done just as it should be for the management of the hotel had plenty of practice in putting on these kinds of parties. In deference to the prohibition laws, drinks were served – with a secrecy which had become ostentatious and pleasurable – in a little side-room to which many people took many trips and always came back with a wink and a joke ('They are serving very good Coca Colas in there'). The producer was in an excellent mood to see his party going so well. He rallied everyone to momentous feats of eating and drinking, joked and slapped backs, clapped his hands with enjoyment, was simultaneously paternal and slyly jovial with all the actresses in white saris. He made a big fuss of Gwen and Maggie who were not really enjoying themselves much – they had been to too many parties like this one by now – but pretended they were. Later there was music, and a playback singer rendered a love-song with so much feeling that it made people shake their heads at the beauty of life and filled them with sadness and longing. The host turned to Gwen and Maggie and asked, 'Did you like it?' They saw that his eyes were swimming in tears.

'Jolly nice,' they replied, embarrassed for him and tactfully looking the other way.

He was not ashamed but proud of his tears: 'What songs we have,' he said, 'what feeling,' and since further words failed him, he shut his eyes and pressed his heart where it hurt him. But then he became cheerful again and, putting an arm round the waist of each girl, said: 'Now we would like to hear an English song.'

Gwen and Maggie looked at each other over the top of his head. They gave the tiniest shrug, their eyebrows were ever so slightly raised.

People clapped and shouted 'Yes yes! Let us have a Beatle song!'

But what Gwen and Maggie chose to give was not a Beatle song. An imperceptible sign passed between them, and then they stood side by side very correctly, and began to sing:

> Go, stranger! track the deep,
> Free, free, the white sails spread!
> Wave may not foam, nor wild wind sweep,
> Where rest not England's dead.

They sang the way they had been taught at school, with spirit and expression. They lifted their heads and their voices high and every time the refrain came round they made a conductor's gesture with their hands as if encouraging their audience to join in. Each rhythmically tapped a foot on the floor. It was rousing and stirring and brave. When they had finished, there was tremendous applause. Many people were laughing; some of the actresses had taken out little lace handkerchiefs and tittered into them. The producer was enchanted, he stretched up and kissed their cheeks and he squeezed their hips ('But how *thin* you are,' he whispered, deeply concerned, when he had done this to Gwen). The girls accepted the applause with a graceful mixture of pride and modesty. They knew their performance could not be judged by the highest standards, but they were happy to have given pleasure. They avoided looking at Suraj.

All the way home in his car he upbraided, scolded them. 'Why did you do it?' he said several times. 'Because we were asked,' they replied, but when he kept repeating his question, they were silent and looked out of the car window at the lights stretching like jewels all round the sea-front.

'Everyone was laughing at you,' he said.

'So what.'

He groaned; he seemed in real pain. 'And not only laughing ... Gwen, Maggie, you don't know what these people are. What thoughts they have.' When they didn't answer but went on looking out of the window, he said desperately, 'Especially about English girls.'

'I nearly got stuck in that Egypt's burning plain bit,' Maggie said to Gwen.

'I know you did.'

'But it went rather well on the whole, don't you think?'

'Frightfully well. I'm proud of us.'

'They think all English girls are loose in their morals,' Suraj said. 'When they look at you, they laugh because of the thoughts they have about you. Such dirty thoughts.'

'Oh do shut up, Suraj.'

'Yes, when truth is to be heard then you say shut up.'

But he did not speak again. He sat between the two of them with his arms folded and staring grimly ahead of him at the back of his chauffeur's neck. He did not move even when they reached the hotel and the girls got out, nor did he answer to their cheerful good-nights. He was angry with them.

But next day he turned up in great excitement at the hotel. A famous American saxophone-player was passing through Bombay, and Suraj had got three tickets. 'You try and get tickets on your own,' he said triumphantly. 'Only try. Even if you pay Rs.500 on the black market you won't be able to get.'

'You are clever.' Then they asked: 'When is it?'

'On the fifteenth.'

They smiled sadly and told him that they had booked their return tickets for the twelfth. Suraj was thunderstruck. He looked from one to the other. He said, 'It is because I was angry with you in the car.'

'Of course not,' they said, laughing a little uneasily and avoiding his eyes.

He insisted it was. He accused himself for his bad temper and then accused them for taking such spiteful revenge on him. He wouldn't listen when they tried to tell him that it was time they went home, they couldn't stay here for ever, and that their decision had nothing to do with what had happened the night before. He knew that wasn't true and wanted to draw them out to admit it. But they just kept on saying no, they had to go, and no, it wasn't because of anything he had said or done. Then he tried to persuade them at least to postpone their departure by two weeks, one week – all right, not a week, just a few days, just till the concert – but here too they would not budge from their position.

Finally he changed. He became resigned and deeply melancholy and recognized that the pain of parting had to be endured. This attitude remained with him in the days that were left. He sighed often, and quoted Urdu couplets about the tears of friends whose paths lie in separate directions. This led him further, and he became even more philosophical and quoted verses about the transience of all worldly pleasures and how nothing ever stayed – not the song of the nightingale nor the bloom of the rose nor the throne of kings – but everything dissolved and disappeared as if it had never been. The girls too became depressed; they said, 'It's going to be awful without you.' When they said that, he became more cheerful and made plans for the future: how they would come back again, or he would go and visit them in England, and meanwhile, of course, there would be letters, many many letters, between them.

The girls did write very often. He loved getting their letters which were very lively and were just the way they spoke. He marvelled at the way they could write like that. When he himself sat down to write, the words came out stiff like words that are written not like words that are spoken. And when he had put down that he was well and hoped that they were also and that the weather was not good and that he was going up to Simla to shoot some scenes in snow, then he didn't know what else to say. Their letters were filled with so many things that happened to them – how they had discovered a marvellous little new restaurant, and that skirts were so short now that they had had to take up all their hems – but he could not think of anything to write. Nothing new ever happened to him: it was just shooting, and sitting with his friends, and premières, always the same. It was not worth writing in a letter all the way to England. He would start writing – slowly and laboriously, with his lips moving – and then he would stop and not know what to say next. When he came back to it a few days later and read it over again, he was dissatisfied because it did not sound very well, nor was he sure of his spelling, and then he tore the letter up and told himself he would start again tomorrow. In the end he didn't write at all, and after a time their letters stopped too.

Sometimes his friends talked about the two English girls. At first they did so hesitantly, looking at him out of the corner of their eyes, but when he said nothing they became bolder and soon they were laughing and everyone had something humorous to contribute. Suraj smiled good-naturedly and allowed himself to be teased. He did not contradict when they made references to events that had never happened, or assumed that there had been more than there actually had been. Sometimes he wondered to himself that there had not been more. At the time he had been proud of this fact, of the purity of their friendship; now he felt slightly ashamed of it, and would not have liked his friends to know. It was like a shortcoming, or like having been cheated. He did not understand how he could have allowed it to happen, and a hint of resentment entered into his memory of the English girls. Indeed, he did not like to think of them much any more, and whenever he could not help doing so, he would go out and visit one of his actress friends.

Rose Petals

He loves being a cabinet minister, he thinks it's wonderful. His bearer comes to wake him with tea early in the morning, and he gets up and starts getting dressed, ready to see the stream of callers who have already begun to gather downstairs. He thinks I'm still asleep but I'm awake and know what he is doing. Sometimes I peep at him as he moves around our bedroom. How fat and old he has become; and he makes an important face even when he is alone like this and thinks no one is watching him. He frowns and thinks of all his great affairs. Perhaps he is rehearsing a speech in Parliament. I see his lips move and sometimes he shakes his head and makes a gesture as if he were talking to someone. He struggles into his cotton tights; he still has not quite got used to these Indian clothes but he wears nothing else now. There was a time when only suits made in London were good enough for him. Now they hang in the closet, and no one ever wears them.

I don't get up till several hours later, when he has left the house. I don't like to get up early, and anyway there is nothing to do. I lie in bed with the curtains drawn. They are golden-yellow in colour, like honey, and so is the carpet, and the cushions and everything; because of this the light in the room is also honey-coloured. After a while Mina comes in. She sits on the bed and talks to me. She is fully dressed and very clean and tidy. She usually has breakfast with her father; she pours the tea for him and any guests there might be and takes an interest in what is being said. She too likes it that her father is a cabinet minister. She wants to be helpful to him in his work and reads all the newspapers and is very well up in current affairs. She intends to go back to college and take a course in political science and economics. We discuss this while she is sitting on my bed. She holds my hand in hers and plays with it. Her hand is broader than mine, and she cuts her nails short and does not use any varnish or anything. I look up into her face. It is so young and earnest; she frowns a little bit the way her father does when he is talking of something serious. I love her so much that I have to shut my eyes. I say, 'Kiss me, darling.' She bends down to do so. She smells of Palmolive soap.

By the time I get up, Mina too has left the house. She has many interests and activities. I'm alone in the house now with the servants. I get up from my bed and walk over to the dressing-table to see myself in the mirror there. I always do this first thing when I get up. It is a habit that has remained with me from the past when I was very interested in my appearance and took so much pleasure in looking in the mirror that I would jump eagerly out of bed to see myself. Now this pleasure has gone. If I don't look too closely and with the curtains drawn and the room all honey-coloured, I don't appear so very different from what I used to be. But sometimes I'm in a mischievous mood with myself. I stretch out my hand and lift the yellow silk curtain. The light comes streaming in straight on to the mirror, and now yes I can see that I do look very different from the way I used to.

Biju comes every day. Often he is already sitting there when I come down. He is reading the papers, but only the cinema and restaurant advertisements and perhaps the local news if there has been a murder or some interesting social engagement. He usually stays all day. He has nowhere to go and nothing to do. Every day he asks, 'And how is the Minister?' Every day he makes fun of him. I enjoy that, and I also make fun of him with Biju. They are cousins but they have always been very different. Biju likes a nice life, no work, good food and drinking. The Minister also likes good food and drinking, but he can't sit like Biju in a house with a woman all day. He always has to be doing something or he becomes restless and his temper is spoiled. Biju's temper is never spoiled although sometimes he is melancholy; then he recites sad poetry or plays sad music on the gramophone.

Quite often we have a lunch or dinner party in the house. Of course it is always the Minister's party and the guests are all his. There are usually one or two cabinet ministers, an ambassador, a few newspaper editors – people like that. Biju likes to stay for these parties, I don't know why, they are not very interesting. He moves round the room talking to everyone. Biju looks distinguished – he is tall and well-built, and though the top of his head is mostly bald he keeps long side-burns; he is always well-dressed in an English suit, just like the Minister used to wear before taking to Indian clothes. The guests are impressed with Biju and talk to him as if he were as clever and important as they themselves are. They never guess that he is not because he speaks in a very grand English accent and is ready to talk on any subject they like.

Mina also enjoys her father's parties and she mingles with the guests and listens to the intelligent conversation. But I don't enjoy them at all. I talk to the wives, but it is tiring for me to talk with strangers about things that are not interesting to me; very soon I slip away, hoping they will think that I have to supervise the servants in the kitchen. Actually, I don't enter the kitchen at all – there is no need because our cooks have been with us a long time; instead I lie down on a sofa somewhere or sit in the garden where no one can find me. Only Biju does find me sooner or later, and then he stays with me and talks to me about the guests. He imitates the accent of a foreign ambassador or shows how one of the cabinet ministers cracks nuts and spits out the shells. He makes me laugh, and I like being there with him in the garden which is so quiet with the birds all asleep in the trees and the moon shining down with a silver light. I wish we didn't have to go back. But I know that if I stay away too long, the Minister will miss me and get annoyed and send Mina to look for me. And when she has found us, she too will be annoyed – she will stand there and look at us severely as if we were two children that were not to be trusted.

Mina is often annoyed with us. She lectures us. Sometimes she comes home earlier than usual and finds me lying on a sofa and Biju by my side with a drink in one hand and a cigar in the other. She says, 'Is this all you ever do?'

Biju says, 'What else *is* there to do?'

'Aren't you awful.' But she can't concentrate on us just now. She is very hungry and is wondering what to eat. I ring for the bearer and order refreshments to be brought for Mina on a tray. She sits with us while she is eating. After a while she feels fit enough to speak to us again. She asks, 'Don't you want to do something constructive?'

Biju thinks about this for a while. He examines the tip of his cigar while he is thinking; then he says, 'No.'

'Well you ought to. Everybody ought to. There's such a lot to do! In every conceivable field.' She licks crumbs off the ends of her fingers – I murmur automatically, 'Darling, use the napkin' – and when she has got them clean she uses them to tick off with: 'Social. Educational. Cultural – that reminds me: are you coming to the play?'

'What play?'

'I've been telling you for *weeks.*'

'Oh yes of course,' I say. 'I remember.' I don't really, but I know vaguely that her friends are always putting on advanced plays translated from French or German or Romanian. Mina has no acting talent herself but she takes great interest in these activities. She often attends rehearsals, and as the time of the performance draws near, she is busy selling tickets and persuading shopkeepers to allow her to stick posters in their windows.

'This is really going to be something special. It's a difficult play but terribly interesting, and Bobo Oberoi is just great as God the Father. What talent he has, that boy, oh.' She sighs with admiration, but next moment she has recollected something and is looking suspiciously at Biju and me: 'You're welcome to buy tickets of course, and I'm certainly going to sell you some, but I hope you'll behave better than last time.'

Biju looks guilty. It's true he didn't behave very well last time. It was a long play, and again a difficult one. Biju got restless – he sighed and crossed his long legs now one way and now another and kept asking me how much longer it was going to be. At last he decided to go out and smoke and pushed his way down the row so that everybody had either to get up or to squeeze in their legs to let him pass, while he said 'Excuse me' in a loud voice and people in the rows behind said 'Shh.'

'Why don't they put on one of the nice musical plays?' Biju asks now, as Mina eats the last biscuit from her tray and washes it down with her glass of milk. She doesn't answer him, but looks exasperated. '*My Fair Lady*,' Biju presses on. '*Funny Girl.*' The expression on Mina's face becomes more exasperated, and I tell him to be quiet.

'If you'd only make an *effort*,' Mina says, doing her best to be patient and in a voice that is almost pleading. 'To move with the times. To understand the modern mind.'

I try to excuse us: 'We're too old, darling.'

'It's nothing to do with age. It's an attitude, that's all. Now look at Daddy.'

'Ah,' says Biju.

'He's the same age as you are.'

'Two years older,' Biju says.

'So you see.'

Biju raises his glass as if he were drinking to someone, and as he does so, his face becomes so solemn and respectful that it is difficult for me not to laugh.

*   *   *

The Minister is very keen to 'move with the times'. It has always been one of his favourite sayings. Even when he was young and long before he entered politics, he was never satisfied doing what everyone else did – looking after the estates, hunting and other sports, entertaining guests – no, it was not enough for him. When we were first married, he used to give me long lectures like Mina does now – about the changing times and building up India and everyone putting their shoulder to the wheel – he would talk to me for a long time on this subject, getting all the time more and more excited and enthusiastic; only I did not listen too carefully because, as with Mina, I was so happy only looking at him while he talked that it didn't matter to me what he said. How handsome he was in those days! His eyes sparkled, and he was tall and strong and always appeared to be in a great hurry as if difficult tasks awaited him. When he went up any stairs it was two, three steps at a time, doors banged behind him, his voice was loud and urgent like a king in battle even when he was only calling to the servant for his shoes. He used to get very impatient with me because he said I was slow and lazy like an elephant, and if he was walking behind me, he would prod my hips (which were always rather heavy) and say, 'Get moving' In those days he wanted me to do everything with him. At one time he had imported a new fertilizer which was going to do magic, and together we would walk through the fields to see its effect (which was not good: it partially killed the maize crop). Another time we travelled to Japan to study their system of hotel management because he thought of converting one of our houses into a hotel. Then he had an idea that he would like to start a factory for manufacturing steel tubing, and we went to Russia to observe the process of manufacture. Wherever we went, he drew up a heavy programme for us which I found very tiring; but since he himself never needed any rest, he couldn't understand why I should. He began to feel that I was a hindrance to him on these tours, and as the years went by, he became less eager to take me with him.

Fortunately, just at that time Biju came back from abroad and he began to spend a lot of time with me so I did not feel too lonely. It was said in the family that Biju had been abroad all these years to study, but of course it was well known that he had not done much studying. Even at that age he was very lazy and did not like to do anything except enjoy himself and have a good time. In the beginning, when he first came back, he used to go to Bombay quite often, to meet with friends and dance and go to the races, but later he did not care so much for these amusements and came to stay on his land which was near to ours, or – during the summer when we went up to Simla – he also took a house there. Everyone was keen for him to get married, and his aunts were always finding suitable girls for him. But he didn't like any of them. He says it is because of me that he didn't marry; but that's only his excuse. It is just that he was too lazy to take up any burdens.

It is not easy to be a Minister's wife. People ask me to do all sorts of things that I don't like to do. They ask me to sit on welfare committees and give away prizes at cultural shows. I want to say no, but the Minister says it's my duty, so I go. But I do it very badly. All the other ladies are used to sitting on committees and they make speeches and know exactly what is wanted. Sometimes they get very heated, especially when they have to elect one another on to sub-committees. They all want to be on as many committees and sub-committees as possible. Not for any selfish reasons but because they feel it is necessary for the good of India. Each proves to the other point by point how necessary it is and they hotly debate with one another. Sometimes they turn to me to ask my opinion, but I don't have any opinion, I don't know what it is they are discussing. Then they turn away from me again and go on talking to each other, and although they are polite to me, I know they don't have a high opinion of me and think I'm not worthy to be a Minister's wife. I wish Mina could be there instead of me. She would be able to talk like they do, and they would respect her.

When I have to give a speech anywhere, it is always Mina who writes it for me. She writes a beautiful speech and then she makes me rehearse it. She is very thorough and strict with me. 'No!' she cries, 'Not "today each of us carries a burden of responsibility", but "each of us carries a burden of *responsibility*"!' I start again and say it the way she wants me to say it, and as many times as she wants me to till at last she is satisfied. She is never entirely satisfied: at the end of each rehearsal, she sighs and looks at me with doubtful eyes. And she is right to be doubtful because, when the time comes to make the speech, I forget all about our rehearsal and just read it off as quickly as possible. When I come home, she asks me how did it go, and I tell her that everyone praised the speech and said it was full of beautiful words and thoughts.

But once she was with me. It was a school's sports day, and it was really quite nice, not like some of the other functions I have had to attend. We all sat on chairs in the school grounds and enjoyed the winter sunshine. Mina and I sat in the front row with the headmistress and the school governors and some other people who had been introduced to us but I could not remember who they were. The girls did mass PT, and rhythmic exercises, and they ran various races. They were accompanied by the school band, and one of the teachers announced each item over the microphone which, however, was not in good order so that the announcement could not be heard very well. From time to time the headmistress explained something to me, and I nodded and smiled although – because of the noise from the loudspeaker and the band – I could not hear what she said. The sun was warm on my face, and I half shut my eyes, and the girls were a pretty coloured blur. Mina nudged me and whispered 'Mummy, are you falling asleep?' so I opened my eyes again quickly and clapped loudly at the conclusion of an item and turned to smile at the headmistress who smiled back to me.

When it was time for my speech, I got up quite happily and read it from the paper Mina had got ready for me. The microphone crackled very loudly so I don't think my speech could be heard distinctly, but no one seemed to mind. I didn't mind either. Then I gave away the prizes, and it was all over and we could go home. I was cheerful and relieved, as I always am when one of these functions is finished, but as soon as we were alone in the car together, Mina began to reproach me for the way I had delivered the speech. She was upset not because I had spoiled her speech – that didn't matter, she said – but because I hadn't cared about it; I hadn't cared about the whole function; I was not serious. 'You even fell asleep,' she accused me.

'No no, the sun was in my eyes, so I shut them.'

'Why are you like that? You and Uncle Biju. Nothing is serious for you. Life is just a game.'

I was silent. I was sorry that she was so disappointed in me. We rode along in silence. My head was turned away from her. I looked out of the window but saw nothing. From time to time a sigh escaped my lips. Then, after a while, she laid her hand on mine. I pressed it, and she came closer and put her head on my shoulder. How sweetly she forgave me, how affectionately she clung to me. I laid my lips against her hair and kissed it again and again.

Is life only a game for Biju and me? I don't know. It's true, we laugh a lot together and have jokes which Mina says are childish. The Minister also gets impatient with us, although we are always careful not to laugh too much when he is there. He himself is of course very serious. The important face with which I see him get up in the morning remains with him till he goes to bed at night. But, in spite of all the great affairs with which his day is filled, once he is in bed he falls asleep at once and his face next to me on the pillow is peaceful like a child's. I toss and turn for many hours, and although I try not to, I usually have to take one of my pills. Biju also has to sleep with pills. And he has terrible nightmares. Often his servant has to rush into his bedroom because he hears him screaming with fear and he shakes him by the shoulder and shouts 'Sahib, Sahib!' till Biju wakes up. Terrible things happen in Biju's dreams: he falls down mountain-sides, tigers jump through his window, he is publicly hanged on a gallows. When his servant shakes him awake, he is trembling all over and wet with perspiration. But he is glad to be awake and alive.

Nothing like that ever happens in the Minister's dreams. He has no dreams. When he goes to sleep at night, there is a complete blank till he wakes up again in the morning and starts to do important things. He always says that he has a great number of worries – his whole life he tells me is one big worry, and sometimes he feels as if he has to carry all the problems of the government and the country on his own shoulders – but all the same he sleeps so soundly. He never seems to be troubled by the sort of thoughts that come to me. Probably he doesn't have time for them. I see him look into the mirror but he appears to do so with pleasure, pulling down his coat and smoothing his hair and turning this way and that to see himself sideways. He smiles at what he sees, he likes it. I wonder – doesn't he remember what he was? How can he like that fat old man that now looks back at him?

It is strange that when you're young you don't think that it can ever happen to you that you'll get old. Or perhaps you do think about it but you don't really believe it, not in your heart of hearts. I remember once we were talking about it, many years ago, Biju and I. We were staying in a house we have by a lake. We never used this house much because it was built as a shooting-box and none of us cared for hunting and shooting. In fact, the Minister had definitely renounced them on what he called humanitarian grounds, and he was always telling people about these grounds and had even printed a pamphlet about them; only it had been done very badly by the local printers and had so many spelling mistakes in it that the Minister felt ashamed and didn't want it distributed. That time we were staying in the shooting-box because he had come on an inspection tour. These inspection tours were another favourite idea of his. He always came on them without any advance notice so as to keep the people who looked after the properties alert all the year round. Sometimes he took a whole party of guests with him, but that time it was only he and I and Biju who had come with us because he thought he would be bored alone at home.

The Minister – of course he wasn't a Minister at that time – was busy going over the house, running his finger along ledges for dust and inspecting dinner services that hadn't been in use for twenty years, while Biju and I rested after our journey in the small red sitting-room. This room had many ornaments in it that my father-in-law, who frequently travelled to Europe, had brought back with him. There were views of Venice in golden frames on the walls, and an ormolu clock on the mantelpiece, and next to it a lacquered musical box that intrigued Biju very much. He kept playing it over and over again. The house was built on a lake and the light from the water filled the room and was reflected from the glass of the pictures of Venice so that the walls appeared to be swaying and rippling as if waves were passing over them. The music box played a very sweet sad tinkling little tune, and Biju didn't seem to get tired of it and I didn't either; indeed, the fact that it was being played over and over again somehow made it even sweeter and sadder so that all sorts of thoughts and feelings rose in the heart. We were drinking orange squash.

Biju said, 'How do you think it'll be when we're old?'

This question was perhaps sudden but I understood how it had come into his head at that particular moment. I said, 'Same as now.'

'We'll always be sitting like this?'

'Why not.'

At that time it wasn't possible for me to think of Biju as old. He was very slim and had a mop of hair and wore a trim little moustache. He was a wonderful dancer and knew all the latest steps. When he heard a snatch of dance music on the radio, at once his feet tapped up and down.

He wound the music box again, and the sad little tune played. The thought of being together like this forever – always in some beautiful room with a view from its long windows of water or a lawn; or hot summer nights in a garden full of scents and overlaid with moonlight so white that it looked like snow – the thought of it was sad and yet also quite nice. I couldn't really think of us as old: only the same as we were now with, at the most, white hair.

'What about the Revolution?' I asked.

Biju laughed: 'No, then we won't be here at all.' He put his head sideways and showed a rope going round his neck: 'Up on a lamp-post.'

The Revolution was one of our jokes. I don't know whether we really thought it would come. I think often we felt it ought to come, but when we talked about it, it was only to laugh and joke. The Minister did sometimes talk about it seriously, but he didn't believe in it. He said India would always remain a parliamentary democracy because that was the best mode of government. Once all three of us were driving in a car when we were held up by some policemen. They were very polite and apologized and asked us please to take another road because some slum houses were being demolished on this one. Our chauffeur tried to reverse but the gear was stuck and for a while we couldn't move. Out of our car window we could see a squad of demolition workers knocking down the hovels made of old tins and sticks and rags, and the people who lived in the hovels picking up what they could from among the debris. They didn't look angry, just sad, except for one old woman who was shaking her fist and shouting something that we couldn't hear. She ran around and got in the way of the workers till someone gave her a push and she fell over. When she got up, she was holding her knee and limping but she had stopped shouting and she too began to dig among the debris. The Minister was getting very impatient with the car not starting, and he was busy giving instructions to the chauffeur. When at last we managed to get away, he talked all the time about the car and that it was a faulty model – all the models of that year were – cars were like vintages he said, some years were good, some not so good. I don't think Biju was paying any more attention than I was. He didn't say anything that time, but later in the day he was making a lot of jokes about the Revolution and how we would all be strung up on lamp posts or perhaps, if we were lucky, sent to work in the salt-mines. The Minister said, 'What salt-mines? At least get your facts straight.'

But to go back to that time in the shooting-box. After finishing his inspection tour, the Minister came striding into the room and asked, 'What are you doing?' and when we told him we were talking about our old age, he said 'Ah,' as if he thought it might be a good subject for discussion. He liked people to have discussions and got impatient with Biju and me because we never had any.

'When I think of my old age,' he said, 'I think mainly: what will I have achieved? That means, what sort of person will I be? Because a person can only be judged by his achievements.' He walked up and down the room, playing an imaginary game of tennis: he served imaginary balls hard across an imaginary net, stretching up so that his chest swelled out. 'I hope I'll have done something,' he said as he served. 'I intend to. I intend to be a very busy person. Not only when I'm young but when I'm old too.' He kept on serving and with such energy that he got a bit out of breath. 'Right-till-the-end,' he said, slamming a particularly hard ball.

'Out,' Biju said.

The Minister turned on him with indignation. 'Absolutely in,' he said. 'And turn off that damn noise, it's getting on my nerves.' Biju shut the music box.

'I'll tell you something else,' said the Minister. 'The point about old age is not to be afraid of it. To meet it head-on. As a challenge that, like everything else, has to be faced and won. The King of Sweden played tennis at the age of *ninety*. I intend to be like that.'

How pleased he would have been at that time if he had known that he was going to be a cabinet minister. Things have not really turned out very different from the way we thought they would. The Minister is busy, and Biju and I are not. We sit in the room and look out into the garden, or sit in the garden and enjoy the trees and flowers. But being old does not mean only white hair. As a matter of fact, we neither of us have all that much white hair (Miss Yvonne takes care of mine, and Biju has lost most of his anyway). We still talk the way we used to, and laugh and joke, but – no, it is not true that life is a game for us. When we were young, we even enjoyed being sad – like when we listened to the music box – and now even when we're laughing, I don't know that we really *are* laughing. Only it is not possible for us to be serious the way the Minister is, and Mina.

Everyone nowadays is serious – all the people who come to the house, and the ladies on committees – they are forever having discussions and talking about important problems. The Minister of course likes it very much, and he hardly ever stops talking. He gives long interviews to the Press and addresses meetings and talks on the radio, and he is always what he calls 'threshing out his ideas' with the people who come to see him and those who come to our parties and with Mina and with Mina's friends. He especially enjoys talking to Mina's friends, and no wonder because they hang on every word he says, and although they argue quite a lot with him, they do so in a very respectful way. He gets carried away talking to them and forgets the time so that his secretary has to come and remind him; then he jumps up with a shout of surprise and humorously scolds them for keeping him from his duties; and they all laugh and say 'Thank you, sir', and Mina kisses his cheek and is terribly proud of him.

The Minister says it is good to be with young people and listen to their ideas. He says it keeps the mind flexible and conditions it to deal with the problems of tomorrow as well as those of today. Biju too would like to talk to Mina's friends. I see him go into the room in which they are all sitting. Before he goes in, he pats his tie, and smoothes his hair to look extra smart. But as a matter of fact he looks rather too smart. He is wearing an English suit and has a handkerchief scented with eau-de-cologne arranged artistically in his top pocket. He seems taller than everyone else in the room. He begins to make conversation. He says 'Any of you seen the new film at the Odeon?' in his clipped, very English accent that always impresses the people at the Minister's parties. But these young people are not impressed. They even look puzzled as if they have not understood what he said, and he repeats his question. They are polite young people and they answer him politely. But no one is at ease. Biju also is embarrassed; he clears his throat and flicks his handkerchief out of his pocket and holds it against his nose for a moment as if to sniff the eau-de-cologne. But he doesn't want to go away, he wants to go on talking. He begins to tell them some long story. Perhaps it is about the film, perhaps it is about a similar film he has once seen, perhaps it is some incident from his past life. It goes on for a long time. Sometimes Biju laughs in the middle and he is disappointed when no one laughs with him. He flicks out his handkerchief again and sniffs it. His story doesn't come to an end; it has no end, he simply trails off and says 'Yes'. The young people patiently wait to see if he wants to say anything more. He looks as if he does want to say more, but before he can do so, Mina says, 'Oh Uncle, I think I hear Mummy calling you.' Biju seems as relieved as everyone else to have an excuse to go away.

Once Mina and her friends rolled up the carpet in the drawing-room and danced to records. The doors of the drawing-room were wide open and the light and music came out into the garden where Biju and I were. We sat on a stone bench by the fountain and looked at them. They were stamping and shaking from side to side in what I suppose were the latest dances. We stayed and watched them for a long time. Biju was very interested, he craned forward and sometimes he said, 'Did you see that?' and sometimes he gave a short laugh as if he didn't believe what he saw. I was only interested in looking at Mina. She was stamping and shaking like all the rest, and she had taken off her shoes and flung her veil over her shoulders so that it danced behind her. She laughed and turned and sometimes flung up her arms into the air.

Biju said, 'Care to dance?' and when I shook my head, he jumped up from the bench and began to dance by himself. He tried to do it the way they were doing inside. He couldn't get it right, but he kept on trying. He wanted me to try too, but I wouldn't. 'Come on,' he said, partly to me, partly to himself, as he tried to get his feet and his hips to make the right movements. He was getting out of breath but he wouldn't give up. I was worried that he might strain his heart, but I didn't say anything because he never likes to be reminded of his heart. Suddenly he said, 'There, now see!' and indeed when I looked he was doing it absolutely right, just like they were doing inside. Only he looked more graceful than they did because probably he was a better dancer. He was enjoying himself; he laughed and spun round on his heel several times and how he shook and glided – round the rim of the fountain, on the grass, up and down the path; he had really got into the rhythm of it now and wouldn't stop though I could see he was getting more and more out of breath. Sometimes he danced in the light that came out of the drawing-room, sometimes he moved over into the dark and was illumined only by faint moonlight. But suddenly there was a third light, a great harsh beam that came from the Minister's car bringing him home from a late-night meeting. I hoped Biju would stop now but, on the contrary, he went on dancing right there in the driveway and only jumped out of the way before the advancing car at the last possible moment, and then he continued on the grass, at the same time saluting the Minister as he passed in the back-seat of the car. The Minister pretended not to see but seemed preoccupied with thoughts of the highest importance.

Sometimes Biju doesn't come for several days to the house. I don't miss him at all – on the contrary, I'm quite glad. I do all sorts of little things that I wouldn't do if he were there. For instance, I stick photographs of Mina into an album, or I tidy some drawers in the Minister's cupboard. I wait for them both to come home. Mina is there first. She talks to me about what she has been doing all day and about her friends. I do her hair in various attractive styles. She looks so nice, but when I have finished, she takes it all down again and plaits it back into a plain pigtail. I ask her whether she wouldn't like to get married but she laughs and says what for. I'm partly relieved but partly also worried because she is nearly twenty-two now. At one time she wanted to be a doctor but kept getting headaches on account of the hard studying she had to do, so she left it. I was glad. I never liked the idea of her becoming a doctor and having to work so hard and seeing so much suffering. The Minister was keen on it because he said the country needed a lot of doctors, but now he says what it needs even more is economists. So Mina often talks to me about becoming an economist.

On those days when Biju is not there, I seem to see more of the Minister. If he is late, I wait up for him to come. He is full of whatever he had been doing – whether attending a meeting or a dinner or some other function – and convinced that it was an event of great importance to the nation. Perhaps it was, I don't know. He tells me about it, and then it is like it was in the old days: I don't listen carefully but I'm glad to have him there. He still speaks with the same enthusiasm and moves with the same energy while he is speaking, often bumping into things in his impatience. He continues to talk when we go up to bed and while he is undressing, but then he gets into bed and is suddenly fast asleep, almost in the middle of a sentence. I leave the light on for a while to look at him; I like to see him sleeping so peacefully, it makes me feel safe and comfortable.

When I get up next morning, I'm half hoping that Biju will not come that day either; but if there is no sign of him by afternoon, I get restless. I wonder what has happened. I telephone to his house, but his old servant is not much used to the telephone and it is difficult to understand or make him understand anything. In the end I have to go to Biju's house and see for myself. Usually there is nothing wrong with him and it is only one of his strange moods when he doesn't feel like getting out of bed or doing anything. After I have been with him for some time, he feels better and gets up and comes home with me. I'm glad to get him out of his house. It is not a cheerful place and he takes no care of it and his servant is too old to be able to keep it nicely. It is a rented house which he has taken only so that he can live in Delhi and be near us. It has cement floors, and broken-down servant quarters at the back, and no one ever looks after the garden so that when entering the gate one has to be careful not to get scratched by the thorny bushes that have grown all over the path.

Once I found him ill. He had a pain in his back and had not got up but kept lying there, not even allowing his bed to be made. It looked very crumpled and untidy and so did he, and this was strange and sad because when he is up he is always so very careful of himself. Now he was unshaven and his pyjama jacket was open, showing tangled grey hair growing on his chest. He looked at me with frightened eyes. I called the doctor, and then Biju was taken away to a nursing home, and he had to stay there for several weeks because they discovered he had a weak heart.

When he came out of the nursing home, the Minister wanted him to give up his house and come and live with us. But he wouldn't. It is strange about Biju: he has always gone where we have gone, but he has always taken a place on his own. He says that if he didn't live away from us, then where would he go every day and what would he do? I don't like to think of him alone at night in that house with only the old servant and with his violent dreams and his weak heart. The Minister too doesn't like it. Ever since he has heard about Biju's heart, he has been worried. And not only about Biju. He thinks of himself too, for he and Biju are about the same age, and he is afraid that anything that was wrong with Biju could be wrong with him too. In the days after Biju was taken to the nursing home, the Minister began not to feel well. He even woke up at nights and wanted me to put my hand on his heart. It felt perfectly all right to me, but he said no, it was beating too fast, and he was annoyed with me for not agreeing. He was convinced now that he too had a weak heart, so we called in the doctor and a cardiogram was taken and it was discovered that his heart was as healthy and sound as that of a fifteen-year-old boy. Then he was satisfied, and didn't have any more palpitations, and indeed forgot all about his heart.

I had an old aunt who was very religious. She was always saying her prayers and went to the temple to make her offerings. I was not religious at all. I never thought there is anything other than what there is every day. I didn't speak of these matters, and I don't speak of them today. I never like anyone to mention them to me. But my old aunt was always mentioning them, she could speak of nothing else. She said that even if I did not feel prayerful, I should at least go through the form of prayer, and if I only repeated the prescribed prayers every day, then slowly something would waken in my heart. But I wouldn't listen to her, and behind her back I laughed at her with Biju. He also did not believe in these things. Neither did the Minister, but whereas Biju and I only laughed and did not care about it much, the Minister made a great issue out of it and said a lot about religion retarding the progress of the people. He even told my aunt that for herself she could do what she liked, but he did not care for her to bring these superstitions into his house. She was shocked by all he said, and after that she never liked to stay with us, and when she did she avoided him as much as she could. She didn't avoid Biju and me, but continued to try and make us religious. One thing she said I have always remembered and sometimes I think about it. She said that yes, now it was easy for us not to care about religion, but later when our youth had gone, and our looks, and everything that gave us so much pleasure now had lost its savour, then what would we do, where would we turn?

Sometimes I too, like Biju, don't feel like getting up. Then I stay in bed with the curtains drawn all day. Mina comes in and is very concerned about me. She moves about the room and pulls at the curtains and rearranges things on my bedside table and settles my pillows and does everything she can to make me comfortable. She fully intends to stay with me all day, but after a while she gets restless. There are so many things for her to do and places to go to. She begins to telephone her friends and tells them that she can't meet them today because she is looking after her mother. I pretend to be very drowsy and ask why doesn't she go out while I'm asleep, it would be much better. At first she absolutely refuses, but after a while she says if I'm quite sure, and I urge her to go till at last she agrees. She gives me many hurried instructions as to rest and diet, and in saying goodbye she gathers me in her arms and embraces me so hard that I almost cry out. She leaves in a great hurry as if there was a lot of lost time to be made up. Then Biju comes in to sit with me. He reads the newspaper to himself, and when there is anything specially interesting he reads it aloud to me. He stays the whole day. Sometimes he dozes off in his chair, sometimes he lays cards out for patience. He is not at all bored or restless, but seems quite happy to stay not only for one day but for many more. I don't mind having him there; it is not very different from being by myself alone.

But when the Minister comes in, it is a great disturbance. 'Why is it so dark in here?' he says and roughly pulls apart the curtains, dispelling the soothing honey-coloured light in which Biju and I have been all day like two fish in an aquarium. We both have to shut our eyes against the light coming in from the windows. My head begins to hurt; I suffer. 'But what's the matter with you?' the Minister asks. He wants to call the doctor. He says when people are ill, naturally one calls a doctor. Biju asks, 'What will *he* do?' and this annoys the Minister. He gives Biju a lecture on modern science, and Biju defends himself by saying that not everything can be cured by science. As usual when they talk together for any length of time, the Minister gets more and more irritated with Biju. I can understand why. All the Minister's arguments are very sensible but Biju's aren't one bit sensible – in fact, after a while he stops answering altogether and instead begins to tear up the newspaper he has been reading and makes paper darts out of it. I watch him launching these darts. He looks very innocent while he is doing this, like a boy; he smiles to himself and his tie flutters over his shoulder. When people have a weak heart they can die quite suddenly, one has to expect it. I think of my old aunt asking where will you turn to? I look at the Minister. He too has begun to take an interest in Biju's paper darts. He picks one up and throws it into the air with a great swing of his body like a discus thrower; but it falls down on the carpet very lamely. He tries again and then again, always attempting this great sportsman's swing though not very successfully because he is so fat and heavy. It gives me pleasure to watch him; it also gives me pleasure to think of his strong heart like a fifteen-year-old boy's. There is a Persian poem. It says human life is like the petals that fall from the rose, and lie soft and withering by the side of the vase. Whenever I think of this poem, I think of Biju and myself. But it is not possible to think of the Minister and Mina as rose petals. No, they are something much stronger. I'm glad! They are what I have to turn to, and it is enough for me. I need nothing more. My aunt was wrong.

A Course of English Studies

Nalini came from a very refined family. They were all great readers, and Nalini grew up on the classics. They were particularly fond of the English romantics, and of the great Russians. Sometimes they joked and said they were themselves like Chekhov characters. They were well off and lived gracious lives in a big house in Delhi, but they were always longing for the great capitals of Europe – London, Paris, Rome – where culture flourished and people were advanced and sophisticated.

Mummy and Daddy had travelled extensively in Europe in easier times (their honeymoon had been in Rome), and the boys had, one by one, been abroad for higher studies. At last it was Nalini's turn. She had finished her course in English literature at Delhi's exclusive Queen Alexandra College and now she was going to the fountainhead of it all, to England itself. She tried for several Universities, and finally got admission in a brand-new one in a Midland town. They were all happy about this, especially after someone told them that the new Universities were better than the old ones because of the more modern, go-ahead spirit that prevailed in them.

'Dearest Mummy, I'm sorry my last letters haven't been very cheerful but please don't get upset! Of course I love it here – who wouldn't! – and it was only because I was missing you darlings all so much that I sounded a bit miserable. Now that I know her better I can see Mrs Crompton is a very nice lady, she is from a much better class than the usual type of landlady and I'm really lucky to be in her house. I have a reading list as long as my arm from classes! It's a stiff course but terribly exciting and I can hardly wait to get started on it all. The lecturers are very nice and the professor is a darling! Social and cultural activities have begun to be very hectic, there are so many societies to choose from it is difficult to know where to start. There are two music societies, one for classical music and the other for pop. You won't have to guess very hard which is the one I joined . . . '

Yes, there was the classical music society, and more, a poetry society, and the town had symphony concerts and a very good repertory company playing in a brand-new theatre financed by the Arts Council. It was a good place, full of cultural amenities and intelligent people, and the University was, as Nalini and her family had been told, modern and go-ahead, with a dynamic youngish Vice-Chancellor in charge. Nalini's letters home – she wrote three or four times a week – were full of everything that went on, and her mother lived it all with her. Sometimes, sitting in her drawing-room in Delhi on the yellow silk sofa, the mother, reading these letters, had tears in her eyes – tears of joy at the fullness and rapture of life and her own daughter a young girl at the very centre of it.

But Nalini was not as happy as she should have been. She did everything that she had always dreamed of doing, like going for walks in the English countryside and having long discussions over cups of coffee, but all the same something that she had expected, some flavour that had entered into her dreams, was not there. It was nothing to do with the weather. She had expected it to be bleak and raining, and she had spirits high enough to soar above that. She had also learned to adjust to her landlady, Mrs Crompton, who had 'moods' – as indeed it was her right to have for she had been the injured party in a divorce suit – and to be sympathetic when Mrs Crompton did not feel up to cooking a hot meal. Of course, she missed Mummy and Daddy and the boys and the house and everything and everyone at home – *dreadfully*! – but it was the price she had been, and still was, willing to pay for the privilege of being in England.

Besides, there was always the satisfaction of writing to them and as often hearing from them, and not only from them but from all the others too, her cousins and her college friends, with all of whom she was in constant correspondence. Every time the postman came, it was always with at least one letter for Nalini, so that Mrs Crompton – who wasn't really expecting anything but nevertheless felt disappointed to have nothing – sometimes became quite snappish.

Nalini was not lonely in England. She got to know the people at college quite quickly, and even had her own group of special friends. These were all girls: they were friendly with the men students, and of course saw a lot of them during classes and the many extra-curricular activities, but special friendships were usually with members of one's own sex. So it was with a number or just a single girl friend that Nalini roamed over the college grounds, or sat in the canteen, or went to a concert, or out for a walk; and very pleasant and companionable it always was. Yet something was missing. She never wrote home about anything being missing so they all thought she was having as grand a time as her letters suggested. But she wasn't. Really, in spite of everything, all England at her disposal, she was disappointed.

One day she was out walking with her friend Maeve. They had left the town behind them and were walking down the lanes of an adjoining village. Sometimes these lanes were narrow and hemmed in by blackberry bushes that were still wet with water drops from recent rains; sometimes they opened up to disclose pale yellow fields, and pale green ones, and little hills, and brindled cows, and a pebbled church. The air was clear and moist. It was the English countryside of which the English poets – Shakespeare himself – had sung, and of which Mummy had so often spoken and tried to describe to Nalini. Maeve was talking about Anglo-Saxon vowel changes and the impossibility of remembering them; she was worried about this because there was a test coming up and she didn't know how she was ever going to get through it. Nalini also did not expect to get through, but quite other thoughts occupied her mind. Although she was fond of Maeve – who was a tall strong girl and looked like a big robin with her ruddy cheeks and brown coat and brown knitted stockings – Nalini could not help wishing that she was not there. She wanted to be alone, in order to give vent to the melancholy thoughts with which she felt oppressed. If she had been alone, perhaps she would have run through the fields, with the wind whipping her face; or she might have leaned her head against a tree, in which a thrush was singing, and sighed, and allowed the tears to flow down her cheeks.

The men students at the University were all very nice boys: eager and gentle and rather well-mannered in spite of the long hair and beards and rough shirts that so many of them affected. One could imagine a charming brother and sister relationship with them, and indeed that seemed to be what they themselves favoured when they went as far as establishing anything more personal with any of the girls. It would not have done for Nalini. She had enough brothers at home, and what she had (even if she didn't at the time know it) come to England for, what she expected from the place, what everything she had read had promised her, was love and a lover.

A girl in such a mood is rarely disappointed. One of the lecturers was Dr Norman Greaves. He took the classes on Chaucer and his Age as well as on the Augustans, and although neither of these periods had ever been among Nalini's favourites, she began to attend the lectures on them with greater enthusiasm than any of the others. This was because Dr Greaves had become her favourite teacher. At first she had liked the professor best – he was handsome, elegant, and often went up to London to take part in television programmes – but, after she had written her first essay for Dr Greaves, she realized that it was he who was by far the finer person.

He had called her to his office and, tapping her essay with the back of his hand, said, 'This won't do, you know.'

Nalini was used to such reactions from the lecturers after they had read her first essays. She could not, like the other English students, order her thoughts categorically, point by point, with discussion and lively development, but had to dash everything down, not thoughts but emotions, and moreover she could only do so in her own words, in the same way in which she wrote her letters home. But all the lecturers said that it wouldn't do, and when they said that, Nalini hung her head and didn't know what to answer. The others had just sighed and handed her essay back to her, but Dr Greaves, after sighing, said, 'What are we going to do about you.' He was really worried.

'I'll work harder, sir,' Nalini promised.

'Yes well, that's nice of you,' said Dr Greaves, but he still looked worried and as if he thought her working harder wouldn't do all that much good. Nalini looked back at him, also worried; she bit her lip and her eyes were large. She feared he was going to say she wasn't good enough for the course.

'"In *Troilus and Criseyde*," ' read Dr Greaves, '"Chaucer shows how well he knows the feelings in a woman's heart." That's all right, but couldn't you be a bit more specific? What passages in particular did you have in mind?'

Nalini continued to stare at him; she was still biting her lip.

'Or didn't you have any in mind?'

'I don't know,' she said miserably; and added – not, as far as she was concerned, at all inconsequentially – 'I think I'm a very emotional sort of person.'

He had given her essay back to her without any further comment; but there had been something in his manner as he did so which made her feel that a bad essay, though unfortunate, was not the end of the world. The others had not made her feel that way. Dr Greaves soared above them all. He was not handsome like the professor, but she found much charm in him. He was rather short – which suited Nalini who was small herself – and thin, and exceptionally pale; his hair was pale too, and very straight and fine, of an indeterminate colour which may have been blond shading into grey. He was no longer young – in his thirties, at the end of his thirties indeed, perhaps even touching forty.

Nalini's life took on colour and excitement. She woke up early every morning and lay in bed wondering joyfully how many times she would see him that day. Tuesdays, Thursdays, and Fridays she was secure because those were days when he lectured; the other two days she was dependent on glimpses in corridors. These had the charm of sudden surprises, and there was always a sort of exquisite suspense as to what the next moment or the next corner turned might not reveal. But of course the best were lecture days. Then she could sit and look at him and watch and adore an hour at a time. He walked up and down the dais as he talked, and his pale hands fidgeted ceaselessly with the edges of his gown. His head was slightly to one side with the effort of concentration to get his thoughts across: he strove to be honest and clear on every point. His gown was old and full of chalk, and he always wore the same shabby tweed jacket and flannel trousers and striped college tie. He was not, unlike the professor and several others of the lecturers, a successful academic.

Weekends would have been empty and boring if she had not got into the habit of walking near his house. He lived on the outskirts of town in a Victorian house with a derelict garden. There had been several rows of these old houses, but most of them had been pulled down and replaced by new semi-detached villas which were sold on easy instalments to newly-weds. Dr Greaves was not newly-wed; he had many children who ran all round the house and down the quiet lanes and out into the fields. These children were never very clean and their clothes were obviously handed down from one to the other. The babies of the young couples in the villas wore pink and blue nylon and were decorated with frills. All the young couples had shiny little cars but Dr Greaves only had a bicycle.

One Saturday Nalini met him coming out of his house wheeling his bicycle. He was surprised to see her and wondered what she was doing there; and although she did not quite have the courage to tell him that she had been lingering around for him, neither did she stoop to tell him a lie. They walked together, he wheeling his bicycle. He called, 'Mervyn!' to a little boy who came dashing round a corner and was, to judge by his unkempt appearance, a son of his, but the boy took no notice and Dr Greaves walked on patiently and as if he did not expect to have any notice taken.

It was a sunny day. Dr Greaves was going into town on a shopping tour and Nalini accompanied him. They went into a supermarket and Dr Greaves took a little wire basket and piled it up with a supply of washing soap and vinegar and sliced loaf and many other things which he read out from a list his wife had prepared for him. Nalini helped him find and take down everything from the shelves; sometimes she brought the wrong thing – a packet of dog biscuits instead of baby rusks – and that made them laugh quite a bit. Altogether it was fun; they were both slow and inexpert and got into other people's way and were grumbled at. Dr Greaves was always very apologetic to the people who grumbled, but Nalini began to giggle. She giggled again at the cash desk where he dropped some money and they had to scrabble for it, while everybody waited and the cashier clicked her tongue. Dr Greaves went very pink and kept saying, to the cashier and to the people whom he kept waiting, 'I'm most awfully sorry, do forgive me, I am so sorry.' Finally they got out of the shop and he stood smiling at her, blinking his eyes against the sun which was still shining, and thanked her for her help. Then he rode away, rather slowly because of the heavy load of shopping he had to carry from the handlebars.

The next Saturday it was raining, but nevertheless Nalini stood and waited for him outside his house. At first he did not seem to be very pleased to see her, and it was only when they had walked away from the house for some distance, that he made her sit on the cross-bar of his bicycle. They rode like that together through the rain. It was like a dream, she in his arms and feeling his breath on her face, and everything around them, the trees and the sky and the tops of the houses, melting away into mist and soft rain. They went to the same shop and bought almost the same things, but this time, when they came out and she already saw the smile of farewell forming on his lips, she quickly said, 'Can't we have coffee somewhere?' They went to a shop which served home-made rock cakes and had copper urns for decoration. It was full of housewives having their coffee break, so the only table available was one by the coat rack, which was rather uncomfortable because of all the dripping coats and umbrellas. Nalini didn't mind, but Dr Greaves sat hunched together and looking miserable. His thin hair was all wet and stuck to his head and sometimes a drop came dripping down his face. Nalini looked at him: 'Cold?' she asked, with tender concern.

'How can you bear it here,' he said. 'In this dreadful climate.' There was an edge to his voice, and his hand fidgeted irritably with the china ashtray.

'Oh I don't mind,' said Nalini. 'I've had so much sun all my life, it makes a change really.' She smiled at him, and indeed as she did so, she radiated such warmth, such a sun all of her own, that he, who had looked up briefly, had at once to look down again as if it were too strong for him.

'And besides,' she added after a short silence, 'it's not what the weather is like outside that matters, but what you feel here, inside you.' Her hand was pressed between her charming little breasts. Her eyes sought his.

'I hope,' he said foolishly clearing his throat, 'that you're happy in your work.'

'Of course I am.'

'Good. I thought your last essay showed some improvement, actually. Of course there's still a long way to go.'

'I'll work hard, I promise!' she cried. 'Only you see, I'm such a funny thing, oh dear, I simply can't learn anything, I'm stupid, my mind is like a stone – till I find someone who can *inspire* me. Now thank goodness,' and she dropped her eyes and fidgeted with the other side of the ashtray, and then she raised her eyes again and she smiled, 'I've found such a person.' She continued to smile.

'You mean me,' he said brusquely.

This put her off. She ceased to smile. She had expected more delicacy.

'My dear girl, I'm really not a fit person to inspire anyone. I'm just a hack, a work-horse. Don't expect anything from me. Oh my God, please,' he said and held his head between his hands as if in pain, 'don't look at me with those *eyes*.'

'Are they so awfully ugly?'

'Leave me alone,' he begged. 'Let me be. I'm all right. I haven't complained, have I? I'm happy.'

'No, you're not.' She sagely shook her head. 'I've read it in your face long ago. Why are these lines here,' and she put out her finger and traced them, those lines of suffering running along the side of his mouth which she had studied over many lectures.

'Because I'm getting old. I'll be forty in May. *Forty*, mind you.'

'Sometimes you look like a little boy. A little boy lost and I want to comfort him.'

'Please let me go home now. I've got to buy fish and chips for Saturday lunch. They'll all be waiting.'

'If you promise to meet me tomorrow. Promise? Norman?' She lightly touched his hand, and the look with which she met his was a teasing, victorious one as if she were challenging him to say no, if he could.

At home her landlady, Mrs Crompton, was feeling unwell. She hadn't cooked anything and lay in bed in the dark, suffering. Nalini turned on the lights and the fires and went down to the kitchen and made scrambled eggs on toast. Then she carried a tray up to Mrs Crompton's bedroom and sat on the side of Mrs Crompton's bed and said, 'Oh you poor thing you,' and stroked the red satin eiderdown. Mrs Crompton sat up in bed in her bedjacket and ate the scrambled egg. She was a woman in early middle age and had a rather heavy, English face, with a strong nose and thin lips and a lowish forehead: it looked even heavier than usual because of the lines of disappointment and grief that seemed to pull it downwards. From time to time, as she ate, she sighed. Her bedroom was very attractively furnished, with ruffled curtains and bedcovers and a white rug, but it was sad on account of the empty twin bed which had been Mr Crompton's and now just stood there parallel with Mrs Crompton's, heavily eloquent under the bedcover which would never again be removed.

Nalini felt sorry for her and tried to cheer her up. She held one of Mrs Crompton's large, cold hands in between her own small, brown, very warm ones and fondled it, and told her everything amusing that she could think of, like how she forgot her sari out on the washing line and it got soaking wet again in the rain, all six yards of it. Mrs Crompton did not get cheered up much, her face remained long and gloomy, and at one point a tear could be seen slowly coursing its way along the side of her nose. Nalini watched its progress and suddenly, overcome with pity for the other's pain, she brought her face close to Mrs Crompton's and kissed that dry, large-pored skin (how strange it felt! Nalini at once thought of Mummy's skin, velvet-smooth and smelling of almond oil) and as she did so, she murmured, 'Don't be sad'; she kept her face down on the pillow with Mrs Crompton's and hidden against it, which was just as well, for although she really was so full of sympathy, none of this showed on her face which was blooming with joy.

'Dearest Mummy, Sorry sorry sorry! Yes you're right I've been awful about letters lately but if you knew how much work they pile on us! I've been working like a slave but it's fun.

My favourites now are the Augustans. Yes darling, I know you're surprised and at first sight they do look cold like we've always said but they are very passionate underneath. I go out quite often into the country, it is so peaceful and beautiful. Sometimes it is windy and cold but it's funny, you know I always feel *hot*, everyone is surprised at it.'

Norman usually wore a polo-neck sweater under his sports jacket, but Nalini never more than an embroidered shawl thrown lightly over her silk sari. Whenever they met, they went out into the country. They had found a place for themselves. It was a bus ride away from town, and when they got off the bus, they had to walk for about half a mile through some fields and finally through a lane which wound down into a small valley. Here there were four cottages, hidden away among trees and quite separate from each other. At the rear their gardens ran out into a little wood. The owners of the fourth and last cottage – a devoted old couple whom Norman had known and sometimes visited – had both died the year before and their cottage was for sale. At the bottom of its garden, just where the wood began, there was a little hut built, plank by loving plank, by the old dead owners themselves as a playroom for visiting grandchildren. Now it served as a secret, hidden shelter for Norman and Nalini. No one ever came there – at most a cat or a squirrel scratching among the fallen leaves; and the loudest sounds were those of woodpeckers and, very occasionally, an aeroplane flying peacefully overhead. Nalini, who was really in these matters quite a practical girl, always brought all necessary things with her: light rugs and air cushions, packets of biscuits and sausage rolls. If it was cold and wet, they carpeted the hut with the rugs and stayed inside; on fine days, they sat in the wood with their backs leaning against the trunk of a tree and watching the squirrels.

Nalini loved picnics. She told Norman about the marvellous picnics they had at home, how the servants got the hampers ready and packed them in the back of the car, and then they drove off to some lovely spot – it might be a deserted palace, or an amphitheatre, or a summer tank always some romantic ruin overgrown with creepers and flowers – and there rugs were spread for them and they lay on them and looked at the sky and talked of this and that, recited poetry and played jokes on each other; when the hampers were unpacked, they contained roast chickens, grapes, and chocolate cake.

'Yes,' said Nalini, 'it was lovely but this,' she said and ate a dry Marie biscuit, 'this is a million billion times better.'

She meant it. He lay beside her on the rug they had spread; it was a fine day, so they were under a tree. Dead leaves crunched under the rug every time they moved; there weren't many left up on the branches, and some of them were bright red and hung in precarious isolation on their stalks.

Norman too sighed with contentment. 'Tell me more,' he said. He never tired of hearing about her family life in their house in Delhi or, in the summer, up in Simla.

'But you've heard it all hundreds of times! Tell me about you now. You never tell me anything.'

'Oh me,' said Norman. 'My life's tended to be rather dowdy up till now.'

'And now?'

He groaned with excess of feeling and gathered her into his arms. He kissed her shoulder, her neck, one temple; he murmured from out of her hair, 'You smell of honey.'

'Do you think of me when I'm not there?'

'Constantly.'

'When you're lecturing?'

'Yes.'

'When you're with your wife?'

He released her, and lay down again, and shut his eyes. She bent close over him; her coil of hair had come half undone and she made it brush against his cheek. 'Tell me how you think of me,' she said.

'As a vision and a glory,' he said without opening his eyes. She drank in his face: how fine it looked, the skin thin and pale as paper with a multitude of delicate lines traced along the forehead, and the two deeply engraved lines that ran from his nose to his lips. It was a face, she felt, designed to register only the highest emotions known to mankind.

'What sort of a vision?' she asked. And when he didn't answer, she begged him: 'I want to hear it from you, tell me in beautiful words.'

He smiled at that and sat up and kissed her again; he said, 'There aren't any words beautiful enough.'

'Oh yes, yes! Think of Chaucer and Pope! Do you ever write poetry, Norman? You don't have to tell me – I know you do. You're a poet really, aren't you? At heart you are.'

'I haven't written anything in years.'

'But now you'll start again, I know it.'

He smiled and said, 'It's too late to start anything again.'

But she would never let him talk like that. If he referred to his forty years, his family, the moderateness of his fortunes, she would brush him aside and say that from now on everything would be different. She did not say how it would be different, nor did she think about it much; but she saw grand vistas opening before them both. Certainly it was inconceivable that, after the grand feelings that had caught them up, anything could ever be the same for either of them again. For the time being, however, she was content to let things go on as they were. She would be here for another two years, finishing her course; and although of course it would have been marvellous if they could have lived together in the same house, since that could not be, she would carry on with Mrs Crompton and he with his family. When the two years were up, they would see. Meanwhile, they had their hut and one another's hearts – what else mattered? She was perfectly happy and wanted, for the moment, nothing more.

It was he who was restless and worried. She noticed during lectures that his hands played even more nervously with the edges of his gown than before; his face looked drawn, and quite often nowadays he seemed to have cut himself shaving so that the pallor of his cheeks was enhanced by a little blob of dried blood. Once in her anxiety she even approached him after lectures and, under cover of asking some academic question, whispered, 'Is something wrong? Are you ill?' A frightened expression came into his eyes.

Afterwards, when they were alone together in their own place, he begged her never again to talk to him like that in class. She laughed: 'What's it matter? No one noticed.'

'I don't care if they noticed or not. I don't want it. It simply frightens me to death.'

'You're so timid,' she teased him, 'like a little mouse.'

'That's true. I always have been. All my life I've been terrified of being found out.'

At that she tossed her head. She certainly had no such fears and did not ever expect to have them.

Then he said, 'I rather think I *have* been found out'; and added 'It's Estelle.'

'Have you told her?'

'When you've been married to someone as long as that, they don't need to be told anything.'

After a short pause, she said, 'I'm glad. Now everything is in the open.'

She knew certain steps would have to be taken, but was not sure what they were. It was no use consulting with Norman, he was in no state to plan anything; and besides, she wanted to spare him all the anxiety she could. In previous dilemmas of her life, she had always had Mummy by her side, and how they would discuss and talk and weigh the pros and cons, sitting up in Mummy's large, cool bedroom with the air-conditioner on. Now Mummy was not there, and even if she had been, this was a matter on which she would not be able to give advice. Poor Mummy, Nalini thought affectionately, how restricted her life had always been, how set in its pattern of being married and having children and growing older, and tasting life only through books and dreams.

Her English friends at college were also not fit to be let into an affair of such magnitude. Nalini was fond of them, of Maeve and the rest, but she could no longer take them quite seriously. This was because they were not serious people. Their concerns were of a superficial order, and even when they had connections with the men students, these too remained on a superficial level; never, at any point, did their lives seem to touch those depths of human involvement where Nalini now had her being. Once she had a long heart-to-heart talk with Maeve. Actually, it was Maeve who did most of the talking. They were in her room, which was very cosy, with a studio couch and an orange-shaded lamp and an open fire in the grate. They sat on the floor by the fire and drank coffee out of pottery mugs. Maeve talked of the future, how she hoped to get a research studentship and write a thesis on the political pamphlets of the early eighteenth century; for this she would have to go to London and spend a lot of time in the British Museum Reading Room. She spoke about all this very slowly and seriously, sitting on the floor with her long legs in brown knitted stockings stretched out in front of her and her head leaned back to rest against a chair; she blew smoke from her cigarette with a thoughtful air. Nalini had her legs tucked under her, which came easily to her, and her sari billowed around her in pale blue silk; sometimes she put up her hand to arrange something – her hair, a fold of her sari – and then the gold bangles jingled on her arms. There was something almost frivolous in her presence in that room with all the books and the desk full of notes and Maeve's favourite Henry Moore study on the wall. Yet it wasn't Nalini who was frivolous, it was large, solid Maeve. How could anyone, thought Nalini, endeavouring to listen with a sympathetic expression to what her friend was saying, talk with so serious an air of so unserious a future – indeed, how could a future spent in the British Museum Reading Room be considered as a future at all? She pitied Maeve, who looked healthy and human enough with her bright red cheeks and her long brown hair, but who did not appear to have as much as an inkling of what riches, what potentialities, lay waiting within a woman's span of life.

Mrs Crompton seemed to know more about it. She carried, at any rate, a sense of loss, the obverse side of which postulated a sense of possibilities: she knew a woman's sorrow and so must have, Nalini inferred, some notion of a woman's joy. Mrs Crompton was not an easy person to get along with. She was hard and autocratic, and ran her household with an iron discipline. Every single little thing had its place, every action of the day its time: no kettle to be put on between ten in the morning and five in the afternoon, no radio to be switched on before noon She did not encourage telephone calls. Nalini, who at home was used to a luxuriantly relaxed way of life, did not, after the initial shock, find it too difficult to fall in with Mrs Crompton's rigid regime and always did her best to humour her. As a result, Mrs Crompton trusted her, even perhaps liked her as far as she was capable of liking (which was not, on the whole, very far – she was not by nature an affectionate person). They spent quite a lot of their evenings together, which suited both of them for, strangely enough, Nalini discovered that she was beginning to prefer Mrs Crompton's company to that of the girls at college.

Indeed, in the evenings Mrs Crompton became a somewhat different person. When the day was done and its duties fulfilled, when the curtains were drawn and chairs arranged closer to the fire, at this cosy domestic hour her normally stern daytime manner began if not to crumble then at any rate to soften. Memories surged up in her, memories of Mr Crompton – though not so much of their life together as of their final parting. This seemed to have been the event in her life which stirred her deeper than anything that had ever gone before or come after. It had played, and was still playing, all her chords and made her reverberate with feelings of tremendous strength. Nalini admired these feelings: it was living, it was passion, it was the way a woman should be. She never tired of listening to Mrs Crompton's story, she was the unfailing attendant and sympathizer of the tears that were wrung from this strong person. Nalini heard not only about Mr Crompton but also, a lot, about the other woman who had taken him away. There was one incident especially that Mrs Crompton often rehearsed and that Nalini listened to with special interest. It was when the other woman had come to visit Mrs Crompton (quite unexpectedly, one morning while she was hoovering in the back bedroom) and had asked her to give Mr Crompton up. Mrs Crompton had been at a disadvantage because she was only in her housedress and a turban tied round her head while the other woman had had her hair newly done and was in a smart red suit with matching bag and shoes; nevertheless Mrs Crompton had managed to carry off the occasion with such dignity – without showing anger, without even once raising her voice, doing nothing more in fact than in a firm voice enunciating right principles – that it was the other woman who had wept and, before leaving, had had to go to the bathroom to repair her make-up.

Nalini was careful to wear her plainest sari when she went to call on Estelle Greaves. She had no desire to show Norman's wife up to an even greater disadvantage than she guessed she already would be. She had not, however, expected to find quite so unattractive a person. She was shocked, and afterwards kept asking Norman: 'But how did you ever get married to her?'

Norman didn't answer. There were dark patches of shadow under his eyes, and he kept running his hand through his hair.

'She can't ever have been pretty. It's not possible, how can she? Of course, probably she wasn't so fat before but even so – *and* she's older than you.'

'She's the same age.'

'She looks years older.'

'For God's sake,' Norman said suddenly, 'shut up.'

Nalini was surprised, but she saw it was best to humour him. And it was such a beautiful day, they ought really to be doing nothing but enjoy it. There was a winter stillness in the air, and a hint of ice in its sharp crystal clearness against which the touches of autumn that still lingered in fields, trees, and hedges looked flushed and exotic. 'Let's walk a bit,' she said, tucking her hand under his arm.

He disengaged himself from her: 'Why did you do it?' he said in a puzzled, tortured way. 'Whatever possessed you?'

'I wanted to clear the air,' she said grandly; and added, even more grandly, 'I can't live with a lie.'

He gave a shout of exasperation; then he asked, 'Is that the sort of language you used with her?'

'Oh, with her.' Nalini shrugged and pouted. 'She's just impossible to talk to. Whenever you try and start on anything serious with her, she jumps up and says the shepherd's pie is burning. Oh Norman, Norman, how do you stand it? How can you live with her and in such an atmosphere? Your house is so – I don't know, uncared for. Everything needs cleaning and repairing. I can't bear to think of you in such a place, you with your love for literature and everything that's lovely –'

He winced and walked away from her. He did not walk through the wood but along the edge of it, in the direction of the next house. This was a way they usually avoided, for they wanted to steer clear of the old people living around. But today he seemed too distraught to care.

'Why are you annoyed with me?' she asked, following him. 'I did right, Norman.'

'No,' he said; he stopped still and looked at her, earnestly, in pain: 'You did very, very wrong.'

She touched his pale cheek, pleadingly. Her hand was frail and so was her wrist round which she wore three gold bangles.

Suddenly he seized her hand and kissed its palm many times over. They went back to their hut where they bolted the door, and at once he was making love to her with the same desperate feverishness with which he had kissed her hand.

She was well pleased, but he more guilty and downcast than before. As he fastened his clothes, he said, 'You know, I really mustn't see you any more.'

She laughed; 'Silly Billy,' she said, tenderly, gaily, in her soft Indian accent.

But from this time on, he often declared that it was time they parted. He blamed himself for coming to meet her at all and said that, if he had any resolution in him, he would not show up again. She was not disturbed by these threats – which she knew perfectly well he could never carry out – but sometimes they irritated her.

She told him, 'It's your wife who's putting you up to this.' He looked at her for a moment as if she were mad. 'She hates me,' Nalini said.

'She hasn't said so. But of course you can't expect –'

'Well I hate her too,' Nalini said. 'She is stupid.'

'No one could call Estelle stupid.'

'I've met her, so you can't tell me. She has nothing to say and she doesn't even understand what's said to her. It's impossible to talk to her intelligently.'

'What did you expect her to talk to you intelligently *about*?'

'About you. Us. Everything.'

He was silent, so she assumed she had won her point. She began to do her hair. She took out all her pins and gave them to him to hold. But it turned out that he had more to say.

'It was so wrong of you to come to our house like that. And what did you want? Some great seething scene of passion and renunciation, such as Indians like to indulge in?'

'Don't dare say anything bad against my country!'

'I'm not, for God's sake, saying anything bad against your country!'

'Yes, you are. And it's your wife who has taught you. I could see at one glance that she was anti-Indian.'

'Please don't let's talk about my wife any more.'

'Yes, we will talk about her. I'll talk about her as much as I like. What do you think, I'm some fallen woman that I'm not allowed to speak your wife's name? Give me my pins.' She plucked them from out of his hand and stabbed them angrily into her coil of hair. 'And I'll tell you something more. From now on everything is going to change. I'm tired of this hole and corner business. You must get a divorce.'

'A splendid idea. You're not forgetting that I have four children?'

'You can have ten for all I care. You must leave that woman! It is she or I. Choose.'

Norman got up and let himself out of the hut. At the door he turned and said in a quiet voice, 'You know I'm no good at these grand scenes.'

He walked away through the garden up on to the path which would lead him to the bus-stop. He had a small, lithe figure and walked with his head erect, showing some dignity; he did not look back nor lose that dignity even when she shouted after him: 'You're afraid! You're a coward! You want to have your cake and eat it!'

They made it up after a day or two. But their separate ideas remained, his that they must part, hers that he must get a divorce. They began to quarrel quite frequently. She enjoyed these fights, both for themselves and for the lovely sensations involved in making them up afterwards. He found them exasperating, and called her a harridan and a fishwife: a preposterous appellation, for what could be further from the image of a harridan and a fishwife than this delicate little creature in silk and gold, with the soft voice and the soft, tender ways. Once he asked her: 'All right – supposing I get a divorce, what next? What do you suggest? Do we stay here, do I go on teaching at the University and support two families on my princely salary? You tell me.'

'Oh no,' she said at once, 'I'll take you with me to India.'

This idea amused him immensely. He saw himself taken away as a white slave-boy, cozened and coddled and taught to play the flute. He asked her to describe how they would live in India, and she said that she would dress him up in a silk pyjama and she would oil his hair and curl it round her finger and twice a day, morning and evening, she would bathe him in milk. It became one of their pastimes to play at being in India, a game in which he would loll on the rug spread on the floor of their hut and she would hold his head in her lap and comb him and pet him and massage his cheeks: this was fun, but it did not, Nalini reflected, get them any further.

'Dearest Mummy, How I long for one of our cosy chats up in the bedroom. I have so much to tell you. Darling Mummy, I have someone with whom I want to share my life and I know you too will love him. He is exactly the sort of person we have always dreamed of, so sensitive and intelligent like an English poet.' But she never sent that letter. Mummy was so far away, it might be difficult for her to understand. Besides, she could not really do anything yet to solve their practical problems. One of these was particularly pressing just now. Winter had come on, and it was beginning to get too cold to use their hut. Icy blasts penetrated through the wooden boards, and Norman's teeth never stopped chattering. But where else could they go? Norman said nowhere, it just meant that they must not see each other any more, that the cycle of seasons was dictating what moral right had already insisted on long ago. Nalini had learned to ignore such defeatist talk.

It was around this time that she first confided in Mrs Crompton. This came about quite naturally, one evening when they were both sitting by the fire, Mrs Crompton with her large hands in her lap, Nalini crocheting a little rose bedjacket for herself. Sometimes Nalini lowered her work and stared before her with tragic eyes. It was silent in the room, with a low hum from the electric fire. Nalini sighed, and Mrs Crompton sighed, and then Nalini sighed again. Words were waiting to be spoken, and before long they were. Nalini told her everything: about Norman, and Estelle, and the children, and the hut, and the cold weather. Also how Norman was going to get a divorce and go away with her to India. Mrs Crompton listened without comment but with, it seemed, sympathy. Later, when they had already said good night and Nalini had gone up to her room and changed into her brushed nylon nightie, Mrs Crompton came in to tell her that it would be all right if she brought Norman to the house. Nalini gave a big whoop and flung her arms round Mrs Crompton's neck, just as she used to do to Mummy when Mummy had done something lovely and nice, crying in a voice chock-full of gratitude, 'Oh you darling, you darling you!'

Norman hated coming to the house. He kept saying he was sure Mrs Crompton was listening outside the door: Once Nalini abruptly opened the door of her room, to convince him that no one was there, but he only shook his head and said that she was listening through the ceiling from downstairs. Certainly, they were both of them – even Nalini – very much aware of Mrs Crompton's presence in the house. Sometimes they heard her moving about and that put them out, and sometimes they didn't hear any sound from her at all and that put them out even more. When it was time for Norman to leave and they came down the stairs, she was invariably there, waiting for them in the hall. 'Do have a cup of tea before you go,' she would say, but he always made some excuse and left hurriedly. Then she would be disappointed, even a little surly, and Nalini would have to work hard to soothe her.

Nalini had made her room so attractive with lots of photographs of the family and embroidered cushions and an Indian wall-hanging, but Norman was always uncomfortable, all the time he was there. Sometimes even he would make an excuse not to come, he would send a note to say he had a lecture to deliver at an evening class, or that he was suffering from toothache and had to visit the dentist. Then Mrs Crompton and Nalini would both be disappointed and turn off the lights and the fires and go to bed early.

She boldly went up to him after classes and said, 'You haven't been for a *week*.' He raised his eyes – which were a very pale, almost translucent blue, and remarkably clear amid the dark shadows left around them by anxiety and sleepless nights – and he looked with them not at her but directly over her head. But he came that evening. He said, 'I told you you mustn't ever do that.'

'I had to – you didn't come so long.'

He sighed and passed his hand over his eyes and down his face.

'You're tired,' she said. 'My poor darling, you've been working too hard.' With swift, graceful movements, which set her bangles jingling, she settled pillows on her bed and smoothed the counterpane invitingly. But he didn't he down. He hadn't even taken his coat off.

'Please let me go, Nalini,' he said in a quiet, grave voice.

'Go where, my own darling?'

'I want us not to see each other any more.'

'Again!'

'No, this time really – please.' He sank into an armchair, as if in utter exhaustion.

'You've been talking to your wife,' she said accusingly.

'Who would I talk to if not to my wife. She *is* my wife, you know, Nalini. We've been together for a long time and through all sorts of things. That does mean a lot. I'm a wretchedly weak person and you must forgive me.'

'You're not weak. You're sensitive. Like an artist.'

He made a helpless, hopeless gesture with his hand. Then he got up and quickly went downstairs. Mrs Crompton was waiting at the foot of the stairs. She said, 'Do have a cup of tea before you go.' Norman didn't answer but hurried away. He had his coat collar up and there was something guilty and suspicious about him which made Mrs Crompton look after him with narrowed eyes.

Mrs Crompton told Nalini about men: that they were selfish and grasping and took what they wanted, and then they left. She illustrated all this with reference to Mr Crompton. But Nalini did not believe that Norman was like Mr Crompton. Norman was suffering. She could hardly bear to look at him during lectures because she saw how he suffered. These were terrible days. It was the end of winter, and whatever snow there had been, was now melting and the same slush colour as the sky that drooped spiritlessly over the town. Nalini felt the cold at last, and wore heavy sweaters and coats over her sari, and boots on her small feet. She hated being muffled up like that and sometimes she felt she was choking. She didn't know what to do with herself nowadays – she did not care to be much with the girls at college and she had lost the taste for Mrs Crompton's company. She hardly worked at all and got very low marks in all her subjects. Once the professor called her and told her that she would either have to do better or leave the course. She burst into tears and he thought it was because of what he was saying, but it wasn't that at all: she often cried nowadays, tears spurting out of her eyes at unexpected moments. She spent a lot of time in bed, crying. She tossed from side to side, thinking, wondering. She could not understand how it could all have ended like that, so abruptly and for nothing. They had been happy, and it had been radiant and wonderful, and after that how could he go back to that house with the leaking taps and the ungainly woman in it and all those children?

The weather was warmer. It was a good spring that year, and crocuses appeared even in Mrs Crompton's garden. Nalini began to feel better – not happy, but better. She went out for walks again with one or two friends, and sometimes they had tea together, or went to the music society. It was all very much like before. One fine Sunday she and Maeve took a walk outside the town. There were cows in the fields, and newly-shorn sheep, and the hedges were brimming with tiny buds. Nalini remembered how she had walked with Maeve the year before, and how dissatisfied she had felt while Maeve, in her brown knitted stockings, talked of Anglo-Saxon vowel changes. Today Maeve wore patterned stockings, and she talked of her chances of a research studentship; there were several other strong candidates in the field – for instance, Dorothy Horne whose forte was the metaphysicals. Nalini listened to her with kindly interest. The air was full of balmy scents and the sky of little white clouds like lambs. Nalini felt sorry for Maeve and, after that, she felt sorry for all of them – Dorothy Horne and the other girls, and Mrs Crompton and Norman.

'Dearest Mummy, What a clever clever little thing you are! Yes you are right, I have not been happy lately . . . You know me so well, our hearts are open to each other even with such a distance between us. Here people are not like that. I don't believe that Shakespeare or Keats or Shelley or any of them can have been English! I think they were Indians, at least in their previous birth!!! Darling, please talk to Daddy and ask him to let me come home for the long vac. I miss you and long for you and want to be with you all soon. I don't think the teaching here is all that good, there is no one like Miss Subramaniam at the dear old Queen Alex with such genuine love for literature and able to inspire their pupils. A thousand million billion kisses, my angel Mummy.'

The Housewife

She had her music lesson very early in the morning before anyone else was awake. She had it up on the roof of the house so no one was disturbed. By the time the others were up, she had already cooked the morning meal and was supervising the cleaning of the house. She spent the rest of the day in seeing to the family and doing whatever had to be done, so no one could say that her music in any way interfered with her household duties. Her husband certainly had no complaints. He wasn't interested in her singing but indulged her in it because he knew it gave her pleasure. When his old aunt, Phuphiji, who lived with them, hinted that it wasn't seemly for a housewife, a matron like Shakuntala, to take singing lessons, he ignored her. He was good at ignoring female relatives, he had had a lot of practice at it. But he never ignored Shakuntala. They had been married for twenty-five years and he loved her more year by year.

It wasn't because of anything Phuphiji said but because of him, who said nothing, that Shakuntala sometimes felt guilty. And because of her daughter and her little grandson. She loved all of them, but she could not deny to herself that her singing meant even more to her than her feelings as wife and mother and grandmother. She was unable to explain this, she tried not to think of it. But it was true that with her music she lived in a region where she felt most truly, most deeply herself. No, not herself, something more and higher than that. By contrast with her singing, the rest of her day, indeed of her life, seemed insignificant. She felt this to be wrong but there was no point in trying to struggle against it. Without her hour's practice in the morning, she was as if deprived of food and water and air.

One day her teacher did not come. She went on the roof and practised by herself but it was not the same thing. By herself she felt weak and faltering. She *was* weak and faltering, but when he was there it didn't matter so much because he had such strength. Later, when her husband had gone to his place of work (he was a building contractor) and she had arranged everything for the day's meals and left Phuphiji entertaining some friends from the neighbourhood with tea, she went to find out what had happened. She took her servant-boy with her to show her the way, for although she often, sent messages to her teacher's house, she had not been there before. The house was old and in a narrow old alley. There was some sort of workshop downstairs and she had to step over straw and bits of packing-cases; on the first floor was a music school consisting of a long room in which several people sat on the floor playing on drums. Her teacher lived on the second storey. He had only one room and everything was in great disorder. There was practically no furniture but a great many discarded clothes were hung up on hooks and on a line strung across the room. A bedraggled, cross woman sat on the floor, turning the handle of a sewing-machine. The teacher himself lay on a mat in a corner, tossing and groaning; when Shakuntala, full of concern, bent over him, he opened his eyes and said, 'I'm going now.' He wore a red cloth tied round his brow and this gave him a rather gruesome appearance.

Shakuntala tried to rally him, but the more she did so, the sicker he became. 'No,' he insisted, 'I'm going.' Then he added, 'I'm not afraid to die.'

His wife, turning the handle of her sewing-machine, snorted derisively. This did rally him; he gathered sufficient strength to prop himself up on one elbow. 'There's no food,' he said to Shakuntala, making pathetic gestures towards his mouth to show

how he lacked sustenance to put into it. 'She doesn't know how to cook for a sick person.'

His wife stopped sewing in order to laugh heartily. 'Soup!' she laughed. 'That's what he's asking for. Where has he ever tasted soup? In his father's house? They thought themselves lucky if they could get a bit of dal with their dry bread. *Soup*,' she repeated in a shaking voice, her amusement abruptly changing into anger.

Shakuntala, who had not anticipated being caught in a domestic quarrel, was embarrassed. But she also felt sorry for the teacher. She did not believe him to be very ill but she saw he was very uncomfortable. The room was hot, and dense with various smells, and full of flies; there was thumping from the workshop downstairs, drums and some thin stringed instruments from the music school, and inside the room the angry whirring of the sewing-machine. In spite of the heat, the sick man was covered with a sheet under which he tossed and turned – not with pain, Shakuntala saw, but with irritation.

After that her own home seemed so sweet and orderly to her. They had recently built a new bungalow with shiny woodwork and pink and green terrazzo floors. Their drawing-room was furnished with a blue rexine-covered sofa-set. She wished she could have brought her teacher here to nurse him; she could have made him so comfortable. All day she was restless, thinking of that. And as always when Shakuntala was restless and her mind turned away from her household affairs, Phuphiji noticed and pursued her through the house and insisted on drawing her attention to various deficiencies such as the month's sugar supply running out too quickly or a cooking vessel not having been scoured to shine as it should. Shakuntala had lived with Phuphiji long enough to remain calm and answer her calmly, but Phuphiji had also lived with Shakuntala long enough to know that these answers were desultory and that Shakuntala's thoughts remained fixed elsewhere. She continued to follow her, to circle her, to fix her with her bright old eyes.

Later in the day Shakuntala's daughter Manju came with little Baba. Of course Shakuntala was happy to see them and played with and kissed Baba as usual; but, like Phuphiji, Manju noticed her mother's distraction. Manju became querulous and had many complaints. She said she had a headache every morning, and Baba sometimes was very naughty and woke them all up in the night and wanted to play. For all this she required her mother's sympathy, and Shakuntala gave it but Manju noticed that she couldn't give it with all her heart and that made her more querulous. And Phuphiji joined in, encouraging Manju, pitying her, drawing the subject out more and more and all the time keeping her eyes on Shakuntala to make sure she participated as keenly as she was in duty bound to. Between them, they drove Shakuntala quite crazy; and the worst of it was that she was on their side, she knew that she ought to be absorbed in their problems and blamed herself because she wasn't.

It was a relief to her when her husband came home, for he was the one person who was always satisfied with her. Unlike the others, he wasn't interested in her secret thoughts. For him it was enough that she dressed up nicely before his arrival home and oiled her hair and adorned it with a wreath of jasmine. She was in her early forties but plump and fresh. She loved jewellery and always wore great quantities of it, even in the house. Her arms were full of bangles, she had a diamond nose-ring and a gold necklace round her smooth, soft neck. Her husband liked to see all that; and he liked her to stand beside him to serve him his meal, and then to he next to him on the bed while he slept. That night he fell asleep as usual after eating large helpings of food. He slept fast and sound, breathing loudly for he was a big man with a lot of weight on him. Sometimes he tossed himself from one side to the other with a grunt. Then Shakuntala gently patted him as if to soothe him; she wanted him to be always entirely comfortable and recognized it to be her mission in life to see that he was. When she fell asleep herself, she slept badly and was disturbed by garbled dreams.

But the next morning the teacher was there again. He wasn't ill at all any more, and when she inquired after his health, he shrugged as if he had forgotten there had ever been anything wrong with it. She sang so well that day that even he was satisfied – at least he didn't make the sour face he usually wore while listening to her. As she sang, her irritation and anxiety dissolved and she felt entirely clear and happy. The sky was translucent with dawn and birds woke up and twittered like fresh gurgling water. No one else was up in the whole neighbourhood, only she and the teacher and the birds. She sang and sang, her voice rose high and so did her heart; sometimes she laughed with enjoyment and saw that in response the shadow of a smile flitted over the teacher's features as well. Then she laughed again and her voice rose – with what ease – to even greater feats. And the joy that filled her at her own achievement and the peace that entered into her with that pure clear dawn, these sensations stayed with her for the rest of the day. She polished all the mirrors and brass fittings with her own hands, and afterwards she cooked sweet vermicelli for her husband which was his favourite dish. Phuphiji, at once aware of her change of mood, was suspicious and followed her around as she had done the previous day and looked at her in the same suspicious way; but today Shakuntala didn't mind, in fact she even laughed at Phuphiji within herself.

Her teacher always went away after the early morning lesson, but about this time, after his illness, he began to visit her in the afternoons as well. Shakuntala was glad. Now that she had seen his home, she realized what a relief it must be to him to have a clean and peaceful room to sit in; and she did her best to make him comfortable and served him with tea and little fried delicacies. But he was never keen on these refreshments and often did not touch anything she set before him, simply letting his eyes glance over it with the expression of distaste that was so characteristic of him. Phuphiji was amazed. She thought he was being excessively and unwarrantably honoured by having these treats placed before him and could not understand why he did not fall upon them as eagerly as she expected him to. She looked from them to him and back again. Tantalized beyond endurance, she even pushed the dishes towards him, saying, 'Eat, eat,' as if he were some bizarre animal whose feeding habits she wished to observe. He treated her in the same way as he did the refreshments, ignoring her after a swift contemptuous glance in her direction. But she was fascinated by him. Whenever he came, she hurried and placed herself in a strategic position in order to look her fill into his face. Sometimes as she gazed she shook her head in wonder and murmured to herself and even gave herself incredulous little laughs. He wasn't bothered by her in the least. He sat there for as long as he felt like it, often in complete silence, and then departed, still in silence.

Occasionally, however, he talked. His conversation was as arbitrary as his silence; he needed no stimulus to start him off and always ended as abruptly as he had begun. Shakuntala loved listening to him, everything he said was of interest to her. She was especially fascinated when he talked about his own teacher who had been a very great and famous and temperamental musician. He often spoke of him, for a good many years of his life and certainly the most formative part of it had been spent under the old man's tutelage. All the disciples had lived with their guru and his family in an old house in Benaras. There had been strict discipline as far as the hours of practice were concerned and all were expected to get up before dawn and spend most of their day in improving their technique; but in between their way of life was entirely without constraint. They ate when they liked, slept when they liked, chewed opium in their betel, loved and formed friendships. When the old man was invited to perform at private or public concerts in other parts of India, most of the disciples travelled with him. They all crammed together into a railway carriage, and when they got to their destination, they stayed together in the quarters allotted to them. Sometimes these were a dingy room in a rest-house, other times they were ornate chambers in some Maharaja's palace. They were equally happy wherever it was, sleeping on the floor round the great bed on which their guru snored, and eating their fill of the rich meals provided for them. They were up all night listening to and performing in concerts that never ended before dawn. They were most of them quite unattached and had no ties apart from those they had formed with their guru. Some of them – such as Shakuntala's teacher – had run away from their parents to be with their guru, others had left their wives and children for his sake. He was a very hard master. He often beat his disciples, and they had to serve him as his servants, doing the most menial tasks for him; he never lifted a finger for himself and got into a terrible rage if some little comfort of his had been neglected. Once Shakuntala's teacher had forgotten to light his hookah, and for this fault was chased all round the house and at last out into the street where he had to stay for three days, sitting on the doorstep like a beggar and being fed on scraps till he was forgiven and admitted inside again. Phuphiji was shocked to hear of such treatment and called the guru by many harsh names; but to Shakuntala, as to her teacher, it did not seem so deplorable – on the contrary, she thought it a reasonable price to pay for the privilege of being near so great and blessed a man.

Whenever a famous musician came to the town to give a performance, Shakuntala did her best to attend. It was not easy for her because she had no one willingly to go with. her. She didn't want to trouble her husband. He cared nothing for music and, in any case, would have found it an ordeal to sit upright on a chair for so many hours. Once or twice she asked Phuphiji to be her chaperone. Phuphiji was quite glad, she always enjoyed an outing.

At first she was interested in everything, she looked round eagerly, craning her neck this way and that. But when the concert started and went on, she became restless. She yawned and slid about on the chair to show how uncomfortable she was; she asked often how much longer they would have to stay, and then she said, 'Let's go,' and when Shakuntala tried to soothe and detain her, she became plaintive and said her back was hurting unbearably. So they always had to come home early, just as the best part of the concert was beginning. And it wasn't much better when Shakuntala took her daughter with her, for although Manju didn't complain the way Phuphiji did, she was obviously bored and made a suffering face. It was usually necessary to take Baba along too, and if they were lucky, he fell asleep quite soon, but if they weren't, he made a lot of disturbance and kicked and struggled and finally he would begin to cry so that there was nothing for it, they had to leave. Shakuntala always tried to put a good face on it and hide her disappointment, but later, when she was at home and in bed beside her husband who had been asleep these many hours, then her thoughts kept reverting to the concert. She wondered what raga was being sung now – Raga Yaman, serene and sublime, Raga Kalawati, full of sweet yearning? – and saw the brightly lit stage on which the musicians sat: the singer in the middle, the accompanists grouped all round, the disciples forming an outer ring, and all of them caught up in a mood of exaltation inspired by the music. Their heads slowly swayed, they exchanged looks and smiles, their hearts were open and sweet sensations flowed in them like honey. And thinking of this, alone in the silent bedroom beside her sleeping husband, she turned her face and buried it deep into her pillow as if she hoped thereby to bury her feelings of bitter disappointment.

One morning her teacher surprised her. It was at the end of their lesson when she had sung as usual and he had listened to her with his usual pained face. But before he went, he suddenly said it was time she sang before an audience. She was so astonished, she couldn't answer for a while, and when she could, it was only to say, 'I didn't know.' She meant she didn't know he thought she was good enough for that. He seemed to understand and it annoyed him. He said, 'Why do you think I come here,' and got up to go downstairs. She followed him but he didn't turn back and didn't speak to her again, he was so irritated with her. And she longed for him to say more, to tell her *why* he came, for once to hear from him that she had talent: but he left the house and turned down the street and she looked after him. He was tall, lean, and rather shabby, and walked like a person who is hot in a hurry and has no particular destination. She didn't know where he went after he left her or how he spent his time; she guessed, however, that he didn't spend much of it at his home. When he had turned the corner she went back into the house. She was triumphant that day with joy. She even had visions of the marquee where the concerts took place and saw herself sitting on the stage, in the centre of a group of musicians. There would only be a thin and scattered audience – most people didn't bother to come till later when it was time for the important musician to start – nor would they be paying much attention, the way audiences don't pay much attention to the preliminaries before the big fight. But she would be there, singing, and not only for herself and her teacher. Yes, that was beautiful too, she loved it, but there had to be something more, she knew that; she had to give another dimension to her singing by performing before strangers. Now she realized she longed to do so. But she also knew it was not to be thought of. She was a housewife from a fine respectable middle-class family – people like her didn't sing in public. It would be an outrage, to her husband, to Phuphiji, to Manju's husband and Manju's inlaws. Even little Baba would be shocked, he wouldn't know what to think if he saw his granny singing before a lot of strangers.

That day she had another surprise. Her husband came home with a packet which he threw in her direction, saying laconically, 'Take.' She opened it and, when she saw the contents, a lightning flash of pleasure passed through her. It was a pair of earrings, 24-carat gold set with rubies and pearls. Her husband watched her hooking them into her ears, pleased with her and pleased with his purchase. He explained to her how he had got them cheaply, as a bargain, from a fellow contractor who was in difficulties and had been forced to sell his wife's jewellery. Shakuntala locked them away carefully in her steel safe in which she kept all her other ornaments. Next day she took them out again and wore them and looked at herself this side and that. While she was doing this, Phuphiji came in and, seeing the earrings, let out a cry. 'Hai, hai!' she cried, and came up and touched them as they dangled from Shakuntala's ears. Shakuntala took them off and locked them up again with the other things, though not before Phuphiji's eyes had devoured them in every detail. 'He brought for you?' Phuphiji inquired and Shakuntala nodded briefly and turned the key of the safe and fastened the bunch back to the string at her waist. Suddenly Phuphiji was sitting on the bed, weeping. She wept over the good fortune of some and the ill fortune of others who had been left widows at an early age and had no one to care for them. When Shakuntala had nothing to say to comfort her, she comforted herself and, wiping the corners of her eyes with the end of her sari, said it was fate, there was nothing to be done about it. It was the way things were ordained in this particular life – though next time, who knew, everything might come out quite differently; wheels always came full circle and those that were kings and queens now might, at the next turn, find themselves nothing more than ants or some other form of lowly insect. This thought cheered her, and she went out and sat on the veranda and called to the servant-boy for a glass of hot tea.

Over the next few days, Shakuntala kept taking out her new earrings. She also took out some of her other pieces and admired them and put them on before the mirror. She loved gold and precious stones and fine workmanship; she also loved to see these things sparkling on herself and the effect they made against her skin and set off all her good points. She preened herself before the mirror and smiled like a girl. One afternoon, when she had spent some time in this pleasant way, she came out and found her teacher sitting on the blue sofa in the drawing-room. Phuphiji had as usual taken up her place near him. She was staring at him and he was yawning widely. They looked like two people who had been sitting there for a long time with nothing to say to each other. Shakuntala went out into the kitchen and quickly got some refreshments ready. Phuphiji followed her. 'What's the use?' she said. 'He won't eat, his stomach is not accustomed to these things.' But that day he did eat, very quickly and ravenously like a man who has had nothing for some time. Shakuntala, watching him, saw that there was something wolf-like about him when he ate like that; she also noticed that he looked more haggard and unkempt than usual. And just before leaving, when he was already by the door, he asked her for an advance of salary. He asked quite casually and without embarrassment; it was she who was embarrassed. She went into the bedroom to take out her money. Phuphiji followed and whispered urgently, 'He asked for money? Don't give him.' Shakuntala ignored her. She went out and gave it to him and he put it in his pocket without counting and walked away without saying anything further.

Next morning, however, after she had finished singing, he said that it was good she had given him that money, it had come in very useful. She didn't ask anything, out of delicacy, but he volunteered the information that there was some 'domestic upset'. He said this with a shrug and a laugh, not out of bravado but really, obviously, because it didn't matter to him. Then also she realized that his whole domestic set-up – his dirty room, his quarrelsome wife – which had so unpleasantly affected her, that too didn't matter to him and her pity was misplaced. On the contrary, today as she watched him walk away down the street, in his shabby grey-white clothes, and his downtrodden slippers, she envied him. She thought how he went where he liked and did what he liked. Her own circumstances were so different. All that day Phuphiji was after her, she nagged at her, she kept asking how much money she had given him, why had she given him, had her husband been told that this money had been given? At last Shakuntala went into her bedroom and bolted the door from inside. It was a very hot day, and the room was close and humid and mosquitoes buzzed inside with stinging noises. Partly out of boredom, partly in the hope of cheering herself up, she unlocked her jewellery again; but now it failed to give her pleasure. It was just things, metal.

Someone rattled at the door, she shouted, 'No, no!' But it was Manju. She unbolted the door and opened it just sufficiently to let Manju in; Phuphiji hovered behind but Shakuntala quickly shut her out. Manju saw her mother's jewellery spread out on the bed. She at once detected the new earrings and picked them up and asked where they had come from. 'Put them on,' Shakuntala invited her, and Manju lost no time in doing so. She looked in the mirror and liked herself very much in them. She went back to the bed and played with the other ornaments. One day they would all be hers but that day was still far off. She looked wistful and Shakuntala guessed what she was thinking and it made her want to pile everything into Manju's lap right now and say, 'Take it.' And indeed when Manju, sighing a bit, put up her hand to take the earrings off again, Shakuntala suddenly said, 'You can keep them.' Manju was astonished, she tried to protest, she said, 'Papa will be angry'; but her mother insisted. Then Manju returned to the mirror, she admired herself more than ever and a pleased smile of proprietorship lit up her somewhat glum features. Shakuntala stood behind her at the mirror. She too smiled with pleasure, though she could see that the earrings didn't suit Manju as well as they suited herself. This made her kiss her all the more tenderly. She was glad to see Manju happy with the gift.

*   *   *

For herself, nothing nowadays seemed to make her happy. Not even her early morning singing. Yet she was making good progress. It was one of those periods when she was beginning to master something that had up till then defeated her: now she saw that it lay within her power, a little more effort and she would be there and then she could begin to set her sights on the next impossible step. But, in spite, of this triumph, she was dissatisfied and she knew her teacher was too. Once or twice he had again broached the subject of her singing in public; each time she had had to put him off, by silence, by a sad smile. He knew her reasons, of course, but did not sympathize with them. Once he even told her, then what is the use? And she knew he was right – what *was* the use – if it was all to be locked up here in. the house and no one to hear, no one to care, no other heart to be touched and respond. And all around her the birds tumbled about in the bright air and sang out lustily, pouring themselves out without stint. She fell into despondency at herself, but her teacher was angry. He said what did she expect, that he came here to waste his time on training *housewives*? Then she began to be afraid that he would stop coming and every morning she got up and went on the roof with her heart beating in fear; and how it leaped in relief when he did come – cross usually, and sour, and displeased with her, but he was there, he hadn't yet given her up.

  He didn't come so often in the afternoons any more, and when he did come, he stayed for a shorter time. It seemed he was bored and restless there. Now his glance of disdain fell not only on the refreshments but on all the shiny furniture and the calendars and the pictures on the wall. And most of all on Phuphiji. Her presence, which he had before accepted with such equanimity, now irritated him intensely. He made no attempt to hide this, but Phuphiji did not care: she kept right on sitting there, and when any comment occurred to her she made it. His visit usually ended in his jumping up and hurrying away, muttering to himself. Once, when he had got outside the door, he said to Shakuntala, 'You should burn her, that's the only thing old women are good for, burning.' Shakuntala's mouth corners twitched with amusement, but he was not in a joking mood. Next morning he asked her for another loan and she was glad to give it. He frequently asked her for money now. He ceased to make the excuse that it was an advance on salary, he just asked for the money and then pocketed it as if it were his right. He never counted it, the transaction was too trifling for him to bother that much about it.

It was not in the least trifling to Phuphiji. Although Shakuntala tried to keep these loans secret, it was not easy – indeed not possible – to keep anything that went on in the house secret from Phuphiji. She kept asking questions about the teacher's salary and whether he had taken any advance and, if so, how much; and when Shakuntala said she didn't remember, Phuphiji reproached her, she said that was not the way to deal with her husband's money. Once she caught them at it. She had hidden herself behind the water-butt in the courtyard and came pouncing out just as Shakuntala untied a bundle of notes and passed them to the teacher. Oh, asked Phuphiji, she was paying him his salary? That was strange, she said, it wasn't the first of the month, it wasn't anywhere near the first, it was somewhere about the middle of the month and surely that wasn't the time for paying anyone's, salary? Before she could get any further, the teacher had taken out the money and flung it at her feet. Phuphiji jumped back a step or two as if it were some dangerous explosive. 'Look at that,' she cried, 'see how he behaves!' But Shakuntala swooped down on the notes and picked them up and ran after him. He was already half-way down the street and didn't turn round. She had to implore him to stop. When he did, she thrust the money into his hand and he took it and stuffed it carelessly into his pocket and then continued his progress down the street.

Phuphiji would have dearly liked to complain to Shakuntala's husband, but she dared not. Indeed, she could not, for Shakuntala's husband never listened to her; if she wanted anything from him, she always had to approach him through Shakuntala. All she could do now was hover around him while he sat and ate his food. She shook out cushions that didn't need shaking, she waved away flies that weren't there, and talked to herself darkly in soliloquy. When she became too obtrusive, he turned to Shakuntala and asked, 'What's she say? What does the old woman want?' Then Phuphiji left off and went to sit outside, squatting on the floor with her knees hunched up and her head supported on her fist like a woman in mourning. Sometimes she used the supporting fist to strike her brow.

But she was more successful with Manju. She managed, by hints rather than by direct narration, to convey a sense of unease, even danger to Manju. She mentioned no figures but gave the impression that large sums of money were changing hands and that the teacher and all his family were being kept in luxury on money supplied by Shakuntala. 'I hear they are buying a television set,' Phuphiji whispered. 'Can you imagine people like that, who never had five rupees to their name? A television set! Where do they get it from?' And Manju drew back from Phuphiji's face thrust close into hers, in shock and fright. Shakuntala came in and found them like that. 'What's the matter?' she asked, looking from one to the other. 'We're just having a talk,' Phuphiji said.

Another day Phuphiji hinted that it was not only money that was going out of the house but other things too.

'What?' Manju, who was not very quick, asked her.

'Very precious things,' Phuphiji said.

Manju faltered: 'Not –?'

Phuphiji nodded and sighed.

'Her *jewellery*?' Manju asked, hand on heart.

Phuphiji stared into space.

'Oh God,' Manju said. She caught up little Baba and held him in a close embrace as if to protect him against unscrupulous people out to rob him of his inheritance. Baba began to cry.

Manju cried with him, and so did Phuphiji, two hard little tears dropping from her as if squeezed from eyes of stone.

'It's true, she's in a strange mood,' Manju said. She told Phuphiji how her mother had given her the new earrings: for no reason at all, had just waved her hand and said casually, 'Take them.' That was not the way to give away jewellery, no not even to your own daughter. It showed a person was strange. And who knew, if she was in that kind of mood, what she would do next – was perhaps already doing – perhaps she was already telling other people, 'Take them,' in that same casual way, waving her hand negligently over all that was most precious to a woman and a family. The thought struck horror into Phuphiji and Manju, and when Shakuntala came in, they both looked up at her as if she were someone remote from and dangerous to them.

Shakuntala hardly noticed them. Her thoughts were day and night elsewhere, and she longed only to be sitting on the roof practising her singing while her teacher listened to her. But nowadays he seemed to be bored with her. He tended to stay for shorter periods, he yawned and became restless and left her before she had finished. When he left her like that, she ceased to sing but continued to sit on the roof by herself; she breathed heavily as if in pain, and indeed her sense of unfulfilment was like pain and stayed with her for the rest of the day. The worst was when he did not turn up at all. This was happening more and more frequently. Days passed and she didn't see him and didn't sing; then he came again – she would step up on the roof in the morning, almost without hope, and there he would be. He had no explanation to offer for his absence, nor did she ask for one. She began straightaway to sing, grateful and happy. She was also grateful and happy when he asked her for money; it seemed such a small thing to do for him. Phuphiji noticed everything – his absences, her loans. She said nothing to Shakuntala but watched her. Manju came often and the two of them sat together and Phuphiji whispered into Manju's ear and Manju cried and looked with red, reproachful eyes at her mother.

*   *   *

One evening Manju and Phuphiji were both present while Shakuntala was serving her husband his meal. When he had finished and was dabbling his hand in the finger-bowl held for him by his wife, Phuphiji suddenly got up and, stepping close to Shakuntala, stood on tiptoe to look at her ears. She peered and squinted as if she couldn't see very well: she with eyes as sharp as little needles! 'Are they new?' she asked.

'He gave them to me when Manju was born,' Shakuntala replied quite calmly and even smiled a bit at the transparency of Phuphiji's tactics.

'Ah,' said Phuphiji and paused. Her nose itched, she scratched it by pressing the palm of her hand against it and rubbing it round and round. When she had finished and emerged with her nose very red and tears in her eyes from this exertion, she said, 'But he gave you some new ones?'

'Yes,' Shakuntala said.

'I haven't seen them,' Phuphiji said. She turned to Manju: 'Have you?'

Manju was silent. Shakuntala could feel that she was very tense, and so was Phuphiji. Both of them were anxious as to the outcome of this scene. But Shakuntala found herself to be completely indifferent.

Phuphiji turned to Shakuntala's husband: 'Have you seen them?' she asked. 'Where are they? Those new earrings you gave her?'

Shakuntala knew that Phuphiji and Manju were both waiting for her to speak so that they could deny what she was going to say. But she said nothing and only handed the towel to her husband to dry his hands. She didn't want Manju to have to say or do anything that would make her feel very bad afterwards.

'Why don't you ask her?' Phuphiji said. 'Go on, ask her: where are those new earrings I gave you? Ask. Let's hear what she has to say.'

For one second her husband looked at Shakuntala; his eyes were like those of an old bear emerging from his winter sleep.

But the next moment he had flung down the towel and stamped on it in rage. He shouted at Phuphiji and abused her. He said he didn't come home to be pestered and needled by a pack of women that's not what he expected after his hard day's work. He also shouted at Manju and asked her why sit on his back, let her go home and sit on her husband's back, what else had she been married off for at enormous expense? Manju burst into tears, but that was nothing new and no one tried to comfort her, not even Phuphiji who busied herself with clearing away the dirty dishes, patient and resigned in defeat.

That night passed slowly for Shakuntala. She lay beside her husband and was full of restless thoughts. But when morning came and her teacher again failed to show up, then she did not hesitate any longer. She went straight to his house. She walked through his courtyard where they were hammering pieces of plywood together, up the stairs, past the music school, and up to his door. It had a big padlock on it. She was put out, but only for a moment. She went down to the music school. Several thin men in poor clothes sat on the floor testing out drums and tuning stringed instruments; they looked at her curiously, and even more curiously when she asked for him. They shrugged at each other and laughed. 'God knows,' they said. 'Ever since she went, he's here and there.' 'Who went?' Shakuntala asked. They looked at her again and wondered. 'His wife,' one of them said at last. Shakuntala was silent and so. were they.

She didn't know what else to ask. She turned and went down the stairs. One of them followed and looked down at her from the landing. As if in afterthought he called: 'He sits around in the restaurants!' She walked through the courtyard where they stopped hammering and also looked after her with curiosity.

Shakuntala had lived in the town all her life, but she was only familiar with certain restricted areas of it. There were others that she knew of, had seen and of necessity passed through on her way to somewhere else, but which remained mysterious and out of bounds to her. One of these was the street where the singing and dancing girls lived, and another was the street where the restaurants were. The two were connected, and to get to the restaurants Shakuntala had first to pass through the other street. This was lined with shops selling coloured brassieres, scents, and filigree necklaces, and on top of the shops were balconies on which the girls sat. Downstairs stood little clusters of men with betel-stained mouths; they looked at Shakuntala and some of them made sweet sounds as she passed. Here and there from upstairs came the sound of ankle-bells and a few bars tapped out for practice on a drum. The street of the restaurants was much quieter. No sounds came out from behind the closed doors of the restaurants. They were called *Bombay House, Shalimar, Monna Lisa, Taj Mahal.* Shakuntala hesitated only before the first one and even then only for a moment before pushing open the door. They were mostly alike from inside with a lot of peeling plaster-of-paris decorations and a smell of fried food, tobacco, and perfumed oil. The clientele was alike too. There was no woman among them, and Shakuntala's presence attracted attention. There was some laughter and, despite her age, also the sweet sounds she had heard from the men in the streets.

She found him in the third one she entered (*Bombay House*). He was one of a group lounging against the wall on a red leather bench behind a table cluttered with plates and glasses. He was drumming one hand rhythmically on the table and swaying and dipping his head in time to a tune playing inside it. When Shakuntala stepped up to the table, the other men sitting with him were astonished; their jaws stopped chewing betel and dropped open. Only he went on swaying and drumming to the tune in his mind. He let her stand there for a while, then he said to the others, 'She's my pupil. I teach her singing.' He added, 'She's a housewife,' and sniggered. No one else said anything nor moved. She noticed that his eyes were heavy and with a far-away blissful look in them.

He got up and, tossing some money on the table, left the restaurant. She followed him, back the same way she had come past the restaurants and through the street of the singing and dancing girls. He walked in front all the time. He was still singing the same tune to himself and was still at the introductory stage, letting the raga develop slowly and spaciously. His hand made accompanying gestures in the air. He also waved this hand at people who greeted him on the way and sometimes to the girls when they called down to him from the balconies. He seemed to be a well-known figure. Walking behind him, Shakuntala remembered the many times she had stood in the doorway of her house watching him as he walked, slowly and casually like someone with all time at his disposal, away from her down the street; only now she did not have to turn back into her house, no she was following him and going where he was going. The tune he was singing began in her mind too and she smiled to it and let it unfold itself in all its glory.

He led the way back to his house and they walked up the stairs, and first the men in the courtyard and then the men in the music school looked after them. He unfastened the big padlock on his door. Inside everything was as before when she had visited him in his sickness except that the sewing-machine was gone and the air was denser because no one had opened the window for a long time. His bedding, consisting of a mat and tumbled sheet, was as he must have left it in the morning. He wasted no time but at once came close to her and fumbled at her clothes and at his own. He was about the same age as her husband but lean, hard, and eager; as he came on top of her, she saw his drugged eyes so full of bliss and he was still smiling at the tune he was playing to himself. And this tune continued to play in her too. He entered her at the moment when, the structure of the raga having been expounded, the combination of notes was being played up and down, backwards and forwards, very fast. There was no going back from here, she knew. But who would want to go back, who would exchange this blessed state for any other?

Suffering Women

Anjana had never been a top film star, but she had done well enough to be able to retire comfortably. Now she lived in a very nice flat with lofty ceilings in one of the old Bombay houses and her daughter Kiku went to college and even spoke of going to America for higher studies. Anjana didn't intend to send her to America, but she liked to hear her talk about it. Many of Kiku's friends also intended to go to America for higher studies.

Anjana was proud of the friends Kiku had. They all came from very good backgrounds; their parents were professional or business people, and some of them belonged to Bombay's smart social set. Anjana was amazed at the freedom their children were allowed. Boys and girls who not only were not related but even came from different castes and communities went out together wherever they liked and with the full consent of their parents. Kiku had a boy friend too – Rahul – and it was so sweet to see them go out together, dancing or parties or a day on the beach; both of them were quite tall and very slim and wore the latest gay clothes.

When Kiku had first proposed going out with Rahul, Anjana had forbidden her to do so. She had shouted at Kiku and told her how she would be getting a bad name. Kiku had shouted back and they had had one of their scenes. On this occasion, as on most others, Kiku had won. Anjana had begun to be persuaded that times had changed and that everyone went out with boy friends now. Many impressive examples were cited (Shirin Mehta of the oil Mehtas, Leila Handa who had gone to school in Switzerland); finally Rahul himself was brought to the flat and made such a superb impression that the last shreds of the mother's fears could not but be blown away. Anjana saw at once that both her daughter and her daughter's reputation were absolutely safe with Rahul. A more well-bred, careful, *harmless* boy did not exist.

Long after Anjana had resigned herself to Rahul and had indeed learned to rejoice in him, Thakur Sahib was still dissatisfied. Thakur Sahib was Anjana's lover. They had been together for many years. Thakur Sahib was married and had several daughters of his own. Although he was a film producer and moved among easy-living people, he kept his daughters very strictly – perhaps more strictly than a man less conversant with what went on in the world might have done. He didn't care for the freedom Kiku was allowed, and he especially didn't care for her to go out with Rahul. Anjana explained about the modern world and changing society, just as Kiku had explained to her, but Thakur Sahib pushed out his lips in a sceptical way. Anjana became annoyed with him. She said he was old and stubborn and his attitude made him ridiculous in the eyes of intelligent people. His only reply was to push out his lips further.

He was lying on Anjana's bed in her bedroom on her pink velvet bedspread. She would have liked to fold it back to prevent it from getting spoiled, but she didn't care to disturb him once he had made himself comfortable. And he was very comfortable: his paunch, with his hands folded on top of it, rose mightily above the bed and breathed up and down.

Anjana said, 'There is no harm at all. They're just two children – a little boy and girl playing together.'

Thakur Sahib's lids had sunk like rolling shutters to cover his eyes, leaving only a small knowing glint shining out at her from underneath. He said, in a calm, comfortable voice, that there was only one game little boys and girls played together. Anjana got very angry and shouted at him for his bad thoughts. But he was unrepentant and continued to lie there, unmoving, so that she knew it was no use shouting any further. He was one of the few people she had had in her life who would not participate in a scene. When she tried to start one with him, he always shrugged her off – with an indifference which, in spite of the fury it inspired in her, she could not help admiring: for its strength, its manliness.

She sank down by the side of the bed and, taking his feet between her hands, began to massage them. They were surprisingly small and delicate feet. She loved them. She pressed and squeezed them and pulled each toe till it ticked and he cried out in ecstasy. Each cry was an inspiration to her. She knew that never in his life had he had anyone who knew how to massage the way she did. His wife had no skill at all, Now Anjana massaged him even when she went to visit him in his own house (and she was an unquestioned visitor there now; after initial difficulties, everything had settled down very nicely). His wife watched and didn't mind. She had accepted the fact that it was not in her power to give him pleasure and had become indifferent to seeing him get it from others. Sometimes, watching, she shrugged and smiled in a superior way, as one who had long since left all such things behind her.

'Last night they went dancing,' Anjana said, while he lay there made helpless and soft. 'All the young people go.' She gave his ankles a squeeze so delicate, so refined that any man's soul would have been charmed out of his body. 'I wish you could have seen them. He came to fetch her in his father's car. He was wearing trousers – tight, tight!' She showed how tight and laughed. 'Such a slim boy. Not like some people'; she laughed again and hit her fist against Thakur Sahib's hips which shook like a woman's. But then she made a kissing sound into the air to show how much all the same she loved him. More than all the slim boys in the world! 'And Kiku had her new orange silk kameez with pearl embroidery all down here. She has such taste, that child, like a princess. And you should hear her talking with the tailor. Each little stitch has to be just right, or she makes him open it all up again. Oh she's strict with them! Of course they charge – everybody charges – the material, if I told you what it cost. But I'm there for the bill, why worry.' She had worked her way up from his feet to his knees now: he lay and enjoyed; she could say anything she liked. She knew he did not approve of Kiku's extravagant taste or of the very modern way she dressed either. His own girls' wardrobe was much more modest in both price and style. Of course their looks too were not like Kiku's.

'He brought flowers for her and chocolate marzipan from Bombelli's,' she said. 'He's such a sweet boy. And what a *gentleman.* But she treats him – well, you know how she is with everybody. She's the queen and the rest of the world has to be her slave. She didn't even say thank you for the flowers and chocolates – didn't look at them, as if they were nothing. But I know she was pleased, don't I know her. And she was pleased to be fetched in a car and she could hardly *wait* to get to that place they go for dancing, though she pretended it wasn't anything and she would just as soon stay at home. She even said to him: "Why don't we stay home and play cards with Mamma." Yes, in her new kameez – I can just see her staying at home to play cards with me!' She had been merry up till then, but on that she sighed and became philosophical: 'Let the old stay at home, when you're young, that's the time. It won't come back again. Do you like it?' she whispered to him, her fingers sinking deep into his thighs. 'Am I doing it well?' He put out his hand and – fond, familiar, and grateful – he patted her.

'Why grudge their happiness,' she said. 'What's left for us? Now at this age.'

Then he said something which a man of means and standing like Thakur Sahib will only say to his most intimate friend in their most intimate moments. For decency's sake, she suppressed a smile, though it would hardly be suppressed; and to punish him, she touched him in that place between his thighs her ministrations, had now reached. In spite of what she had said, she felt at that moment that she and Thakur Sahib were not old at all but, on the contrary, quite young and mischievous.

Anjana's best friend was a lady called Sultana. Anjana had long since retired as a film actress, but Sultana still kept going. Of course she could no longer play the heroine's part, but was mostly cast in a subsidiary elderly role such as mother-in-law. She had made a speciality of that kind of part so that when she appeared on the screen everyone knew what to expect. She was a lot in demand and never dared to turn a part down for fear of not being asked again. As a result she was much busier than at her age she ought to have been and got quite worn out by the constant long shooting schedules and travelling to and fro.

'Why don't you give it up?' Anjana asked her one day when Sultana came to her looking even more tired than usual. She had come straight from the set and now lay reclining with her shoes off in Anjana's drawing-room. They were having tea and rather a lot to eat with the tea: stuffed pancakes, Bengali milk puffs swimming in cream, cashew nuts spiced with chili powder, egg sandwiches, and cakes covered with pink icing. Anjana kept pushing the dishes towards Sultana but Sultana only nibbled a bit here and there without appetite, while it was Anjana herself who enjoyed everything as food should be enjoyed.

Anjana advised her friend: 'You ought to retire and just lead a nice fat lazy life like I do.' She smiled in a fat lazy way.

Sultana didn't smile. Her mouth corners turned down further and she shrugged: 'Yes, and what about this?' she asked with some bitterness, rubbing two fingers together to suggest money.

Anjana spoke a drawn-out 'Oh' and made a deprecatory gesture with her hand: 'A rich woman like you.'

'Ha,' laughed Sultana with more bitterness.

Anjana knew very well that Sultana, in spite of her considerable earnings in the past and present, was not rich at all. She could have been, but she had one terrible extravagance: she was always falling in love with young men. Some of these young men were aspiring film actors, others liked to lead a life devoted to art and culture. In either case, they were rather demanding and had expensive tastes. So Sultana had to go on working.

'How is Sayyid?'

'He is redecorating the apartment,' Sultana replied without pleasure. Sayyid was the latest young man, an interior decorator.

'What, again!' cried Anjana.

'He says he needs practice.'

There was an unhappy silence. Anjana imagined how Sultana came home exhausted from the set to find her apartment full of paint and workmen and Sayyid running around irritably giving orders. There would be nowhere for her to sit and be comfortable, the way she was comfortable here with Anjana. If she tried to stretch out on a sofa in a corner, Sayyid would tell her, 'Not there please, darling,' and he would order the workmen to push the sofa away before she had quite had time to get up again. And afterwards, when it was all done, what prospect of comfort did she have even then? Sayyid went in for very modern furniture; he also liked very modern pictures on the wall, mostly painted by his friends.

Anjana got up and tucked a huge satin cushion behind the other's back. She ran her fingers lovingly over Sultana's face: how tired she looked, her poor friend. 'Rest now,' she murmured. 'Be quite comfortable.' Sultana gratefully shut her eyes and murmured back, 'It's so nice here.'

It *was* nice. Kiku was always trying to get her mother to have the room redone in a modern style, but Anjana liked it the way it was. She had done up everything in royal blue velvet – she loved velvet best of all, it was almost alive it was so soft and sensuous – and where there wasn't velvet there was satin, and a carpet with flowers and vines and tigers and parrots woven into it; the furniture was heavy and intricately carved the way she had glimpsed it in rich people's houses when she was young; there were many ornaments such as vases with Japanese ladies on them, and china dogs, and dolls in quaint costumes. On the wall hung Anjana's favourite picture: a pale lady draped in diaphanous white sitting on a rock and looking out over the sea with wild, sad eyes, her arms clasped about her knees, her long hair blowing in the wind.

While Sultana rested, Anjana told her about Kiku and Rahul. But Sultana did not even make a pretence of being interested; she lay with her eyes shut and only opened them to look at her nails and blow a speck of dust off them. It was always like that with her. She wasn't interested in Kiku, and whenever Anjana spoke about her, she became bored. Of course this was because she had never had a child of her own and did not have a heart big enough to rejoice in the happiness of others.

Aajana gave a great sigh both of resignation and contentment: 'What other pleasure is there left to us except what we get from our children?'

Sultana yawned. She didn't open her mouth to do so, but instead she swallowed the yawn and made a pained face as if it were something unpleasant she had swallowed.

'It's a pity,' Anjana said, 'you don't have some young people about you. It would help you to keep yourself young and not feel so tired all the time.'

Of course as soon as she had said this, Anjana realized her mistake. Sultana threw her a quick ironic look. She had always been famous for her eyes which were not full, dark, and passionate like Anjana's, but disturbingly light-coloured (Sultana claimed Persian ancestry) and flecked with cold, fierce lights like those of a tigress.

Anjana's anger grew at having these famous eyes used on her. She cried, 'The only way to know and love the young is as a mother!'

Sultana also became angry but, as usual when this happened, she did not shout but smiled (showing her small, slightly pointed teeth which were still as white as in her youth and almost as perfect) and sent lights to flicker from her eyes.

'Look at you,' said Anjana, holding out her hand and waving it to and fro to indicate her friend's reclining figure. 'So tired you can hardly breathe and now you have to go home and play with your Sayyid. I *pity* you,' she added, twisting her lips in a contemptuous rather than pitying way.

'Thank you,' said Sultana, 'but I'd rather have someone to laugh and play with than a fat old man snoring on my bed.'

Anjana could not, on the spur of the moment, think of anything insulting enough to reply, so she said in a very mean voice and with a mean expression on her face: 'If you knew how people talked about you.'

'Let them talk,' said Sultana. She sat up on the sofa and began to grope for her shoes with her feet.

'I feel ashamed when I hear the things that are said about you. I want to get angry with people, to say she is my friend, it's not true, but how can I when it *is* true. Lie down, what are you sitting up for.'

Sultana wriggled her feet into her shoes, one at a time, wearily.

'Now I suppose you want to run away. A little bit of truth and you run. Go on, lie *down*.' She leaned forward and gave the other a push that sent her sprawling back on the sofa. Sultana lay where she fell and made no further attempt to move.

Anjana said, 'Who else will tell you if I don't? Who else have you got in this world to care for you the way I care? Ridiculous – working like a – like a – and for what? So that you can keep some young – some little – no all right, I'll be quiet!' she cried as Sultana opened her dangerous eyes. 'I'll say nothing!' She poured more tea into Sultana's cup and said in a fury, 'Drink this.'

'I don't want,' Sultana said with closed eyes.

'*Drink* it!'

Sultana turned her face away. Her eyes remained closed. Anjana knew she would not take the tea. She stood holding it and looking down into Sultana's face, exasperated by its expression of obstinacy and both exasperated and pained by the exhaustion so clearly written there.

'Don't drink,' Anjana said, setting the cup down with a clatter and bang. 'Don't eat, don't drink. Kill yourself. That's the best way.'

Anjana and Sultana had known each other for more than thirty years. During that time their relationship had had many ups and downs. Years had passed during which they had not been on speaking terms. Other years they had been like sisters. In their youth, in the heyday of their careers, they had been professional rivals. They had both played heroines in the same kind of second-grade films; both had been very popular among taxi-drivers, wrestlers, and small boys queueing up for the four-anna seats on Saturday mornings. Sultana, with her tigress eyes and lithe figure, had played bold, manly parts and had been cheered out of thousands of throats as she galloped over the Khyber Pass, clutching in her arms the infant king whom she had rescued in the nick of time from his black-bearded murderers. Anjana, on the other hand, all soft bosom and melting eyes, had been made love to in trellissed bowers and danced ankle-deep in meadows of white primroses. Off-screen, they were both equally romantic and had been remarkable for the number and intensity of their love affairs. It was here, and not in their professional lives, that their rivalry had for a time turned into bitter enmity.

The cause had been Kiku's father. They had both been in love with him, and he had inclined first to one and then to the other. Finally, when she became pregnant, Anjana had got him to marry her. Sultana's rage and anguish had known no bounds, although it became clear quite soon that it was Anjana who had had the worst of it. Kiku's father had never forgiven her for their marriage. It was not only that he was a Muslim and she a Hindu, but also that he came from an old Lucknow family claiming descent from courtiers, while Anjana's mother and grandmother (like Sultana's) had been dancing-girls. He could not forget his fall, and she too had become deeply imbued with feelings of guilt. She did all she could to make it up to him, keeping him in the luxury that he loved and pampering him in all his desires and manifold tastes. Nothing did any good. Sick with self-disgust, he became more slothful, more bitter, drank all night and slept all day, wrote poetry squashy with too many nightingales and roses and laments for the transience of all worldly delights: till finally he was found dead from taking a combination of drink and drugs which he may or may not have known to be fatal in effect. Anjana and Sultana had a reconciliation scene over his bier worthy of one of their own films; but their high-flown language, the torn hair and clothes, the wailing and the breast-beating were real. Passion and grief had torn their hearts in two, and when they mended again they were found to have grown together in a rough jagged way and could not be parted again.

Kiku was not ready when Rahul came to fetch her, so Anjana made him comfortable in the drawing-room and sat by him to keep him company. But she did not feel easy. It may have been his too good, too deferential manners; and the thought of his aristocratic parents in their fashionable home and what they would think if they saw him sitting there talking to her; and what if she said something wrong, which might undermine his opinion not only of her but of Kiku too on her account? It was a relief to her when Kiku was ready at last and came into the drawing-room, clicking on high heels, a flower cunningly entwined in her hair. She did not apologize for having kept him waiting, but on the contrary made it seem as if he were keeping her: 'Well come on! What are you waiting for? New Year?'

Anjana watched them leave from her bedroom window. His car was parked on the pavement several storeys below her. She watched him open the car door for her, watched Kiku glide gracefully in. They drove off. Anjana looked up to the sky and prayed: God, bless them. From the sky her eyes reluctantly came down again to the building opposite. Once she had had a wonderful view of the sea from her bedroom window, but some five years ago a building as tall as her own had been built on the site opposite. It was a private nursing-home. Some of the patients were permanent inmates and had probably been placed there by rich relatives unwilling to keep them at home. The same woman had stood at the window facing Anjana's ever since the place had opened. Hour after hour she looked out over the iron bars which reached half-way up the window. At first Anjana had tried to make friendly overtures to her but when she got no response at all, when the woman had simply gone on staring in the same blank way, Anjana had realized that she was not right in her mind.

Anjana drew the curtains, she turned on the lamps. The curtains were of pink velvet, the lampshades pink satin. She should have felt cosy and safe, but she felt neither. She knew too well what terrible things can happen. Kiku didn't know anything about that. She thought that if you had money and lived in a comfortable home nothing could touch you. Again Anjana raised her eyes in prayer, begging blessing and protection for her child. If only she could have been sure that there was someone to hear her! But all she saw was her white ceiling with a basket of roses moulded on it in plaster-of-paris. Sighing with pain, she went to the telephone and rang up Thakur Sahib. She needed him so much.

Thakur Sahib was not as young as he had been, and he got very tired running around all day dealing with financiers, film stars, and distributors. So it was not a small request, Anjana knew, to get him out again in the evening when he had settled down comfortably at home and had eaten his meal and was ready to go to sleep. All the same, he came at her call, and she was so grateful that she could not do enough for him. She made herself be gay and lively, talked a lot, and ran to and fro plying him with drinks and refreshments. He sat in the most comfortable chair in the room, propped up from every side by her satin cushions; behind him on the wall hung her favourite picture of the lady in white gazing over the sea. Anjana sat on the carpet at Thakur Sahib's feet and leaned her head against his knee; from time to time she took a sip from his glass, making a face at the taste of the whisky.

'Where's Kiku?' he asked.

'She's gone out.' But she changed the subject quickly; she didn't want to have an argument with him today on the subject of Kiku. Instead she began talking to him about Sultana, telling him about her friend's money worries and the hard life she led.

Thakur Sahib said, 'Whose fault is that.' He wasn't very sympathetic towards Sultana. As a matter of fact, he wasn't sympathetic towards any actress. He had to have a lot to do with them and of course made his money through them, but he didn't like them or approve of the way they lived.

'Poor thing,' said Anjana, 'she's looking so tired and old.'

Thakur Sahib shrugged and took a drink from his glass. Then he said, 'That one came to see me today.'

'Who?'

'What's her name – Tara Bai.'

'Tara Bai!'

'I didn't recognize her. She looks like an old beggar-woman. The servants nearly drove her away.'

'What did she want?'

'What do they always want.'

'Money?'

'What else.'

Anjana turned her face from him so that he would not see the expression on it. Tara Bai had been a very famous actress, a bigger star than either Sultana or Anjana. But she had had a troubled life, like so many others.

'Where is she living?' Anjana asked. Thakur Sahib didn't know and didn't care. Unable to stop herself, Anjana went on asking

How I Became a Holy Mother and Other Stories

questions in a frightened, frenzied way: 'What about her son? She had a son, from that musician she was with. Where is he? Why isn't he looking after his mother?'

'I gave her fifty rupees and didn't ask any questions. I was glad to get rid of her.' He noticed the look on Anjana's face: 'What's the matter with you? Why should you care about these people?'

Anjana kept quiet. She didn't want to remind him that she too had been one of them. It was all different now – she had saved money and bought shares and lived respectably on the interest. Her daughter went to college. Why should she be afraid? She got up and refilled his glass, then perched on his knees and held the glass to his lips to make him drink. She pressed herself so closely against him that he could feel her heart beating through her ample warm flesh.

The telephone rang. Anjana went out to answer it. It was one of Thakur Sahib's daughters. After apologizing for disturbing auntie (as she called Anjana), she asked to have a message delivered to her father. Anjana went to tell him: it was some business matter, a meeting to be arranged in the morning. At once the expression on his face changed and he became the busy film producer. He began to give her instructions what to reply on the telephone, but midway changed his mind and got up to answer himself. Anjana followed and listened to him talking to his daughter. She pointed to herself to indicate that she too would like to talk. He nodded, but at the end of his conversation he put down the receiver and returned to the room, engrossed in his thoughts.

'I wanted to talk,' she said, following him.

'What?'

'I wanted to talk to her about her exam. Poor child, she was so worried. I wanted to ask her how she got on. And then you put it down. How does it look?'

'It doesn't matter.'

'To you no, but what will the child think? She will say to herself, "Just see, auntie doesn't care about me, she doesn't even ask."'

'No one will think.'

He spoke with curt authority, but she continued to brood. She thought of his family, his wife and daughters, and how wrong it was of her to call him away from them like this in the evening. She knew herself to be guilty. But her need of him was so great. She could not live without Thakur Sahib. If they parted, her life would be a dark tunnel, she would grope here and there and be lost and afraid. But what right, she asked herself, had she compared with *their* right? If they hated and cursed her, it would only be what she deserved. Suddenly she threw back her head and, flinging her hands before her face, rocked herself to and fro.

Thakur Sahib started forward in his chair and shouted, 'What is it? What is it?'

'You put it down on purpose! You don't want me to talk to her!'

'Madwoman!'

'You think I'm like Tara Bai, that I've led a bad life. And you're right: I *have* led a bad life. Very bad. Oh God!' She sobbed.

Thakur Sahib was angry. He tried to force her to uncover her face and look at him; but she wouldn't, and the angrier he grew, the more she said he was right to be angry with her. She said what she really deserved was for him to go away, go back to his family, leave her for ever. But when, cursing her obstinacy, he turned from her for a moment, she leaped up and, throwing herself on the floor, clasped her arms around his knees and declared that if he went, if he left her, she would kill herself. She even described how she would kill herself, committing suttee for his departure in the best tradition by pouring kerosene over her clothes and setting herself on fire.

She let go of his legs and stretched herself flat on the floor. 'Yes leave me,' she said. 'Let me lie here and die.' And indeed, she lay quite still on the floor, as one dead already.

'Enough now,' Thakur Sahib said quite calmly and sat down in his armchair again. He drank what was left of his whisky. Anjana sat up. She dried her eyes with the end of her sari and scrambled up from the floor, groaning as she did so for her knee was somewhat stiff and hurt her. She got back into her former position on his lap, her arms entwined about his neck. Over his shoulder she could see her picture of the lady sitting on a rock and looking with suffering eyes out over the sea. It was not hard to guess why she was suffering. There was only one thing could fill a woman's eyes with such expression, or indeed make her hair fly with such wild abandon in the wind. Anjana laid her lips on Thakur Sahib's cheek and left them there. He had a strong growth and should by rights have shaved twice a day, but she loved the tough bristles poking her skin. She laid one hand on the back of his head to bring him closer to her face. She didn't like the taste of whisky, but she loved the smell of it after he had drunk it.

When Sultana did not come to see her for more than a week, Anjana became worried about her and went to visit her. Sultana lived right on top of a very new tall white apartment building from where she had a wonderful view of the sea and other tall white apartment buildings. The apartment was very expensive, and the constant redecorating to which Sayyid subjected it also cost a great deal. On this visit Anjana found everything quite different from the last time she had been there. Sayyid had now entered a very austere stage: the walls were painted stark white, and what little furniture he had allowed himself was made of metal in sharp geometrical shapes.

Sultana was sitting on a comfortless, wrought-iron sofa, smoking a cigarette. She was wearing slacks in a leopard skin design and a shirt. Sultana was not fat, but she had the hips and bosom of an Indian woman and these burgeoned within the tight confines of her unaccustomed Western clothes. She looked up briefly when Anjana came in and went on smoking. Anjana knew at once that something had happened and that Sultana was in a very gloomy mood.

Anjana asked, 'Where's Sayyid?'

'God knows.' Sultana shrugged bitterly.

So that was it: of course Anjana had easily guessed. Sultana had great shadows under her eyes and looked as if she had not slept for several nights. Anjana imagined her lying in bed, staring into the dark. Sultana hardly ever wept. Instead her tigress eyes became dry and hard, and one could imagine them gleaming in the dark like green stones.

'When did he go?' Anjana said.

'Four days ago.' Sultana took a deep drag from her cigarette.

Anjana sighed; it was by no means a new situation. Not only Sayyid but earlier young men too had tended to disappear from time to time and then Sultana sat at home and smoked and waited and suffered.

'He'll come back,' Anjana said.

'Of course. When he's tired.'

'Some girl?'

'Or boy.' Sultana shrugged again.

Anjana's heart hurt for her so much she had to lay her hand on it and hold it. She knew what it was to have to wait for someone, pace the house and wonder what he was doing and with whom. Kiku's father used to disappear in the same way, before he had become too sunk in sloth and drink to want to move. And, with him too, one could never be sure in what company he had spent his time, whether it was some young girl or boy that had engaged his fancy.

Anjana asked, 'Did you have a quarrel?'

'We always have quarrels.'

'No, but anything special?'

'Everything is special. If I do my hair in a way he doesn't like, it's special. If I don't smile enough at his friends, that's special too. I must run here and there to serve them, otherwise I'm showing him disrespect. *I* show *him* disrespect! Can you imagine! That boy, half my age! Look!' She pushed up her sleeve; there was a scratch on her arm – nothing very bad, but Anjana cried out.

'That was for showing him disrespect. To teach me a lesson. But don't worry, he got plenty in return.' She laughed horribly. 'Wherever he's gone, he's taken a few marks with him to show.'

Anjana shook her head. God knew, she had gone through enough such scenes herself, but that had been long ago, when she was young and full of strength and spirit. 'At your age,' she told Sultana.

'I know! When all I want is peace and quiet! You know how I feel when I come home from shooting. But no, every night he's got some programme. And if I say I'm tired, then what scenes! Then how I'm spoiling, ruining his life! The names he calls me. Of course his favourite is old hag. It's all his own fault he says for getting himself entangled with an old hag.'

'No,' Anjana said, 'it's not his fault. It's yours.' She shifted uncomfortably on the little wrought-iron chair and it increased her temper. 'How can you live like this? Not even a place to sit! No wonder you're going mad. I would go mad. Anyone would. And don't smoke so much,' she added; for Sultana, having just ground out one half-smoked cigarette in the overflowing ashtray, had at once lit another.

'There's no taste in them,' Sultana said, filling herself up with smoke and blowing it out again in disgust through her nostrils.

It was Sayyid who had made her take to cigarettes. Before that she had smoked a hookah. She had had a very elaborate one with an enamelled base and a tube so long that it coiled and twisted into many rings. Sultana had reclined in her wide silk trousers on a silk-covered mattress, sucking at the silver mouthpiece while the hookah made soft soothing bubbling noises. In those days her room had always been thick and fragrant with a mixed smell of incense and tobacco. Now it didn't smell of anything.

'Listen,' Anjana said, leaning urgently towards her friend. 'You come home with me. Lock up this place, rent it out, do anything you like. But come with me. Now – at once! Where's Ayah? Let her pack your things.'

Sultana's eyes glittered with pleasure: 'What a shock he'll have when he comes home and finds me gone! Oh I would like to see his face! Just to see his face!'

'Never mind about him. Where are your keys? Give them to me.'

She held out her hand. Sultana lifted her shirt and fumbled for her keys which – in spite of her Western clothes – she kept on a string round her waist. She dropped them into Anjana's palm. But as soon as Anjana's fingers closed on them, she said, 'No, give them back.'

'I won't. I'll take out your jewels and a few clothes and then we're going. Ayah can bring the rest tomorrow.'

'I'll come tomorrow. I'll pack everything myself, that will be much better. Ayah doesn't know anything, she's so clumsy and stupid.'

'We're going *now.*'

Anjana held on tight to the keys. Sultana kept sitting and looking up at her with eyes which, in spite of their dry hard glitter, were almost appealing.

'Supposing he comes today –'

'So let him come. Very good.'

'Yes but I want to see his face! When I tell him it's finished, I'm renting out the apartment, there's no place for you here any more. For you *or* your friends. How will he look then? What will he do?' Sultana ground her teeth: 'I know what he'll do,' she said with vicious pleasure. 'He'll *cry.* He always cries when I'm really angry with him. Big tears.' She showed with her fingers how the tears coursed down his cheeks. 'Well this time I'll let him cry. I'll stand there and watch him.' She folded her arms in satisfaction and fixed her eyes in space as if she actually saw him standing there crying. Anjana didn't say anything but she had her hands on hips and one foot tapped up and down and there was a cynical expression on her face.

'He'll have a surprise,' Sultana said. 'He thinks it will be like always – that I'll take him in my arms, lay his head in my lap and beg him, don't cry. When I say that he always cries more. He presses his face into my thighs and sobs and sobs. And I stroke his head.' She stroked the air, with great tenderness.

Anjana opened the hand in which she had been clutching the keys and flung them towards Sultana. Sultana picked them up and fastened them back to the string at her waist. She laughed. She said, 'Well what can I do? He's so young, so lovely. Do you know he doesn't have one single hair on his chest? Smooth, smooth, like satin. Velvet,' she said in a voice like velvet.

At home Kiku was busy with the tailor. She was wearing another new outfit – in rose silk – but something had displeased her about the fit of the trousers. The tailor had been summoned and now he crouched on the floor sewing at her ankles while she looked down at him severely. She was ready to go out, ready to the last exquisite detail, with brand-new varnish on each finger and toe-nail. Her hair was swept up and garnished with a rose.

'Is Rahul coming to fetch you?' Anjana asked.

'I suppose so.' She stifled a yawn, then frowned down at the tailor who responded by crouching lower and plying his needle with redoubled energy. Appeased, she looked up again and at her mother. Anjana sat enjoying a little snack she had ordered for herself. Now Kiku frowned at her: 'Mamma, of course if you eat so much you must expect to get fat.'

'But I'm fat already.'

Kiku gave her a little lecture. She told her that even in middle age women had to keep themselves trim and slim and up to the mark. She gave her mother a few hints how to achieve this end, dwelling mainly on diet and exercise. Anjana respectfully listened. She was proud of Kiku's expertise and the forceful way in which she expounded it. Although so young, Kiku already knew so much and on so many interesting subjects.

Rahul arrived exactly on time. Anjana hastily sat up from her reclining position and fumbled at her dishevelled hair. He asked her permission to sit down and this flustered her, and in any case she was prevented from replying by having hair-pins in her mouth.

As always with Rahul, Anjana felt compelled to make conversation; She asked after his studies, his friends, his exams. He answered patiently; he was quite at his ease and sat with one leg crossed over the other. Anjana admired his calm, his confidence. It was obvious that here was a boy born to a good position in life which would be his without struggle or effort. He knew it himself, and consequently there was a smile of good-nature always hovering on his lips. Clearly he would never give trouble to any woman – would not fight with her or run off, worrying her to death where he was gone and who he was with. One could always be sure of him. A golden boy! Anjana smiled and shook her head to herself: she admired him so much. Yet at the same time as she looked at him with this wistful admiration, there was some other expression in her eyes as she – instinctively, almost unconsciously – weighed him up to herself. Yes, it was true, he wouldn't give trouble to a woman – but was he the type to give her much pleasure either? And her lips curled a little bit differently from a smile of approval as her eyes measured him up and down quite frankly now, so that he noticed and was surprised and shifted a little bit on his chair. He had never been looked at like that.

'Ready at last!' cried Kiku as the tailor bit off the end of his thread. Rahul jumped to his feet. 'Come on, hurry up!' Kiku told him. She made her veil brush over his face and teasingly trod on his foot. She burst out laughing at her joke and could still be heard laughing on the stairs.

Anjana went to her place at the bedroom window to watch them leave. It had rained during the day, and now the evening was cool and moist. Crowds had come out to enjoy a promenade by the sea, and with the crowds came the beggars lucky enough to have the sea-front for their beat: the man with the twisted limbs who wound himself like a creeper round the long pole he carried, the very respectable woman who wore shoes and spoke English and hadn't eaten for three days. Anjana saw a few crippled children clinging to Rahul's car and tapping on the windows, but Rahul swiftly drove off so that the children fell back and hobbled as fast as they could to surround some other car. The woman in the nursing-home opposite was at her post, her blank face gazing over the iron bars. She looked like a good housewife, enjoying a little respite from her duties after the day's chores. Probably she *had* been a good housewife – before she couldn't carry on any longer and her relatives had had to bring her here. Anjana understood how this could happen. She thought of poor Sultana – sitting at home in her horrible apartment, smoking and suffering, wearing youthful leopard pants – and asked herself, is it any wonder we go mad? She looked at the sky laid like a benediction over the housetops. The moon was up and there was one star. As usual, on seeing the sky, Anjana prayed: today not for Kiku and Rahul but for people who suffered – like herself, and Sultana, and Tara Bai. She prayed, her lips moving devoutly, her eyes upturned in humble supplication. But she didn't feel she was getting an answer.

She went to the telephone. Thakur Sahib answered himself and, at the sound of his voice, she was so overcome that she couldn't speak. 'Hallo?' he said, twice, and 'Hallo!' getting annoyed.

'Yes yes it's me,' she said to him at last.

He grunted.

She shut her eyes, in bliss, in safety.

An Experience of India

Today Ramu left. He came to ask for money and I gave him as much as I could. He counted it and asked for more, but I didn't have it to give him. He said some insulting things, which I pretended not to hear. Really I couldn't blame him. I knew he was anxious and afraid, not having another job to go to. But I also couldn't help contrasting the way he spoke now with what he had been like in the past: so polite always, and eager to please, and always smiling, saying, 'Yes sir,' 'Yes madam please.' He used to look very different too, very spruce in his white uniform and his white canvas shoes. When guests came, he put on a special white coat he had made us buy him. He was always happy when there were guests – serving, mixing drinks, emptying ashtrays – and I think he was disappointed that more didn't come. The Ford Foundation people next door had a round of buffet suppers and Sunday brunches, and perhaps Ramu suffered in status before their servants because we didn't have much of that. Actually, coming to think of it, perhaps he suffered in status anyhow because we weren't like the others. I mean, I wasn't. I didn't look like a proper memsahib or dress like one – I wore Indian clothes right from the start – or ever behave like one. I think perhaps Ramu didn't care for that. I think servants want their employers to be conventional and put up a good front so that other people's servants can respect them. Some of the nasty things Ramu told me this morning were about how everyone said I was just someone from a very low sweeper caste in my own country and how sorry they were for him that he had to serve such a person.

He also said it was no wonder Sahib had run away from me. Henry didn't actually run away, but it's true that things had changed between us. I suppose India made us see how fundamentally different we were from each other. Though when we first came, we both came we thought with the same ideas. We were both happy that Henry's paper had sent him out to India. We both thought it was a marvellous opportunity not only for him professionally but for both of us spiritually. Here was our escape from that Western materialism with which we were both so terribly fed up. But once he got here and the first enthusiasm had worn off, Henry seemed not to mind going back to just the sort of life we'd run away from. He even didn't seem to care about meeting Indians any more, though in the beginning he had made a great point of doing so; now it seemed to him all right to go only to parties given by other foreign correspondents and sit around there and eat and drink and talk just the way they would at home. After a while, I couldn't stand going with him any more, so we'd have a fight and then he'd go off by himself. That was a relief. I didn't want to be with any of those people and talk about inane things in their tastefully appointed air-conditioned apartments.

I had come to India to *be* in India. I wanted to be changed. Henry didn't – he wanted a change, that's all, but not to be changed. After a while because of that he was a stranger to me and I felt I was alone, the way I'm really alone now. Henry had to travel a lot around the country to write his pieces, and in the beginning I used to go with him. But I didn't like the way he travelled, always by plane and staying in expensive hotels and drinking in the bar with the other correspondents. So I would leave him and go off by myself. I travelled the way everyone travels in India, just with a bundle and a roll of bedding which I could spread out anywhere and go to sleep. I went in third-class railway carriages and in those old lumbering buses that go from one small dusty town to another and are loaded with too many people inside and with too much scruffy baggage on top. At the end of my journeys, I emerged soaked in perspiration, soot, and dirt. I ate anything anywhere and always like everyone else with my fingers (I became good at that) – thick, half-raw chapattis from wayside stalls and little messes of lentils and vegetables served on a leaf, all the food the poor eat; sometimes if I didn't have anything, other people would share with me from out of their bundles. Henry, who had the usual phobia about bugs, said I would kill myself eating that way. But nothing ever happened. Once, in a desert fort in Rajasthan, I got very thirsty and asked the old caretaker to pull some water out of an ancient disused well for me. It was brown and sort of foul-smelling, and maybe there was a corpse in the well, who knows. But I was thirsty so I drank it, and still nothing happened.

People always speak to you in India, in buses and trains and on the streets, they want to know all about you and ask you a lot of personal questions. I didn't speak much Hindi, but somehow we always managed, and I didn't mind answering all those questions when I could. Women quite often used to touch me, run their hands over my skin just to feel what it was like I suppose, and they specially liked to touch my hair which is long and blonde. Sometimes I had several of them lifting up strands of it at the same time, one pulling this way and another that way and they would exchange excited comments and laugh and scream a lot; but in a nice way, so I couldn't help but laugh and scream with them. And people in India are so hospitable. They're always saying, 'Please come and stay in my house,' perfect strangers that happen to be sitting near you on the train. Sometimes, if I didn't have any plans or if it sounded as if they might be living in an interesting place, I'd say, 'All right thanks,' and I'd go along with them. I had some interesting adventures that way.

I might as well say straight off that many of these adventures were sexual. Indian men are very, very keen to sleep with foreign girls. Of course men in other countries are also keen to sleep with girls, but there's something specially frenzied about Indian men when they approach you. Frenzied and at the same time shy. You'd think that with all those ancient traditions they have – like the Kama Sutra, and the sculptures showing couples in every kind of position – you'd think that with all that behind them they'd be very highly skilled, but they're not. Just the opposite. Middle-aged men get as excited as a fifteen-year-old boy, and then of course they can't wait, they *jump* and before you know where you are, in a great rush, it's all over. And when it's over, it's over, there's nothing left. Then they're only concerned with getting away as soon as possible before anyone can find them out (they're always scared of being found out). There's no tenderness, no interest at all in the other person as a person; only the same kind of curiosity that there is on the buses and the same sort of questions are asked, like are you married, any children, why no children, do you like wearing our Indian dress . . . There's one question though that's not asked on the buses but that always inevitably comes up during sex, so that you learn to wait for it: always, at the moment of mounting excitement, they ask, 'How many men have you slept with?' and it's repeated over and over, 'How many? How many?' and then they shout, 'Aren't you ashamed?' and, 'Bitch!' – always that one word which seems to excite them more than any other, to call you that is the height of their love-making, it's the last frenzy, the final outrage: 'Bitch!' Sometimes I couldn't stop myself but had to burst out laughing.

I didn't like sleeping with all these people, but I felt I had to. I felt I was doing good, though I don't know why, I couldn't explain it to myself. Only one of all those men ever spoke to me: I mean the way people having sex together are supposed to speak, coming near each other not only physically but also wanting to show each other what's deep inside them. He was a middle-aged man, a fellow-passenger on a bus, and we got talking at one of the stops the bus made at a wayside tea-stall. When he found

I was on my way to X — and didn't have anywhere to stay, he said, as so many have said before him, 'Please come and stay in my house.' And I said, as I had often said before, 'All right.' Only when we got there he didn't take me to his house but to a hotel. It was a very poky place in the bazaar and we had to grope our way up a steep smelly stone staircase and then there was a tiny room with just one string-cot and an earthenware water jug in it. He made a joke about there being only one bed. I was too tired to care much about anything. I only wanted to get it over with quickly and go to sleep. But afterwards I found it wasn't possible to go to sleep because there was a lot of noise coming up from the street where all the shops were still open though it was nearly midnight. People seemed to be having a good time and there was even a phonograph playing some cracked old love-song. My companion also couldn't get to sleep: he left the bed and sat down on the floor by the window and smoked one cigarette after the other. His face was lit up by the light coming in from the street outside and I saw he was looking sort of thoughtful and sad, sitting there smoking. He had rather a good face, strong bones but quite a feminine mouth and of course those feminine suffering eyes that most Indians have.

I went and sat next to him. The window was an arch reaching down to the floor so that I could see out into the bazaar. It was quite gay down there with all the lights; the phonograph was playing from the cold-drink shop and a lot of people were standing around there having highly coloured pop-drinks out of bottles; next to it was a shop with pink and blue brassieres strung up on a pole. On top of the shops were wrought-iron balconies on which sat girls dressed up in tatty georgette and waving peacock fans to keep themselves cool. Sometimes men looked up to talk and laugh with them, and they talked and laughed back. I realized we were in the brothel area; probably the hotel we were in was a brothel too.

I asked, 'Why did you bring me here?'

He answered, 'Why did you come?'

That was a good question. He was right. But I wasn't sorry I came. Why should I be? I said, 'It's all right. I like it.'

He said, 'She likes it,' and he laughed. A bit later he started talking: about how he had just been to visit his daughter who had been married a few months before. She wasn't happy in her in-laws' house, and when he said goodbye to her she clung to him and begged him to take her home. The more he reasoned with her, the more she cried, the more she clung to him. In the end he had had to use force to free himself from her so that he could get away and not miss his bus. He felt very sorry for her, but what else was there for him to do. If he took her away, her in-laws might refuse to have her back again and then her life would be ruined. And she would get used to it, they always did; for some it took longer and was harder, but they all got used to it in the end. His wife too had cried a lot during the first year of marriage.

I asked him whether he thought it was good to arrange marriages that way, and he looked at me and asked how else would you do it. I said something about love and it made him laugh and he said that was only for the films. I didn't want to defend my point of view; in fact, I felt rather childish and as if he knew a lot more about things than I did. He began to get amorous again, and this time it was much better because he wasn't so frenzied and I liked him better by now too. Afterwards he told me how when he was first married, he and his wife had shared a room with the whole family (parents and younger brothers and sisters), and whatever they wanted to do, they had to do very quickly and quietly for fear of anyone waking up. I had a strange sensation then, as if I wanted to strip off all my clothes and parade up and down the room naked. I thought of all the men's eyes that follow one in the street, and for the first time it struck me that the expression in them was like that in the eyes of prisoners looking through their bars at the world outside; and then I thought maybe I'm that world outside for them – the way I go here and there and talk and laugh with everyone and do what I like – maybe I'm the river and trees they can't have where they are. Oh, I felt so sorry, I wanted to do so much. And to make a start, I flung myself on my companion and kissed and hugged him hard, I lay on top of him, I smothered him, I spread my hair over his face because I wanted to make him forget everything that wasn't me – this room, his daughter, his wife, the women in georgette sitting on the balconies – I wanted everything to be new for him and as beautiful as I could make it. He liked it for a while but got tired quite quickly, probably because he wasn't all that young any more.

It was shortly after this encounter that I met Ahmed. He was eighteen years old and a musician. His family had been musicians as long as anyone could remember and the alley they lived in was full of other musicians, so that when you walked down it, it was like walking through a magic forest all lit up with music and sounds. Only there wasn't anything magic about the place itself which was very cramped and dirty; the houses were so old that, whenever there were heavy rains, one or two of them came tumbling down. I was never inside Ahmed's house or met his family – they'd have died of shock if they had got to know about me – but I knew they were very poor and scraped a living by playing at weddings and functions. Ahmed never had any money, just sometimes if he was lucky he had a few coins to buy his betel with. But he was cheerful and happy and enjoyed everything that came his way. He was married, but his wife was too young to stay with him and after the ceremony she had been sent back to live with her father who was a musician in another town.

When I first met Ahmed, I was staying in a hostel attached to a temple which was free of charge for pilgrims; but afterwards he and I wanted a place for us to go to, so I wired Henry to send me some more money. Henry sent me the money, together with a long complaining letter which I didn't read all the way through, and I took a room in a hotel. It was on the outskirts of town which was mostly waste land except for a few houses and some of these had never been finished. Our hotel wasn't finished either because the proprietor had run out of money, and now it probably never would be for the place had turned out to be a poor proposition, it was too far out of town and no one ever came to stay there. But it suited us fine. We had this one room, painted bright pink and quite bare except for two pieces of furniture – a bed and a dressing-table, both of them very shiny and new. Ahmed loved it, he had never stayed in such a grand room before; he bounced up and down on the bed which had a mattress and stood looking at himself from all sides in the mirror of the dressing-table.

I never in all my life was so gay with anyone the way I was with Aimed; I'm not saying I never had a good time at home; I did. I had a lot of friends before I married Henry and we had parties and danced and drank and I enjoyed it; But it wasn't like with Ahmed because no one was ever as *carefree* as he was, as light and easy and just ready to play and live. At home we always had our problems, personal ones of course, but on top of those there were universal problems – social, and economic, and moral, we really cared about what was happening in the world around us and in our own minds, we felt a responsibility towards being here alive at this point in time and wanted to do our best. Ahmed had no thoughts like that at all; there wasn't a shadow on him. He had his personal problems from time to time, and when he had them, he was very downcast and sometimes he even cried. But they weren't anything really very serious – usually some family quarrel, or his father was angry with him – and they passed away, blew away like a breeze over a lake and left him sunny and sparkling again. He enjoyed everything so much: not only our room, and the bed and the dressing-table, and making love, but so many other things like drinking Coca Cola and spraying scent and combing my hair and my combing his; and he made up games for us to play like indoor cricket with a slipper for a bat and one of Henry's letters rolled up for a ball. He taught me how to crack his toes, which is such a great Indian delicacy, and yelled with pleasure when I got it right; but when he did it to me, I yelled with pain so he stopped at once and was terribly sorry. He was very considerate and tender. No one I've ever known was sensitive to my feelings as he was. It was like an instinct with him, as if he could feel right down into my heart and know what was going on there; and without ever having to ask anything or my ever having to explain anything, he could sense each change of mood and adapt himself to it and feel with it. Henry would always have to ask me, 'Now what's up? What's the matter with you?' and when we were still all right with each other, he would make a sincere effort to understand. But Ahmed never had to make an effort, and maybe if he'd had to he wouldn't have succeeded because it wasn't ever with his mind that he understood anything, it was always with his feelings. Perhaps that was so because he was a musician and in music everything is beyond words and explanations anyway; and from what he told me about Indian music, I could see it was very, very subtle, there are effects that you can hardly perceive they're so subtle and your sensibilities have to be kept tuned all the time to the finest, finest point; and perhaps because of that the whole of Ahmed was always at that point and he could play me and listen to me as if I were his sarod.

After some time we ran out of money and Henry wouldn't send any more, so we had to think what to do. I certainly couldn't bear to part with Ahmed, and in the end I suggested he'd better come back to Delhi with me and we'd try and straighten things out with Henry. Ahmed was terribly excited by the idea; he'd never been to Delhi and was wild to go. Only it meant he had to run away from home because his family would never have allowed him to go, so one night he stole out of the house with his sarod and his little bundle of clothes and met me at the railway station. We reached

Delhi the next night, tired and dirty and covered with soot the way you always get in trains here. When we arrived home, Henry was giving a party; not a big party, just a small informal group sitting around chatting. I'll never forget the expression on everyone's faces when Ahmed and I came staggering in with our bundles and bedding. My blouse had got torn in the train all the way down the side, and I didn't have a safety-pin so it kept flapping open and unfortunately I didn't have anything underneath. Henry's guests were all looking very nice, the men in smart bush-shirts and their wives in little silk cocktail dresses; and although after the first shock they all behaved very well and carried on as if nothing unusual had happened, still it was an awkward situation for everyone concerned.

Ahmed never really got over it. I can see now how awful it must have been for him, coming into that room full of strange white people and all of them turning round to stare at us. And the room itself must have been a shock to him, he can never have seen anything like it. Actually, it was quite a shock to me too. I'd forgotten that that was the way Henry and I lived. When we first came, we had gone to a lot of trouble doing up the apartment, buying furniture and pictures and stuff, and had succeeded in making it look just like the apartment we have at home except for some elegant Indian touches. To Ahmed it was all very strange. He stayed there with us for some time, and he couldn't get used to it. I think it bothered him to have so many *things* around, rugs and lamps and objets d'art; he couldn't see why they had to be there. Now that I had travelled and lived the way I had, I couldn't see why either; as a matter of fact I felt as if these things were a hindrance and cluttered up not only your room but your mind and your soul as well, hanging on them like weights.

We had some quite bad scenes in the apartment during those days. I told Henry that I was in love with Ahmed, and naturally that upset him, though what upset him most was the fact that he had to keep us both in the apartment. I also realized that this was an undesirable situation, but I couldn't see any way out of it because where else could Ahmed and I go? We didn't have any money, only Henry had, so we had to stay with him. He kept saying that he would turn both of us out into the streets but I knew he wouldn't. He wasn't the type to do a violent thing like that, and besides he himself was so frightened of the streets that he'd have died to think of anyone connected with him being out there. I wouldn't have minded all that much if he *had* turned us out: it was warm enough to sleep in the open and people always give you food if you don't have any. I would have preferred it really because it was so unpleasant with Henry; but I knew Ahmed would never have been able to stand it. He was quite a pampered boy, and though his family were poor, they looked after and protected each other very carefully; he never had to miss a meal or go dressed in anything but fine muslin clothes, nicely washed and starched by female relatives.

Ahmed bitterly repented having come. He was very miserable, feeling so uncomfortable in the apartment and with Henry making rows all the time. Ramu, the servant, didn't improve anything by the way he behaved, absolutely refusing to serve Ahmed and never losing an opportunity to make him feel inferior. Everything went out of Ahmed; he crumpled up as if he were a paper flower. He didn't want to play his sarod and he didn't want to make love to me, he just sat around with his head and his hands hanging down, and there were times when I saw tears rolling down his face and he didn't even bother to wipe them off. Although he was so unhappy in the apartment, he never left it and so he never saw any of the places he had been so eager to come to Delhi for, like the Juma Masjid and Nizamuddin's tomb. Most of the time he was thinking about his family. He wrote long letters to them in Urdu, which I posted, telling them where he was and imploring their pardon for running away; and long letters came back again and he read and read them, soaking them in tears and kisses. One night he got so bad he jumped out of bed and, rushing into Henry's bedroom, fell to his knees by the side of Henry's bed and begged to be sent back home again. And Henry, sitting up in bed in his pyjamas, said all right, in rather a lordly way I thought. So next day I took Ahmed to the station and put him on the train, and through the bars of the railway carriage he kissed my hands and looked into my eyes with all his old ardour and tenderness, so at the last moment I wanted to go with him but it was too late and the train pulled away out of the station and all that was left to me of Ahmed was a memory, very beautiful and delicate like a flavour or a perfume or one of those melodies he played on his sarod.

I became very depressed. I didn't feel like going travelling any more but stayed home with Henry and went with him to his diplomatic and other parties. He was quite glad to have me go with him again; he liked having someone in the car on the way home to talk to about all the people who'd been at the party and compare their chances of future success with his own. I didn't mind going with him, there wasn't anything else I wanted to do. I felt as if I'd failed at something. It wasn't only Ahmed. I didn't really miss him all that much and was glad to think of him back with his family in that alley full of music where he was happy. For myself I didn't know what to do next though I felt that something still awaited me. Our apartment led to an open terrace and I often went up there to look at the view which was marvellous. The house we lived in and all the ones around were white and pink and very modern, with picture windows and little lawns in front, but from up here you could look beyond them to the city and the big mosque and the fort. In between there were stretches of waste land, empty and barren except for an occasional crumbly old tomb growing there. What always impressed me the most was the sky because it was so immensely big and so unchanging in colour, and it made everything underneath it – all the buildings, even the great fort, the whole city, not to speak of all the people living in it – seem terribly small and trivial and passing somehow. But at the same time as it made me feel small, it also made me feel immense and eternal. I don't know, I can't explain, perhaps because it was itself like that and this thought – that there *was* something like that – made me feel that I had a part in it, I too was part of being immense and eternal. It was all very vague really and nothing I could ever speak about to anyone; but because of it I thought well maybe there is something more for me here after all. That was a relief because it meant I wouldn't have to go home and be the way I was before and nothing different or gained. For all the time, ever since I'd come and even before, I'd had this idea that there was something in India for me to *gain*, and even though for the time being I'd failed, I could try longer and at last perhaps I would succeed.

I'd met people on and off who had come here on a spiritual quest, but it wasn't the sort of thing I wanted for myself. I thought anything I wanted to find, I could find by myself travelling around the way I had done. But now that this had failed, I became interested in the other thing. I began to go to a few prayer-meetings and I liked the atmosphere very much. The meeting was usually conducted by a swami in a saffron robe who had renounced the world, and he gave an address about love and God and everyone sang hymns also about love and God. The people who came to these meetings were mostly middle-aged and quite poor. I had already met many like them on my travels, for they were the sort of people who sat waiting on station platforms and at bus depots, absolutely patient and uncomplaining even when conductors and other officials pushed them around. They were gentle people and very clean though there was always some slight smell about them as of people who find it difficult to keep clean because they five in crowded and unsanitary places where there isn't much running water and the drainage system isn't good. I loved the expression that came into their faces when they sang hymns. I wanted to be like them, so I began to dress in plain white saris and I tied up my hair in a plain knot and the only ornament I wore was a string of beads not for decoration but to say the names of God on. I became a vegetarian and did my best to cast out all the undesirable human passions, such as anger and lust. When Henry was in an irritable or quarrelsome mood, I never answered him back but was very kind and patient with him. However, far from having a good effect, this seemed to make him worse. Altogether he didn't like the new personality I was trying to achieve but sneered a lot at the way I dressed and looked and the simple food I ate. Actually, I didn't enjoy this food very much and found it quite a trial eating nothing but boiled rice and lentils with him sitting opposite me having his cutlets and chops.

The peace and satisfaction that I saw on the faces of the other hymn-singers didn't come to me. As a matter of fact, I grew rather bored. There didn't seem much to be learned from singing hymns and eating vegetables. Fortunately just about this time someone took me to see a holy woman who lived on the roof of an old overcrowded house near the river. People treated her like a holy woman but she didn't set up to be one. She didn't set up to be anything really, but only stayed in her room on the roof and talked to people who came to see her. She liked telling stories and she could hold everyone spellbound listening to her, even though she was only telling the old mythological stories they had known all their lives long, about Krishna, and the Pandavas, and Rama and Sita. But she got terribly excited while she was telling them, as if it wasn't something that had happened millions of years ago but as if it was all real and going on exactly now. Once she was telling about Krishna's mother who made him open his mouth to see whether he had stolen and was eating up her butter. What did she see then, inside his mouth?

'Worlds!' the holy woman cried. 'Not just this world, not just one world with its mountains and rivers and seas, no, but world upon world, all spinning in one great eternal cycle in this child's mouth, moon upon moon, sun upon sun!'

She clapped her hands and laughed and laughed, and then she burst out singing in her thin old voice, some hymn all about how great God was and how lucky for her that she was his beloved. She was dancing with joy in front of all the people. And she was just a little shrivelled old woman, very ugly with her teeth gone and a growth on her chin: but the way she carried on it was as if she had all the looks and glamour anyone ever had in the world, and was in love a million times over. I thought well whatever it was she had, obviously it was the one thing worth having and I had better try for it.

I went to stay with a guru in a holy city. He had a house on the river in which he lived with his disciples. They lived in a nice way: they meditated a lot and went out for boat rides on the river and in the evenings they all sat around in the guru's room and had a good time. There were quite a few foreigners among the disciples, and it was the guru's greatest wish to go abroad and spread his message there and bring back more disciples. When he heard that Henry was a journalist, he became specially interested in me. He talked to me about the importance of introducing the leaven of Indian spirituality into the lump of Western materialism. To achieve this end, his own presence in the West was urgently required, and to ensure the widest dissemination of his message he would also need the full support of the mass media. He said that since we live in the modern age, we must avail ourselves of all its resources. He was very keen for me to bring Henry into the ashram, and when I was vague in my answers – I certainly didn't want Henry here nor would he in the least want to come – he became very pressing and even quite annoyed and kept returning to the subject.

He didn't seem a very spiritual type of person to me. He was a hefty man with big shoulders and a big head. He wore his hair long but his jaw was clean-shaven and stuck out very large and prominent and gave him a powerful look like a bull. All he ever wore was a saffron robe and this left a good part of his body bare so that it could be seen at once how strong his legs and shoulders were. He had huge eyes which he used constantly and apparently to tremendous effect, fixing people with them and penetrating them with a steady beam. He used them on me when he wanted Henry to come, but they never did anything to me. But the other disciples were very strongly affected by them. There was one girl, Jean, who said they were like the sun, so strong that if she tried to look back at them something terrible would happen to her like being blinded or burned up completely.

Jean had made herself everything an Indian guru expects his disciples to be. She was absolutely humble and submissive. She touched the guru's feet when she came into or went out of his presence, she ran eagerly on any errand he sent her on. She said she gloried in being nothing in herself and living only by his will. And she looked like nothing too, sort of drained of everything she might once have been. At home her cheeks were probably pink but now she was quite white, waxen, and her hair too was completely faded and colourless. She always wore a plain white cotton sari and that made her look paler than ever, and thinner too, it seemed to bring out the fact that she had no hips and was utterly flat-chested. But she was happy – at least she said she was – she said she had never known such happiness and hadn't thought it was possible for human beings to feel like that. And when she said that, there was a sort of sparkle in her pale eyes, and at such moments I envied her because she seemed to have found what I was looking for. But at the same time I wondered whether she really had found what she thought she had, or whether it wasn't something else and she was cheating herself, and one day she'd wake up to that fact and then she'd feel terrible.

She was shocked by my attitude to the guru – not touching his feet or anything, and talking back to him as if he was just an ordinary person. Sometimes I thought perhaps there was something wrong with me because everyone else, all the other disciples and people from outside too who came to see him, they all treated him with this great reverence and their faces lit up in his presence as if there really was something special. Only I couldn't see it. But all the same I was quite happy there – not because of him, but because I liked the atmosphere of the place and the way they all lived. Everyone seemed very contented and as if they were living for something high and beautiful. I thought perhaps if I waited and was patient, I'd also come to be like that. I tried to meditate the way they all did, sitting crosslegged in one spot and concentrating on the holy word that had been given to me. I wasn't ever very successful and kept thinking of other things. But there were times when I went up to sit on the roof and looked out over the river, the way it stretched so calm and broad to the opposite bank and the boats going up and down it and the light changing and being reflected back on the water: and then, though I wasn't trying to meditate or come to any higher thoughts, I did feel very peaceful and was glad to be there.

The guru was patient with me for a long time, explaining about the importance of his mission and how Henry ought to come here and write about it for his paper. But as the days passed and Henry didn't show up, his attitude changed and he began to ask me questions. Why hadn't Henry come? Hadn't I written to him? Wasn't I going to write to him? Didn't I think what was being done in the ashram would interest him? Didn't I agree that it deserved to be brought to the notice of the world and that to this end no stone should be left unturned? While he said all this, he fixed me with his great eyes and I squirmed – not because of the way he was looking at me, but because I was embarrassed and didn't know what to answer. Then he became very gentle and said never mind, he didn't want to force me, that was not his way, he wanted people slowly to turn towards him of their own accord, to open up to him as a flower opens up and unfurls its petals and its leaves to the sun. But next day he would start again, asking the same questions, urging me, forcing me, and when this had gone on for some time and we weren't getting anywhere, he even got angry once or twice and shouted at me that I was obstinate and closed and had fenced in my heart with seven hoops of iron. When he shouted, everyone in the ashram trembled and afterwards they looked at me in a strange way. But an hour later the guru always had me called back to his room and then he was very gentle with me again and made me sit near him and insisted that it should be I who handed him his glass of milk in preference to one of the others, all of whom were a lot keener to be selected for this honour than I was.

Jean often came to talk to me. At night I spread my bedding in a tiny cubby-hole which was a disused store-room, and just as I was falling asleep, she would come in and lie down beside me and talk to me very softly and intimately. I didn't like it much, to have her so close to me and whispering in a voice that wasn't more than a breath and which I could feel, slightly warm, on my neck; sometimes she touched me, putting her hand on mine ever so gently so that she hardly was touching me but all the same I could feel that her hand was a bit moist and it gave me an unpleasant sensation down my spine. She spoke about the beauty of surrender, of not having a will and not having thoughts of your own. She said she too had been like me once, stubborn and ego-centred, but now she had learned the joy of yielding, and if she could only give me some inkling of the infinite bliss to be tasted in this process – here her breath would give out for a moment and she couldn't speak for ecstasy. I would take the opportunity to pretend to fall asleep, even snoring a bit to make it more convincing; after calling my name a few times in the hope of waking me up again, she crept away disappointed. But next night she'd be back again, and during the day too she would attach herself to me as much as possible and continue talking in the same way.

It got so that even when she wasn't there, I could still hear her voice and feel her breath on my neck. I no longer enjoyed anything, not even going on the river or looking out over it from the top of the house. Although they hadn't bothered me before, I kept thinking of the funeral pyres on the bank, and it seemed to me that the smoke they gave out was spreading all over the sky and the river and covering them with a dirty yellowish haze. I realized that nothing good could come to me from this place now. But when I told the guru that I was leaving, he got into a great fury. His head and neck swelled out and his eyes became two coal-black demons rolling around in rage. In a voice like drums and cymbals, he *forbade* me to go. I didn't say anything but I made up my mind to leave next morning. I went to pack my things. The whole ashram was silent and stricken, no one dared speak. No one dared come near me either till late at night when Jean came as usual to lie next to me. She lay there completely still and crying to herself. I didn't know she was crying at first because she didn't make a sound but slowly her tears seeped into her side of the pillow and a sensation of dampness came creeping over to my side of it. I pretended not to notice anything.

Suddenly the guru stood in the doorway. The room faced an open courtyard and this was full of moonlight which illumined him and made him look enormous and eerie. Jean and I sat up. I felt scared, my heart beat fast. After looking at us in silence for a while, he ordered Jean to go away. She got up to do so at once. I said, 'No, stay,' and clung to her hand but she disengaged herself from me and, touching the guru's feet in reverence, she went away. She seemed to dissolve in the moonlight outside, leaving no trace. The guru sat beside me on my bedding spread on the floor. He said I was under a delusion, that I didn't really want to leave; my inmost nature was craving to stay by him – he knew, he could hear it calling out to him. But because I was afraid, I was attempting to smother this craving and to run away. 'Look how you're trembling,' he said. 'See how afraid you are.' It was true, I was trembling and cowering against the wall as far away from him as I could get. Only it was impossible to get very far because he was so huge and seemed to spread and fill the tiny closet. I could feel him close against me, and his pungent male smell, spiced with garlic, overpowered me.

'You're right to be afraid,' he said: because it was his intention, he said, to batter and beat me, to smash my ego till it broke and flew apart into a million pieces and was scattered into the dust. Yes, it would be a painful process and I would often cry out and plead for mercy, but in the end – ah, with what joy I would step out of the prison of my own self, remade and reborn! I would fling myself to the ground and bathe his feet in tears of gratitude. Then I would be truly his. As he spoke, I became more and more afraid because I felt, so huge and close and strong he was, that perhaps he really had the power to do to me all that he said and that in the end he would make me like Jean.

I now lay completely flattened against the wall, and he had moved up and was squashing me against it. One great hand travelled up and down my stomach', but its activity seemed apart from the rest of him and from what he was saying. His voice became lower and lower, more and more intense. He said he would teach me to obey, to submit myself completely, that would be the first step and a very necessary one. For he knew what we were like, all of us who came from Western countries: we were self-willed, obstinate, *licentious*. On the last word his voice cracked with emotion, his hand went further and deeper. *Licentious,* he repeated, and then, rolling himself across the bed so that he now lay completely pressed against me, he asked, 'How many men have you slept with?' He took my hand and made me hold him: how huge and hot he was! He pushed hard against me. 'How many? Answer me!' he commanded, urgent and dangerous. But I was no longer afraid: now he was not an unknown quantity nor was the situation any longer new or strange. 'Answer me, answer me!' he cried, riding on top of me, and then he cried 'Bitch!' and I laughed in relief.

I quite liked being back in Delhi with Henry. I had lots of baths in our marble bathroom, soaking in the tub for hours and making myself smell nice with bath-salts. I stopped wearing Indian clothes and took out all the dresses I'd brought with me. We entertained quite a bit, and Ramu scurried around in his white coat, emptying ashtrays. It wasn't a bad time. I stayed around all day in the apartment with the air-conditioner on and the curtains drawn to keep out the glare. At night we drove over to other people's apartments for buffet suppers of boiled ham and potato salad; we sat around drinking in their living-rooms, which were done up more or less like ours, and talked about things like the price of whisky, what was the best hill station to go to in the summer, and servants. This last subject often led to other related ones like how unreliable Indians were and how it was impossible ever to get anything done. Usually this subject was treated in a humorous way, with lots of funny anecdotes to illustrate, but occasionally someone got quite passionate; this happened usually if they were a bit drunk, and then they went off into a long thing about how dirty India was and backward, riddled with vile superstitions – evil, they said – corrupt – corrupting.

Henry never spoke like that – maybe because he never got drunk enough – but I know he didn't disagree with it. He disliked the place very much and was in fact thinking of asking for an assignment elsewhere. When I asked where, he said the cleanest place he could think of. He asked how would I like to go to Geneva. I knew I wouldn't like it one bit, but I said all right. I didn't really care where I was. I didn't care much about anything these days. The only positive feeling I had was for Henry. He was so sweet and good to me. I had a lot of bad dreams nowadays and was afraid of sleeping alone, so he let me come into his bed even though he dislikes having his sheets disarranged and I always kick and toss about a lot. I lay close beside him, clinging to him, and for the first time I was glad that he had never been all that keen on sex. On Sundays we stayed in bed all day reading the papers and Ramu brought us nice English meals on trays. Sometimes we put on a record and danced together in our pyjamas. I kissed Henry's cheeks which were always smooth – he didn't need to shave very often – and sometimes his lips which tasted of toothpaste.

Then I got jaundice. It's funny, all that time I spent travelling about and eating anything anywhere, nothing happened to me, and now that I was living such a clean life with boiled food and boiled water, I got sick. Henry was horrified. He immediately segregated all his and my things, and anything that I touched had to be sterilized a hundred times over. He was for ever running into the kitchen to check up whether Ramu was doing this properly. He said jaundice was the most catching thing there was, and though he went in for a whole course of precautionary inoculations that had to be specially flown in from the States, he still remained in a very nervous state. He tried to be sympathetic to me, but couldn't help sounding reproachful most of the time. He had sealed himself off so carefully, and now I had let this in. I knew how he felt, but I was too ill and miserable to care. I don't remember ever feeling so *ill*. I didn't have any high temperature or anything, but all the time there was this terrible nausea. First my eyes went yellow, then the rest of me as if I'd been dyed in the colour of nausea, inside and out. The whole world went yellow and sick. I couldn't bear anything: any noise, any person near me, worst of all any smell. They couldn't cook in the kitchen any more because the smell of cooking made me scream. Henry had to live on boiled eggs and bread. I begged him not to let Ramu into my bedroom for, although Ramu always wore nicely laundered clothes, he gave out a smell of perspiration which was both sweetish and foul and filled me with disgust. I was convinced that under his clean shirt he wore a cotton vest, black with sweat and dirt, which he never took off but slept in at night in the one-room servant quarter where he lived crowded together with all his family in a dense smell of cheap food and bad drains and unclean bodies.

I knew these smells so well – I thought of them as the smells of India, and had never minded them; but now I couldn't get rid of them, they were like some evil flood soaking through the walls of my air-conditioned bedroom. And other things I hadn't minded, had hardly bothered to think about, now came back to me in a terrible way so that waking and sleeping I saw them. What I remembered most often was the disused well in the Rajasthan fort out of which I had drunk water. I was sure now that there had been a corpse at the bottom of it, and I saw this corpse with the flesh swollen and blown but the eyes intact: they were huge like the guru's eyes and they stared, glazed and jellied, into the darkness of the well. And worse than seeing this corpse, I could taste it in the water that I had drunk – that I was still drinking – yes, it was now, at this very moment, that I was raising my cupped hands to my mouth and feeling the dank water lap around my tongue. I screamed out loud at the taste of the dead man and I called to Henry and clutched his hand and begged him to get us sent to Geneva quickly, quickly. He disengaged his hand – he didn't like me to touch him at this time – but he promised. Then I grew calmer, I shut my eyes and tried to think of Geneva and of washing out my mouth with Swiss milk.

I got better, but I was very weak. When I looked at myself in the mirror, I started to cry. My face had a yellow tint, my hair was limp and faded; I didn't look old but I didn't look young any more either. There was no flesh left, and no colour. I was drained, hollowed out. I was wearing a white night-dress and that increased the impression. Actually, I reminded myself of Jean. I thought so this is what it does to you (I didn't quite know at that time what I meant by it – jaundice in my case, a guru in hers; but it seemed to come to the same). When Henry told me that his new assignment had come through, I burst into tears again; only now it was with relief. I said let's go now, let's go quickly.

I became quite hysterical so Henry said all right; he too was impatient to get away before any more of those bugs he dreaded so much caught up with us. The only thing that bothered him was that the rent had been paid for three months and the landlord refused to refund. Henry had a fight with him about it but the landlord won. Henry was furious but I said never mind, let's just get away and forget all about all of them. We packed up some of our belongings and sold the rest; the last few days we lived in an empty apartment with only a couple of kitchen chairs and a bed. Ramu was very worried about finding a new job.

Just before we were to leave for the airport and were waiting for the car to pick us up, I went on the terrace. I don't know why I did that, there was no reason. There was nothing I wanted to say goodbye to, and no last glimpses I wanted to catch. My thoughts were all concentrated on the coming journey and whether to take air-sickness pills or not. The sky from up on the terrace looked as immense as ever, the city as small. It was evening and the light was just fading and the sky wasn't any definite colour now: it was sort of translucent like a pearl but not an earthly pearl. I thought of the story the little saintly old woman had told about Krishna's mother and how she saw the sun and the moon and world upon world in his mouth. I liked that phrase so much – world upon world – I imagined them spinning around each other like glass balls in eternity and everything as shining and translucent as the sky I saw above me. I went down and told Henry I wasn't going with him. When he realized – and this took some time – that I was serious, he knew I was mad. At first he was very patient and gentle with me, then he got in a frenzy. The car had already arrived to take us. Henry yelled at me, he grabbed my arm and began to pull me to the door. I resisted with all my strength and sat down on one of the kitchen chairs. Henry continued to pull and now he was pulling me along with the chair as if on a sleigh. I clung to it as hard as I could but I felt terribly weak and was afraid I would let myself be pulled away. I begged him to leave me. I cried and wept with fear – fear that he would take me, fear that he would leave me.

Ramu came to my aid. He said it's all right Sahib, I'll look after her. He told Henry that I was too weak to travel after my illness but later, when I was better, he would take me to the airport and put me on a plane. Henry hesitated. It was getting very late, and if he didn't go, he too would miss the plane. Ramu assured him that all would be well and Henry need not worry at all. At last Henry took my papers and ticket out of his inner pocket. He gave me instructions how I was to go to the air company and make a new booking. He hesitated a moment longer – how sweet he looked all dressed up in a suit and tie ready for travelling, just like the day we got married – but the car was hooting furiously downstairs and he had to go. I held on hard to the chair. I was afraid if I didn't I might get up and run after him. So I clung to the chair, trembling and crying. Ramu was quite happily dusting the remaining chair. He said we would have to get some more furniture. I think he was glad that I had stayed and he still had somewhere to work and live and didn't have to go tramping around looking for another place. He had quite a big family to support.

I sold the ticket Henry left with me but I didn't buy any new furniture with it. I stayed in the empty rooms by myself and very rarely went out. When Ramu cooked anything for me, I ate it, but sometimes he forgot or didn't have time because he was busy looking for another job. I didn't like living like that but I didn't know what else to do. I was afraid to go out: everything I had once liked so much – people, places, crowds, smells – I now feared and hated. I would go running back to be by myself in the empty apartment. I felt people looked at me in a strange way in the streets; and perhaps I was strange now from the way I was living and not caring about what I looked like any more; I think I talked aloud to myself sometimes – once or twice I heard myself doing it. I spent a lot of the money

I got from the air ticket on books. I went to the bookshops and came hurrying back carrying armfuls of them. Many of them I never read, and even those I did read, I didn't understand very much. I hadn't had much experience in reading these sort of books – like the Upanishads and the Vedanta Sutras – but I liked the sound of the words and I liked the feeling they gave out. It was as if I were all by myself on an immensely high plateau breathing in great lungfuls of very sharp, pure air. Sometimes the landlord came to see what I was doing. He went round all the rooms, peering suspiciously into corners, testing the fittings. He kept asking how much longer I was going to stay; I said till the three mouths' rent was up. He brought prospective tenants to see the apartment, but when they saw me squatting on the floor in the empty rooms, sometimes with a bowl of half-eaten food which Ramu had neglected to clear away, they got nervous and went away again rather quickly. After a time the electricity got cut off because I hadn't paid the bill. It was very hot without the fan and I filled the tub with cold water and sat in it all day. But then the water got cut off too. The landlord came up twice, three times a day now. He said if I didn't clear out the day the rent was finished he would call the police to evict me. I said it's all right, don't worry, I shall go. Like the landlord, I too was counting the days still left to me. I was afraid what would happen to me.

Today the landlord evicted Ramu out of the servant quarter. That was when Ramu came up to ask for money and said all those things. Afterwards I went up on the terrace to watch him leave. It was such a sad procession. Each member of the family carried some part of their wretched household stock, none of which looked worth taking. Ramu had a bed with tattered strings balanced on his head. In two days' time I too will have to go with my bundle and my bedding. I've done this so often before – travelled here and there without any real destination – and been so happy doing it; but now it's different. That time I had a great sense of freedom and adventure. Now I feel compelled, that I *have* to do this whether I want to or not. And partly I don't want to, I feel afraid. Yet it's still like an adventure, and that's why besides being afraid I'm also excited, and most of the time I don't know why my heart is beating fast, is it in fear or in excitement, wondering what will happen to me now that I'm going travelling again.

How I Became a Holy Mother

On my twenty-third birthday when I was fed up with London and all the rest of it – boyfriends, marriages (two), jobs (modelling), best friends that are suddenly your best enemies – I had this letter from my girl friend Sophie who was finding peace in an ashram in South India:

> . . . oh Katie you wouldn't know me I'm such a changed person. I get up at 5 – *a.m.*!!! I am an absolute vegetarian let alone no meat no eggs either and am making fabulous progress with my meditation. I have a special mantra of my own that Swamiji gave me at a special ceremony and I say it over and over in my mind. The sky here is blue all day long and I sit by the sea and watch the waves and have good thoughts . . .

But by the time I got there Sophie had left – under a cloud, it seemed, though when I asked what she had done, they wouldn't tell me but only pursed their lips and looked sorrowful. I didn't stay long in that place. I didn't like the bitchy atmosphere, and that Swamiji was a big fraud, anyone could see that. I couldn't understand how a girl as sharp as Sophie had ever let herself be fooled by such a type. But I suppose if you want to be fooled you are. I found that out in some of the other ashrams I went to. There were some quite intelligent people in all of them but the way they just shut their eyes to certain things, it was incredible. It is not my role in life to criticize others so I kept quiet and went on to the next place. I went to quite a few of them. These ashrams are a cheap way to live in India and there is always company and it isn't bad for a few days provided you don't get involved in their power politics. I was amazed to come across quite a few people I had known over the years and would never have expected to meet here. It is a shock when you see someone you had last met on the beach of St Tropez now all dressed up in a saffron robe and meditating in some very dusty ashram in Madhya Pradesh. But really I could see their point because they were all as tired as I was of everything we had been doing and this certainly was different.

I enjoyed myself going from one ashram to the other and travelling all over India. Trains and buses are very crowded – I went third class, I had to be careful with my savings – but Indians can tell when you want to be left alone. They are very sensitive that way. I looked out of the window and thought my thoughts. After a time I became quite calm and rested. I hadn't brought too much stuff with me, but bit by bit I discarded most of that too till I had only a few things left that I could easily carry myself. I didn't even mind when my watch was pinched off me one night in a railway rest-room (so-called). I felt myself to be a changed person. Once, at the beginning of my travels, there was a man sitting next to me on a bus who said he was an astrologer. He was a very sensitive and philosophical person – and I must say I was impressed by how many such one meets in India, quite ordinary people travelling third class. After we had been talking for a time and he had told me the future of India for the next forty years, suddenly out of the blue he said to me, 'Madam, you have a very sad soul.' It was true. I thought about it for days afterwards and cried a bit to myself. I did feel sad inside myself and heavy like with a stone. But as time went on and I kept going round India – the sky always blue like Sophie had said, and lots of rivers and fields as well as desert – just quietly travelling and looking, I stopped feeling like that. Now I was as a matter of fact quite light inside as if that stone had gone.

Then I stopped travelling and stayed in this one place instead. I liked it better than any of the other ashrams for several reasons. One of them was that the scenery was very picturesque. This cannot be said of all ashrams as many of them seem to be in sort of dust bowls, or in the dirtier parts of very dirty holy cities or even cities that aren't holy at all but just dirty. But this ashram was built on the slope of a mountain, and behind it there were all the other mountains stretching right up to the snow-capped peaks of the Himalayas; and on the other side it ran down to the river which I will not say can have been very clean (with all those pilgrims dipping in it) but certainly looked clean from up above and not only clean but as clear and green as the sky was clear and blue. Also along the bank of the river there were many little pink temples with pink cones and they certainly made a pretty scene. Inside the ashram also the atmosphere was good which again cannot be said of all of them, far from it. But the reason the atmosphere was good here was because of the head of this ashram who was called Master. They are always called something like that – if not Swamiji then Maharaj-ji or Babaji or Maharishiji or Guruji; but this one was just called plain Master, in English.

He was full of pep and go. Early in the morning he would say, 'Well what shall we do today!' and then plan some treat like all of us going for a swim in the river with a picnic lunch to follow. He didn't want anyone to have a dull moment or to fall into a depression which I suppose many there were apt to do, left to their own devices. In some ways he reminded me of those big business types that sometimes (in other days!) took me out to dinner. They too had that kind of superhuman energy and seemed to be stronger than other people. I forgot to say that Master was a big burly man, and as he didn't wear all that many clothes – usually only a loincloth – you could see just how big and burly he was. His head was large too and it was completely shaven so that it looked even larger. He wasn't ugly, not at all. Or perhaps if he was one forgot about it very soon because of all that dynamism.

As I said, the ashram was built on the slope of a mountain. I don't think it was planned at all but had just grown: there was one little room next to the other and the Meditation Hall and the dining-hall and Master's quarters – whatever was needed was added and it all ran higgledy-piggledy down the mountain. I had one of the little rooms to myself and made myself very snug in there. The only furniture provided by the ashram was one string bed, but I bought a handloom rug from the Lepers Rehabilitation Centre and I also put up some pictures, like a Tibetan Mandala which was very colourful. Everyone liked my room and wanted to come and spend time there, but I was a bit cagey about that as I needed my privacy. I always had lots to do, like writing letters or washing my hair and I was also learning to play the flute. So I was quite happy and independent and didn't really need company though there was plenty of it, if and when needed.

There were Master's Indian disciples who were all learning to be swamis. They wanted to renounce the world and had shaved their heads and wore an orange sort of toga thing. When they were ready, Master was going to make them into full swamis. Most of these junior swamis were very young – just boys, some of them – but even those that weren't all that young were certainly so at heart. Sometimes they reminded me of a lot of school kids, they were so full of tricks and fun. But I think basically they were very serious – they couldn't not be, considering how they were renouncing and were supposed to be studying all sorts of very difficult things. The one I liked the best was called Vishwa. I liked him not only because he was the best looking, which he undoubtedly was, but I felt he had a lot going for him. Others said so too – in fact, they all said that Vishwa was the most advanced and was next in line for full initiation. I always let him come and talk to me in my room whenever he wanted to, and we had some interesting conversations.

Then there were Master's foreign disciples. They weren't so different from the other Europeans and Americans I had met in other ashrams except that the atmosphere here was so much better and that made them better too. They didn't have to fight with each other over Master's favours – I'm afraid that was very much the scene in some of the other ashrams which were like harems, the way they were all vying for the favour of their guru. But Master never encouraged that sort of relationship, and al-though of course many of them did have very strong attachments to him, he managed to keep them all healthy. And that's really saying something because, like in all the other ashrams, many of them were not healthy people; through no fault of their own quite often, they had just had a bad time and were trying to get over it.

Once Master said to me, 'What about you, Katie?' This was when I was alone with him in his room. He had called me in for some dictation – we were all given little jobs to do for him from time to time, to keep us busy and happy I suppose. Just let me say a few words about his room and get it over with. It was *awful*. It had linoleum on the floor of the nastiest pattern, and green strip lighting, and the walls were painted green too and had been decorated with calendars and pictures of what were supposed to be gods and saints but might as well have been Bombay film stars, they were so fat and gaudy. Master and all the junior swamis were terribly proud of this room. Whenever he acquired anything new – like some plastic flowers in a hideous vase – he would call everyone to admire and was so pleased and complacent that really it was not possible to say any thing except 'Yes very nice.'

When he said 'What about you, Katie?' I knew at once what he meant. That was another thing about him – he would suddenly come out with something as if there had already been a long talk between you on this subject. So when he asked me that, it was like the end of a conversation, and all I had to do was think for a moment and then I said, 'I'm okay.' Because that was what he had asked: was I okay? Did I want anything, any help or anything? And I didn't. I really was okay now. I hadn't always been but I got so travelling around on my own and then being in this nice place here with him.

This was before the Countess came. Once she was there, everything was rather different. For weeks before her arrival people started talking about her: she was an important figure there, and no wonder since she was very rich and did a lot for the ashram and for Master when he went abroad on his lecture tours. I wondered what she was like. When I asked Vishwa about her, he said, 'She is a great spiritual lady.'

We were both sitting outside my room. There was a little open space round which several other rooms were grouped. One of these – the biggest, at the corner – was being got ready for the Countess, It was the one that was always kept for her. People were vigorously sweeping in there and scrubbing the floor with soap and water.

'She is rich and from very aristocratic family,' Vishwa said, 'but when she met Master she was ready to give up everything.' He pointed to the room which was being scrubbed: 'This is where she stays. And see – not even a bed – she sleeps on the floor like a holy person. Oh Katie, when someone like me gives up the world, what is there? It is not such a great thing. But when *she* does it –' His face glowed. He had very bright eyes and a lovely complexion. He always looked very pure, owing no doubt to the very pure life he led.

Of course I got more and more curious about her, but when she came I was disappointed. I had expected her to be very special, but the only special thing about her was that I should meet her *here.* Otherwise she was a type I had often come across at posh parties and in the salons where I used to model. And the way she walked towards me and said, 'Welcome!' – she might as well have been walking across a carpet in a salon. She had a full-blown, middle-aged figure (she must have been in her fifties) but very thin legs on which she took long strides with her toes turned out. She gave me a deep searching look – and that too I was used to from someone like her because very worldly people always do that: to find out who you are and how usable. But in her case now I suppose it was to search down into my soul and see what that was like.

I don't know what her conclusion was, but I must have passed because she was always kind to me and even asked for my company quite often. Perhaps this was partly because we lived across from each other and she suffered from insomnia and needed someone to talk to at night. I'm a sound sleeper myself and wasn't always very keen when she came to wake me. But she would nag me till I got up. 'Come on, Katie, be a sport,' she would say. She used many English expressions like that: she spoke English very fluently though with a funny accent. I heard her speak to the French and Italian and German people in the ashram very fluently in their languages too. I don't know what nationality she herself was – a sort of mixture I think – but of course people like her have been everywhere, not to mention their assorted governesses when young.

She always made me come into her room. She said mine was too *luxurious*, she didn't feel right in it as she had given up all that. Hers certainly wasn't luxurious. Like Vishwa had said, there wasn't a stick of furniture in it and she slept on the floor on a mat. As the electricity supply in the ashram was very fitful, we usually sat by candlelight. It was queer sitting like that with her on the floor with a stub of candle between us. I didn't have to do much talking as she did it all. She used her arms a lot, in sweeping gestures, and I can still see them weaving around there by candlelight as if she was doing a dance with them; and her eyes which were big and baby-blue were stretched wide open in wonder at everything she was telling me. Her life was like a fairy tale, she said. She gave me all the details though I can't recall them as I kept dropping off to sleep (naturally at two in the morning). From time to time she'd stop and say sharply, 'Are you asleep, Katie,' and then she would poke me till I said no I wasn't. She told me how she first met Master at a lecture he had come to give in Paris. At the end of the lecture she went up to him – she said she had to elbow her way through a crowd of women all trying to get near him – and simply bowed down at his feet. No words spoken. There had been no need. It had been predestined.

She was also very fond of Vishwa. It seemed all three of them – i.e. her, Master, and Vishwa – had been closely related to each other in several previous incarnations. I think they had been either her sons or her husbands or fathers, I can't remember which exactly but it was very close so it was no wonder she felt about them the way she did. She had big plans for Vishwa. He was to go abroad and be a spiritual leader. She and Master often talked about it, and it was fascinating listening to them, but there was one thing I couldn't understand and that was why did it have to be Vishwa and not Master who was to be a spiritual leader in the West? I'd have thought Master himself had terrific qualifications for it.

Once I asked them. We were sitting in Master's room and the two of them were talking about Vishwa's future. When I asked 'What about Master?' she gave a dramatic laugh and pointed at him like she was accusing him: 'Ask him! Why don't you ask him!'

He gave a guilty smile and shifted around a bit on his throne. I say throne – it really was that: he received everyone in this room so a sort of dais had been fixed up at one end and a deer-skin spread on it for him to sit on; loving disciples had painted an arched back to the dais and decorated it with stars and symbols stuck on in silver paper (hideous!).

When she saw him smile like that, she really got exasperated. 'If you knew, Katie,' she said, 'how I have argued with him, how I have fought, how I have begged and pleaded on my *knees*. But he is as stubborn as–as–'

'A mule,' he kindly helped her out.

'Forgive me,' she said (because you can't call your guru names, that just isn't done!); though next moment she had worked herself up again: 'Do you know,' she asked me, 'how many people were waiting for him at the airport last time he went to New York? Do you know how many came to his lectures? That they had to be turned away from the *door* till we took a bigger hall! And not to speak of those who came to enrol for the special three-week Meditation-via-Contemplation course.'

'She is right,' he said. 'They are very kind to me.'

'Kind! They want him – need him – are crazy with love and devotion –'

'It's all true,' he said. 'But the trouble is, you see, I'm a very, very lazy person.' And as he said this, he gave a big yawn and stretched himself to prove how lazy he was: but he didn't look it – on the contrary, when he stretched like that, pushing out his big chest, he looked like he was humming with energy.

That evening he asked me to go for a stroll with him. We walked by the river which was very busy with people dipping in it for religious reasons. The temples were also busy – whenever we passed one, they seemed to be bursting in there with hymns, and cymbals, and little bells.

Master said: 'It is true that everyone is very kind to me in the West. Oh they made a big fuss when I come. They have even made a song for me – it goes – wait, let me see –'

He stopped still and several people took the opportunity to come up to ask for his blessing. There were many other holy men walking about but somehow Master stood out. Some of the holy men also came up to be blessed by him.

'Yes it goes: "*He's here! Our Master ji is here Jai jai Master! Jai jai He!*" They stand waiting for me at the airport, and when I come out of the customs they burst into song. They carry big banners and also have drums and flutes. What a noise they make! Some of them begin to dance there and then on the spot, they are so happy. And everyone stares and looks at me, all the respectable people at the airport, and they wonder "Now who is this ruffian?"'

He had to stop again because a shopkeeper came running out of his stall to crouch at Master's feet. He was the grocer – everyone knew he used false weights – as well as the local moneylender and the biggest rogue in town, but when Master blessed him I could see tears come in his eyes, he felt so good.

'A car has been bought for my use,' Master said when we walked on again. 'Also a lease has been taken on a beautiful residence in New Hampshire. Now they wish to buy an aeroplane to enable me to fly from coast to coast.' He sighed. 'She is right to be angry with me. But what am I to do? I stand in the middle of Times Square or Piccadilly, London, and I look up and there are all the beautiful beautiful buildings stretching so high up into heaven: yes I look at them but it is not them I see at all, Katie! Not them at all!'

He looked up and I with him, and I understood that what he saw in Times Square and Piccadilly was what we saw now – all those mountains growing higher and higher above the river, and some of them so high that you couldn't make out whether it was them with snow on top or the sky with clouds in it.

Before the Countess's arrival, everything had been very easy-going. We usually did our meditation, but if we happened to miss out, it never mattered too much. Also there was a lot of sitting around gossiping or trips to the bazaar for eats. But the Countess put us on a stricter regime. Now we all had a time-table to follow, and there were gongs and bells going off all day to remind us. This started at 5 a.m. when it was meditation time, followed by purificatory bathing time, and study time, and discussion time, and hymn time, and so on till lights-out time. Throughout the day disciples could be seen making their way up or down the mountain-side as they passed from one group activity to the other. If there was any delay in the schedule, the Countess got impatient and clapped her hands and chivied people along. The way she herself clambered up and down the mountain was just simply amazing for someone her age. Sometimes she went right to the top of the ashram where there was a pink plaster pillar inscribed with Golden Rules for Golden Living (a sort of Indian Ten Commandments): from here she could look all round, survey her domain as it were. When she wanted to summon everyone, she climbed up there with a pair of cymbals and how she beat them together! Boom! Bang! She must have had military blood in her veins, probably German.

She had drawn up a very strict time-table for Vishwa to cover every aspect of his education. He had to learn all sorts of things; not only English and a bit of French and German, but also how to use a knife and fork and even how to address people by their proper titles in case ambassadors and big church people and such were drawn into the movement as was fully expected. Because I'd been a model, I was put in charge of his deportment. I was supposed to teach him how to walk and sit nicely. He had to come to my room for lessons in the afternoons, and it was quite fun though I really didn't know what to teach him. As far as I was concerned, he was more graceful than anyone I'd ever seen. I loved the way he sat on the floor with his legs tucked under him; he could sit like that without moving for hours and hours. Or he might lie full length on the floor with his head supported on one hand and his ascetic's robe falling in folds round him so that he looked like a piece of sculpture you might see in a museum. I forgot to say that the Countess had decided he wasn't to shave his hair any more like the other junior swamis but was to grow it and have long curls. It wasn't long yet but it was certainly curly and framed his face very prettily.

After the first few days we gave up having lessons and just talked and spent our time together. He sat on the rug and I on the bed. He told me the story of his life and I told him mine. But his was much better than mine.

His father had been the station master at some very small junction, and the family lived in a little railway house near enough the tracks to run and put the signals up or down as required. Vishwa had plenty of brothers and sisters to play with, and friends at the little school he went to at the other end of town; but quite often he felt like not being with anyone. He would set off to school with his copies and pencils like everyone else, but half way he would change his mind and take another turning that led out of town into some open fields. Here he would lie down under a tree and look at patches of sky through the leaves of the tree, and the leaves moving ever so gently if there was a breeze or some birds shook their wings in there. He would stay all day and in the evening go home and not tell anyone. His mother was a religious person who regularly visited the temple and sometimes he went with her but he never felt anything special. Then Master came to town and gave a lecture in a tent that was put up for him on the Parade Ground. Vishwa went with his mother to hear him, again not expecting anything special, but the moment he saw Master something very peculiar happened: he couldn't quite describe it, but he said it was like when there is a wedding on a dark night and the fireworks start and there are those that shoot up into the sky and then burst into a huge white fountain of light scattering sparks all over so that you are blinded and dazzled with it. It was like that, Vishwa said. Then he just went away with Master. His family were sad at first to lose him; but they were proud too like all families are when one of them renounces the world to become a holy man.

Those were good afternoons we had, and we usually took the precaution of locking the door so no one could interrupt us. If we heard the Countess coming – one good thing about her, you could always *hear* her a mile off, she never moved an inch without shouting instructions to someone – the moment we heard her we'd jump up and unlock the door and fling it wide open: so when she looked in, she could see us having our lesson – Vishwa walking up and down with a book on his head, or sitting like on a dais to give a lecture and me showing him what to with his hands.

When I told him the story of *my* life, we both cried. Especially when I told him about my first marriage when I was only sixteen and Danny just twenty. He was a bass player in a group and he was really good and would have got somewhere if he hadn't freaked out. It was terrible seeing him do that, and the way he treated me after those first six months we had together which were out of this world. I never had anything like that with anyone ever again, though I got involved with many people afterwards. Everything just got worse and worse till I reached an all-time low with my second marriage which was to a company director (so-called, though don't ask me what sort of company) and a very smooth operator indeed besides being a sadist. Vishwa couldn't stand it when I came to that part of my story. He begged me not to go on, he put his hands over his ears. We weren't in my room that time but on top of the ashram by the Pillar of the Golden Rules. The view from here was fantastic, and it was so high up that you felt you might as well be in heaven, especially at this hour of the evening when the sky was turning all sorts of colours though mostly gold from the sun setting in it. Everything I was telling Vishwa seemed very far away. I can't say it was as if it had never happened, but it seemed like it had happened in someone else's life. There were tears on Vishwa's lashes, and I couldn't help myself, I had to kiss them away. After which we kissed properly. His mouth was as soft as a flower and his breath as sweet; of course he had never tasted meat nor eaten anything except the purest food such as a lamb might eat.

The door of my room was not the only one that was locked during those hot afternoons. Quite a few of the foreign disciples locked theirs for purposes I never cared to inquire into. At first I used to pretend to myself they were sleeping, and afterwards I didn't care what they were doing. I mean, even if they weren't sleeping, I felt there was something just as good and innocent about what they actually *were* doing. And after a while – when we had told each other the story of our respective lives and had run out of conversation – Vishwa and I began to do it too. This was about the time when preparations were going on for his final Renunciation and Initiation ceremony. It's considered the most important day in the life of a junior swami, when he ceases to be junior and becomes a senior or proper swami. It's a very solemn ceremony. A funeral pyre is lit and his junior robe and his caste thread are burned on it. All this is symbolic – it means he's dead to the world but resurrected to the spiritual life. In Vishwa's case, his resurrection was a bit different from the usual. He wasn't fitted out in the standard senior swami outfit – which is a piece of orange cloth and a begging bowl – but instead the Countess dressed him up in the clothes he was to wear in the West. She had herself designed a white silk robe for him, together with accessories like beads, sandals, the deer skin he was to sit on, and an embroidered shawl.

Getting all this ready meant many trips to the bazaar, and often she made Vishwa and me go with her. She swept through the bazaar the same way she did through the ashram, and the shopkeepers leaned eagerly out of their stalls to offer their salaams which she returned or not as they happened to be standing in her books. She was pretty strict with all of them – but most of all with the tailor whose job it was to stitch Vishwa's new silk robes. We spent hours in his little shop while Vishwa had to stand there and be fitted. The tailor crouched at his feet, stitching and restitching the hem to the Countess's instructions. She and I would stand back and look at Vishwa with our heads to one side while the tailor waited anxiously for her verdict. Ten to one she would say, 'No! Again!'

But once she said not to the tailor but to me, 'Vishwa stands very well now. He has a good pose.'

'Not bad,' I said, continuing to look critically at Vishwa and in such a way that he had a job not to laugh.

What she said next however killed all desire for laughter: 'I think we could end the deportment lessons now,' and then she shouted at the tailor: 'What is this! What are you doing! What sort of monkey-work do you call that!'

I managed to persuade her that I hadn't finished with Vishwa yet and there were still a few tricks of the trade I had to teach him. But I knew it was a short reprieve and that soon our lessons would have to end. Also plans were now afoot for Vishwa's departure. He was to go with the Countess when she returned to Europe in a few weeks' time; and she was already very busy corresponding with her contacts in various places, and all sorts of lectures and meetings were being arranged. But that wasn't the only thing worrying me: what was even worse was the change I felt taking place in Vishwa himself, especially after his Renunciation and Initiation ceremony. I think he was getting quite impressed with himself. The Countess made a point of treating him as if he were a guru already, and she bowed to him the same way she did to Master. And of course whatever she did everyone else followed suit, especially the foreign disciples. I might just say that they're always keen on things like that – I mean, bowing down and touching feet – I don't know what kick they get out of it but they do, the Countess along with the rest. Most of them do it very clumsily – not like Indians who are *born* to it – so sometimes you feel like laughing when you look at them. But they're always very solemn about it and afterwards, when they stumble up again, there's a sort of holy glow on their faces. Vishwa looked down at them with a benign expression and he also got into the habit of blessing them the way Master did.

Now I stayed alone in the afternoons, feeling very miserable, especially when I thought of what was going on in some of the other rooms and how happy people were in there. After a few days of this I couldn't stand being on my own and started wandering around looking for company. But the only person up and doing at that time of day was the Countess who I didn't particularly want to be with. So I went and sat in Master's room where the door was always open in case any of us needed him any time.

Like everybody else, he was often asleep that time of afternoon but it didn't matter. Just being in his presence was good. I sat on one of the green plastic benches that were ranged round his room and looked at him sleeping which he did sitting upright on his throne. Quite suddenly he would open his eyes and look straight at me and say, 'Ah Katie,' as if he'd known all along that I was sitting there.

One day there was an awful commotion outside. Master woke up as the Countess came in with two foreign disciples, a boy and a girl, who stood hanging their heads while she told us what she had caught them doing. They were two very young disciples; I think the boy didn't even have to shave yet. One couldn't imagine them doing anything really evil, and Master didn't seem to think so. He just told them to go away and have their afternoon rest. But because the Countess was very upset he tried to comfort her which he did by telling about his early life in the world when he was a married man. It had been an arranged marriage of course, and his wife had been very young, just out of school. Being married for them had been like a game, especially the cooking and housekeeping part which she had enjoyed very much. Every Sunday she had dressed up in a spangled sari and high-heeled shoes and he had escorted her on the bus to the cinema where they stood in a queue for the one-rupee seats. He had loved her more than he had ever loved anyone or anything in all his life and had not thought it possible to love so much. But it only lasted two years at the end of which time she died of a miscarriage. He left his home then and wandered about for many years, doing all sorts of different jobs. He worked as a motor mechanic, and a salesman for medical supplies, and had even been in films for a while on the distribution side. But not finding rest anywhere, he finally decided to give up the world. He explained to us that it had been the only logical thing to do.

Having learned during his two years of marriage how happy it was possible for a human being to be, he was never again satisfied to settle for anything less; but also seeing how it couldn't last on a worldly plane, he had decided to look for it elsewhere and help other people to do so with him.

I liked what he said, but I don't think the Countess took much of it in. She was more in her own thoughts. She was silent and gloomy which was *very* unusual for her. When she woke me that night for her midnight confessions, she seemed quite a different person: and now she didn't talk about her fairy tale life or her wonderful plans for the future but on the contrary about all the terrible things she had suffered in the past. She went right back to the time she was in her teens and had eloped with and married an old man, a friend of her father's, and from there on it was all just one long terrible story of bad marriages and unhappy love affairs and other sufferings that I wished I didn't have to listen to. But I couldn't leave her in the state she was in. She was crying and sobbing and lying face down on the ground. It was eerie in that bare cell of hers with the one piece of candle flickering in the wind which was very strong, and the rain beating down like fists on the tin roof.

The monsoon had started, and when you looked up now, there weren't any mountains left, only clouds hanging down very heavily; and when you looked down, the river was also heavy and full. Every day there were stories of pilgrims drowning in it, and one night it washed over one bank and swept away a little colony of huts that the lepers had built for themselves. Now they no longer sat sunning themselves on the bridge but were carted away to the infectious diseases hospital. The rains came gushing down the mountain right into the ashram so that we were all wading ankle-deep in mud and water. Many rooms were flooded and their occupants had to move into other people's rooms resulting in personality clashes. Everyone bore grudges and took sides so that it became rather like the other ashrams I had visited and not liked.

The person who changed the most was the Countess. Although she was still dashing up and down the mountain, it was no longer to get the place in running order. Now she tucked up her skirts to wade from room to room to peer through chinks and see what people were up to. She didn't trust anyone but appointed herself as a one-man spying organization. She even suspected Master and me! At least me – she asked me what I went to his room for in the afternoon and sniffed at my reply in a way I didn't care for. After that one awful outburst she had, she didn't call me at night any more but she was certainly after me during the day.

She guarded Vishwa like a dragon. She wouldn't even let me pass his room, and if she saw me going anywhere in that direction, she'd come running to tell me to take the other way round. I wasn't invited any more to accompany them to the bazaar but only she and Vishwa set off, with her holding a big black umbrella over them both. If they happened to pass me on the way, she would tilt the umbrella so he wouldn't be able to see me. Not that this was necessary as he never seemed to see me anyway. His eyes were always lowered and the expression on his face very serious. He had stopped joking around with the junior swamis, which I suppose was only fitting now he was a senior swami as well as about to become a spiritual leader. The Countess had fixed up a throne for him at the end of Master's room so he wouldn't have to sit on the floor and the benches along with the rest of us. When we all got together in there, Master would be at one end on his throne and Vishwa at the other on his. At Master's end there was always lots going on – everyone laughing and Master making jokes and having his fun – but Vishwa just sat very straight in the lotus pose and never looked at anyone or spoke, and only when the Countess pushed people to go and touch his feet, he'd raise a hand to bless them.

With the rains came flies and mosquitoes, and people began to fall sick with ah sorts of mysterious fevers. The Countess – who was terrified of germs and had herself pumped full of every kind of injection before coming to India – was now in a great hurry to be off with Vishwa. But before they could leave, he too came down with one of those fevers. She took him at once into her own room and kept him isolated in there with everything shut tight. She wouldn't let any of us near him. But I peeped in through the chinks, not caring whether she saw me or not. I even pleaded with her to let me come in, and once she let me but only to look at him from the door while she stood guard by his pillow. His eyes were shut and he was breathing heavily and moaning in an awful way. The Countess said I could go now, but instead I rushed up to Vishwa's bed. She tried to get between us but I pushed her out of the way and got down by the bed and held him where he lay moaning with his eyes shut. The Countess shrieked and pulled at me to get me away. I was shrieking too. We must have sounded and looked like a couple of madwomen. Vishwa opened his eyes and when he saw me there and moreover found that he was in my arms, *he* began to shriek too, as if he was frightened of me and that perhaps I was the very person he was having those terrible fever dreams about that made him groan.

It may have been this accidental shock treatment but that night Vishwa's fever came down and he began to get better. Master announced that there was going to be a Yagna or prayer-meet to give thanks for Vishwa's recovery. It was to be a really big show. Hordes of helpers came up from the town, all eager to take part in this event so as to benefit from the spiritual virtue it was expected to generate. The Meditation Hall was repainted salmon pink and the huge holy *OM* sign at one end of it was lit up all round with coloured bulbs that flashed on and off. Everyone worked with a will, and apparently good was already beginning to be generated because the rains stopped, the mud lanes in the ashram dried up, and the river flowed back into its banks. The disciples stopped quarrelling which may have been partly due to the fact that everyone could move back into their own rooms.

The Countess and Vishwa kept going down into the town to finish off with the tailors and embroiderers. They also went to the printer who was making large posters to be sent abroad to advertise Vishwa's arrival. The Countess often asked me to go with them: she was really a good-natured person and did not want me to feel left out. Especially now that she was sure there wasn't a dangerous situation working up between me and Vishwa. There she was right. I wasn't in the least interested in him and felt that the less I saw of him the better. I couldn't forget the way he had shrieked that night in the Countess's room as if I was something impure and dreadful. But on the contrary to me it seemed that it had been *he* who was impure and dreadful with his fever dreams. I didn't even like to think what went on in them.

The Great Yagna began and it really was great. The Meditation Hall was packed and was terribly hot not only with all the people there but also because of the sacrificial flames that sizzled as more and more clarified butter was poured on them amid incantations. Everyone was smiling and singing and sweating. Master was terrific – he was right by the fire stark naked except for the tiniest bit of loincloth. His chest glistened with oil and seemed to reflect the flames leaping about. Sometimes he jumped up on his throne and waved his arms to make everyone join in louder; and when they did, he got so happy he did a little jig standing up there. Vishwa was on the other side of the Hall also on a throne. He was half reclining in his spotless white robe; he did not seem to feel the heat at all but lay there as if made out of cool marble. He reminded me of the god Shiva resting on top of his snowy mountain. The Countess sat near him, and I saw how she tried to talk to him once or twice but he took no notice of her. After a while she got up and went out which was not surprising for it really was not her scene, all that noise and singing and the neon lights and decorations.

It went on all night. No one seemed to get tired – they just got more and more worked up and the singing got louder and the fire hotter. Other people too began to do little jigs like Master's. I left the Hall and walked around by myself. It was a fantastic night, the sky sprinkled all over with stars and a moon like a melon. When I passed the Countess's door, she called me in. She was lying on her mat on the floor and said she had a migraine. No wonder, with all that noise. I liked it myself but I knew that, though she was very much attracted to Eastern religions, her taste in music was more for the Western classical type (she loved string quartets and had had a long *affaire* with a cellist). She confessed to me that she was very anxious to leave now and get Vishwa started on his career. I think she would have liked to confess more things, but I had to get on. I made my way uphill past all the different buildings till I had reached the top of the ashram and the Pillar of the Golden Rules. Here I stood and looked down.

I saw the doors of the Meditation Hall open and Master and Vishwa come out. They were lit up by the lights from the Hall. Master was big and black and naked except for his triangle of orange cloth, and Vishwa was shining in white. I saw Master raise his arm and point it up, up to the top of the ashram. The two of them reminded me of a painting I've seen of I think it was an angel pointing out a path to a pilgrim. And like a pilgrim Vishwa began to climb up the path that Master had shown him. I stood by the Pillar of the Golden Rules and waited for him. When he got to me, we didn't have to speak one word. He was like a charged dynamo; I'd never known him like that. It was more like it might have been with Master instead of Vishwa. The drums and hymns down in the Meditation Hall also reached their crescendo just then. Of course Vishwa was too taken up with what he was doing to notice anything going on round him, so it was only me that saw the Countess come uphill. She was walking quite slowly and I suppose I could have warned Vishwa in time but it seemed a pity to interrupt him, so I just let her come on up and find us.

*   *   *

Master finally settled everything to everyone's satisfaction. He said Vishwa and I were to be a couple, and whereas Vishwa was to be the Guru, I was to embody the Mother principle (which is also very important). Once she caught on to the idea, the Countess rather liked it. She designed an outfit for me too – a sort of flowing white silk robe, really quite becoming. You might have seen posters of Vishwa and me together, both of us in these white robes, his hair black and curly, mine blonde and straight. I suppose we do make a good couple – anyway, people seem to like us and to get something out of us. We do our best. It's not very hard; mostly we just have to sit there and radiate. The results are quite satisfactory – I mean the effect we seem to have on people who need it. The person who really has to work hard is the Countess because she has to look after all the business and organizational end. We have a strenuous tour programme. Sometimes it's like being on a one-night stand and doing your turn and then packing up in a hurry to get to the next one. Some of the places we stay in aren't too good – motels where you have to pay in advance in case you flit – and when she is very tired, the Countess wrings her hands and says, 'My God, what am I doing here?' It must be strange for her who's been used to all the grand hotels everywhere, but of course really she likes it. It's her life's fulfilment. But for Vishwa and me it's just a job we do, and all the time we want to be somewhere else and are thinking of that other place. I often remember what Master told me, what happened to him when he looked up in Times Square and Piccadilly, and it's beginning to happen to me too. I seem to *see* those mountains and the river and temples; and then I long to be there.

In the Mountains

When one lives alone for most of the time and meets almost nobody, then care for one's outward appearance tends to drop away. That was what happened to Pritam. As the years went by and she continued living by herself, her appearance became rougher and shabbier, and though she was still in her thirties, she completely forgot to care for herself or think about herself as a physical person.

Her mother was just the opposite. She was plump and pampered, loved pastries and silk saris, and always smelled of lavender. Pritam smelled of – what was it? Her mother, enfolded in Pritam's embrace after a separation of many months, found herself sniffing in an attempt to identify the odour emanating from her. Perhaps it was from Pritam's clothes, which she probably did not change as frequently as was desirable. Tears came to the mother's eyes. They were partly for what her daughter had become and partly for the happiness of being with her again.

Pritam thumped her on the back. Her mother always cried at their meetings and at their partings, Pritam usually could not help being touched by these tears, even though she was aware of the mixed causes that evoked them. Now, to hide her own feelings, she became gruffer and more manly, and even gave the old lady a push towards a chair. 'Go on, sit down,' she said. 'I suppose you are dying for your cup of tea.' She had it all ready, and the mother took it gratefully, for she loved and needed tea, and the journey up from the plains had greatly tired her.

But she could not drink with enjoyment. Pritam's tea was always too strong for her – a black country brew such as peasants drank, and the milk was also that of peasants, too newly rich and warm from the buffalo. And they were in this rough and barely furnished room in the rough stone house perched on the mountainside. And there was Pritam herself. The mother had to concentrate all her energies on struggling against more tears.

'I suppose you don't like the tea,' Pritam said challengingly. She watched severely while the mother proved herself by drinking it up to the last drop, and Pritam refilled the cup. She asked, 'How is everybody? Same as usual? Eating, making money?'

'No, no,' said the mother, not so much denying the fact that this was what the family was doing as protesting against Pritam's saying so.

'Aren't they going up to Simla this year?'

'On Thursday,' the mother said, and shifted uncomfortably.

'And stopping here?'

'Yes. For lunch.'

The mother kept her eyes lowered. She said nothing more, though there was more to say. It would have to wait till a better hour. Let Pritam first get over the prospect of entertaining members of her family for a few hours on Thursday. It was nothing new or unexpected, for some of them stopped by every year on their way farther up the mountains. However much they may have desired to do so, they couldn't just drive past; it wouldn't be decent. But the prospect of meeting held no pleasure for anyone. Quite often there was a quarrel, and then Pritam cursed them as they drove away, and they sighed at the necessity of keeping up family relationships, instead of having their lunch comfortably in the hotel a few miles farther on.

Pritam said, 'I suppose you will be going with them,' and went on at once, 'Naturally, why should you stay? What is there for you here?'

'I want to stay.'

'No, you love to be in Simla. It's so nice and jolly, and meeting everyone walking on the Mall, and tea in Davico's. Nothing like that here. You even hate my tea.'

'I want to stay with you.'

'But I don't want you!' Pritam was laughing, not angry. 'You will be in my way, and then how will I carry on all my big love affairs?'

'What, what?'

Pritam clapped her hands in delight. 'Oh no. I'm telling you nothing, because then you will want to stay and you will scare everyone away.' She gave her mother a sly look and added, 'You will scare poor Doctor Sahib away.'

'Oh Doctor Sahib,' said the old lady, relieved to find it had all been a joke. But she continued with disapproval, 'Does he still come here?'

'Well, what do you think?' Pritam stopped laughing now and became offended. 'If he doesn't come, then who will come? Except some goats and monkeys, perhaps. I know he is not good enough for you. You don't like him to come here. You would prefer me to know only goats and monkeys. And the family, of course.'

'When did I say I don't like him?' the mother said.

'People don't have to say. And other people are quite capable of feeling without anyone saying. Here.' Pritam snatched up her mother's cup and filled it, with rather a vengeful air, for the third time.

Actually, it wasn't true that the mother disliked Doctor Sahib. He came to visit the next morning, and as soon as she saw him she had her usual sentiment about him – not dislike but disapproval. He certainly did not look like a person fit to be on terms of social intercourse with any member of her family. He was a tiny man, shabby and even dirty. He wore a kind of suit, but it was in a terrible condition and so were his shoes. One eye of his spectacles, for some reason, was blacked out with a piece of cardboard.

'Ah!' he exclaimed when he saw her. 'Mother has come!' And he was so genuinely happy that her disapproval could not stand up to him – at least, not entirely.

'Mother brings us tidings and good cheer from the great world outside,' Doctor Sahib went on. 'What are we but two mountain hermits? Or I could even say two mountain bears.'

He sat at a respectful distance away from the mother, who was ensconced in a basket chair. She had come to sit in the garden. There was a magnificent view from here of the plains below and the mountains above; however, she had not come out to enjoy the scenery but to get the benefit of the morning sun. Although it was the height of summer, she always felt freezing cold inside the house, which seemed like a stone tomb.

'Has Madam told you about our winter?' Doctor Sahib said. 'Oh, what these two bears have gone through! Ask her.'

'His roof fell in,' Pritam said.

'One night I was sleeping in my bed. Suddenly – what shall I tell you – crash, bang! Boom and bang! To me it seemed that all the mountains were falling and, let alone the mountains, heaven itself was coming down into my poor house. I said, "Doctor Sahib, your hour has come."'

'I told him, I told him all summer, "The first snowfall and your roof will fall in." And when it happened all he could so was stand there and wring his hands. What an idiot!'

'If it hadn't been for Madam, God knows what would have become of me. But she took me in and all winter she allowed me to have my corner by her own fireside.'

The mother looked at them with startled eyes.

'Oh yes, all winter,' Pritam said, mocking her. 'And all alone, just the two of us. Why did you have to tell her?' she reproached Doctor Sahib. 'Now she is shocked. Just look at her face. She is thinking we are two guilty lovers.'

The mother flushed, and so did Doctor Sahib. An expression of bashfulness came into his face, mixed with regret, with melancholy. He was silent for some time, his head lowered. Then he said to the mother, 'Look, can you see it?' He pointed at his house, which nestled farther down the mountainside, some way below Pritam's. It was a tiny house, not much more than a hut. 'All hale and hearty again. Madam had the roof fixed, and now I am snug and safe once more in my own little kingdom.'

Pritam said, 'One day the whole place is going to come down, not just the roof, and then what will you do?'

He spread his arms in acceptance and resignation. He had no choice as to place of residence. His family had brought him here and installed him in the house; they gave him a tiny allowance but only on condition that he wouldn't return to Delhi. As was evident from his fluent English, Doctor Sahib was an educated man, though it was not quite clear whether he really had qualified as a doctor. If he had, he may have done something disreputable and been struck off the register. Some such air hung about him. He was a great embarrassment to his family. Unable to make a living, he had gone around scrounging from family friends, and at one point had sat on the pavement in New Delhi's most fashionable shopping district and attempted to sell cigarettes and matches.

Later, when he had gone, Pritam said, 'Don't you think I've got a dashing lover?'

'I know it's not true,' the mother said, defending herself. 'But other people, what will they think – alone with him in the house all winter? You know how people are.'

'What people?'

It was true. There weren't any. To the mother, this was a cause for regret. She looked at the mountains stretching away into the distance – a scene of desolation. But Pritam's eyes were half shut with satisfaction as she gazed across the empty spaces and saw birds cleaving through the mist, afloat in the pure mountain sky.

'I was waiting for you all winter,' the mother said. 'I had your room ready, and every day we went in there to dust and change the flowers.' She broke out. 'Why didn't you come? Why stay in this place when you can be at home and lead a proper life like everybody else?'

Pritam laughed. 'Oh but I'm not like everybody else! That's the last thing!'

The mother was silent. She could not deny that Pritam was different. When she was a girl, they had worried about her and yet they had also been proud of her. She had been a big, handsome girl with independent views. People admired her and thought it a fine thing that a girl could be so emancipated in India and lead a free life, just as in other places.

Now the mother decided to break her news. She said, 'He is coming with them on Thursday.'

'Who is coming with them?'

'Sarla's husband.' She did not look at Pritam after saying this.

After a moment's silence Pritam cried, 'So let him come! They can all come – everyone welcome. My goodness, what's so special about him that you should make such a face? What's so special about any of them? They may come, they may eat, they may go away again, and goodbye. Why should I care for anyone? I don't care. And also you! You also may go – right now, this minute, if you like – and I will stand here and wave to you and laugh!'

In an attempt to stop her, the mother asked, 'What will you cook for them on Thursday?'

That did bring her up short. For a moment she gazed at her mother wildly, as if she were mad herself or thought her mother mad. Then she said, 'My God, do you ever think of anything except food?'

'I eat too much,' the old lady gladly admitted. 'Dr Puri says I must reduce.'

Pritam didn't sleep well that night. She felt hot, and tossed about heavily, and finally got up and turned on the light and wandered around the house in her nightclothes. Then she unlatched the door and let herself out. The night air was crisp, and it refreshed her at once. She loved being out in all this immense silence. Moonlight lay on top of the mountains, so that even those that were green looked as if they were covered in snow.

There was only one light – a very human little speck, in all that darkness. It came from Doctor Sahib's house, some way below hers. She wondered if he had fallen asleep with the light on. It happened sometimes that he dozed off where he was sitting and when he woke up again it was morning. But other times he really did stay awake all night, too excited by his reading and thinking to be able to sleep. Pritam decided to go down and investigate. The path was very steep, but she picked her way down, as sure and steady as a mountain goat. She peered in at his window. He was awake, sitting at his table with his head supported on his hand, and reading by the light of a kerosene lamp. His house had once had electricity, but after the disaster last winter it could not be got to work again. Pritam was quite glad about that, for the wiring had always been uncertain, and he had been in constant danger of being electrocuted.

She rapped on the glass to rouse him, then went round to let herself in by the door. At the sound of her knock, he had jumped to his feet; he was startled, and no less so when he discovered who his visitor was. He stared at her through his one glass lens, and his lower lip trembled in agitation.

She was irritated. 'If you're so frightened, why don't you lock your door? You should lock it. Any kind of person can come in and do anything he wants.' It struck her how much like a murder victim he looked.

He was so small and weak – one blow on the head would do it. Some morning she would come down and find him lying huddled on the floor.

But there he was, alive, and, now that he had got over the shock, laughing and flustered and happy to see her. He fussed around and invited her to sit on his only chair, dusting the seat with his hand and drawing it out for her in so courtly a manner that she became instinctively graceful as she settled herself on it and pulled her nightdress over her knees.

'Look at me, in my nightie,' she said, laughing. 'I suppose you're shocked. If Mother knew. If she could see me! But of course she is fast asleep and snoring in her bed. Why are you awake? Reading one of your stupid books – what stuff you cram into your head day and night. Anyone would go crazy.'

Doctor Sahib was very fond of reading. He read mostly historical romances and was influenced and even inspired by them. He believed very strongly in past births, and these book helped him to learn about the historical eras through which he might have passed.

'A fascinating story,' he said. 'There is a married lady – a queen, as a matter of fact – who falls hopelessly in love with a monk.'

'Goodness! Hopelessly?'

'You see, these monks – naturally – they were under a vow of chastity and that means – well – you know . . .'

'Of course I know.'

'So there was great anguish on both sides. Because he also felt burning love for the lady and endured horrible penances in order to subdue himself. Would you like me to read to you? There are some sublime passages.'

'What is the use? These are not things to read in books but to experience in life. Have you ever been hopelessly in love?'

He turned away his face, so that now only his cardboard lens was looking at her. However, it seemed not blank but full of expression.

She said, 'There are people in the world whose feelings are much stronger than other people's. Of course they must suffer. If you are not satisfied only with eating and drinking but want something else . . . You should see my family. They care for nothing – only physical things, only enjoyment.'

'Mine exactly the same.'

'There is one cousin, Sarla – I have nothing against her, she is not a bad person. But I tell you it would be just as well to be born an animal. Perhaps I shouldn't talk like this, but it's true.'

'It is true. And in previous births these people really were animals.'

'Do you think so?'

'Or some very low form of human being. But the queens and the really great people, they become – well, they become like you. Please don't laugh! I have told you before what you were in your last birth.'

She went on laughing. 'You've told me so many things,' she said.

'All true. Because you have passed through many incarnations. And in each one you were a very outstanding personality, a highly developed soul, but each time you also had a difficult life, marked by sorrow and suffering.'

Pritam had stopped laughing. She gazed sadly at the blank wall over his head.

'It is the fate of all highly developed souls,' he said. 'It is the price to be paid.'

'I know.' She fetched a sigh from her innermost being.

'I think a lot about this problem. Just tonight, before you came, I sat here reading my book. I'm not ashamed to admit that tears came streaming from my eyes, so that I couldn't go on reading, on account of not being able to see the print. Then I looked up and I asked, "Oh, Lord, why must these good and noble souls endure such torment, while others, less good and noble, can enjoy themselves freely?"'

'Yes, why?' Pritam asked.

'I shall tell you. I shall explain.' He was excited, inspired now. He looked at her fully, and even his cardboard lens seemed radiant. 'Now, as I was reading about this monk – a saint, by the way – and how he struggled and battled against nature, then

I could not but think of my own self. Yes, I too, though not a saint, struggle and battle here alone in my small hut. I cry out in anguish, and the suffering endured is terrible but also – oh, Madam – glorious! A privilege.'

Pritam looked at a crack that ran right across the wall and seemed to be splitting it apart. One more heavy snowfall, she thought, and the whole hut would come down. Meanwhile he sat here and talked nonsense and she listened to him. She got up abruptly.

He cried, 'I have talked too much! You are bored!'

'Look at the time,' she said. The window was milk-white with dawn. She turned down the kerosene lamp and opened the door. Trees and mountains were floating in a pale mist, attempting to surface like swimmers through water. 'Oh my God,' she said, 'it's time to get up. And I'm going to have such a day today, with all of them coming.'

'They are coming today?'

'Yes, and you needn't bother to visit. They are not your type at all. Not one bit.'

He laughed. 'All right.'

'Not mine, either,' she said, beginning the upward climb back to her house.

Pritam loved to cook and was very good at it. Her kitchen was a primitive little outbuilding in which she bustled about. Her hair fell into her face and stuck to her forehead; several times she tried to push it back with her elbow but only succeeded in leaving a black soot mark. When her mother pointed this out to her, she laughed and smeared at it and made it worse.

Her good humour carried her successfully over the arrival of the relatives. They came in three carloads, and suddenly the house was full of fashionably dressed people with loud voices. Pritam came dashing out of the kitchen just as she was and embraced everyone indiscriminately, including Sarla and her husband, Bobby. In the bustle of arrival and the excitement of many people, the meeting went off easily. The mother was relieved. Pritam and Bobby hadn't met for eight years – in fact, not since Bobby had been married to Sarla.

Soon Pritam was serving a vast, superbly cooked meal. She went around piling their plates, urging them to take, take more, glad at seeing them enjoy her food. She still hadn't changed her clothes, and the smear of soot was still on her face. The mother – whose main fear had been that Pritam would be surly and difficult – was not relieved but upset by Pritam's good mood. She thought to herself, why should she be like that with them – what have they ever done for her that she should show them such affection and be like a servant to them? She even looked like their servant. The old lady's temper mounted, and when she saw Pritam piling rice on to Bobby's plate – when she saw her serving *him* like a servant, and the way he turned round to compliment her about the food, making Pritam proud and shy and pleased – then the mother could not bear any more. She went into the bedroom and lay down on the bed. She felt ill; her blood pressure had risen and all her pulses throbbed. She shut her eyes and tried to shut out the merry, sociable sounds coming from the next room.

After a while Pritam came in and said, 'Why aren't you eating?'

The old lady didn't answer.

'What's, the matter?'

'Go. Go away. Go to your guests.'

'Oh my God, she is sulking!' Pritam said, and laughed out loud – not to annoy her mother but to rally her, the way she would a child. But the mother continued to lie there with her eyes shut.

Pritam said, 'Should I get you some food?'

'I don't want it,' the mother said. But suddenly she opened her eyes and sat up. She said, 'You should give food to him. He also should be invited. Or perhaps you think he is not good enough for your guests?'

'Who?'

'Who. You know very well. You should know. You were with him the whole night.'

Pritam gave a quick glance over her shoulder at the open door, then advanced toward her mother. 'So you have been spying on me,' she said. The mother shrank back. 'You pretended to be asleep, and all the time you were spying on me.'

'Not like that, Daughter –'

'And now you are having filthy thoughts about me.'

'Not like that!'

'Yes, like that!'

Both were shouting. The conversation in the next room had died down. The mother whispered, 'Shut the door,' and Pritam did so.

Then the mother said in a gentle, loving voice, 'I'm glad he is here with you. He is a good friend to you.' She looked into Pritam's face, but it did not lighten, and she went on, 'That is why I said he should be invited. When other friends come, we should not neglect our old friends who have stood by us in our hour of need.'

Pritam snorted scornfully.

'And he would have enjoyed the food so much,' the mother said. 'I think he doesn't often eat well.'

Pritam laughed. 'You should see what he eats!' she said. 'But he is lucky to get even that. At least his family send him money now. Before he came here, do you want to hear what he did? He has told me himself. He used to go to the kitchens of the restaurants and beg for food. And they gave him scraps and he ate them – he has told me himself. He ate leftover scraps from other people's plates like a sweeper or a dog. And you want such a person to be my friend.'

She turned away from her mother's startled, suffering face. She ran out of the room and out through the next room, past all the guests. She climbed up a path that ran from the back of her house to a little cleared plateau. She lay down in the grass, which was alive with insects; she was level with the tops of trees and with the birds that pecked and called from inside them. She often came here. She looked down at the view but didn't see it, it was so familiar to her. The only unusual sight was the three cars parked outside her house. A chauffeur was wiping a windscreen. Then someone came out of the house and, reaching inside a car door, emerged with a bottle. It was Bobby.

Pritam watched him, and when he was about to go back into the house, she aimed a pebble that fell at his feet. He looked up. He smiled. 'Hi, there!' he called.

She beckoned him to climb up to her. He hesitated for a moment, looking at the bottle and towards the house, but then gave the toss of his head that she knew well, and began to pick his way along the path. She put her hand over her mouth to cover a laugh as she watched him crawl up toward her on all fours. When finally he arrived, he was out of breath and dishevelled, and there was a little blood on his hand where he had grazed it. He flung himself on the grass beside her and gave a great 'Whoof!' of relief.

She hadn't seen him for eight years, and her whole life had changed in the meantime, but it didn't seem to her that he had changed all that much. Perhaps he was a little heavier, but it suited him, made him look more manly than ever. He was lying face down on the grass, and she watched his shoulder-blades twitch inside his finely striped shirt as he breathed in exhaustion.

'You are in very poor condition,' she said.

'Isn't it terrible?'

'Don't you play tennis any more?'

'Mostly golf now.'

He sat up and put the bottle to his mouth and tilted back his head. She watched his throat moving as the liquid glided down. He finished with a sound of satisfaction and passed the bottle to her, and without wiping it she put her lips where his had been and drank. The whisky leaped up in her like fire. They had often sat like this together, passing a bottle of Scotch between them.

He seemed to be perfectly content to be there with her. He sat with his knees drawn up and let his eyes linger appreciatively over the view. It was the way she had often seen him look at attractive girls. 'Nice,' he said, as he had said on those occasions. She laughed, and then she too looked and tried to imagine how he was seeing it.

'A nice place,' he said. 'I like it. I wish I could live here.'

'You!' She laughed again.

He made a serious face. 'I love peace and solitude. You don't know me. I've changed a lot.' He turned right round towards her, still very solemn, and for the first time she felt him gazing full into her face. She put up her hand and said quickly, 'I've been cooking all day.'

He looked away, as if wanting to spare her, and this delicacy hurt her more than anything. She said heavily, 'I've changed.'

'Oh no!' he said in haste. 'You are just the same. As soon as I saw you, I thought: Look at Priti, she is just the same.' And again he turned towards her to allow her to see his eyes, stretching them wide open for her benefit. It was a habit of his she knew well; he would always challenge the person to whom he was lying to read anything but complete honesty in his eyes.

She said, 'You had better go. Everyone will wonder where you are.'

'Let them.' And when she shook her head, he said, in his wheedling voice, 'Let me stay with you. It has been such a long time. Shall I tell you something? I was so excited yesterday thinking: Tomorrow I shall see her again. I couldn't sleep all night. No, really – it's true.'

Of course she knew it wasn't. He slept like a bear; nothing could disturb that. The thought amused her, and her mouth corners twitched. Encouraged, he moved in closer. 'I think about you very often,' he said. 'I remember so many things – you have no idea. All the discussions we had about our terrible social system. It was great.'

Once they had had a very fine talk about free love. They had gone to a place they knew about, by a lake. At first they were quite frivolous, sitting on a ledge overlooking the lake, but as they got deeper into their conversation about free love (they both, it turned out, believed in it) they became more and more serious and, after that, very quiet, until in the end they had nothing more to say. Then they only sat there, and though it was very still and the water had nothing but tiny ripples on it, like wrinkles in silk, they felt as if they were in a storm. But of course it was their hearts beating and their blood rushing. It was the most marvellous experience they had ever had in their whole lives. After that, they often returned there or went to other similar places that they found, and as soon as they were alone together that same storm broke out.

Now Bobby heaved a sigh. To make himself feel better, he took another drink from his bottle and then passed it to her. 'It's funny,' he said. 'I have this fantastic social life. I meet such a lot of people, but there isn't one person I can talk with the way I talk with you. I mean, about serious subjects.'

'And with Sarla?'

'Sarla is all right, but she isn't really interested in serious subjects. I don't think she ever thinks about them. But I do.'

To prove it, he again assumed a very solemn expression and turned his face towards her, so that she could study it. How little he had changed!

'Give me another drink,' she said, needing it.

He passed her the bottle. 'People think I'm an extrovert type, and of course I do have to lead a very extrovert sort of life,' he said. 'And there is the business too – ever since Daddy had his stroke, I have to spend a lot of time in the office. But very often, you know what I like to do? Just lie on my bed and listen to nice tunes on my cassette. And then I have a lot of thoughts.'

'What about?'

'Oh, all sorts of things. You would be surprised.'

She was filled with sensations she had thought she would never have again. No doubt they were partly due to the whisky; she hadn't drunk in a long time. She thought he must be feeling the way she did; in the past they had always felt the same. She put out her hand to touch him – first his cheek, which was rough and manly, and then his neck, which was soft and smooth. He had been talking, but when she touched him he fell silent. She left her hand lying on his neck, loving to touch it. He remained silent, and there was something strange. For a moment, she didn't remove her hand – she was embarrassed to do so – and when at last she did she noticed that he looked at it. She looked at it too. The skin was rough and not too clean, and neither were her nails, and one of them was broken. She hid her hands behind her back.

Now he was talking again, and talking quite fast. 'Honestly, Priti, I think you're really lucky to be living here,' he said. 'No one to bother you, no worries, and all this fantastic scenery.' He turned his head again to admire it and made his eyes sparkle with appreciation. He also took a deep breath.

'And such marvellous air,' he said. 'No wonder you keep fit and healthy. Who lives there?' He pointed at Doctor Sahib's house below.

Pritam answered eagerly. 'Oh, I'm very lucky – he is such an interesting personality. If only you could meet him.'

'What a pity,' Bobby said politely. Down below, there was a lot of activity around the three cars. Things were being rolled up and stowed away in preparation for departure.

'Yes, you don't meet such people every day. He is a doctor, not only of medicine but all sorts of other things too. He does a lot of research and thinking, and that is why he lives up here. Because it is so quiet.'

Now people could be seen coming out of Pritam's house. They turned this way and that, looking up and calling Pritam's name.

'They are looking for you,' Bobby said. He replaced the cap of his whisky bottle and got up and waited for her to get up too. But she took her time.

'You see, for serious thinking you have to have absolute peace and quiet,' she said. 'I mean, if you are a real thinker, a sort of philosopher type.'

She got up. She stood and looked down at the people searching and calling for her. 'Whenever I wake up at night, I can see his light on. He is always with some book, studying, studying.'

'Fantastic,' Bobby said, though his attention was distracted by the people below.

'He knows all about past lives. He can tell you exactly what you were in all your previous births.'

'Really?' Bobby said, turning towards her again.

'He has told me all about my incarnations.'

'Really? Would he know about me too?'

'Perhaps. If you were an interesting personality. Yes all right, coming!' she called down at last.

She began the steep climb down, but it was so easy for her that she could look back at him over her shoulder and continue talking. 'He is only interested in studying highly developed souls, so unless you were someone really quite special in a previous birth he wouldn't be able to tell you anything.'

'What were you?' Bobby said. He had begun to follow her. Although the conversation was interesting to him, he could not concentrate on it, because he had to keep looking down at the path and place his feet with caution.

'I don't think I can tell you,' she said, walking on ahead. 'It is something you are supposed to know only in your innermost self.'

'What?' he said, but just then he slipped, and it was all he could do to save himself from falling.

'In your innermost self!' she repeated in a louder voice, though without looking back. Nimbly, she ran down the remainder of the path and was soon among the people who had been calling her.

*　　　*　　　*

They were relieved to see her. It seemed the old lady was being very troublesome. She refused to have her bag packed, refused to get into the car and be driven up to Simla. She said she wanted to stay with Pritam.

'So let her,' Pritam said.

Her relatives exchanged exasperated glances. Some of the ladies were so tired of the whole thing that they had given up and sat on the steps of the veranda, fanning themselves. Others, more patient, explained to Pritam that it was all very well for her to say let her stay, but how was she going to look after her? The old lady needed so many things – a masseuse in the morning, a cup of Horlicks at eleven and another at three, and one never knew when the doctor would have to be called for her blood pressure. None of these facilities was available in Pritam's house, and they knew exactly what would happen – after a day, or at the most two, Pritam would send them an SOS, and they would have to come back all the way from Simla to fetch her away.

Pritam went into the bedroom, shutting the door behind her. The mother was lying on her bed, with her face to the wall. She didn't move or turn round or give any sign of life until Pritam said, 'It's me.' Then her mother said, 'I'm not going with them.'

Pritam said, 'You will have to have a cold bath every day, because I'm not going to keep lighting the boiler for you. Do you know who has to chop the wood? Me, Pritam.'

'I don't need hot water. If you don't need it, I don't.'

'And there is no Horlicks.'

'Tcha!' said her mother. She was still lying on the bed, though she had turned round now and was facing Pritam. She did not look very well. Her face seemed puffed and flushed.

'And your blood pressure?' Pritam asked.

'It is quite all right.'

'Yes, and what if it isn't? There is not Dr Puri here, or anyone like that.'

The mother shut her eyes, as if it were a great effort. After a time, she found the strength to say, 'There is a doctor.'

'God help us!' Pritam said, and laughed out loud.

'He *is* a doctor.' The mother compressed her little mouth stubbornly over her dentures. Pritam did not contradict her, though she was still laughing to herself. They were silent together but not in disagreement. Pritam opened the door to leave.

'Did you keep any food for him?' the mother said.

'There is enough to last him a week.'

She went out and told the others that her mother was staying. She wouldn't listen to any arguments, and after a while they gave up. All they wanted was to get away as quickly as possible. They piled into their cars and waved at her from the windows. She waved back. When she was out of sight, they sank back against the car upholstery with sighs of relief. They felt it had gone off quite well this time. At least there had been no quarrel. They discussed her for a while and felt that she was improving; perhaps she was quietening down with middle age.

Pritam waited for the cars to reach the bend below and then – quite without malice but with excellent aim – she threw three stones. Each one squarely hit the roof of a different car as they passed, one after the other. She could hear the sound faintly from up here. She thought how amazed they would be inside their cars, wondering what had hit them, and how they would crane out of the windows but not be able to see anything. They would decide that it was just some stones crumbling off the hillside – perhaps the beginning of a landslide; you never could tell in the mountains.

She picked up another stone and flung it all the way down at Doctor Sahib's corrugated tin roof. It landed with a terrific clatter, and he came running out. He looked straight up to where she was standing, and his one lens glittered at her in the sun.

She put her hands to her mouth and called, 'Food!' He gave a sign of joyful assent and straightaway, as nimble as herself, began the familiar climb up.

Bombay

Sometimes the Uncle did not visit his niece for several days. He stayed in his bare, unventilated lodging and fed himself with food from the bazaar. Once, after such an absence, there was a new servant in the niece's house, who refused to let him in. 'Not at home!' the servant said, viewing the Uncle with the utmost suspicion. And indeed who could blame him; certainly not the Uncle himself.

But Nargis, the niece, the mistress of the house, was annoyed – not with the servant but with her uncle. In any case, she was usually annoyed with him when he reappeared after one of his absences. It was resentment partly at his having stayed away, partly at his having reappeared.

'Look at you,' she said. 'Like a beggar. And I suppose you have been eating that dirty bazaar food again. Or no food at all.'

She rang the bell and gave orders to a servant, who soon returned with refreshments. The Uncle enjoyed them; sometimes he did enjoy things in that house, though only if he and she were alone together.

That could never be for long. Khorshed, one of her unmarried sisters-in-law, was soon with them, greeting the Uncle with the formal courtesy – a stately inclination of the head – that she extended to everyone. Since he was family, she also smiled at him. She had yellow teeth and was yellow all over; her skin was like thin old paper stretched over her bones. She sat in one of the winged armchairs by the window – her usual place, which enabled her to keep an eye on the road and anything that might be going on there. She entertained them with an account of a charity ball she had witnessed at the Taj Mahal Hotel the day before. Soon she was joined by her sister Pilla, who took the opposite armchair in order to see the other end of the road. They always shared a view between them in this way. They had done the same the day before at the Taj Mahal Hotel. They themselves had not bought tickets – it had not been one of their charities – but had taken up a vantage point on the velvet bench on the first landing of the double staircase. Khorshed had watched the people who had come up from the right-hand wing, and Pilla those from the left. Now they described who had been there, supplementing each other's account and sometimes arguing whether it had been Lady Ginwala who had worn a tussore silk or Mrs Homy Jussawala. They quarrelled over it ever so gently.

Rusi came in much later. He had only just got up. He always got up very late; he couldn't sleep at night, and moved around the house and played his record-player at top volume. When he came in – in his brocade dressing-gown and with his hair tousled – everyone in the room became alert and intense, though they tried to hide it. His two aunts bade him good morning in sweet fluting voices; his mother inquired after his breakfast. He ignored them all. He sank into a chair, scowling heavily and supporting his forehead on his hand, as if weighted down by thoughts too lofty for anyone there to understand.

'Look, look,' said Pilla to create a diversion, 'here she is again!'

'Where!' cried Khorshed, helping her sister.

'There. In *another* new sari. Walking like a princess – and they owe rent and bills everywhere.'

'Just see – a new parasol too, matching the sari.'

Both shook their heads. The boy, Rusi, took his hand from his brow, and his scowling eyes swept around the room and rested on the Uncle.

'Oh, back again,' he said. 'Thought we'd got rid of you.' He gave one of his short, mad laughs.

'Yes,' said the Uncle, 'here you see me again. I had no food at home, so I came. Because of this,' he said, patting his thin stomach.

'All dogs are like that,' Rusi said. 'Where there is food to be got, there they run. Have you heard of Pavlov? Of course not. You people are all so ignorant.'

'Tell us, darling,' said Nargis, his mother.

'Please teach us, Rusi darling,' the aunts begged eagerly.

He relapsed into silence. He sat hunched in the chair and, drawing his feet out of his slippers, held them up one by one and studied them, wriggling the toes. He did this with great concentration, so that no one dared speak for fear of disturbing him.

The Uncle now forced himself to look at him. Every time he came here, it seemed to him that the boy had deteriorated further. Rusi had a shambling, flabby body, and though he was barely twenty his hair was beginning to fall out in handfuls. He was dreadful. The Uncle, instead of feeling sorry for this sick boy, hated him more than any other human being on earth. Rusi looked up. Their eyes met; the Uncle looked away. Rusi gave another of his laughs and said, 'When Pavlov rang a bell, saliva came out of the dog's mouth.' He tittered and pointed at the Uncle. 'We don't even have to ring a bell! Khorshed, Pilla – look at him! Not even a bell!'

The women laughed with him, and so did the Uncle, though only after he had caught his niece's eye and had read the imploring look there. Then it was not so difficult for him to join in; in fact, he wanted to.

Everyone always thought of the Uncle as a bachelor, but he had once been married. His wife had been dull and of a faded colour, and soon he sent her back to her parents and went to live with his brother and with Nargis, the brother's daughter. The brother's wife had also been dull and faded; she did not have to be sent away, but died, leaving the two brothers alone with the girl. These three had lived together very happily in a tiny house with a tiny garden that had three banana plants and a papaya tree in it. This was in an outlying suburb of Bombay, with a lot of respectable neighbours who did not quite know what to make of the household. It included an ancient woman servant, who was sometimes deaf, sometimes dumb, sometimes both. Whatever the truth of her disability, it prevented her from communicating with anyone outside the house and quite often with anyone in it. The two brothers didn't work much, though Nargis's father was a journalist and the Uncle a lawyer. They only went out to practise their respective professions when money ran very low. Then Nargis's father made the rounds of the newspaper offices, and the Uncle sat outside the courts to draw up documents and write legal letters. The rest of the time, they stayed at home and amused Nargis. They were both musical, and one sang while the other accompanied him on the harmonium. The whole household kept very odd hours, and sometimes when they got excited over their music they stayed up all night and slept through the day, keeping the shutters closed. Then the neighbours, wondering whether something untoward had happened, stood outside the little house and peered through the banana plants, until at last, towards evening, the shutters would be thrown open and a brother would appear at each window, fresh and rested and smiling at the little crowd gathered outside.

Both were passionate readers of Persian poetry and Victorian poetry and prose. They taught Nargis everything they could, and since she was in any case not a keen scholar, there was no necessity to send her to school. Altogether they kept her so much to themselves that no one realized she was growing up, till one day, there she was – a lush fruit, suddenly and perfectly ready. The two brothers carried on as if nothing had happened – singing, reading poetry, amusing her to the best of their ability. They bought her all sorts of nice clothes too, and whatever jewellery they could afford, so that it became necessary for them to go out to work rather more frequently than in the past. Nargis's father began to accept commissions to write biographies of prominent members of their own Parsi community. He wrote these in an ornate, fulsome style, heaping all the ringing superlatives he had gathered from his Victorian readings on to these shrewd traders in slippers and round hats. In this way, he was commissioned to write a biography of the founder of the great commercial house of Paniwala & Sons. The present head of the house took a keen interest in the project and helped with researches into the family archives. Once he got so excited over the discovery of a document that he had himself driven to the little house in the suburb. That was how he first saw Nargis, and how he kept coming back again even after the biography had been printed and distributed.

Nargis had no objections to marrying him. He wasn't really old – in his late thirties – though he was already perfectly bald, with his head and face the same pale yellow colour. His hands were pale too, and plump like a woman's, with perfectly kept fingernails. He was a very kind man – very kind and gentle – with a soft voice and soft ways. He wanted to do everything for Nargis. She moved into the family mansion with him and his two sisters and with his servants and the treasures he had bought from antique dealers all over Europe. Positions were found in the house of Paniwala for Nargis's father and the Uncle, so that they no longer had to go out in order to work but only to collect their cheques. Everyone should have been happy, and no one was. The little house in the suburb died the way a tree dies and all its leaves drop off and the birds fly away. It was the old woman who felt the blight first and had herself taken to hospital to die there. Next, Nargis's father lay down with an ailment that soon carried him off. Then the Uncle moved out of the house and into his quarters in the city.

*　　　　*　　　　*

Nargis had once visited him there, to persuade him to come and live in the family mansion. He wouldn't hear of it. He also said, 'Who asked you to come here?' He was quite angry. Her arrival had thrown the whole house – indeed, the whole neighbourhood – into commotion. A crowd gathered around her large car parked outside, and some lay waiting on the stairs, and children even opened the door of his room to peep in at the grand lady who had come. He bared his teeth at them and made bloodcurdling noises.

'Come,' Nargis pleaded. She looked round the room, which was quite squalid, though it had a patterned marble floor and coloured-glass panes set in a fan above the door. The house had once been a respectable merchant's dwelling, but now, like the whole neighbourhood, it was fast turning into a slum.

'You needn't talk with anyone,' she promised. 'Only with me.'

'And Khorshed?' he asked. 'And Pilla?' He opened his mouth wide to laugh. He got great amusement out of the two sisters.

'Only with me.'

He gave an imitation of Khorshed and Pilla looking out of the window. Then he laughed at his joke. He jumped up and cackled and hopped up and down on one foot with amusement.

'You haven't come for four days,' she accused him, above this.

He pretended not to hear, and went on laughing and hopping.

'What's wrong? Why not?' she persisted. 'Don't you want to see me?'

'How is Paniwala?'

'He says bring Uncle. Get the big room upstairs ready. Send a car for him.'

'Oh go away,' he said, his laughter suddenly gone. 'Leave me alone.'

She wouldn't. Usually complaisant, even phlegmatic, she became quite obstinate. She sat on his rickety string bed and folded her hands in her lap. She said if he wasn't coming, then she was staying. She wouldn't move till he had promised that, even if he wouldn't go and live in the house, he would visit there every day. Then at last she consented to be led back to her car. He went in front, clearing a way for her by poking his stick at all the sightseers.

He kept his promise for a while and went to the house every day. But he was always glad to come back home again. He walked up and down in the bazaar, looking at the stalls and the people, and then he sat outside the sweetmeat seller's and had tea and milk sweets and read out of his little volume of Sufi poetry. Sometimes he was so stirred that he read out loud for the benefit of the other customers and passers-by, even though they couldn't understand Persian:

> 'When you lay me in my grave,
> don't say, "Farewell, farewell."
> For the grave is a screen hiding the
> cheers and welcome of the
> people of Paradise.
> Which seed was cast but did not
> sprout?
> And why should it be otherwise for
> the seed of man?
> Which bucket went down but
> came not up full of water?'

Then it seemed to him that everything had become suffused in purity and brightness – yes, even this bazaar where people haggled and made money and passed away their time in idle, worldly pursuits. He walked slowly home and up the wooden stairs, which were so dark (he often reproached the landlady) that one could fall and break one's neck. He went past the common lavatory and the door of the paralytic landlady, which was left open so that she could look out. He sat by the open window in his room, looking at the bright stars above and the bright street below, and couldn't sleep for hours because of feeling so good.

In the Paniwala house, it always seemed to be mealtime. A great deal of food was cooked. Paniwala himself could only eat very bland boiled food, on account of his weak digestion. Khorshed had a taste for Continental food masked in cheese sauces, while for Pilla a meal was not a meal if it was not rice with various curries of fish and meat and a great number of spicy side dishes. Servants passed around the table with dishes catering to all these various tastes. The sideboard that ran the length of the wall carried more dishes under silver covers, and there were pyramids of fruits, bought fresh every morning, that were so polished and immaculate that they appeared artificial. The meals lasted for hours. Plates kept getting changed and everyone chewed very slowly, and it got hotter and hotter, so that the Uncle, eating all he could, felt as if he were in a fever. The sisters talked endlessly, but their conversation seemed an activity indistinguishable from masticating. By the time the meal was over, the Uncle felt his mind and body bathed in perspiration, and in this state he had to retire with them into the drawing-room, where sleep overtook everyone except Nargis and himself. The afternoon light that filtered through the slatted blinds made the room green and dim like an ocean bed; and uncle and niece sat staring at eachother among the marble busts and potted plants, while the snores of the sleeping family lapped around them.

Once, as they sat like that, the Uncle saw tears oozing out of Nargis's eyes. It took him some time to realize they *were* tears – he stared at her as they dropped – and then he said in exasperation, 'But what do you want?'

'Come and live here.'

'No!' he cried like a drowning man.

All that had been a long time ago, before Rusi was born. After that event, although the Uncle continued to live in his slum house and the Paniwala family continued to eat their succession of meals, there was a change in both establishments. During one very heavy

Bombay monsoon, an upper balcony of the Uncle's house collapsed and the whole tenement suffered a severe shock, so that the cracks on the staircase walls gaped wider and plaster fell in flakes from the ceilings. What remained of the coloured window-panes dropped out, and some were replaced with plain glass and some with cardboard and some were simply forgotten till more rain came. Also, in the same year as this heavy monsoon, the Uncle's skin began to discolour. This was not unexpected; leucoderma was a family disease and, indeed, very prevalent in the Parsi community. The Uncle first noticed the small telltale spot on his thumb. Of course, the affliction continued to spread and then the spots broke out all over him like mildew, so that within a few years he was completely discoloured. It was neither a painful nor a dangerous disease, only disfiguring.

The change in the Paniwala family was both more positive and more far-reaching. Somehow no one had expected any offspring, so that when Rusi nevertheless appeared, everyone was too excited to notice that his head was rather big or that it took him a long time to sit up. He was three before he could walk. 'Let him take his time,' they all said, and his slowness became a virtue, like the growth of a very special flower that one must wait upon to unfold. Only the Uncle did not much like to look at him. Rusi was always the centre around which the rest of the family was, quite literally, grouped. With his big head shaking, he tottered around on the carpet making guttural sounds, while they formed a smiling circle around him, encouraging him, calling his name, reciting long-forgotten baby rhymes, holding out loving fingers for him to steady himself on. They nodded at each other, and their soft, yellow, middle-aged faces beamed. And Nargis was one of them. The Uncle did not, as far as he could help it, look at the child; he looked at her. She had changed. Motherhood had ripened and extended her, and she was almost fat. But it suited her, and her eyes, which had once been tender and misty and shining as if through a veil, were now luminous with fulfilment. They never looked at the Uncle – only at her son.

The Uncle tried staying away. At first he thought he liked it. He sat for hours outside the sweetmeat seller's and read and talked to everyone who had time. He also talked to the people who lived in the tenement with him – especially with the paralytic landlady. She had as much time as he did. She had spent over twenty years lying on her bed, looking out of the open door at the people going up and down on the stairs. Sometimes he went in and sat with her and listened to her reflections on the transient stream of humanity flowing past her door. She was a student of palmistry and astrology and was always keen to tell his fortune. She grasped his discoloured hand and studied it very earnestly and ignored his jokes about how the only fortune still left to him was the further fading of his pigmentation. She traced the lines of his palm and said she still saw a lot of beautiful living left. Then he turned the joke and said, 'What about you?' Quite seriously, she stretched out her palm and interpreted its lines, and they too, it seemed, were as full of promise as a freshly sown field.

However long he stayed away now, Nargis never came to visit him or sent him any messages. If he wanted to see her, he had to present himself there. When he did, she rarely seemed pleased. His clothes were very shabby – he only possessed two shirts and two patched trousers, and never renewed them till they were past all wear – but whereas before Rusi's birth Nargis had taken his appearance entirely for granted, now she often asked him, 'Why do you come like that? How do you think it looks?' He feigned surprise and looked down at himself with an innocent expression. She was not amused. Once she even lost her temper and shouted at him that if he did not have enough money to buy clothes, then please take it from her; she said she would be glad to give it to him. Of course, he did have enough, as she knew; his cheques came in regularly. Suddenly she became more angry and pulled out some rupee notes and flung them at his feet, and rushed out of the room. There was a moment's silence; everyone was surprised, for she was usually so calm. Then one of the sisters bent down to pick up the money, gently clicking her tongue as she did so.

'She is upset,' she said.

'Yes, because of Rusi,' said the other sister.

'He had a little tummy trouble last night.'

'Naturally, she is upset.'

'Naturally.'

'A mother . . . '

'Of course.'

They went on like that, like a purling, soothing stream. They did this partly to cover up for Nargis, and partly for him, so that he might have time to collect himself. Although he sat quite still and with his gaze lowered to the carpet, he was trembling from head to foot. After a time, ignoring the sisters, he got up to leave. He walked very slowly down the stairs and was about to let himself out when Nargis called to him. He looked up. She was leaning over the curved banister with Rusi, whom she was dancing up and down in her arms. 'Ask Uncle to come up and play with us!' she told Rusi. 'Say, "Please, Uncle! Please, Uncle dear!"' For reply, Rusi opened his mouth wide and screamed. The Uncle did not look up again but continued his way towards the front door, which a servant was holding open for him. Nargis called down loudly, 'Where are you going!'

At that the child was beside himself. His face went purple and his mouth was stretched open as wide as it would go, but no screams came out. This made him more frantic, and he caught his fingers in his mother's hair, pulling it out of its pins, and then flailed his hands against her breasts. He was only three years old but as strong as a demon. She fell to the floor, with him on top of her. The Uncle ran up the stairs as fast as he could. He tried to help her up, tugging at her from under the child, who now began to flail his fists at the Uncle.

'Yes yes, I'm all right,' Nargis said, to reassure them both. She managed to sit up; her hair was about her shoulders and there were scratches on her face. 'Where are you going?' she asked the Uncle.

'I'm not going,' he said. 'I'm here. Can't you see?' he shouted, 'I'm here! Here!' very loudly, in order to make himself heard above the child's screams.

As Rusi grew up, it was decided that he was too brilliant. He did too much thinking. His mother and aunts were disturbed to see him sitting scowling and hunched in an armchair, sunk in deep processes of thought. Occasionally he would emerge with some fragment dredged up from that profundity. 'There will be a series of natural disasters due to the explosion of hitherto undiscovered minerals from under the earth's surface,' he might say. He would fix his aunts with his brooding eyes and say, 'You look out.' Then they became very disturbed – not because of his prophecy but because they feared the damage so much mental activity might do his brain. They would try and bring him some distraction – share some exciting piece of news with him regarding a wedding or a tea party, or feed him some sweet thing that he liked. Sometimes he accepted their offering graciously, sometimes not. He was unpredictable, though very passionate in his likes and dislikes.

The person to whom Rusi took the deepest dislike was the Uncle. He baited him mercilessly and had all sorts of unpleasant names for him. The one he used most frequently was the Leper, on account of the Uncle's skin disease. Sometimes he said he could not bear to be in the house with him and that either the Uncle or he himself must leave. Then the Uncle would leave. Next time he came, Rusi might be quite friendly to him – it was impossible to tell. The Uncle tried not to mind either way, and the rest of the family did all they could to make it up to him. At least Paniwala and his sisters did; Nargis was more unpredictable. Sometimes, when Rusi had been very harsh, she would follow the Uncle to the door and be very nice to him, but other times she would encourage Rusi and clap her hands and laugh loudly in applause and then jeer when the Uncle got up to go away. On such occasions, the Uncle did not take the train or bus but walked all the way home through the city in the hope of tiring himself out. He never did, though, but lay awake half the night, saying to himself over and over, 'Now enough, now enough.' Then he thought of the landlady downstairs eagerly reading in his palm that great things were still in store for him. It made him laugh, for he was in his seventies now.

Rusi ordered a lot of books, though he did not do much reading. His aunts said he didn't have to, because he had it all in his head already. For the same reason, there was not much point in his going to school; he only quarrelled with the teachers, who were very ignorant and not at all up to his standards. In all the schools he tried, everyone eventually agreed that it would be better for him to leave. Then came a succession of private tutors, but here too there was the same trouble – there was just no one who knew as much as he did. Those who did not leave quite soon of their own accord had to be told to go, because their inferior qualities made him take such a dislike to them. Once he got so angry with one of them that he stabbed him with a penknife. Although everyone was disturbed by this incident, still no one said anything beyond what they always said: the boy was too highly strung. It came, his aunts explained, from having too active a mind. They recommended more protein in his diet and some supplementary vitamin pills. Nargis listened to them eagerly and went out to buy the pills. The three women tried to coax him to take them, but he laughed in derision and told them how he had a method, evolved by himself, of storing extra energy in his body through his own mineral deposits. He had plans to patent this method and expected to make a large fortune out of it. The aunts shook their heads behind his back and tapped their foreheads to indicate that he had too much brilliance for his own good. When he looked at them, they changed their expression, to appear as interested and intelligent as possible. He said that they were a couple of foolish old women who understood nothing, so what was the use of talking to them; the only person in the house who might understand something of what he was saying was his father, who was going to put up the money for the project.

His father was not seen very much in the house nowadays. It seemed he was very busy in the office and spent almost all his time there. Weeks passed when the Uncle did not meet him at all. When he did, he found him more gentle than ever, but there was something furtive about him now and he did not like to meet anyone's eye. If he was present while Rusi was baiting the Uncle, he tried to remonstrate. He said, 'Rusi, Rusi,' but so softly that his son probably failed to hear him. After a while, he would get up and quietly leave the room and not come back. Once, though, when this happened, the Uncle found him waiting for him downstairs by the door. 'One moment,' Paniwala said and drew him into his study; he pressed the Uncle's hand as he did so. The Uncle wondered what he was going to say, and he waited and Paniwala also waited. A gold clock could be heard ticking in a very refined way.

When Paniwala at last did speak, it was on an unexpected subject. He informed the Uncle that the oil painting on the wall above his desk – it was of the Paniwala ancestor who had founded their fortune – was not done from life but had been copied from a photograph. Even the photograph was the only one of him known to be in existence; he had not been a man who could be induced to pose very often in a photographer's studio.

'He came to Bombay from a village near Surat,' Paniwala said. 'To the end of his days, what he relished most was the simple village food of chapati and pickle. He built this house with many bathrooms, but still he liked to take his bath in a bucket out in the garden, thereby also watering the plants.'

Paniwala chuckled, and both of them looked up at the portrait, which showed a shrivelled face with a big bony Parsi nose sticking out of it. Paniwala also had a big nose, but his was not bony; it was soft and fleshy. Altogether he looked very different from his ancestor, being very much softer and gentler in the contours of his face and in expression.

'He was a very strict man,' Paniwala said. 'With himself and also with others. Everyone had to work hard, no slacking allowed. My grandfather also got this discipline from him. Yes, in those days they were different men – a different breed of men.' He passed his hands over his totally bald head. When he spoke again, it was to say, 'Your expenses must have gone up; money is not what it was. I wonder if your cheque . . . You'll excuse me.' He lowered his eyes.

The Uncle waved his hand in a gesture that could mean anything.

'You'll allow me,' said Paniwala, terribly ashamed. 'From the first of next month. Thank you. The little house where he was born, near Surat, is still there. It is so small you would not believe that the whole family lived there. There were nine children, and all grew up healthy and well. Later he brought his brothers and brothers-in-law to Bombay, and everyone did well and they too had large families . . . You are going? No, you must take one of the cars – what are they all standing there for? Allow me.' But the Uncle wanted to walk, so Paniwala escorted him to the door. He told him how his grandfather had always insisted on walking to the warehouse, even when he was very old and quite unsteady, so that the family had made arrangements for a carriage and an attendant to follow him secretly.

The two sisters also often spoke about their family – not about past generations but about the present one. They were always visiting relatives, many of whom were bedridden, and then they would come home and discuss the case. Sometimes they predicted an early end, but this rarely came to pass. The family tended to be very long-lived, and though crippled by a variety of diseases, the invalids lingered on for years and years. They stayed in their mahogany bedsteads and were fed and washed by servants. There was also an imbecile called Poor Falli, who had lived in the same Edwardian house for over fifty years, though confined to one room with bars on the windows; he was not dangerous, but his personal habits made it difficult for other people. The two sisters spoke about all these family matters quite openly now before the Uncle. It had not always been so. True, they had always been scrupulously polite to him – ignoring his shabby clothes, calling him by his first name, never omitting a greeting to him on entering or leaving a room – but he had remained an outsider. Nor had they forgotten the difference between his family and theirs. But as the years passed they regarded him more and more as one of themselves. This happened not all at once, but gradually, and only after Rusi's birth – an event, in the eyes of the sisters, that had finally drawn the two families together and made them as one.

The Uncle fell ill with fever. He lay in his room, tossing on his string bed, which had no sheets but only a cotton mat and a little pillow hard as a stone. Neighbours came in and, because he was shivering so much, covered him with a blanket and tried to make him drink milk and soup. He let them do whatever was necessary. His body felt as if it were being broken up bone by bone by someone wielding a stone hammer. He wondered whether he was going to die now. All the time he was smiling – not outwardly, for he groaned and cried out so much that the neighbours were very worried and sent messages to the Paniwala house, but inside himself. Sometimes he thought he was at the sweetmeat seller's, sometimes he saw himself back in the little house in the suburb with his brother and the old woman and Nargis ripening like a fruit in sunshine. It didn't matter in which of these places he fancied himself, for they were both wonderful, a foretaste of Paradise. He thought if he were really going to die now, he would never need to return to the Paniwala house at all. When he thought of this, tears welled into his eyes and flowed down his cheeks, so that the neighbours exclaimed in pity.

When Nargis came, he was better. The fever had abated and he lay exhausted. He had not died and yet he felt dead, as if everything were spent. Nargis wasted no time. She paid what was left of his rent and reimbursed the neighbours. They helped her pack up his things. He kept wanting to say no, but he didn't have the strength. Instead he wept again; only now the tears were cold and hard. The neighbours, not seeing the difference, told Nargis that he had been weeping like that all through his sickness, and when she heard this, she also wept. At last he was carried down the stairs, and as they passed the door of the paralytic landlady, she called out to him in triumph, 'You see! It has come true what I said! It was all written in your hand.'

Sometimes, as he lay in the large fourposter in the Paniwala bedroom, he looked at his hand and wondered which were the lines that had told the landlady about the new life awaiting him. It was very still and quiet in that room. He gazed at the painting on the opposite wall; it had been specially commissioned and showed a scene in the Paniwala counting house at the beginning of the century. The Paniwala founder sat at a desk high up on a dais, and his sons at other desks on a slightly lower dais, and they overlooked a hall full of clerks sitting crosslegged in rows and writing in ledgers. It had been done in dark, murky colours, to look like a Renaissance painting. When he was tired of it, he looked at the other wall, where there was a window and the top of a tree just showing against it. Nargis had engaged a servant for him, who made his bed and washed him and performed other personal functions. Khorshed and Pilla came in at least once a day and sat on either side of him and told him everything that was happening, in the family and in Bombay society in general. Rusi also came in; he had been warned to be good to his uncle, and for quite some time he observed this injunction. But as the weeks and then the months passed and the Uncle still lay there, Rusi could not help himself and reverted to his former manner. He was especially gleeful if he happened to come in while the Uncle was being fed. This had to be done very carefully and with a specially curved spoon, and even then quite a lot went to waste and trickled down the Uncle's chin.

It was usually his servant who fed the Uncle, but sometimes Nargis did it herself. Although she was less satisfactory than the servant and got impatient quite quickly, the Uncle much preferred her to do it. Then he would linger over his food as long as possible. Then Rusi could stand there and say what he liked – the Uncle didn't care at all. He just looked into Nargis's face. She always sat with her back to the window and the tree. Even when she got annoyed with him – saying, 'You are doing it on purpose,' when the food dropped on his chin – still he loved to have her sitting here. At such times it seemed to him that his landlady had been right and that his life was not over by any means.

On Bail

Although I get tired working in the shop all day, once I reach home I forget all about it. I change into an old cotton sari and tuck it round my waist and I sing as I cook. Sometimes he is at home but not often, and usually only if he is sick with a cold. What a fuss he makes then; I have to take his temperature many times and prepare hot drinks and crush pills in honey and altogether feel very sorry for him. That's the best time, especially since he forgets quite soon about being sick and wants to amuse himself and me. How we laugh then, what a fine time we have! He doesn't seem to miss his friends and coffee houses and all those places one bit but is as happy to be at home with me as I am to be with him. Next evening, of course, he is off again, but I don't mind, for I know it's necessary – not only because he is a very sociable person but because it is for business contacts too.

I'm used to waiting up for him quite late, so I was not worried that night at all. When my cooking was finished, I sat at the table waiting for him. I love these hours; it is silent and peaceful and the clock ticks and I have many pleasant thoughts. I know that soon I will hear his step on the stairs, and the door will open and he will be there. I smile to myself, sitting there at the table with my head supported on my hand, full of drowsy thoughts. Sometimes I nod off and those thoughts turn into dreams on the same subject. But I always start up at the sound of his steps – only *his* steps, because that night Daddy was already in the room, calling my name, before I woke up. Then I jumped to my feet. I knew something terrible had happened.

When Daddy said that Rajee had been arrested, I sank down again on to my chair. I couldn't stand, I couldn't speak. Daddy thought it was with shock, but of course it was out of relief. I had imagined far worse. It took me some time to realize that this too was very bad. I knew Daddy thought it was the worst thing there could be. He was so badly affected that I had to make him lie down while I prepared tea for him. I also served him the meal I had cooked for Rajee and myself. Daddy ate both our portions. Now that he is old, he seems to need a great deal of food and is always ready to eat at any hour, whatever his state of mind may be.

But when he had finished this time, he became very upset again. He pushed away the dish and said, 'Yes, yes, yes, I knew how it would be.'

Of course, this was no time to start defending Rajee. In any case, I have long stopped doing so. I know it isn't so much Rajee that Daddy doesn't like but the fact that I'm married to him and have not become any of the grand things Daddy wanted.

'A case of cheating and impersonation,' Daddy said now. 'A criminal case.'

I cried, 'But where is he?'

'In jail! In prison! Jail!'

Daddy moaned, and so did I. I thought of Rajee sitting in a cell. I could see him sitting there and the expression on his face. I put my head down on the table and sobbed. I could not stop.

After a while Daddy began to pat my back. He didn't know what else to do; unlike Rajee, he has never been good at comforting people. I wiped my eyes and said as steadily as I could, 'What about bail?'

That made Daddy excited again; he cried, 'Five thousand rupees! Where should we take it from?'

No, we didn't have five thousand rupees. Daddy only had his pension, and Rajee and I only had my salary from the shop. Again I saw Rajee sitting there, but I quickly shut my eyes against this unbearable vision.

I made Daddy comfortable on our bed and told him I would be back soon. He wanted to know where I was going. He asked how I could go alone in the streets at this time of night, but he was too tired to protest much. I think he was already asleep when I left. I had to walk all the way through the empty streets. I wasn't frightened, although there had lately been some bad cases in the newspapers of women being attacked. I had other things to think about, and chief among them at the moment was how I could wake up Sudha without waking the rest of her household. But this turned out to be no problem at all, because it was she who came to the door as soon as I knocked. I think she hadn't gone to sleep yet, although it was two o'clock in the morning. No one else stirred in the house.

When I told her, she had a dreadful shock. I think she had the same vision of him that I had. I put out my hand to touch her, but she pushed me away. The expression of pain on her face turned to one of anger. She said, 'Why do you come here? What should I do?' Of course she knew what it was I wanted. She said, 'I haven't got it.' Then she shouted, 'Do you know how long I haven't seen him! How many days!'

I looked around nervously, and she laughed. She said, 'Don't worry. He wouldn't wake up if the house fell down.' She was right; I could hear her husband snoring, with those fat sounds fat people make in their sleep. 'Listen,' she said. 'It's the same every night. He eats his meal and then –' She imitated the snoring sounds. 'And I can't sleep. I walk round the house, thinking. Does Rajee talk about me to you? What does he say?'

I didn't know what to answer. I had already suspected that Rajee did not like to be with her as much as before, but I didn't want to hurt her feelings. Also, this was not the time to talk about it. I had to have the money from her. I had to. There was no other way.

When I said nothing, her face became hard. She and I have known each other for a long time – we were at college together –

but I have always been a bit afraid of her. She is a very passionate person. 'Go!' she said to me now, and her voice was hard. 'How dare you come here? Aren't you ashamed?'

'Where else can I go?'

We were silent. Her husband snored.

I said, 'I had cooked fish curry for him tonight, he loves it so much. Do you think they gave him anything to eat there? You know how particular he is about his food.'

She shrugged, like someone to whom this is of no concern. But I knew these were not her true feelings, so I continued. 'Will he be able to sleep? I don't know if they give beds. Perhaps there are other people with him in the cell – bad characters. I've heard there are many people who share each cell, there is such overcrowding nowadays. And there are no facilities for them, only one bucket, and they take away their belts and shoelaces, because they are afraid that –'

'Be quiet!'

She went out of the room, stumbling over a footstool in her hurry, I could hear her in the bedroom, rattling keys and banging drawers. She took absolutely no care about making a noise, but the sounds from her husband went on undisturbed. I waited for her. I didn't like being here. The room was furnished with costly things, but they were not in good taste. I have always disliked coming here. The atmosphere is not good, probably because she and her husband don't like each other.

At last she came back. She didn't have cash, but she gave me some jewellery. She had wrapped it in a cloth, which she thrust into my hands. Then she said, 'Go, go, go,' but that was not necessary, for I was already on my way out.

Rajee came home the next evening. I wished we could have been alone, but Daddy and Sudha were also there. Rajee smiled at them, but they both averted their eyes from him and then his smile faded. He didn't know what to say. Neither did I.

Rajee is so good-humoured and sociable that he hates it when the atmosphere is like that, and he feels he has to do something to cheer everyone up again. He rubbed his hands and said, 'Nice to be home,' in a cheerful, smiling voice.

Sudha shot him a burning look. Her eyes are already large enough, but they look even larger because of the kohl with which she outlines them.

'North, South, East, West, home is best,' Rajee said.

'Fool! Idiot!' Sudha screamed.

There was a silence, in which we seemed to be listening to the echo of this scream. Then Rajee said, 'Please let me explain.'

'What is there to explain?' Daddy said. 'Cheating, impersonation –'

'A mistake,' Rajee said.

They were silent in a rather grim way, as if waiting to hear what he had to say. He cleared his throat a few times and spread his hands and began a long story. It was very involved and got more and more so as he went on. It was all about some man he had met in the coffee house who had seemed an honest, decent person but had turned out not to be so. It was he who had drawn Rajee into this deal, which also had turned out not to be as honest and decent as Rajee had thought. I didn't listen very carefully; I was watching the two others to see what impression he was making on them. Rajee too was watching them, and every now and again he stopped to scan their faces, and then he ran his tongue over his lips and went on talking faster. He didn't once look at me, though; he knew it didn't make any difference to me what he said, because I was on his side anyway.

Rajee is a very good talker, and I could see that Sudha and Daddy were wavering. But of course they weren't happy yet, and they continued to sit there with very glum faces. So then Rajee, sincerely anxious to cheer them up, said to me, 'How about some tea? And a few biscuits, if you have any?' He smiled and winked at me, and I also smiled and went away to make the tea.

When I came back, Daddy was arguing with Rajee. Daddy was saying, 'But is this the way to do business? In a coffee house, with strangers, is this the way to make a living?' Rajee was proving to him that it was. He told him all big deals were made that way. He gave him a lot of examples of fortunes that had been made just by two or three people meeting by chance – how apartment houses had been bought and sold, and a new sugar mill set up with all imported machinery by special government licence. It was all a matter of luck and skill and being there at the right time. I knew all these stories, for Rajee had told them to me many times. He loves telling them and thinking about them; they are his inspiration in life. It is because of them, I think, that he gets up in such good humour every day and hums to himself while shaving and dresses up smartly and goes out with a shining, smiling face.

But Daddy remained glum. It is not in his nature to believe such stories. He is retired now, but all through his working life he never got up in good humour or ever went to his office with high expectations. All he ever expected was his salary, and afterwards his pension, and that is all he ever got.

'Do you know about Verma Electricals, how they started – have you any idea?' Rajee said, flushed with excitement. But Daddy said, 'It would be better to get some regular job.'

Rajee smiled politely. He could have pointed out – only he didn't, because he is always very careful of people's feelings – that the entire salary that Daddy had earned throughout his thirty-five years of government service was less than Rajee can expect to make out of one of his deals.

Now Daddy started to get excited. His lips trembled and his hands fumbled about in the air. He said, 'If you – then she – she – she –' He pointed at me with a shaking finger. We all knew what he meant. If Rajee got a job, then I wouldn't have to go to work in the shop.

I said, 'I like it.'

Daddy got more excited. He stammered and his hands waved frantically in the air as if they were searching for the words that wouldn't come to him. Rajee tried to soothe him. He kept saying, 'Please, Daddy.' He was afraid for his heart.

And, indeed, Daddy's hands suddenly left off fumbling in the air and clutched his side instead. He must have got one of his tremors. He started whimpering like a child. Rajee jumped up and kept saying, 'Oh my goodness.' He took Daddy's arm to lead him to our sofa and make him lie down there. Rajee said several times, 'Now keep quite calm,' but in fact it was he who was the most excited.

I got Daddy's pills and Sudha got water and Rajee ran for pillows. Daddy lay on the sofa, with his eyes shut. He looked quite exhausted, as if he didn't want to say or think anything more. Rajee kept fussing over him, but after a time there was nothing more to be done. Daddy was all right and fast asleep. Rajee said to me, 'Sit with him.' I took a cane stool and sat by the sofa holding Daddy's hand.

But I wasn't thinking of him, I was watching the other two. There was going to be a big scene between them, I knew. Rajee also knew it, and he was very uncomfortable. Sudha lounged in a chair in the middle of the room, with her legs stretched out before her under her sari. She was wearing a brilliant emerald silk sari and gold-and-diamond earrings. She seemed too large and too splendid for our little room. Everything in the room appeared very shabby – the old black oilcloth sofa with the white cotton stuffing bulging out where the material has split; the rickety little table with the cane unwinding like apple peel from the legs; last year's free calendar hanging from a nail on the wall, which hasn't been whitewashed for a long time. I only notice these things when she is here. She makes everything look shabby – me included. Only Rajee matches up to her. Even now, after a night in jail, he looked plump and prosperous and he shone, the way she did.

He was waiting for her to say something, but she only looked at him from under her big lids, half lowered over her big eyes. It seemed she was waiting for him to speak first. He started telling her about Daddy's heart – about the attack last year and how careful we have had to be since then and how we always keep his pills handy. Suddenly she interrupted him. She did this in a strange way – by clutching the top part of her sari and pulling it down from her breasts. She commanded, 'Look!'

What was he to look at? At her big breasts that swelled from out of her low-cut blouse? Modestly – because of Daddy and me being in the room – he lowered his eyes, but she repeated, 'Look, look,' in an impatient voice. She struck her hand against her bared throat.

'Your necklace,' he murmured uncomfortably.

She threw a savage look in my direction, so that I felt I had to defend myself. I said to Rajee, 'Where else could I get it from? Five thousand!'

He shook his head, as if rebuking me. This infuriated her, and she began to shout at me. She cried, 'Yes, you should have left him there in jail where he belongs!'

'Sh-h-h, sh-h-h,' said Rajee, afraid she might wake up Daddy.

She lowered her voice but went on with the same fury. 'It's the place where you belong. Because you are not only a cheat but a thief also. Can you deny it? Try. Say, "No, I'm not a thief." No? Then what about that time in my house?' She turned to me. 'I never told you, but now I will show you what sort of a person you are married to.'

I didn't look at her but stared straight in front of me.

'I'll make him tell you himself. Tell her!' she ordered him, but the next moment she was shouting, 'The servant caught him! He called me, "Quick, quick, come quick, Memsahib," and when I went into the room, yes, there he was with his hand right inside my purse. Oh, how he looked then! I will never, never, never forget as long as I live his face at that moment!' She flung her hands before her face like someone who didn't want to see.

'I don't believe you,' I said.

'Ask him!'

'I don't believe you.'

Our clock ticked. It is a round battered old metal clock, and it ticks with a loud metal sound. Usually, when I am alone here sitting quietly at the table waiting for him, I like that sound; it is soothing and homely to me. But now, in the silence that had fallen between us, it was like a sick heart beating.

When Sudha spoke again, it was in quite a different voice. 'It doesn't matter,' she said. 'I don't care at all.' Then she said, 'Whatever you need, you think I wouldn't give? Would I ever say no to you? If you want, take these too. Here –' She put up her hands to her earrings. 'No, take them. Take,' she said as he held out his hand to restrain her, though she did not go any farther in unhooking them. 'That's all nothing. I don't care one jot. I only care that you haven't come. For so long you haven't come to me. Every Tuesday afternoon, every Thursday, I got ready for you and I waited and waited – Why are you looking at her!' she cried, for Rajee had glanced nervously in my direction. 'Who is she to grudge me those few hours with you, when she has taken everything else!'

She got up from where she had been sprawled in the chair. I didn't know what she was going to do. She looked capable of anything; the room seemed too small for all she seemed capable of doing. I think Rajee felt the same, and that is why he took her away.

We have one more room besides this one, but we have to cross an open passage to get to it. This is a nuisance during the rains, when sometimes we have to use an umbrella to go from our bedroom to our sitting-room. We run across the passage under the umbrella, holding each other close. Now he was taking Sudha through our passage. I heard him shut the door and draw the big metal bolt from inside.

I was left alone with Daddy, who was sleeping with his mouth dropped open. He looked an old, old man. The clock ticked, loud as a hammer. I tried not to think of Rajee and Sudha in our bedroom, just as I always tried not to think of them in her house on Tuesday and Thursday afternoons (the days her husband goes to visit his factory at Saharanpur). Sometimes it is not good to think too much. Why dwell on things that can't be helped? Or on those that are over and done with? That is why I also don't look back on the past very much. There was a time when I didn't know Rajee but Sudha did. Of course she often spoke to me about him – I was her best friend – but I didn't meet him till I had to start taking letters between them. That was the time her family was arranging her marriage, and she and Rajee were planning to elope together. Well, it all turned out differently, so what is the use of thinking back now to what was then?

Daddy woke up. He looked round the room and asked where the other two were. I said Sudha had gone home and Rajee was sleeping in the bedroom because he was very tired after last night. Daddy groaned at the mention of last night. He said, 'Do you know what it could mean? Seven years rigorous imprisonment.'

'No, no, Daddy,' I said. I wasn't a bit frightened; I didn't believe it for a moment.

'You may look in the penal code. Cheating and impersonation, Section 420.'

'It was all a mistake, Daddy. While you were sleeping, he explained everything to me.'

I didn't want to hear anything more, and there was only one way I knew to keep him quiet. Although I couldn't find anything except one rather soft banana, he was glad to have even that. I watched him peeling it and chewing slowly, mulling it round in his mouth to make the most of every bite. Whenever I watch him eat nowadays, I feel he is not going to live much longer. I feel the same when I see him looking at the leaves moving on a tree. He enjoys these things like a person for whom they are not going to be there much longer.

He said, 'How will you stay alone for seven years?'

I said, 'No, Daddy.'

I was saying no, it wouldn't happen, Rajee wouldn't be away for seven years, and also I was saying no, Daddy, I won't be alone, you won't die.

But he went on. 'Yes, alone. You will be alone. I won't be here.'

He turned away his face from me. I strained my ears towards the bedroom. But of course it was too far away, with the passage in between, to hear anything.

Daddy said, 'These government regulations are very unfair. If there is a widow, the pension is paid to her, but otherwise it stops. Often I think if I had saved, but how was it possible? With high rent and college fees and other expenses?'

Daddy used to spend a lot of money on me. He sent me to the best school and college, where girls from much richer families went. He also tried to buy me the same sort of clothes that those girls had, so that I should not feel inferior to them.

I said, 'I'm all right. I have my job.'

'Your job!'

Daddy has always hated it that I work as cashier in a shop. Of course, from his point of view, and after all that expense and education, it isn't very much, but it is enough for Rajee and me to live on.

'They wanted a graduate. I couldn't have got it if I weren't a graduate.' I said this to make him feel better and show him his efforts had not been wasted. 'And sometimes there are some quite difficult calculations, so it's good I did all that maths at college.'

'For this?' Daddy said, making the grubbing movement of counting coins with which he always refers to my job.

'Never mind,' I said, 'It doesn't matter.'

Whenever we speak about this subject, we end up in the same way. Daddy used to have very high hopes for me. There were only the two of us, because my mother had died when I was born and Daddy didn't care for the rest of the family and had broken off relations with them. He cared only for me. He was proud because

I did well at school and always stood first in arithmetic and English composition. At that time he used to read a lot. It's funny: nowadays he doesn't read at all; you would think in his retirement he would be reading all the time, but he doesn't – not even the newspaper. But at that time he was particularly fond of reading H.G. Wells and Bernard Shaw, and was keen for me to become like the women in their books. He said there was no need for me to get married; he said why should I be like the common run of girls. No, I must be free and independent and the equal of men in everything. He wanted me to smoke cigarettes, and even, began to smoke himself so as to encourage me. (I didn't like the taste, so we both stopped.)

Now he said, 'If he has to go, it would be better to give up this place and stay somewhere as paying guest.'

'He doesn't have to go!'

'Or perhaps you can stay with a friend. What about her? What is her name?'

'Sudha? You want me to go and stay with her?'

I laughed and laughed; only at some point I stopped. I don't know if he noticed the difference. He may not have, because I was sitting on the floor with my knees drawn up and my face buried in them. All he would be able to see was my shoulders shaking, and that could be laughing *or* crying.

But I think he wasn't taking much notice of me. I think he was more interested in his own thoughts. He has a lot of thoughts always; I can tell because I can see him sunk into them and mumbling to himself and sometimes mumbling out loud. Perhaps that's the reason he doesn't read anymore. I looked at him; he was shaking his head and smiling to himself. Well, at least he was thinking something pleasant that made him happy.

And I could think only of Sudha and Rajee in there in our bedroom! You would have said – anyone would have said – that I had the right to go and bang on the door and shout, 'What are you doing! Come out of there!' I should have done it.

Daddy said, 'The time I liked best was the exams. I watched you go in with the others and I knew you would do better than any of them. I was sure of it.'

He chuckled to himself in the triumphant way he used to when the results came out and I had done well. He had always accompanied me right up to the door of the examination hall, and as I went in he shouted after me, 'Remember! First Class first!' flexing the muscles of his arm as if to give me strength. It used to be rather embarrassing – everyone stared – and I hurried in, pretending not to be the person addressed. But I was glad to see him when I came out again and he was standing there waiting, always with some special thing he knew I liked, such as a bag of chili chips.

He had stopped chuckling. Now his face was sad. He turned up his hand and held it out empty. 'In the end, what is there?' he said. 'Nothing. Ashes.'

Well, I couldn't sit there listening to such depressing talk! I jumped up. I went straight through the passage, and now I did bang on the door. The bolt was drawn back and Rajee opened the door. He said, 'One minute. She is going now.'

I said, 'I told Daddy she has gone home.'

Rajee understood the problem at once. We have only one entrance door, and to get to that Sudha would have to pass through the sitting-room and walk past Daddy. He would be surprised to see her back again.

Rajee told me to wait till he called. He went into the sitting-room. I heard him talk to Daddy in a loud, cheerful voice. I went into the bedroom. Sudha was buttoning up her blouse. She didn't take much notice of me but only glanced at me over her shoulder and went on straightening her sari and fixing her hair. She did not look happy or satisfied; on the contrary, her eyes and cheeks were swollen with tears, and I think she was still crying, without making any sound.

At last Rajee called. Sudha and I walked through the passage and into the sitting-room. I made her walk on the far side of

Daddy, along the wall, and Rajee had also got between us and Daddy to shield us from view. He was stirring something in a cup. 'Just wait till you taste this, Daddy,' he was saying. 'It is called Rajee's Special. Once tasted, never forgotten.' Daddy's attention was all on this cup, and he had even stretched out his hands for it. Sudha walked along the wall with her sari pulled over her head, not looking right or left. I think she was still crying. I took her as far as the stairs and I said, 'Be careful,' because there was no light on the stairs. She managed to grope her way down, though I didn't wait to see. I was in a hurry to get back into the room.

I said, 'Daddy had better go home now, before it gets too late.'

'How can he go?' Rajee said. 'He is not well; he must stay here with us.'

Suddenly I became terribly angry with Rajee. Perhaps I had been angry all the time – only now it came out. I began to shout at him. I shouted about the disgrace of getting arrested, but it wasn't only that; in fact, that was the least of it. Once I get angry, I find it very difficult to stop. New thoughts keep coming up, making me more angry, and I feel shaken through and through. I said many things I didn't mean.

Daddy joined in from time to time, saying what a disgrace it was to the family. The worse things I said the better pleased he was. When I showed signs of running down, he encouraged me to start up again. He listened attentively with his head to one side, so as not to miss anything, and whenever he thought I had scored a good point he thrust his forefinger up into the air and shouted, 'Right! Correct!' He had become quite bright and perky again.

But Rajee sat there hunched together and with his head bowed, letting me say whatever I wanted, even when I called him a cheat and a liar and a thief. He sat there quiet and looking guilty. Then I wished that he would speak and rouse himself and perhaps get angry in return. I stopped every time I had said something very bad, so that he might defend himself. But it was always Daddy who spoke. 'Right,' he said. 'Correct,' till at last I cried, 'Oh, please be quiet, Daddy!'

'No,' Rajee said. 'He is right. I deserve everything you say, all the names you are calling me, for having worried you so much.'

'Worried me about what?'

Rajee looked up in surprise. He made a vague gesture, as if too ashamed to mention what had, happened.

'About what?'

Rajee lowered his eyes again.

'Oh, you think that's all,' I said. 'That you have been in jail. You think that's the worst thing you have done. Ha.'

He looked quite blank. The idiot! Did he think that was nothing – to have been in our bedroom alone with Sudha? Was it so small a thing? Then I longed to do more than only shout at him. I longed really to strike and beat him. If only Daddy would go away!

Daddy said, 'I'm very tired. I will stay here tonight.'

'Yes, yes, quite right.' Rajee jumped up. He got sheets and pillows and made up Daddy's bed on the sofa. Afterwards he turned down the sheet like a professional nurse and helped Daddy undress and arranged him comfortably. He spent rather a long time on all this, and appeared quite engrossed in it. I realized he was putting off being alone with me.

But I could wait. Soon Daddy would be asleep and then we would be alone. He would not be able to get away from me. I crossed the passage into our bedroom. I looked round carefully. It was as usual. There seemed to be no trace of Sudha left. It is strange; she has a very strong smell – partly because she is heavy and perspires heavily and partly because of the strong perfumes she wears – but though I sniffed and sniffed the air, I found that nothing of her remained.

I stepped up close to the mirror to look at myself. I often do it – not so much because I'm interested in myself but because of a desire to check up on how I look to Rajee. I haven't changed much from the time he first knew me. I think small, skinny girls like me don't change as fast as big ones like Sudha. If it weren't for my long hair, I still could be taken either for a boy or a girl. When I was a child, people had difficulty in telling which I was because Daddy always had my hair cut short. He had a theory that it was a woman's long hair that was to blame for her lack of freedom. But later, when I grew bigger, I envied the other girls their thick, long hair, in which they wore ornaments and flowers, and I would no longer allow mine to be cut. It never grew very thick, though. Sometimes I try to wear a flower, but my hair is too thin to hold it and the flower droops and looks odd, so that sooner or later I snatch it out and throw it away.

Rajee called to ask if I wanted tea. I called back no. I realized he only wanted to put off the moment for us to be alone together. I felt angry and grim. But when he did come I stopped feeling like that. He stood in the door, trying to scan my face to see my mood. He tried to smile at me. He looked terribly tired, with rings under his eyes.

'Lie down,' I said. 'Go to sleep now.' My voice shook, I had such deep feeling for him at that moment.

He was very much relieved that I had stopped being angry. He flung himself on the bed like a person truly exhausted. I squatted on the bed beside him and rubbed my fingers to and fro in his soft hair. He had his eyes shut and looked at peace.

After a time, I whispered, 'Was it very bad?'

Without opening his eyes, he answered, 'Only at first. Don't stop. I like it.' I went on rubbing my fingers in his hair. 'At first of course it was a shock, though everyone was quite polite. They allowed me to take a taxi, and two policemen accompanied me.'

'They didn't –?' I asked. I had been thinking about this all the time, and it made me shudder more than anything. So often in the streets I had seen people led away to jail, and their wrists were handcuffed and they were fastened to a policeman with a long chain.

'Oh no,' he said. He knew what I meant at once. 'They could see they were dealing with a gentleman. The policemen were very respectful to me, and they accepted cigarettes from me and smoked them in the taxi, though they were on duty. And when we got there everyone was quite nice. They were quite apologetic that this had to be done.' He opened his eyes and said, 'I wish you hadn't taken the money from Sudha.'

'Then from where?' I cried.

'Yes, I know. But I wish –'

'Should I have left you there?'

'No no, of course not.' He spoke quickly, as if afraid that I would get angry again. And to prevent this from happening he pulled me down beside him and pressed me close and held me.

He seemed eager to tell me about the jail. He always likes to tell me everything, and I sit up for him at night and try and keep awake, however late he comes, because I know he is coming home with a lot to tell. Every day something exciting happens to him, and he loves to repeat it to me in every detail. Well, it seemed that even in jail he had had a good time, and it wasn't at all like what I had thought.

'You see,' he explained, 'before trial we are kept quite separate and we are allowed all sorts of facilities. It's really more like a hotel. Of course, there are guards, but they don't bother you at all. On the contrary, if they see you are a better-class person they like to help you. I met some very interesting people there – really some quite top-notch people; you'd be surprised.'

I *was* surprised. I had no idea it could be like that. But that is one of the wonderful things about Rajee – wherever he goes, whatever he does, something good and exciting happens to him.

'As a matter of fact,' he said, 'I made a very good contact. Something interesting could come of it. Wait, I'll tell you.'

I knew he wanted his cigarettes – he always likes to smoke when he has something nice to tell – so I got out of bed and brought them for him. He lit up, and we lay again side by side on the bed.

'There was this person in the patent-medicine line, who had been in for several days. It took time to arrange for his bail, because it was for a very big amount. There is a big case against him. Everyone – all the guards and everyone – was very respectful to him, and he was good to them too. He knew how to handle them. His food and other things came from outside, and he also had cases of beer and always saw to it that the guards had their share. Naturally, they did everything they could to oblige him. And they were very careful with me too, because they could see he had taken a great liking to me.'

That was nothing new. Wherever he goes, people take a great liking to Rajee and do all sorts of things for him and want to keep him in their company.

'He insisted I should eat with him, though as a matter of fact I wasn't very hungry, I was still rather upset. But the food was so delicious – such wonderful kebabs, I wish you could have tasted them. And plenty of beer with it, and plenty of good company, because there were some other people too, all in for various things but all of them better-class. We were quite a select group. Afterwards we had a game of cards, that was good fun. Why are you laughing?'

It was all so different from what I had thought! I was laughing at myself, for my fears and terrible visions. I asked, 'Did you win anything?'

'No, as a matter of fact I lost, but as I didn't have the money to pay they said it didn't matter, I could pay some other time.'

'How much?' I asked, suddenly suspicious.

'Oh, not very much.'

But he seemed anxious to change the subject, which confirmed my suspicions. My mood was no longer so good now. I began to brood. Here I had been, and Daddy and Sudha, and there he had been all the time, quite enjoying himself and even losing money at cards.

I said, 'If it was so nice, perhaps I should have left you there.'

He gave me a reproachful look and was silent for a while. But then he said, 'I wish it had been possible to get the money from someone else.'

'Why?' I said, and then I felt worse. 'Why?' I repeated. 'She is such a wonderful friend to you. So wonderful,' I cried, 'that you bring her here and lock yourself into our bedroom with her to do God knows what!'

He turned to me and comforted me. He explained everything. I began to see that he had had no alternative – that he *had* to bring her in here because of the way she felt and because of the money she had given. He didn't say so outright, but I realized it was partly my fault also, for taking the money from her.

I felt much better. He went on talking about Sudha, and I liked it, the way he spoke about her. He said, 'She is not a generous person; that is why it is not good to take from her. At heart, she grudges giving – it eats her up.'

'She was always like that,' I said, giving him a swift sideways look. But he agreed with me; he nodded. I saw that his feelings for her had completely changed.

'Every little bit she gives,' he said, 'she wants four times as much in return.'

'It's her nature.'

I remembered what she had said about his taking money from her purse. I felt indignant. To shame him like that, before her servant! Obviously, he would never have taken the money if he had not been in great need. She should have been glad to help him out. I never hide my money from him now. I used to sometimes – I used to put away absolutely necessary amounts, like for the rent – but he always seemed to find out my hiding places, so I don't do it anymore. Now if we run short I borrow it from the cash register in the shop; no one ever notices, and I always put it back when I get my salary. Only once I couldn't put it back – there were some unexpected expenses – but they never found out, so it's all right.

'What's that?' he said. We were both silent, listening. He said, 'I think Daddy is calling.'

'I don't hear anything.'

Rajee wanted to go and see, but I assured him it was all right. Daddy might have called out in his sleep – he often did that. I asked Rajee to tell me more about his adventures last night, so he settled back and lit another cigarette.

'You know, this person I was telling you about – in the patent-medicine line? He wants me to contact him as soon as he comes out. He says he will put some good things in my way. He was very keen to meet me again and wanted to have my telephone number . . . You know, it is very difficult without a telephone; it is the biggest handicap in my career. It is not even necessary to have an office, but a telephone – you can't do big business without one. Do you know that some of the most important deals are concluded over the telephone only? I could tell you some wonderful stories.'

'I know,' I said. He had already told me some wonderful stories on this subject, and I know how much he longed for and needed a telephone, but where could I get it from?

'Never mind,' he said. He didn't want me to feel bad. 'When we move into a better place, we shall install all these things. Telephone, refrigerator – I think he *is* calling.'

Rajee went to see. I also got off the bed and looked under it for my slippers. As I did so, I remembered a terrible dream I used to have as a child. I used to dream Daddy was dead. Then I screamed and screamed, and when I woke up Daddy was holding me and I had my arms round his neck. Afterwards I was always afraid to go on sleeping by myself and got into his bed. But I would never tell him my dream. I was frightened to speak it out.

When I came into the sitting-room, I found Daddy sitting up on the sofa, and Rajee was holding him up under the arms – sort of propping him up. It was that time of the night when everything looks dim and depressing. We have only one light bulb, and it looked very feeble and even ghostly and did not shed much light. Dawn wasn't far off – it was no longer quite night and it was not yet day – and the light coming in through the window was rather dreary. Perhaps it was because of this that Daddy's face looked so strange; he lay limp and lolling in Rajee's arms.

And he was very cross. He said he had been shouting for hours and no one came. In the end, he had had to get up himself and get his pills and the water to swallow them with. If it hadn't been for that – if he hadn't somehow got the strength together – then who knew what state we might have found him in later when we woke up from our deep sleep? Rajee kept apologizing, trying to soothe him, but that only seemed to make him more cross. He went on and on.

'Yes,' he said, 'and if something happens to me now, then what about her?' He pointed at me in an accusing way.

'Nothing will happen, Daddy,' Rajee said, soothing him. 'You are all right.'

Daddy snorted with contempt. 'Feel this,' he said, guiding Rajee's hand to his heart.

'You are all right,' Rajee repeated.

Daddy made another contemptuous sound and pushed Rajee's hand away. 'You would have made a fine doctor. And who is going to look after her when you go? What will she do all alone for seven years?'

'He is *not going*, Daddy,' I said, spacing my words very distinctly. I didn't like it, that he should still be thinking about that.

'Not going where?' Rajee asked.

That made Daddy so angry that he became quite energetic. He stopped lolling in Rajee's arms and began to abuse him, calling him the same sort of names I had called him earlier. And Rajee listened to him as he had listened to me, respectfully, with his head lowered.

I tried to bear it quietly for a while but couldn't. Then I interrupted Daddy. I said, 'It is not like that at all.'

'No?' he said. 'To go to jail is not like that? Perhaps it's a nice thing. Perhaps we should say, "Well done, Son. Bravo."'

'He wasn't in jail,' I said. 'It was more like a hotel. And he met some very fine people there. You don't understand anything about these things, Daddy, so it's better not to talk.'

Daddy was quiet. I didn't look at him, I was too annoyed with him. He had no right to meddle in things he didn't know about; he was old now, and should just eat and sleep.

'Lie down,' I told him. 'Go to sleep.'

'All right,' Daddy said in a meek voice.

But in fact he couldn't lie down, because Rajee had dropped off to sleep on the sofa. He was sitting up, but his head had dropped to his chest and his eyes were shut. Naturally, after two sleepless nights, I couldn't disturb him, so I told Daddy he had better go and sleep in our bedroom. Daddy said all right again, in the same meek voice. He carried his pillow under his arm and went away.

I lifted Rajee's legs on to the sofa and arranged his head. He didn't wake up. I looked at him sleeping. I thought that even if he had to go away for a while he would be coming back to me. And even if it were for a longer time there are always remissions for good conduct and other concessions, and meanwhile visits are allowed and I could take him things and also receive letters from him. So even if it is for longer, I shall wait and not do anything to myself. I would never do anything to myself now, never. I wouldn't think of it.

I did try it once. I got the idea from two people. One of them was Rajee. It was the time when Sudha's marriage was being arranged, and he came daily to our house and cried and said he could not bear it and would kill himself. I think he felt better with being able to talk to me, but after I told him my feelings for him he didn't come so often anymore, and after a time he stopped coming altogether. Then I began to remember all he had said about what was the use of living. It so happened that just at this time there was a girl in the neighbourhood who committed suicide – not for love but because of cruel treatment from her in-laws. She did it in the usual way, by pouring kerosene over her clothes and setting herself on fire. It is a crude method and perhaps not suitable for a college girl like me, but it was the only way I could think of and also the easiest and cheapest, so I decided on it.

Only that day, when everything was ready, Daddy came home early and found me. Although he never wanted me to get married, he saw then that there was no other way and he sent for Rajee. When Daddy saw that Rajee was reluctant to get married to me, he did a strange thing – the sort of thing he has never, never in his whole life done to anyone. He got down on the floor and touched Rajee's feet and begged him to marry me. Rajee, who is always very respectful to elders, was shocked, and he bent down to raise him and cried, 'Daddy, what are you doing!' As soon as I heard him say Daddy, I knew it would be all right. I mean, he wouldn't call him Daddy, would he, unless he was going to be his son-in-law?

Prostitutes

Tara's house was in a newly developed area on the outskirts of town. It had been one of the first houses there, but in the last few years others had been coming up and tenants had moved into them. Tara didn't know any of these people and had no interest in making their acquaintance. She had got used to being on her own. She did not even miss her daughter, Leila; indeed, in many ways it was a relief not to have her there.

Leila's father, Mukand Sahib, came every day – often twice a day. He too was relieved to have Leila away at boarding school, for in recent years the girl had taken a dislike to him. It had been a difficult situation, and the cause of half the fights between mother and daughter. The other half had been due to the presence of Bikki, although, unlike Mukand Sahib, Bikki had not at all minded the girl's tantrums. On the contrary, he seemed to enjoy teasing her into them. Bikki did not increase his visits when Leila was sent away. In fact, nowadays Tara saw nowhere near enough of him. Sometimes, hearing some noise at the door, she thought he had come and hurried out to meet him. But it was usually only Mukand Sahib. Then she found it difficult to curb her irritation.

Mukand Sahib did everything he could to placate her. He had become very humble with her, which irritated her more than ever. She watched him sitting in her living-room one hot summer day, panting with heat and not even daring to ask her for a glass of water. She did not offer him one. She was too angry and disappointed with him for not being Bikki. She sat with her face averted, though she was aware of his imploring looks.

He was wiping his forehead with his handkerchief. He appeared to be really suffering, but all he said was, 'It is very hot outside.'

It was as if she had been waiting for this. 'Then why come here?' she cried. 'I'm sure your wife will be very happy to keep you at home! Why come and sit on my head?'

When he did not reply, she glanced at him out of the corner of her eye. He was trembling, and he looked terribly old. She began to be nervous. What if he were to have a stroke here and now, in her house? She realized she would have to be more careful. She forced herself to say, 'Should the servant bring water for you?' He nodded, unable to speak, though his eyes now gazed at her in gratitude.

She shouted for the servant, but he did not come. She went to the door and shouted in a voice so loud that the thin little house seemed to shake. Still he did not come; he was a new servant and very unreliable. Soon she would have to change him (she often changed her servant). She went out to the water jug and filled a glass for Mukand Sahib. He drank it off at once, and she went to get another. When she came back with that, he seized her hand and kissed it.

Although she overcame her desire to snatch her hand away, she felt she could not stay with him a moment longer. Mumbling that she was going to make tea for him, she swiftly left the room. She went up on the roof. It was intensely hot there, with the sun beating down in a white hot glare, but she felt it was the only place where she could breathe. She found it difficult to draw in sufficient breath. She laid her hand on her breasts – large and still firm, though she was nearing forty – and took great gulps of air. The spot on her hand where his lips had been felt like a sore, and she wiped it again and again on her sari. She sank down by the parapet and buried her head in her knees. She did not know what to do. She did not think she could ever go back into that house, back into the room where he was waiting for her to return. Yet it was unbearable on the roof; the bricks burned like fire. All around the landscape was arid, as desolate as a desert, and the new houses scattered over it, some of them half finished, looked like skeletons picked bare and bleached in the sun.

When Mukand Sahib had first bought this house for her, almost ten years ago, she had been very happy to live in it. She had not felt lonely at all, although at that time there had been only one other building near by (a contractor's office, since abandoned). She had eaten and slept and played with Leila, and in the evenings she had dressed herself up to wait for Mukand Sahib. Quite often he had not been able to come. He had been busy in those years – not only with his law practice and his family obligations but also with his various honorary positions, such as vice-president of the local Rotary Club. She had been very proud of him and of his attachment to her and of everything he did for her and their daughter. No other woman in her family had ever been so well settled – not her mother or her grandmother or anyone else. Of course, they had all had admirers in their youth, and had borne children to them, and had even been kept by them for a while, but none of them had been taken out of her surroundings and provided for and kept in a good position, the way she had been by Mukand Sahib.

He was calling her now; she could hear his plaintive, old man's voice from the house below. She wiped the tears and perspiration from her face and after a while managed to pull herself together sufficiently to go down to him. He was sitting in the same place she had left him, on the mattress in one corner. When she came in, he said, 'Why do you leave me? Don't leave me.' He didn't ask about the tea she had promised him. He only wanted her to be there, as near to him as possible. 'Here,' he pleaded, feebly patting the mattress. Again overcoming herself, she approached him, sat by him. He laid his hand in her lap and sighed with contentment. 'Don't leave me,' he said again.

'Why should I leave you?' she said in the gruff way in which she usually spoke to him nowadays. 'Where should I go? I was right here, in the kitchen.' Then, cunningly, taking advantage of his contentment, she said, 'But today I have to go and visit my mother.' When she saw the pain and disappointment on his face, she shouted, 'I have to! Don't you understand!'

'Yes yes, I understand,' he said quickly.

'My God, how selfish you are. Naturally, Maji wants to see me. She is lonely, now that he has gone.' Her mother's companion – an old man who had been with her for many years – had recently died.

'You think you are the only person who needs me,' Tara went on. 'You have no thought for anyone but yourself. That is the sort of person you are – I have always known it.'

There was a silence. Then he said, 'You should take a little present for your mother.'

'All right.'

'Please take it from my pocket.'

She put her hand in and drew out his money and counted it. She kept all of it except for one rupee, which she put back. The rest she folded and thrust down into her bosom – but with rather a stern air, as if she were doing him a favour. And he really seemed to feel it was a favour, for he took up the hand with which she had taken the money and kissed it again. This time she was quite complaisant about it. Poor old man, she thought – though absently, for she was already looking forward to the expedition to her mother's house.

Her mother still lived in the Quarter, just behind the street of the silversmiths. She was the oldest tenant in her building, and everyone knew her and called her Maji. The other tenants were all much younger women who still practised their profession, and the house was always ringing with the noise of musical instruments and ankle bells. At night there was a lot of coming and going; men chewing betel felt their way up the dark stairs, and quite often there were brawls. Music came from the mother's room too, for she still liked to entertain herself with singing. Now, however, all her songs were devotional. Sometimes the other tenants came in to listen to her – they sighed and looked thoughtful – but she didn't care if anyone was there or not; she sang anyway. She was singing when Tara arrived, and though she smiled and nodded at her daughter, she didn't stop till the song had ended. She was accompanying herself on the harmonium. It was strange seeing her do that, because in the past the old man, her companion, had always been there to play for her.

The last time Tara had been in this room had been the day the old man had died. His corpse had lain there on a plank, covered with red cloth up to the chin. His face was exposed, not looking much different from when he was alive. The room was crowded, mostly with the other tenants. They were crying bitterly, although they had all disliked him. He used to lurk on the stairs, waiting for them in order to start quarrelling over some trifle. Of course all that was forgotten now that he was a corpse draped with marigolds. Loud wailing broke out when the plank was lifted up, to be carried downstairs and through the streets on its way to the burning ground. All the women rushed to the top of the stairs for a last look. Maji, of course, wailed the loudest and had to be supported under both arms while she beat her breasts and struck her head against the wall.

But now, two weeks later, she was singing and smiling and really just the same as ever. The room too was the same – the most comfortable place Tara knew on earth. It was crowded with objects: musical instruments, brass vessels, a hookah, a birdcage, a faded screen with a hole in the silk. It was also fragrant with incense and scented betel. Tara stretched herself out on the mattress on the floor in an attitude of complete relaxation. Her large limbs were sprawled in all directions. She could never relax like that in her own house.

As soon as Maji had finished her song, Tara asked, 'Has Bikki been here?'

'Yes. And the child? Has a letter come? What does she say? Are they giving sufficient food in the school?'

Maji was passionately fond of Leila, her only grandchild, and did not seem to mind at all that Leila hardly ever came to see her, or that when she did she was very surly with her.

When Tara had given all the news of Leila, she asked again about Bikki. Again Maji's reply was brief and evasive. Tara asked many more questions: When had he come? How long had he stayed? Was he so busy that he had no time to visit Tara?

When Maji found it impossible to be evasive any longer, she made excuses for Bikki. Yes, she said, he had been busy, but it was for her sake, for Maji. He had been very kind to her and had done some of the little errands for her that the old man used to do. Tara became calmer and was even able to think of her mother instead of Bikki. 'It must be difficult for you,' she said. 'After so many years.'

Maji and the old man had been together from before the time when Tara was born. He was not Tara's father – that had been someone else, long since vanished – but he had served Maji in many capacities; as musician, pimp, errand boy, lover when there had been no one else and she had still needed someone. In his last years he had done whatever small services he could in return for being allowed to live here with Maji and eat her food.

Maji said, 'He was old. And I'm old, too. Perhaps it will be my turn next.' She cackled rather gleefully, as if this were a treat to be looked forward to.

Tara snapped her fingers in the air several times, to keep ill luck away. 'Will he come today?' she asked.

'Who?'

'Bikki.'

Maji changed the subject. 'And Mukand Sahib?' she asked. She murmured a blessing upon the air, as was her habit when speaking of her daughter's benefactor.

'He sent this for you.' Tara fumbled in her bosom for the money.

'Where was the need?' protested Maji, quickly tucking it into her own bodice.

'Do you know where Bikki is? Can you send for him?' Tara was no longer relaxed on the mattress but straining forward to hear her mother's reply.

At last Maji said, 'Leave it.'

Tara sank back on to the mattress. She lay there like a sick woman. 'I *have* to see him,' she said, with such anguish that Maji realized there was no help for it.

Bikki came very quickly – too quickly – but Tara was so relieved to see him that she did not start thinking about that. In any case, Bikki did not give her much time to think. He came into the room with his usual bounce and high spirits, ready to charm and please. Soon he had them all in a festive mood. He was so gallant with Maji that she simpered and turned aside to hide her face behind her hand in a gesture of coquetry that sprang fresh from her youth. As for Tara, all the pain of longing and separation was forgotten, as the pangs of childbirth are forgotten in the moment of delivery. Her face was radiant; her eyes were only on him. She feasted on him. He was a rather stocky, broad-shouldered young man, with a round face blooming with smiles, sparkling black eyes, and glossy black hair that nestled low on the nape of his neck. He was dressed very beautifully, as always, in wide white freshly starched muslin and embroidered slippers. Tara took his hand in hers and turned his ring around and around on the little finger on which he wore it She had bought that ring for him with money that Mukand Sahib had given her to pay a dentist's bill. She kissed the ring, and then he kissed it, and then they smiled at each other and their eyes spoke.

Suddenly Bikki jumped up and said, 'Listen!' He squatted on the floor by the harmonium and began to play a new tune and sing the words to it. He didn't know it very well, but he had quite a sweet voice and sang with so much pleasure that they had to like it too. He broke off in the middle and cried, 'It is wonderful,

wonderful! Oh! "*Didn't you hear my heart cry out as you plucked it?*" Oh, oh!' He threw himself down on the floor and rolled around there while clutching his heart, like one suffering excruciating pain. The two women laughed, and he was satisfied and sat up, smiling to have given pleasure.

He said to Tara, 'Now it is your turn. Make us happy with a beautiful song sung in your own beautiful voice.'

'Get away!' She pretended to hit him. Tara was quite unmusical. Her mother and grandmother had worked hard to train her, but whenever she had begun to sing they covered their ears with their hands. Actually, it had not mattered. Tara in her heyday had brought more professional engagements into the family than they had ever had before. When men saw her, they forgot about singing and dancing and were content just to look.

Maji said, 'But our little Leila, our angel, she has the true gift.'

Tara shrugged. It was true that Leila seemed to have inherited her grandmother's voice rather than her mother's looks. But she had never cared to learn the family tradition of singing; she hated it above everything.

'Ah, when is she coming?' cried Bikki. 'I miss our little Missie Sahib so much.'

'You are very cruel to her,' Tara said.

'No, it is she who is cruel to me.' He rubbed his forehead ruefully. During her last holidays, she had thrown a cup at him. It had broken, and a piece had cut him and he had bled. Leila had run into the bedroom and locked the door. Then Tara ran about, alternately sponging Bikki's head and pounding on the door to get Leila to come out. But Leila did not emerge till late in the evening, after Bikki had left. Her face was swollen and she refused to speak to Tara for several days afterwards – in fact, not until it was time to return to school and Tara took her to the railway station.

Now Bikki decided that he was hungry. He told them of a new place he had discovered, not far away at all, where excellent meat pilao was to be had. He would go and get some for the three of them straightaway, and some carrot halwa as well. He waited tactfully for Tara to give him money, and the way he took it was very tactful too, his palm closing over it in a delicate, unobtrusive manner. He was already running down the stairs when Tara called him back; he stopped and looked up at her, and she ran down to meet him and threw her arms around his neck on the dark stairs. She wouldn't let go of him, though he tried to disengage himself. 'Someone will come,' he whispered. He looked up apprehensively, but she didn't care at all. She was stroking his neck and discovered a thin gold chain around it. Surprised, she drew it out to look at it. 'Who gave this to you?' she asked. Then he managed to free himself and ran as quickly as he could down the stairs.

Tara returned to her mother in a pensive mood. All sorts of suspicions now arose in her mind. She brooded while Maji played the harmonium and softly sang to herself. At last Tara said, 'Where was he when you sent for him?' She had recollected how quickly Bikki had appeared; he must have been somewhere in the building to appear so quickly. What was he doing there? And with whom? These thoughts were like thorns.

'*Where?*' she shouted.

Maji stopped playing. The last note hung on the air, together with Tara's shout.

'Upstairs,' Maji answered at last.

'Who with? Tell me . . . No, you must.' Tara was struggling to speak calmly, and struggling also to keep herself together. She suffered from high blood pressure, and in moments of agitation her heart thumped as if it wanted to burst through her body.

Maji said, 'What does it matter? What is it to you?' Although Tara made a feeble gesture, asking her to stop saying such things, Maji went on bravely. 'You can wait for seven births and plead and pray with folded hands, and still you will not meet again a person like Mukand Sahib,' she said. She repeated her customary blessing on him.

Tara managed to prop herself on her elbow. 'Who is he with? Which one?' she said. 'Is it Salima?' Maji did not reply, and Tara sank back and said, 'I thought so.'

Salima was a woman who had moved into the house a few months before. She was rather charming and had quite a few customers. She could well afford to keep Bikki and give him gold chains. She may have been a few years older than Bikki, but of course she was still many years younger than Tara.

Now Tara was cursing Bikki and Salima both. She swore what she would do to them – hack their bones into tiny pieces, pluck out their eyes to feed to vultures. She acted out how she would do these dreadful things. Maji tried to calm her. She shouted above Tara's shouts, she held Tara's arms, which were flailing in the air. It was as if she were struggling with devils that possessed her daughter.

Tara was exhausted, She lay still and allowed Maji to brush away the strands of hair that clung with perspiration to her forehead. Maji murmured endearments. She also kept repeating the name and virtues of Mukand Sahib, as if he were some kind of balm that she was applying to her daughter's hurt.

But Tara said, 'I don't want to see him ever again. I hate him. He makes me –' She thrust out her tongue; she really felt overcome with nausea. The spot on her hand he had kissed that morning began to tingle again with unpleasant sensations. She said, 'I'm not going back there. I shall stay with you.'

'Very fine. Very good,' Maji said, and she laughed ironically.

She left her daughter's side and went back to sit by her harmonium. She began to play, but broke off after a few bars. She talked. Her voice rambled on. Sometimes she laughed, sometimes she sighed. Tara did not listen carefully, but it was good to hear the familiar voice and other familiar sounds as well – the incessant beating of little hammers on metal from the street of the silversmiths, women calling to each other in lazy morning voices, and their slippers slipslopping along the stone floors.

Maji was talking about the dead old man. 'Sometimes I couldn't stand him anymore. Several times I drove him away. "Don't show your face here again," I said. Then he rolled up his few things and left. But sooner or later he always came back again. One day he would be there, and I would say, "Oh, you have come." And then he stayed.'

Tara yawned. The subject was not interesting to her; the old man had always been there, like this mattress, like that birdcage.

Maji said, 'This is what happened one night. It was long ago, when I was still young and had visitors. We were sitting; I was singing. A few people were there. Your grandmother was there too. She sat and listened, with her head going up and down to my singing. Then a man came in – I think he had been upstairs with Phul Devi. Perhaps his business with her was finished, or perhaps they had thrown him out. He was a very third-class person, and his behaviour was also very third-class. Everyone told him to leave, but he said why should he leave – he was ready to spend money too. He drew a big bundle out of his pocket, but he only threw down one or two rupees. "Here," he said. "Take it, be quick." And Grandmother was quick; she picked up the money at once and tucked it away. I was ready to continue singing, but he would not let me. He touched me in a coarse way. I said, "Please leave." I hoped the old man would do something – I say old man, but of course he was young then – but all he did was play his drum a bit louder, with his head down, and pretended to be too busy to hear or see anything. I felt angry with him, because it was his duty to make this person leave. Why else did we keep him and give him all that food and let him live here in the room with us? But he did nothing, he was afraid, and I don't know what would have happened if Mithu had not been here.'

'Who?' Tara said out of her deep drowsiness.

'No, I have not spoken to you much about Mithu. It is long ago.' But Maji was smiling as if it were not long ago at all. 'Oh, he was a rascal, a layabout, no good at all. But that day he was a blessing to us, for once. When this person would not leave, Mithu slapped his face and then he pushed him out of the door and gave him a kick down the stairs. Of course, Mithu always loved a fight. But that day even your grandmother was quite pleased with him. And as for me – what shall I tell you!' Maji flung her hands before her face.

Tara recognized her mother's feelings, and this sharpened her own. 'Is he always up there with Salima?' she asked.

'Leave it, Daughter,' Maji counselled again.

'She must be giving him presents and money. He would run anywhere, to anyone who can give him presents and money, even if she were a hundred years old and ugly as the devil.'

'One thing I could not get out of my mind,' Maji said. 'The way the old man had sat there playing the drum, with his head bent down. I hated him for that. I could not put up with him one moment longer. So he had to roll up his little bundle again and go elsewhere. And then Mithu moved in. I did not care what your grandmother said. I would not listen to her, or to anyone. I was stone-deaf, except to *his* voice. And I thought this happiness would never come to an end.'

Maji usually did not talk about things that were finished. Today, however, she went on and on, as if Tara did not have enough on her mind without having to hear all that.

'Then one day I found I was pregnant,' Maji said. 'God forgive me for everything I tried. But it was no use – you were determined to come and eat your share in this world. It was a very difficult time. There were complications; doctors and medicines had to be paid for. I lay here on this mat, and your grandmother wrung her hands and said we would all die. We cried day and night, not knowing where to turn. Don't ask about Mithu. With no clients, nothing going on, no food in the house, naturally it was too dull for him here. Then one day the old man was back again. Grandmother nearly fell over him on the stairs, where he was sleeping. She brought him in. You will say, What use was that, just one more belly to starve. Of course you are right, he couldn't help much. But he would get up very early – three, four o'clock, it must have been, though we never heard him, he went so quietly. He went to the wholesale fruit-and-vegetable market and bought bananas to sell from door to door. Why only bananas I don't know, but it brought in a little bit. We ate, and quite often there was even milk for me.'

Tara sat up, her ears strained towards the stairs. She rushed to the door and opened it suddenly, as if trying to catch someone by surprise. But it was the wrong person.

'Who is it?' Maji said.

'Only that policeman who visits Roxana. I thought it was *him*, trying to sneak upstairs. Just let him try!' She clenched her teeth.

'Lie down. Rest yourself.'

Tara lay down, but she did not rest. She said, 'Everything will be different from now on. I shall be here, and then let me see how he goes upstairs.'

She had spoken in a grim, threatening tone, but now this began to change. 'Perhaps it is my fault also,' she said in a forgiving voice. 'He is a person you have to watch all the time. If the child goes astray, who is to be blamed? Not the child but the mother who has been failing in her duty.' She did not look at Maji, whom she knew to be making a sceptical face. 'When I am with him, he wants nothing and no one else. He is content. How often he has put his head here to rest and said, "Now I am happy." He loves my breasts very much. He says I carry two big pillows specially for him.' She laughed and looked down at them, and then fidgeted them into position within her huge brassiere. 'The elastic is going,' she said. 'I shall have to buy new brassieres. Leila also wrote to say send new ones. She sent a long list of things. Every day there is something new to buy and send.'

'Well, thank God the money is there,' Maji said, and invoked her usual blessings on Mukand Sahib. She ignored Tara's frowns. 'He has been sent to us from above.'

Tara laughed scornfully. 'Yes, a fine angel,' she said. Then, interpreting Maji's silence as a reproach, she cried, 'You don't know! Day and night he is there, sitting there. And I have to sit with him so that he can look at me. He drops off to sleep, but if I try and move away he wakes up at once. "Tara! Tara!" All the time I hear his voice calling, "Tara! Tara!" Even in my dreams sometimes I think I hear him. And when Leila is home from school, it is worst. I am with her for a few moments, and at once we hear "Tara! Tara!" And Leila catches hold of me and says, "Don't go." But I have to go – to *run*! – because he is shouting so loud I'm afraid he will have a stroke.' She clutched her head. 'All I want is that he should leave me alone, leave me in peace,' she pleaded. 'I must have *some peace*.'

The door burst open. It was Bikki back again, triumphantly holding up some little earthenware pots. He wasted no time but set everything out for them to eat, talking all the while and telling them of acquaintances he had met in the bazaar and the conversation he had had with them. He began to eat with relish, commenting on the excellence of the pilao. He didn't notice that he was eating most of it. Tara was more interested in him than in the food. She kept stroking him, and he thought she was pleased with him because of what he had brought. This added to his own enjoyment, and he took more and more, saying, 'Good, hmm?' and licked each of his fingers. Tara brought water for him to wash in, and she wiped his hands on a towel, and then she sat close to him again and ran her hands over his face and neck. She could not get enough of him. She toyed with his new gold chain and pulled it out of his shirt to look at. She held it in the palm of her hand, but she did not say anything, and tucked it back again and went on stroking him. At last she said to Maji, 'No, I'm not going back.'

Maji did not reply.

'Not going back where?' Bikki asked.

'Why should I?' Tara demanded of Maji, who still did not reply. 'Maji is lonely,' Tara said. 'She wants me to come and live with her.'

'Here?' Bikki asked, unable to keep a tremor out of his voice.

'Yes.' She was still fondling him, but now her caresses were those of a moody tigress. 'Are you happy?' she asked him. 'Now you will not have to come so far to visit me.'

He nodded. Her caressing hand had got to his gold chain again. Again she drew it out and weighed it on her palm. 'Who gave you this?' she asked him lightly.

After a moment, he said, 'My auntie.' He stared back at her boldly.

Maji began to speak in the ensuing silence. She talked about the old man. She said she had not expected him to die. He had always enjoyed excellent health, and right till the end he had kept up his good appetite. In fact, the day before he died he had asked for a sugar melon. But in these last months he could never bear to let her out of his sight. If she left him for five minutes, she would find him crying on her return. 'With tears,' she said, and with her fingers she showed how they had coursed their way down his cheeks. It had irritated her terribly.

But it was strange to be without him, she said. Sometimes she woke up in the night and called his name. Of course no one answered. She supposed she would get used to it in time – that is, if she still had time. No one was here forever. When your ticket of departure was issued to you, then you went. Well, she was packed and ready. Everything was in order. Her daughter was well settled – and as for the granddaughter! There were just no words to describe the good fortune that girl was born with.

'You said you had to go and buy things to send to her school?' she asked Tara. 'New brassieres? What else?'

Tara was still holding the end of Bikki's chain in her palm. Her hand was trembling. Bikki continued to look defiant. His hard young eyes challenged her to say something further; but she dared not.

'What else?' Maji repeated stubbornly.

'Oh, so many things. Even a racket to play a game with.'

'A princess!' Maji clapped her hands together in delight. She was full of gratitude for the favours showered on her family. First she cried out her thanks to God for them, and after that to Mukand Sahib.

Tara tucked Bikki's chain back into his shirt. He became good-humoured again and began to take an interest in the racket that had to be bought for Leila. Was it for tennis or badminton? He decided he had better go with Tara and help her buy it. He jumped up. 'Let's hurry before the shops shut,' he said. He always loved shopping.

Tara hesitated. She said Mukand Sahib would be waiting for her at home. He worried if she stayed away too long.

'Not long,' Bikki said in a wheedling way. 'We shall just go to the shops for the racket – and perhaps one or two other things for Leila.'

Tara smiled. 'Only for Leila?'

'Of course, if you see something you might like to give to me . . . ' He shrugged, leaving the whole thing to her.

Tara looked at Maji as if for advice. Maji nodded. 'Go along,' she said. 'Buy him something nice, and then you can go home.'

Bikki bent down and kissed the bald patch on top of Maji's head. Almost before Maji could cry 'Get out!', he was out of the door, pulling Tara along with him. Maji could hear them laughing together on the stairs, but she forgot them the next moment. She began to play the harmonium again and to sing a devotional song.

Two More under the Indian Sun

Elizabeth had gone to spend the afternoon with Margaret. They were both English, but Margaret was a much older woman and they were also very different in character. But they were both in love with India, and it was this fact that drew them together. They sat on the veranda, and Margaret wrote letters and Elizabeth addressed the envelopes. Margaret always had letters to write; she led a busy life and was involved with several organizations of a charitable or spiritual nature. Her interests were centred in such matters, and Elizabeth was glad to be allowed to help her.

There were usually guests staying in Margaret's house. Sometimes they were complete strangers to her when they first arrived, but they tended to stay weeks, even months, at a time – holy men from the Himalayas, village welfare workers, organizers of conferences on spiritual welfare. She had one constant visitor throughout the winter, an elderly government officer who, on his retirement from service, had taken to a spiritual life and gone to live in the mountains at Almora. He did not, however, very much care for the winter cold up there, so at that season he came down to Delhi to stay with Margaret, who was always pleased to have him. He had a soothing effect on her – indeed, on anyone with whom he came into contact, for he had cast anger and all other bitter passions out of his heart and was consequently always smiling and serene. Everyone affectionately called him Babaji.

He sat now with the two ladies on the veranda, gently rocking himself to and fro in a rocking chair, enjoying the winter sunshine and the flowers in the garden and everything about him. His companions, however, were less serene. Margaret, in fact, was beginning to get angry with Elizabeth. This happened quite frequently, for Margaret tended to be quickly irritated, and especially with a meek and conciliatory person like Elizabeth.

'It's very selfish of you,' Margaret said now.

Elizabeth flinched. Like many very unselfish people, she was always accusing herself of undue selfishness, so that whenever this accusation was made by someone else it touched her closely. But because it was not in her power to do what Margaret wanted, she compressed her lips and kept silent. She was pale with this effort at obstinacy.

'It's your duty to go,' Margaret said. 'I don't have much time for people who shirk their duty.'

'I'm sorry, Margaret,' Elizabeth said, utterly miserable, utterly ashamed. The worst of it, almost, was that she really wanted to go; there was nothing she would have enjoyed more. What she was required to do was take a party of little Tibetan orphans on a holiday treat to Agra and show them the Taj Mahal. Elizabeth loved children, she loved little trips and treats, and she loved the Taj Mahal. But she couldn't go, nor could she say why.

Of course Margaret very easily guessed why, and it irritated her more than ever. To challenge her friend, she said bluntly, 'Your Raju can do without you for those few days. Good heavens, you're not a honeymoon couple, are you? You've been married long enough. Five years.'

'Four,' Elizabeth said in a humble voice.

'Four, then. I can hardly be expected to keep count of each wonderful day. Do you want me to speak to him?'

'Oh no.'

'I will, you know. It's nothing to me. I won't mince my words.' She gave a short, harsh laugh, challenging anyone to stop her from speaking out when occasion demanded. Indeed, at the thought of anyone doing so, her face grew red under her crop of grey hair, and a pulse throbbed in visible anger in her tough, tanned neck.

Elizabeth glanced imploringly towards Babaji. But he was rocking and smiling and looking with tender love at two birds pecking at something on the lawn.

'There are times when I can't help feeling you're afraid of him,' Margaret said. She ignored Elizabeth's little disclaiming cry of horror. 'There's no trust between you, no understanding. And married life is nothing if it's not based on the twin rocks of trust and understanding.'

Babaji liked this phrase so much that he repeated it to himself several times, his lips moving soundlessly and his head nodding with approval.

'In everything I did,' Margaret said, 'Arthur was with me. He had complete faith in me. And in those days – Well.' She chuckled. 'A wife like me wasn't altogether a joke.'

Her late husband had been a high-up British official, and in those British days he and Margaret had been expected to conform to some very strict social rules. But the idea of Margaret conforming to any rules, let alone those! Her friends nowadays often had a good laugh at it with her, and she had many stories to tell of how she had shocked and defied her fellow-countrymen.

'It was people like you,' Babaji said, 'who first extended the hand of friendship to us.'

'It wasn't a question of friendship, Babaji. It was a question of love.'

'Ah!' he exclaimed.

'As soon as I came here – and I was only a chit of a girl, Arthur and I had been married just two months – yes, as soon as I set foot on Indian soil, I knew this was the place I belonged. It's funny isn't it? I don't suppose there's any rational explanation for it. But then, when was India ever the place for rational explanations?'

Babaji said with gentle certainty, 'In your last birth, you were one of us. You were an Indian.'

'Yes, lots of people have told me that. Mind you, in the beginning it was quite a job to make them see it. Naturally, they were suspicious – can you blame them? It wasn't like today. I envy you girls married to Indians. You have a very easy time of it.'

Elizabeth thought of the first time she had been taken to stay with Raju's family. She had met and married Raju in England, where he had gone for a year on a Commonwealth scholarship, and then had returned with him to Delhi; so it was some time before she met his family, who lived about two hundred miles out of Delhi, on the outskirts of a small town called Ankhpur. They all lived together in an ugly brick house, which was divided into two parts – one for the men of the family, the other for the women. Elizabeth, of course, had stayed in the women's quarters. She couldn't speak any Hindi and they spoke very little English, but they had not had much trouble communicating with her. They managed to make it clear at once that they thought her too ugly and too old for Raju (who was indeed some five years her junior), but also that they did not hold this against her and were ready to accept her, with all her shortcomings, as the will of God. They got a lot of amusement out of her, and she enjoyed being with them. They dressed and undressed her in new saris, and she smiled good-naturedly while they stood round her clapping their hands in wonder and doubling up with laughter. Various fertility ceremonies had been performed over her, and before she left she had been given her share of the family jewellery.

'Elizabeth,' Margaret said, 'if you're going to be so slow, I'd rather do them myself.'

'Just these two left,' Elizabeth said, bending more eagerly over the envelopes she was addressing.

'For all your marriage,' Margaret said, 'sometimes I wonder how much you do understand about this country. You live such a closed-in life.'

'I'll just take these inside,' Elizabeth said, picking up the envelopes and letters. She wanted to get away, not because she minded being told about her own wrong way of life but because she was afraid Margaret might start talking about Raju again.

It was cold inside, away from the sun. Margaret's house was old and massive, with thick stone walls, skylights instead of windows, and immensely high ceilings. It was designed to keep out the heat in summer, but it also sealed in the cold in winter and became like some cavernous underground fortress frozen through with the cold of earth and stone. A stale smell of rice, curry, and mango chutney was chilled into the air.

Elizabeth put the letters on Margaret's work-table, which was in the drawing-room. Besides the drawing-room, there was a dining-room, but every other room was a bedroom, each with its dressing-room and bathroom attached. Sometimes Margaret had to put as many as three or four visitors into each bedroom, and on one occasion – this was when she had helped to organize a conference on Meditation as the Modern Curative – the drawing-and dining-rooms too had been converted into dormitories, with string cots and bedrolls laid out end to end. Margaret was not only an energetic and active person involved in many causes but she was also the soul of generosity, ever ready to throw open her house to any friend or acquaintance in need of shelter. She had thrown it open to Elizabeth and Raju three years ago, when they had had to vacate their rooms almost over-night because the landlord said he needed the accommodation for his relatives. Margaret had given them a whole suite – a bedroom and dressing-room and bathroom – to themselves and they had had all their meals with her in the big dining-room, where the table was always ready laid with white crockery plates, face down so as not to catch the dust, and a thick white tablecloth that got rather stained towards the end of the week. At first, Raju had been very grateful and had praised their hostess to the skies for her kind and generous character. But as the weeks wore on, and every day, day after day, two or three times a day, they sat with Margaret and whatever other guests she had round the table, eating alternately lentils and rice or string-beans with boiled potatoes and beetroot salad, with Margaret always in her chair at the head of the table talking inexhaustibly about her activities and ideas – about Indian spirituality and the Mutiny and village uplift and the industrial revolution – Raju, who had a lot of ideas of his own and rather liked to talk, began to get restive. 'But Madam, Madam,' he would frequently say, half rising in his chair in his impatience to interrupt her, only to have to sit down again, unsatisfied, and continue with his dinner, because Margaret was too busy with her own ideas to have time to take in his.

Once he could not restrain himself. Margaret was talking about – Elizabeth had even forgotten what it was – was it the first Indian National Congress? At any rate, she said something that stirred Raju to such disagreement that this time he did not restrict himself to the hesitant appeal of 'Madam' but said out loud for everyone to hear, 'Nonsense, she is only talking nonsense.' There was a moment's silence; then Margaret, sensible woman that she was, shut her eyes as a sign that she would not hear and would not see, and, repeating the sentence he had interrupted more firmly than before, continued her discourse on an even keel. It was the other two or three people sitting with them round the table – a Buddhist monk with a large shaved skull, a welfare worker and a disciple of the Gandhian way of life wearing nothing but the homespun loincloth in which the Mahatma himself had always been so simply clad – it was they who had looked at Raju, and very, very gently one of them had clicked his tongue.

Raju had felt angry and humiliated, and afterwards, when they were alone in their bedroom, he had quarrelled about it with Elizabeth. In his excitement, he raised his voice higher than he would have if he had remembered that they were in someone else's house, and the noise of this must have disturbed

Margaret, who suddenly stood in the doorway, looking at them. Unfortunately, it was just at the moment when Raju, in his anger and frustration, was pulling his wife's hair, and they both stood frozen in this attitude and stared back at Margaret. The next instant, of course, they had collected themselves, and Raju let go of Elizabeth's hair, and she pretended as best she could that all that was happening was that he was helping her comb it. But such a feeble subterfuge would not do before Margaret's penetrating eye, which she kept fixed on Raju, in total silence, for two disconcerting minutes; then she said, 'We don't treat English girls that way,' and withdrew, leaving the door open behind her as a warning that they were under observation. Raju shut it with a vicious kick. If they had had anywhere else to go, he would have moved out that instant.

Raju never came to see Margaret now. He was a proud person, who would never forget anything he considered a slight to his honour. Elizabeth always came on her own, as she had done today, to visit her friend. She sighed now as she arranged the letters on Margaret's work-table; she was sad that this difference had arisen between her husband and her only friend, but she knew that there was nothing she could do about it. Raju was very obstinate. She shivered and rubbed the tops of her arms, goose-pimpled with the cold in that high, bleak room, and returned quickly to the veranda, which was flooded and warm with afternoon sun.

Babaji and Margaret were having a discussion on the relative merits of the three ways towards realization. They spoke of the way of knowledge, the way of action, and that of love. Margaret maintained that it was a matter of temperament, and that while she could appreciate the beauty of the other two ways, for herself there was no path nor could there ever be but that of action. It was her nature.

'Of course it is,' Babaji said. 'And God bless you for it.'

'Arthur used to tease me. He'd say, "Margaret was born to right all the wrongs of the world in one go." But I can't help it. It's not in me to sit still when I see things to be done.'

'Babaji,' said Elizabeth, laughing, 'once I saw her – it was during the monsoon, and the river had flooded and the people on the bank were being evacuated. But it wasn't being done quickly enough for Margaret! She waded into the water and came back with someone's tin trunk on her head. All the people shouted, "Memsahib, Memsahib! What are you doing!" but she didn't take a bit of notice. She waded right back in again and came out with two rolls of bedding, one under each arm.'

Elizabeth went pink with laughter, and with pleasure and pride, at recalling this incident. Margaret pretended to be angry and gave her a playful slap, but she could not help smiling, while Babaji clasped his hands in joy and opened his mouth wide in silent, ecstatic laughter.

Margaret shook her head with a last fond smile. 'Yes, but I've got into the most dreadful scrapes with this nature of mine. If I'd been born with an ounce more patience, I'd have been a pleasanter person to deal with and life could have been a lot smoother all round. Don't you think so?'

She looked at Elizabeth, who said, 'I love you just the way you are.'

But a moment later, Elizabeth wished she had not said this. 'Yes,' Margaret took her up, 'that's the trouble with you. You love everybody just the way they are.' Of course she was referring to Raju. Elizabeth twisted her hands in her lap. These hands were large and bony and usually red, although she was otherwise a pale and rather frail person.

The more anyone twisted and squirmed, the less inclined was Margaret to let them off the hook. Not because this afforded her any pleasure but because she felt that facts of character must be faced just as resolutely as any other kinds of fact. 'Don't think you're doing anyone a favour,' she said, 'by being so indulgent towards their faults. Quite on the contrary. And especially in marriage,' she went on unwaveringly. 'It's not mutual pampering that makes a marriage but mutual trust.'

'Trust and understanding,' Babaji said.

Elizabeth knew that there was not much of these in her marriage. She wasn't even sure how much Raju earned in his job at the municipality (he was an engineer in the sanitation department), and there was one drawer in their bedroom whose contents she didn't know, for he always kept it locked and the key with him.

'I'll lend you a wonderful book,' Margaret said. 'It's called *Truth in the Mind,* and it's full of the most astounding insight. It's by this marvellous man who founded an ashram in Shropshire. Shafi!' She called suddenly for the servant, but of course he couldn't hear, because the servants' quarters were right at the back, and the old man now spent most of his time there, sitting on a bed and having his legs massaged by a granddaughter.

'I'll call him,' Elizabeth said, and got up eagerly.

She went back into the stone-cold house and out again at the other end. Here were the kitchen and the crowded servants' quarters. Margaret could never bear to dismiss anyone, and even the servants who were no longer in her employ continued to enjoy her hospitality. Each servant had a great number of dependents, so this part of the house was a little colony of its own, with a throng of people outside the rows of peeling hutments, chatting or sleeping or quarrelling or squatting on the ground to cook their meals and wash their children. Margaret enjoyed coming out there, mostly to advise and scold – but Elizabeth felt shy, and she kept her eyes lowered.

'Shafi,' she said, 'Memsahib is calling you.'

The old man mumbled furiously. He did not like to have his rest disturbed and he did not like Elizabeth. In fact, he did not like any of the visitors. He was the oldest servant in the house – so old that he had been Arthur's bearer when Arthur was still a bachelor and serving in the districts, almost forty years ago.

Still grumbling, he followed Elizabeth back to the veranda. 'Tea, Shafi!' Margaret called out cheerfully when she saw them coming.

'Not time for tea yet,' he said.

She laughed. She loved it when her servants answered her back; she felt it showed a sense of ease and equality and family irritability, which was only another side of family devotion. 'What a cross old man you are,' she said. 'And just look at you – how dirty.'

He looked down at himself. He was indeed very dirty. He was unshaven and unwashed, and from beneath the rusty remains of what had once been a uniform coat there peeped out a ragged assortment of grey vests and torn pullovers into which he had bundled himself for the winter.

'It's hard to believe,' Margaret said, 'that this old scarecrow is a terrible, terrible snob. You know why he doesn't like you, Elizabeth? Because you're married to an Indian.'

Elizabeth smiled and blushed. She admired Margaret's forthrightness.

'He thinks you've let down the side. He's got very firm principles. As a matter of fact, he thinks I've let down the side too. All his life he's longed to work for a real memsahib, the sort that entertains other memsahibs to tea. Never forgave Arthur for bring home little Margaret.'

The old man's face began working strangely. His mouth and stubbled cheeks twitched, and then sounds started coming that rose and fell – now distinct, now only a mutter and a drone – like waves of the sea. He spoke partly in English and partly in Hindi, and it was some time before it could be made out that he was telling some story of the old days – a party at the Gymkhana Club for which he had been hired as an additional waiter. The sahib who had given the party, a Major Waterford, had paid him not only his wages but also a tip of two rupees. He elaborated on this for some time, dwelling on the virtues of Major Waterford and also of Mrs Waterford, a very fine lady who had made her servants wear white gloves when they served at table.

'Very grand,' said Margaret with an easy laugh. 'You run along now and get our tea.'

'There was a little Missie sahib too. She had two ayahs, and every year they were given four saris and one shawl for the winter.'

'Tea, Shafi,' Margaret said more firmly, so that the old man, who knew every inflection in his mistress's voice, saw it was time to be off.

'Arthur and I've spoiled him outrageously,' Margaret said. 'We spoiled all our servants.'

'God will reward you,' said Babaji.

'We could never think of them as servants, really. They were more our friends. I've learned such a lot from Indian servants. They're usually rogues, but underneath all that they have beautiful characters. They're very religious, and they have a lot of philosophy – you'd be surprised. We've had some fascinating conversations. You ought to keep a servant, Elizabeth – I've told you so often.' When she saw Elizabeth was about to answer something, she said, 'And don't say you can't afford it. Your Raju earns enough, I'm sure, and they're very cheap.'

'We don't need one,' Elizabeth said apologetically. There were just the two of them, and they lived in two small rooms. Sometimes Raju also took it into his head that they needed a servant, and once he had even gone to the extent of hiring an undernourished little boy from the hills. On the second day, however, the boy was discovered rifling the pockets of Raju's trousers while their owner was having his bath, so he was dismissed on the spot. To Elizabeth's relief, no attempt at replacing him was ever made.

'If you had one you could get around a bit more,' Margaret said.

'Instead of always having to dance attendance on your husband's mealtimes. I suppose that's why you don't want to take those poor little children to Agra?'

'It's not that I don't want to,' Elizabeth said hopelessly.

'Quite apart from anything else, you ought to be longing to get around and see the country. What do you know, what will you ever know, if you stay in one place all the time?'

'One day you will come and visit me in Almora,' Babaji said.

'Oh Babaji, I'd love to!' Elizabeth exclaimed.

'Beautiful,' he said, spreading his hands to describe it all. 'The mountains, trees, clouds . . . ' Words failed him, and he could only spread his hands farther and smile into the distance, as if he saw a beautiful vision there.

Elizabeth smiled with him. She saw it too, although she had never been there: the mighty mountains, the grandeur and the peace, the abode of Shiva where he sat with the rivers flowing from his hair. She longed to go, and to so many other places she had heard and read about. But the only place away from Delhi where she had ever been was Ankhpur, to stay with Raju's family.

Margaret began to tell her about all the places she had been to. She and Arthur had been posted from district to district, in many different parts of the country, but even that hadn't been enough for her. She had to see everything. She had no fears about travelling on her own, and had spent weeks tramping around in the mountains, with a shawl thrown over her shoulders and a stick held firmly in her hand. She had travelled many miles by any mode of transport available – train, bus, cycle, rickshaw, or even bullock cart – in order to see some little-known and almost inaccessible temple or cave or tomb: Once she had sprained her ankle and lain all alone for a week in a derelict rest house, deserted except for one decrepit old watchman, who had shared his meals with her.

'That's the way to get to know a country,' she declared. Her cheeks were flushed with the pleasure of remembering everything she had done.

Elizabeth agreed with her. Yet although she herself had done none of these things, she did not feel that she was on that account cut off from all knowledge. There was much to be learned from living with Raju's family in Ankhpur, much to be learned from Raju himself. Yes, he was her India! She felt like laughing when this thought came to her. But it was true.

'Your trouble is,' Margaret suddenly said, 'you let Raju bully you. He's got something of that in his character – don't contradict. I've studied him. If you were to stand up to him more firmly, you'd both be happier.'

Again Elizabeth wanted to laugh. She thought of the nice times she and Raju often had together. He had invented a game of cricket that they could play in their bedrooms between the steel almirah and the opposite wall. They played it with a rubber ball and a hairbrush, and three steps made a run. Raju's favourite trick was to hit the ball under the bed, and while she lay flat on the floor groping for it he made run after run, exhorting her with mocking cries of 'Hurry up! Where is it? Can't you find it?' His eyes glittered with the pleasure of winning; his shirt was off, and drops of perspiration trickled down his smooth, dark chest.

'You should want to do something for those poor children!' Margaret shouted.

'I do want to. You know I do.'

'I don't know anything of the sort. All I see is you leading an utterly useless, selfish life. I'm disappointed in you, Elizabeth. When I first met you, I had such high hopes of you. I thought, Ah, here at last is a serious person. But you're not serious at all. You're as frivolous as any of those girls that come here and spend their days playing mahjong.'

Elizabeth was ashamed. The worst of it was she really had once been a serious person. She had been a school teacher in England, and devoted to her work and her children, on whom she had spent far more time and care than was necessary in the line of duty. And, over and above that, she had put in several evenings a week visiting old people who had no one to look after them. But all that had come to an end once she met Raju.

'It's criminal to be in India and not be committed,' Margaret went on. 'There isn't much any single person can do, of course, but to do nothing at all – no, I wouldn't be able to sleep at nights.'

And Elizabeth slept not only well but happily, blissfully! Sometimes she turned on the light just for the pleasure of looking at Raju lying beside her. He slept like a child, with the pillow bundled under his cheek and his mouth slightly open, as if he were smiling.

'But what are you laughing at!' Margaret shouted.

'I'm not, Margaret.' She hastily composed her face. She hadn't been aware of it, but probably she had been smiling at the image of Raju asleep.

Margaret abruptly pushed back her chair. Her face was red and her hair dishevelled, as if she had been in a fight. Elizabeth half rose in her chair, aghast at whatever it was she had done and eager to undo it.

'Don't follow me,' Margaret said. 'If you do, I know I'm going to behave badly and I'll feel terrible afterwards. You can stay here or you can go home, but *don't follow me.*'

She went inside the house, and the screen door banged after her. Elizabeth sank down into her chair and looked helplessly at Babaji.

He had remained as serene as ever. Gently he rocked himself in his chair. The winter afternoon was drawing to its close, and the sun, caught between two trees, was beginning to contract into one concentrated area of gold. Though the light was failing, the garden remained bright and gay with all its marigolds, its phlox, its pansies, and its sweet peas. Babaji enjoyed it all. He sat wrapped in his woollen shawl, with his feet warm in thick knitted socks and sandals.

'She is a hot-tempered lady,' he said, smiling and forgiving. 'But good, good.'

'Oh, I know,' Elizabeth said. 'She's an angel. I feel so bad that I should have upset her. Do you think I ought to go after her?'

'A heart of gold,' said Babaji.

'I know it.' Elizabeth bit her lip in vexation at herself.

Shafi came out with the tea tray. Elizabeth removed some books to clear the little table for him, and Babaji said, 'Ah,' in pleasurable anticipation. But Shafi did not put the tray down.

'Where is she?' he said.

'It's all right, Shafi. She's just coming. Put it down, please.'

The old man nodded and smiled in a cunning, superior way. He clutched his tray more tightly and turned back into the house. He had difficulty in walking, not only because he was old and infirm but also because the shoes he wore were too big for him and had no laces.

'Shafi!' Elizabeth called after him. 'Babaji wants his tea!' But he did not even turn round. He walked straight up to Margaret's bedroom and kicked the door and shouted, 'I've brought it!'

Elizabeth hurried after him. She felt nervous about going into Margaret's bedroom after having been so explicitly forbidden to follow her. But Margaret only looked up briefly from where she was sitting on her bed, reading a letter, and said, 'Oh, it's you,' and 'Shut the door.' When he had put down the tea, Shafi went out again and the two of them were left alone.

Margaret's bedroom was quite different from the rest of the house. The other rooms were all bare and cold, with a minimum of furniture standing around on the stone floors; there were a few isolated pictures hung up here and there on the whitewashed walls, but nothing more intimate than portraits of Mahatma Gandhi and Sri Ramakrishna and a photograph of the inmates of Mother Theresa's Home. But Margaret's room was crammed with a lot of comfortable, solid old furniture, dominated by the big double bed in the centre, which was covered with a white bedcover and a mosquito curtain on the top like a canopy. A log fire burned in the grate, and there were photographs everywhere – family photos of Arthur and Margaret, of Margaret as a little girl, and of her parents and her sister and her school and her friends. The stale smell of food pervading the rest of the house stopped short of this room, which was scented very pleasantly by woodsmoke and lavender water. There was an umbrella stand that held several alpenstocks, a tennis racket, and a hockey stick.

'It's from my sister,' Margaret said, indicating the letter she was reading. 'She lives out in the country and they've been snowed under again. She's got a pub.'

'How lovely.'

'Yes, it's a lovely place. She's always wanted me to come and run it with her. But I couldn't live in England anymore, I couldn't bear it.'

'Yes, I know what you mean.'

'What do you know? You've only been here a few years. Pour the tea, there's a dear.'

'Babaji was wanting a cup.'

'To hell with Babaji.'

She took off her sandals and lay down on the bed, leaning against some fat pillows that she had propped against the headboard. Elizabeth had noticed before that Margaret was always more relaxed in her own room than anywhere else. Not all her visitors were allowed into this room – in fact, only a chosen few. Strangely enough, Raju had been one of these when he and Elizabeth had stayed in the house. But he had never properly appreciated the privilege; either he sat on the edge of a chair and made signs to Elizabeth to go or he wandered restlessly round the room, looking at all the photographs or taking out the tennis racket and executing imaginary services with it; till Margaret told him to sit down and not make them all nervous, and then he looked sulky and made even more overt signs to Elizabeth.

'I brought my sister out here once,' Margaret said. 'But she couldn't stand it. Couldn't stand anything – the climate, the water, the food. Everything made her ill. There are people like that. Of course, I'm just the opposite. You like it here too, don't you?'

'Very, very much.'

'Yes, I can see you're happy.'

Margaret looked at her so keenly that Elizabeth tried to turn away her face slightly. She did not want anyone to see too much of her tremendous happiness. She felt somewhat ashamed of herself for having it – not only because she knew she didn't deserve it but also because she did not consider herself quite the right kind of person to have it. She had been over thirty when she met Raju and had not expected much more out of life than had up till then been given to her.

Margaret lit a cigarette. She never smoked except in her own room. She puffed slowly, luxuriously. Suddenly she said, 'He doesn't like me, does he?'

'Who?'

'"Who?"' she repeated impatiently. 'Your Raju, of course.'

Elizabeth flushed with embarrassment. 'How you talk, Margaret,' she murmured deprecatingly, not knowing what else to say.

'I know he doesn't,' Margaret said. 'I can always tell.'

She sounded so sad that Elizabeth wished she could lie to her and say that no, Raju loved her just as everyone else did. But she could not bring herself to it. She thought of the way he usually spoke of Margaret. He called her by rude names and made coarse jokes about her, at which he laughed like a schoolboy and tried to make Elizabeth laugh with him; and the terrible thing was sometimes she did laugh, not because she wanted to or because what he said amused her but because it was he who urged her to, and she always found it difficult to refuse him anything. Now when she thought of this compliant laughter of hers she was filled with anguish, and she began unconsciously to wring her hands, the way she always did at such secretly appalling moments.

But Margaret was having thoughts of her own, and was smiling to herself. She said, 'You know what was my happiest time of all in India? About ten years ago, when I went to stay in Swami Vishwananda's ashram.'

Elizabeth was intensely relieved at the change of subject, though somewhat puzzled by its abruptness.

'We bathed in the river and we walked in the mountains. It was a time of such freedom, such joy. I've never felt like that before or since. I didn't have a care in the world and I felt so – light. I can't describe it – as if my feet didn't touch the ground.'

'Yes, yes!' Elizabeth said eagerly, for she thought she recognized the feeling.

'In the evenings we all sat with Swamiji. We talked about everything under the sun. He laughed and joked with us, and sometimes he sang. I don't know what happened to me when he sang. The tears came pouring down my face, but I was so happy I thought my heart would melt away.'

'Yes,' Elizabeth said again.

'That's him over there.' She nodded towards a small framed photograph on the dressing-table. Elizabeth picked it up. He did not look different from the rest of India's holy men – naked to the waist, with long hair and burning eyes.

'Not that you can tell much from a photo,' Margaret said. She held out her hand for it, and then she looked at it herself, with a very young expression on her face. 'He was such fun to be with, always full of jokes and games. When I was with him, I used to feel – I don't know – like a flower or a bird.' She laughed gaily, and Elizabeth with her.

'Does Raju make you feel like that?'

Elizabeth stopped laughing and looked down into her lap. She tried to make her face very serious so as not to give herself away.

'Indian men have such marvellous eyes,' Margaret said. 'When they look at you, you can't help feeling all young and nice. But of course your Raju thinks I'm just a fat, ugly old memsahib.'

'Margaret, Margaret!'

Margaret stubbed out her cigarette and, propelling herself with her heavy legs, swung down from the bed. 'And there's poor old Babaji waiting for his tea.'

She poured it for him and went out with the cup. Elizabeth went after her. Babaji was just as they had left him, except that now the sun, melting away between the trees behind him, was even more intensely gold and provided a heavenly background, as if to a saint in a picture, as he sat there at peace in his rocking chair.

Margaret fussed over him. She stirred his tea and she arranged his shawl more securely over his shoulders. Then she said, 'I've got an idea, Babaji.' She hooked her foot round a stool and drew it close to his chair and sank down on it, one hand laid on his knee. 'You and I'll take those children up to Agra. Would you like that? A little trip?' She looked up into his face and was eager and bright. 'We'll have a grand time. We'll hire a bus, and we'll have singing and games all the way. You'll love it.' She squeezed his knee in anticipatory joy, and he smiled at her and his thin old hand came down on the top of her head in a gesture of affection or blessing.

Picnic with Moonlight and Mangoes

Unfortunately the town in which Sri Prakash lived was a small one so that everyone knew what had happened to him. At first he did not go out at all, on account of feeling so ashamed; but, as the weeks dragged on, sitting at home became very dreary. He also began to realize that, with thinking and solitude, he was probably exaggerating the effect of his misfortune on other people. Misfortune could befall anyone, any time; there was really no need to be ashamed. So one morning when his home seemed particularly depressing he made up his mind to pay a visit to the coffee house. He left while his wife was having her bath – he told her he was going, he shouted it through the bathroom door, and if she did not hear above the running water that was obviously not his fault.

So when he came home and she asked him where he had been, he could say 'I *told* you' with a perfectly good conscience. He was glad of that because he could see she had been worried about him. While she served him his food, he did his best to reassure her. He told her how pleased they had all been to see him in the coffee house. Even the waiter had been pleased and had brought his usual order without having to be told. His wife said nothing but went on patiently serving him. Then he began somewhat to exaggerate the heartiness of the welcome he had received. He said things which, though not strictly true, had a good effect – not so much on her (she continued silently to serve him) as on himself. By the time he had finished eating and talking, he was perfectly reassured as to what had happened that morning. The little cloud of unease with which he had come home was dispelled. He realized now that no one had looked at him queerly, and that there had been no undertones in their 'Just see who is here.' It was only his over-sensitive nature that had made it seem like that.

He had always had a very sensitive nature: a poet's temperament. He was proud of it, but there was no denying that it had been the cause of many troubles to him – including the present one. The facts of the case were these: Sri Prakash, a gazetted government officer, had been suspended from his post in the State Ministry of Telecommunication while an inquiry was instituted regarding certain accusations against him. These were based on the words of a man who was a drunkard, a liar, and a convicted perjurer. His name was Goel and he was the father of a Miss Nimmi. Miss Nimmi had come to Sri Prakash to inquire about a possible vacancy as typist in his office. Sri Prakash had sincerely tried to help the girl, calling her for interviews several times, and the result of his good intentions had been that she had complained of his misbehaviour towards her. The father, after visiting Sri Prakash both in his office and at home and finding him not the man to yield to blackmail and extortion, had carried the complaint to Sri Prakash's superiors in the department. From there on events had taken their course. Naturally it was all extremely unpleasant for Sri Prakash – a family man, a husband and father of three respectably married daughters – but, as he was always telling his wife, he had no doubts that in the end truth and justice would prevail.

She never made any comment when he said that. She was by nature a silent woman: silent and virtuous. How virtuous! She was the ideal of all a mother and wife should be. He thanked God that he had it in him to appreciate her character. He worshipped her. He often told her so, and told everyone else too – his daughters, people in the office, sometimes even complete strangers (for instance, once a man he had shared a rickshaw with). Also how he was ready to tear himself into a thousand pieces, or lie down in the middle of the main bazaar by the clock tower and let all who came trample on him with their feet if by such an action he could save her one moment's anxiety. In this present misfortune there was of course a lot of anxiety. There was not only the moral hardship but also the practical one of having his salary held in arrears while the inquiry took its course. Already they had spent whatever his wife had managed to lay by and had had to sell the one or two pieces of jewellery that still remained from her dowry. Now they were dependent for their household expenses on whatever their sons-in-law could contribute. It was a humiliating position for a proud man, but what was to be done? There was no alternative, he could not allow his wife to starve. But when his daughters came to the house and untied the money from the ends of their saris to give to their mother, he could not restrain his tears from flowing. His daughters were not as sympathetic towards him as his wife. They made no attempts to comfort him but looked at him in a way that made him feel worse. Then he would leave them and go to lie down on his bed. His daughters stayed for a while, but he did not come out again. He could hear them talking to their mother, and sometimes he heard sounds like the mother weeping. These sounds were unbearable to him, and he had to cover his head with the pillow so as not to hear them.

After that first visit to the coffee house, he continued to go every day. It was good to meet his friends again. He had always loved company. In the past, when he was still king in his own office, people had dropped in on him there all day long. At eleven o'clock they had all adjourned to the coffee house where they had drunk many cups of coffee and smoked many cigarettes and talked on many subjects. He had talked the most, and everyone had listened to and applauded him. But nowadays everything was changed. It was not only that he could not afford to drink coffee or pay for his own cigarettes: other things too were not as they had been. He himself was not as he had been. He had always been so gay and made jokes at which everyone laughed. Once he had jumped up on the table and had executed a dance there. He had stamped his feet and made ankle-bell noises with his tongue. And how they had laughed, standing around him in a circle – his friends and other customers, even the waiters: they had clapped their hands and spurred him on till he had jumped from the table – hands extended like a diver – and landed amid cheers and laughter in the arms held out to catch him.

Although nothing like that happened now, he continued to visit the coffee house regularly every morning; soon he was going regularly every evening too. There was usually a large party of friends, but one evening when he went there was no one – only a waiter flicking around with his dirty cloth, and a silent old widower, a regular customer, eating vegetable cutlets. The waiter was surly – he always had been, even in the days when Sri Prakash had still been able to hand out tips – and it was only after repeated inquiries that he condescended to say that, didn't Sri Prakash know? Hadn't they told him? They had all gone to Moti Bagh for a moonlight picnic with mangoes. Sri Prakash slapped his forehead, pretending he had known about it but had forgotten. It was an unconvincing performance and the waiter sneered, but Sri Prakash could not worry about that now. He had to concentrate on getting himself out of the coffee house without showing how he was feeling.

He walked in the street by himself. It was evening, there was a lot of traffic and the shops were full. Hawkers with trays bumped in and out of the crowds on the sidewalks. On one side the sky was melting in a rush of orange while on the other the evening star sparkled, alone and aloof, like a jewel made of ice. Exquisite hour – hour of high thoughts and romantic feelings! It had always been so for Sri Prakash and was so still. Only where was he to go, who was there to share with him the longing for beauty that flooded his heart?

'Oh-ho, oh-ho! Just see who is here!'

Someone had bumped against him in the crowd, now stood and held his arms in a gesture of affectionate greeting. It was the last person Sri Prakash would have wished to meet: Goel, the father of Miss Nimmi, his accuser, his enemy, the cause of his ruin and tears. Goel seemed genuinely delighted by this meeting; he continued to hold Sri Prakash by the arms and even squeezed them to show his pleasure. Sri Prakash jerked himself free and hurried away. The other followed him; he protested at this unfriendliness, demanded to know its cause. He claimed a misunderstanding. He followed Sri Prakash so close that he trod on his heels. Then Sri Prakash stood still and turned round.

'Forgive me,' said Goel. He meant for treading on his heels; he even made the traditional self-humbling gesture of one seeking forgiveness. They stood facing each other. They were about the same height – both were short and plump, though Goel was flabbier. Like Sri Prakash, he also was bald as a ball.

Sri Prakash could hardly believe his ears: Goel was asking him to come home with him. He insisted, he said he had some bottles of country liquor at home, and what good luck that he should have run into Sri Prakash just at this moment when he had been wondering what good friend he could invite to come and share them with him? When Sri Prakash indignantly refused, tried to walk on, Goel held on to him. 'Why not?' he insisted. 'Where else will you go?'

Then Sri Prakash remembered where everyone else had gone. The moonlight picnic at Moti Bagh was an annual outing. The procedure was always the same: the friends hired a bus and, together with their baskets of mangoes and crates of local whisky, had themselves driven out to Moti Bagh. They sang boisterous songs all the way. At Moti Bagh they cut up some of the mangoes and sucked the juice out of others. Their mouths became sticky and sweet and this taste might have become unpleasant if they had not kept washing it out with the whisky. They became very rowdy. They waited for the moon to rise. When it did, their mood changed. Moti Bagh was a famous beauty spot, an abandoned and half-ruined palace built by a seventeenth-century prince at the height of his own glory and that of his dynasty. When the moon shone on it, it became spectral, a marble ghost that evoked thoughts of the passing of all earthly things. Poems were recited, sad songs sung; a few tears flowed. Someone played the flute – as a matter of fact, this was Sri Prakash who had always taken a prominent part in these outings. But this year they had gone without him.

Goel did not live in a very nice part of town. The bazaar, though once quite prosperous, now catered mainly for poorer people; the rooms on top of the shops had been converted into one-night hotels. Goel's house, which was in a network of alleys leading off from this bazaar, would have been difficult to find for anyone unfamiliar with the geography of the locality. The geography of his house was also quite intricate, as every available bit of space – in the courtyard, galleries, and on staircase landings – had been partitioned between different tenants. Goel and his daughter Miss Nimmi had one long narrow room to themselves; they had strung a piece of string halfway across to serve as both clothes-line and partition. At first Sri Prakash thought the room was empty, but after they had been there for some time Goel shouted 'Oy!' When he received no answer, he pushed aside the pieces of clothing hanging from the string and revealed Miss Nimmi lying fast asleep on a mat on the floor.

Goel had to shout several times before she woke up. Then she rose from the mat – very slowly, as if struggling up from the depths of a sea of sleep – and sat there, blinking. Her sari had slipped from her breasts, but she did not notice. She also did not notice that they had a visitor. She was always slow in everything, slow and heavy. Her father had to shout, 'Don't you see who has come!' She blinked a few more times, and then very, very slowly she smiled and very, very slowly she lifted the sari to cover her breasts.

Goel told her to find two glasses. She got up and rummaged around the room. After a time she said there was only one. Sri Prakash said it didn't matter, he had to go anyway; he said he was in a hurry, he had to catch a bus for Moti Bagh where his friends awaited him. He got up but his host pressed him down again, asking what was the point of going now, why not stay here, they would have a good time together. 'Look,' Goel said, 'I've got money.' He emptied out his pockets and he did have money – a wad of bank notes, God knew where they had come from. He let Sri Prakash look his fill at them before putting them back. He said let's go to Badshahbad, we'll take the liquor and mangoes and we'll have a moonlight picnic of our own. He got very excited by this Idea. Sri Prakash said neither yes nor no. Goel told Miss Nimmi to change into something nice, and she disappeared behind the clothes-line and got busy there. Sri Prakash did not look in that direction, but the room was saturated by her the way a store room in which ripe apples are kept becomes saturated by their savour and smell.

Badshahbad was not as far off as Moti Bagh – in fact, it was just at the outskirts of town and could be reached very quickly. It too was a deserted pleasure palace but had been built two centuries later than the one at Moti Bagh and as a rather gaudy imitation of it. However, now in the dark it looked just the same. The surrounding silence and emptiness, the smell of dust, the occasional jackal cry were also the same. At first Sri Prakash felt rather depressed, but his mood changed after he had drunk some of Goel's liquor. Goel was determined to have a good time, and Miss Nimmi, though silent, also seemed to be enjoying herself. She was cutting up the mangoes and eating rather a lot of them. The three of them sat in the dark, waiting for the moon to rise.

Goel fell into a reminiscent mood. He began to recall all the wonderful things he had done in his life: how he had sold a second-hand imported car for Rs.50,000, and once he had arranged false passports for a whole party of Sikh carpenters. All these activities had brought in fat commissions for himself – amply deserved, because everything had been achieved only through his good contacts. That was his greatest asset in life – his contacts, all the important people he had access to. He ticked them off on his fingers: the Under Secretary to the Welfare Ministry, the Deputy Minister of Mines and Fuel, all the top officers in the income tax department . . . He challenged Sri Prakash, he said: 'Name any big name, go as high as you like, and see if I don't know him.'

Sri Prakash got excited, he cried: 'My goodness! Big names – big people – whenever there was anything to be done, everyone said, "Ask Sri Prakash, he knows everyone, he has them all in his pocket." Once there was a function to felicitate our departmental Secretary on his promotion. The principal organizers came to me and said, "Sri Prakash, we need a VIP to grace the occasion." I replied, "I will get you the Chief Minister himself, just wait and see." And I did. I went to him, I said, "Sir, kindly give us the honour of your presence," and he replied, "Certainly, Sri Prakash, with pleasure." There and then he told his secretary to make a note of the appointment.'

'When I go into the Secretariat building,' Goel said, 'the peons stand up and salute. I don't bother with appointments. The personal assistant opens the big shot's door and says, "Sir, Goel has come." They know I don't come with empty hands. I slip it under their papers, no word spoken, they don't notice, I don't notice. The figures are all fixed, no need to haggle: 1,000 to an Under Secretary, 2,000 to a Deputy. Each has his price.'

Goel smiled and drank. Sri Prakash also drank. The liquor, illicitly distilled, had a foul and acrid taste. Sri Prakash remembered reading in the papers quite recently how a whole colony of labourers had been wiped out through drinking illicit country liquor. Nothing could be done for them, it had rotted them through and through.

Goel said: 'Let alone the Secretaries, there are also the Ministers to be taken care of. Some of them are very costly. Naturally, their term is short, no one can tell what will happen at the next elections. So their mouths are always wide open. You must be knowing Dev Kishan –'

'Dev Kishan!' Sri Prakash cried, 'He and I are like that! Like that!' He held up two fingers, pressed close together.

'There was some work in his Ministry, it was rather a tricky job and I was called in. I went to his house and came straight to the point. "Dev Kishan Sahib," I said –'

Sri Prakash suddenly lost his temper: 'Dev Kishan is not this type at all!' When Goel sniggered, he became more excited: 'A person like you would not understand a person like him at all. And I don't believe you went to his house –'

'Come with me right now!' Goel shouted. 'We will go together to his house and then you will see how he receives me –'

'Not Dev Kishan!' Sri Prakash shouted back. 'Someone else – not he –'

'He! The same!'

Although they were both shouting at the tops of their voices, Miss Nimmi went on placidly sucking mangoes. Probably the subject was of no interest to her; probably also she was used to people getting excited while drinking.

'As a matter of fact,' Goel sneered, 'shall I let you into a secret – his mouth is open wider than anyone's, they call him The Pit because he can never get enough, your Dev Kishan.'

'I don't believe you,' Sri Prakash said again, though not so fervently now. He really had no particular interest in defending this man. It was only that the mention of his name had called up a rather painful memory.

When his troubles had first begun, Sri Prakash had run around from one influential person to another. Most people would not receive him, and he had had to content himself with sitting waiting in their outer offices and putting his case to such of their clerical staff as would listen. Dev Kishan, however, was one of the few people who *had* received him. Sri Prakash had been ushered into his ministerial office which had two air-conditioners and an inscribed portrait of the President of India. Dev Kishan had sat behind an enormous desk, but he had not asked Sri Prakash to take the chair opposite. He had not looked at Sri Prakash either but had fixed his gaze above his head. Sri Prakash wanted to plead, to explain – he had come ready to do so – if necessary go down on his knees, but instead he sat quite still while Dev Kishan told him that a departmental inquiry must be allowed to proceed according to rule. Then Sri Prakash had quietly departed, passing through the outer office with his head lowered and with nothing to say for himself whatsoever. He had not spoken for a long while afterwards. He kept thinking – he was still thinking – of the way Dev Kishan had looked above his head. His eyes had seemed to be gazing far beyond Sri Prakash, deep into state matters, and Sri Prakash had felt like a fly that had accidentally got in and deserved to be swatted.

Goel did not want to quarrel any more. He had come on a picnic, he had spent money on liquor and mangoes and the hiring of a horse carriage to bring them here. He expected a good time in return. He refilled their glasses while remembering other outings he had enjoyed in the past. He told Sri Prakash of the time he and some friends had consumed one dozen bottles of liquor at a sitting and had become very merry. He nudged Sri Prakash and said, 'Girls were also brought.' He said this in a low voice, so that Miss Nimmi would not hear, and brought his face close to Sri Prakash. Sri Prakash felt a desire to throw the contents of his glass into this face. He imagined that the liquor contained acid and what would happen. He was filled with such strong emotion that something, some release was necessary: but instead of throwing the liquor in his host's face, he emptied it on the ground in a childishly angry gesture. Goel gave a cry of astonishment, Miss Nimmi stopped halfway in the sucking of a mango.

Just then the moon rose. The palace trembled into view and stood there melting in moonlight. Sri Prakash left his companions and went towards it as one drawn towards a mirage. It did not disappear as he approached, but it did turn out to be locked. He peered through the glass doors and could just make out the sleeping form of a watchman curled up on the floor. The interior was lit only by the palest beams filtering in from outside. By day there were too many curlicued arches and coloured chandeliers, too many plaster leaves and scrolls: but now in the moonlight everything looked as it should. Overcome by its beauty and other sensations, Sri Prakash sat down on the steps and wept. He had his face buried in his hands and could not stop.

After a while Goel joined him. He sat beside him on the steps. Goel began to talk about the passing away of all earthly things, the death of kings and pariah dogs alike. He waved his hand towards the abandoned pleasure palace, he said, 'Where are they all, where have they gone?' Although these reflections were perfectly acceptable – probably at this very moment Sri Prakash's friends were making the same ones at their picnic in Moti Bagh – nevertheless, coming from Goel, Sri Prakash did not want to hear them. He felt Goel had no right to them. What did he know of philosophy and history – indeed of anything except drinking and bribery? Sri Prakash lifted his head; irritation had dried his tears.

He said, 'Do you know what the Nawab Sahib Ghalib Hasan said when they came to tell him the enemy was at the gate?'

Goel did not know – he knew nothing – he hardly knew who the Nawab Sahib Ghalib Hasan was. To cover his ignorance, he waved his hand again and repeated, 'Where are they all, where have they gone?'

Sri Prakash began to instruct him. He knew a lot about the Nawab who had always been one of his heroes. Abandoning the palace at Moti Bagh, the Nawab had built himself this costly new palace here at Badshahbad and filled it with his favourites. There had been poets and musicians and dancing girls, cooks and wine tasters, a French barber, an Irish cavalry officer; also a menagerie which included a lion and an octopus. The Nawab himself wrote poetry which he read aloud to his courtiers and to the girls who massaged his feet and scented them. It was during such a session that messengers had come to tell him the enemy was at the gate. He had answered by reciting these verses which Sri Prakash now quoted to Goel: '*When in her arms, what is the drum of war? the sword of battle? nay, even the ancient whistle of bony-headed Death?*'

'Ah!' said Goel, laying his hand on his chest to show how deeply he was affected.

Quite pleased with this reaction, Sri Prakash repeated the quotation. Then he quoted more verses written by the Nawab. Goel turned out to be an appreciative listener. He swayed his head and sometimes shouted out loud in applause the way connoisseurs shout when a musician plays a note, a dancer executes a step showing more than human skill. Sri Prakash began rather to enjoy himself. It had been a long time since anyone had cared to listen to him reciting poetry. His wife and daughters – he had always regretted it – had no taste for poetry at all; not for music either, which he loved so much.

But then Goel made a mistake. Overcome by appreciation, he repeated a line that Sri Prakash had just quoted to him: '*O rose of my love, where have your petals fallen?*' But Goel's voice, which was vulgar and drunken, degraded these beautiful words. Suddenly Sri Prakash turned on him. He called him all the insulting names he could think of such as liar, swindler, blackmailer, and drunkard. Goel continued to sit there placidly, even nodding once or twice as if he agreed. Perhaps he was too drunk to hear or care; or perhaps he had been called these names so often that he had learned to accept them. But this passive attitude was frustrating for Sri Prakash; he ran out of insults and fell silent.

After a while he said, 'Why did you do it? For myself I don't care – but what about my wife and family? Why should their lives be ruined? Tell me that.'

Goel had no answer except a murmur of sympathy. As if grateful for this sympathy, Sri Prakash began to tell him moving incidents from his married life. They all illustrated the fact that his wife was an angel, a saint. The more Sri Prakash knew her the more he marvelled. In her he had studied all womanhood and had come to the conclusion that women are goddesses at whose feet men must fall down and worship. He himself had got into the habit of doing so quite often. Not now so much any more – his spirits were too low, he felt himself unworthy – but in the past when things were still well with him. Then he would come home from a late night outing with friends to find her nodding in the kitchen, waiting for him to serve him his meal. He would be overcome with love and admiration for her. With a cry that startled her from her sleep, he would fall down at her feet and lift the hem of her garment to press it to his lips. Although she tried to make him rise, he would not do so; he wanted to stay down there to make it clear how humble he was in relation to her greatness. Then she undressed him right there where he lay on the floor and tried to get him to bed. Sometimes she had to lift him up in her arms – he had always been a small man – and he loved that, he lay in her arms with his eyes shut and felt himself a child enfolded in its mother's love. 'Mother,' he would murmur in ecstasy, as she staggered with him to the bed.

Goel had fallen asleep. Sri Prakash was sorry, for although he did not esteem Goel as a person, he felt the need of someone to talk to. Not only about his wife; there were many other subjects, many thoughts he longed to share. It was like that with him sometimes. His heart was so full, so weighted with feeling, that he longed to fling it somewhere – to someone – or, failing someone, up to the moon that was so still and looked down at him from heaven. But there *was* someone; there was Miss Nimmi. She had remained where they had left her by the basket of mangoes and the bottles. She had finished eating mangoes. She did not seem to mind being left alone nor did she seem impatient to go home but just content to wait till they were ready. She sat with her hands folded and looked in front of her at the bare and dusty earth.

This patient pose was characteristic of her. It was the way she had sat in Sri Prakash's office when she had come to ask him for a job. That was why he had kept telling her to come back: to have the pleasure of seeing her in his office, ready to wait for as long as he wanted. She had reminded him of a chicken sitting plump and cooked on a dish on a table. By the third day he had begun to call her his little chicken. 'Fall to!' he would suddenly cry and make the motion of someone who grabbed from a dish and fell to eating. Of course she hadn't known what he meant, but she had smiled all the same.

'Fall to!' he cried now, as he joined her on the ground among the empty bottles. And now too she smiled. Like the palace floating behind her, she was transformed and made beautiful by moonlight. It veiled her rather coarse features and her skin pitted by an attack of smallpox in childhood.

He moved up close to her. Her breasts, as warm as they were plump, came swelling out of her bodice, and he put his hand on them: but respectfully, almost with awe, so that there was no harm in her leaving it there. 'Where is Papa?' she asked.

'Asleep. You need not worry.'

Very gently and delicately he stroked her breasts. Then he kissed her mouth, tasting the mango there. She let all this be done to her. It had been the same in his office – she had always kept quite still, only occasionally glancing over her shoulder to make sure no one was coming. She did the same now, glanced towards her father.

'You need not worry,' Sri Prakash said again. 'He has drunk a lot. He won't wake up.'

'He *is* waking up.'

They both looked towards Goel left alone in front of the palace. He was trying to stretch himself out more comfortably along the steps, but instead he rolled down them. It was not far, and the ground seemed to receive him softly; he did not move but remained lying there.

'Is he all right?' Miss Nimmi asked.

'Of course he is all right. What could happen to *him*?' Sri Prakash spoke bitterly. He took his hand away from her; his mood was spoiled. He said, 'Why did you let him do it to me? What harm have I done to him? Or to you? Answer.'

She had no answer. There was none, he knew. She could not say that he had harmed her, had done anything bad. Was it bad to love a person? To adore and worship the way he had done? Those moments in his office had been pure, and his feelings as sacred as if he were visiting a shrine to place flowers there at the feet of the goddess.

'Why?' he asked again. 'What did I do to you?'

'That is what Papa kept asking: "What did he do to you?" When I said you did nothing, he got very angry. He kept asking questions, he would not stop. Sometimes he woke me up at night to ask.'

Sri Prakash pressed his face into her neck. 'What sort of questions?' he murmured from out of there.

'He asked, "Where did he put his hand?" When I couldn't remember, he asked, "Here?" So I had to say yes. Because you did.'

'Yes,' he murmured. 'Yes I did.' And he did it again, and she let him.

She said, 'Papa shouted and screamed. He hit his head against the wall. But it wasn't only that – there were other things. He was going through a lot of other troubles at that time. Two men kept coming. They told him he would have to go to jail again. Papa is very frightened of going to jail. When he was there before, he came out *so* thin.' She showed how with her finger. 'He lost fifty pounds in there.'

Sri Prakash remembered Goel's demented state in those days. He had come to him many times, threatening, demanding money; he had looked like a madman, and Sri Prakash – still sitting secure behind his desk then, safe in his office – had treated him like one. 'Go to hell,' he had told him. 'Do what you like.' And the last time he had said that, Goel had pounded the desk between them and thrust his face forward into Sri Prakash's: 'Then you will see!' he had screamed. 'You will see and learn!' He had really looked like a madman – even with foam at his mouth. Sri Prakash had felt uneasy but nevertheless had laughed in the other's face and blown a smoke ring.

Miss Nimmi said, 'I was very frightened. Papa was in a terrible mood. He said he would teach you a lesson you would not forget. He said, "Why should I be the only person in this world to suffer blows and kicks? Let someone else also have a few of these." But afterwards those two men stopped coming, and then Papa was much better. He was cheerful again and brought me a present, a little mirror like a heart. And then he was sorry about you. He tried to go to your office again, to change his report, but they said it was too late. I cried when he came back and told me that.'

'You cried? You cried for me?' Sri Prakash was moved.

'Yes, and Papa also was sad for you.'

Goel was still lying at the foot of the steps where he had rolled down. Sri Prakash did not feel unkindly towards him – on the contrary, he even felt quite sorry for him. But his greatest wish with regard to him at the moment was that he would go on sleeping. Sri Prakash did not want to be disturbed in his private conversation with Miss Nimmi. In his mind he prayed for sufficient time, that they might not be interrupted by her father.

'I cried so much that Papa did everything he could to make me feel better. He brought me more presents – sweets and a piece of cloth. When still I went on crying, he said, "What is to be done? It is his fate."'

'He is right,' Sri Prakash said. He too spoke only to soothe her. He did not want Miss Nimmi to be upset in any way. He just wanted her to be as she always was and to keep still so that he could adore her to his heart's content. He raised the hem of her sari to his lips, the way he did to his wife; and he also murmured 'Goddess' to her the way he did to his wife – worshipping all women in her, their goodness and beauty.

In a Great Man's House

The letter came in the morning, but when she told Khan Sahib about it, he said she couldn't go. There was no time for argument because someone had come to see him – a research scholar from abroad writing a thesis on Indian musical theory – so she was left to brood by herself. First she thought bad thoughts about Khan Sahib. Then she thought about the wedding. It was to take place in her home town, in the old house where she had grown up and where her brother now lived with his family. She had a very clear vision of this house and the tree in its courtyard to which a swing was affixed. There was always a smell of tripe being cooked (her father had been very fond of it); a continuous sound of music, of tuning and singing and instrumental practice, came out of the many dark little rooms. Now these rooms would be packed with family members, flocking from all over the country to attend the wedding. They would all have a good time together. Only she was to be left here by herself in her silent, empty rooms – alone except for Khan Sahib and her thieving servants.

Later in the morning her sister Roxana, who of course had also had a letter, came to discuss plans. Roxana came with her eldest daughter and her youngest son and was very excited, looking forward to the journey and the wedding. She cried out when Hamida told her that Khan Sahib would not allow her to go.

Hamida said, 'It is the time of the big Music Conference. He says he needs me here,' She added: 'For what I don't know.'

Roxana shook her head at such behaviour. Then she inclined it towards Khan Sahib's practice room from which she could hear the sound of voices. She asked, 'Who is with him?' Her neck was craned forward, her earrings trembled, she wore the strained expression she always did when she was poking into someone else's business, especially Khan Sahib's.

'An American,' Hamida replied with a shrug. 'He has come to speak about something scholarly with him. Don't, Baba,' she admonished Roxana's little boy who was smearing his fingers against the locked glass cabinet in which she kept precious things for show.

Roxana strained to listen to the voices, but when she could not make out anything, she began to shake her head again. She said, 'He must allow. He can't say no to you.'

'Very big people will be coming for the Conference.'

'But a niece's wedding! A brother's daughter!'

'They will all be coming to the house to visit Khan Sahib. Of course someone will have to be there for the cooking and other arrangements. Who can trust servants,' she concluded with a sigh.

Roxana, who had no servants, puckered her mouth.

'Don't, Baba!' Hamida said again to the child who was doing dreadful damage with his sticky fingers to her polished panes.

'He wants to play,' Roxana said. 'He will need some new little silk clothes for the wedding. And this child also,' she added, indicating her meek daughter sitting beside her. The girl did look rather shabby, but Hamida gave no encouragement. So then Roxana nudged her daughter and said, 'You must ask auntie nicely – nicely,' and she leered to show her how. The girl was ashamed and lowered her eyes. Hamida was both ashamed and irritated. Her gold bangles jingled angrily as she unlocked her cabinet and took out the Japanese plastic doll Baba had been clamouring for. 'Now sit quiet,' she admonished him, and he did so.

Roxana leaned forward again with her greedy look of curiosity. Khan Sahib's visitor was leaving: they could hear Khan Sahib's loud hearty voice seeing him off from the front of the house.

Then Khan Sahib returned into the house and walked through his practice room into the back room where the women sat. Roxana at once pulled her veil over her head and simpered. She always simpered in his presence: not only was he an elder brother-in-law but he was also the great man in the family.

Condescending and gracious, he did honour to both roles. He pinched the niece's cheek and swept Baba up into his arms. He laughed 'Ha-ha!' at Baba who however was frightened of this uncle with the large moustache and loud voice. After laughing at him, Khan Sahib did not know what to do with him so he handed him over to Hamida who put him back on the floor.

'How is my brother?' he asked Roxana. He meant his brother-in-law – Roxana's husband – who was also a musician but in a very small way with a very small job in All India Radio.

'What shall I say: poor man,' Roxana replied. It was her standard reply to Khan Sahib's queries on this subject. Her husband was a very humble, self-effacing man so it was up to her to be on the look-out on his behalf.

Hamida, who felt that all requests to Khan Sahib should come only through herself, did not wish to encourage this conversation. In any case, she now had things of her own to say: 'They are leaving next week,' she informed her husband. 'They are going by train. The others will also be leaving from Bombay at the same time. Everyone is going of course. Sayyida has even postponed her operation.'

Khan Sahib said to Roxana, 'Ask my brother to come and see me. There may be something for him at the Music Conference.'

'God knows it is needed. There will be all sorts of expenses for the wedding. For myself it doesn't matter but at least these children should have some decent clothes to go to my brother's house.'

'Well well,' Khan Sahib reassured her. He looked at the niece with a twinkle: he had very fat cheeks and when he was good-humoured, as now, his eyes quite disappeared in them. But when he was not, then these same eyes looked large and rolled around. He told Hamida: 'You had better take her to the shops. Some pretty little pink veils and blouses,' he promised the girl and winked at her playfully. 'She will look like a little flower.' He had always longed for a daughter, and when he spoke to young girls, he was tender and loving.

'I can leave her with you now,' Roxana said with a sigh of sacrifice.

'No, today I'm busy,' Hamida said.

'See that you are a good girl,' Roxana told the girl. 'I don't want to hear any bad reports.' She got up and adjusted her darned veil. 'Come, Baba,' she said. 'Give that little doll back to auntie, it is hers.'

Baba began to cry and Khan Sahib said, 'No no it belongs to Baba, take it, child.' But Hamida had already taken it away from him and swiftly locked it back into her cabinet. She also lost no time in ushering her sister out of the house. The girl followed them.

'When should I send him to you?' Roxana called back to Khan Sahib. He did not hear her because of Baba's loud cries; but Hamida said, 'I will send word.'

'You can stay till tomorrow or even the day after if she needs you,' Roxana told her daughter.

The girl had blushed furiously. She said, 'Auntie is busy.'

Roxana ignored her and walked out with Baba in her arms. When the girl tried to follow, Hamida said, 'You can stay,' though not very graciously. She didn't look at her again – she had no time, she had to hurry back to Khan Sahib. There was a lot left she had to say to him.

He was lying on his bed, resting. She said, 'I must go. What will people say? Everyone will think there has been some quarrel in the family.'

'It is not possible.' His eyes were shut and his stomach, rising like a dome above the bed, breathed up and down peacefully.

'But my own niece! My own brother's own daughter!'

'You are needed here.'

She turned from him and began to tidy up his crowded dressing-table. Actually, it was very tidy already – she did it herself every morning – but she nervously moved a few phials and jars about while thinking out her next move. She could see him in the mirror. He looked like an immoveable mountain. What chance did she have against him? Her frail hands, loaded with rings, trembled. Then she began to tremble all over. She remembered similar scenes in the past – so many! so many! – when she had desperately wanted something and he had lain like that, mountainously, on his bed.

He said, 'Massage my legs.'

She was holding one of his phials of scent. She was overcome by the desire to fling it into the mirror – and then sweep all his scents and oils and hair-dyes off the table and throw them around and smash a lot of glass. Of course she didn't; she put the bottle down, though her hands trembled more than ever. Nowadays she always overcame these impulses. It had not been so in the past: then she had often been violent. Once she really had smashed all the bottles on his dressing-table. It had been a holocaust, and two servants had had to spend many hours cleaning and picking up the splinters. For weeks afterwards the room was saturated in flowery essences, and some of the stains had never come out. But what good had it done her? None. So nowadays she never threw things.

'The right leg,' he said from the bed.

'I can't,' she said.

'Tcha, you're useless.'

She swung round from the mirror: 'Then why do you want me here? If I'm useless why should I stay for your Conference!'

He continued to look peaceful. It was always that way: he was so confident, so relaxed in his superior strength. 'Come here,' he said. When she approached, he pointed at his right leg. She squatted by the side of his bed and began to massage him. But she really was no good at it. Even when she went to it with good will (which was not the case at present), her arms got tired very quickly. She also tended to become impatient quite soon.

'Harder, *harder*,' he implored. 'At least try.'

Instead she left off. She remained on the floor and buried her head in his mattress. He didn't look at her but groped with his hands at her face; when he felt it wet, he clicked his tongue in exasperation. He said, 'What is the need for this? What is so bad?'

Everything, it seemed to her, was bad. Not only the fact that he wouldn't let her go to the wedding, but so many other things as well: her whole life. She buried her head deeper. She said, 'My son, my little boy.' That was the worst of all, the point it seemed to her at which the sorrow of her life came to a head.

It had been the occasion of their worst quarrel (the time when she had broken all his bottles). Khan Sahib had insisted that the boy be sent away for education to an English-type boarding school in the hills. Hamida had fought him every inch of the way. She could not, would not be parted from Sajid. He was her only child, she could never have another. His birth had been very difficult: she had been in labour for two days and finally there had to be a Caesarian operation and both of them had nearly died. For his first few years Sajid had been very delicate, and she could not bear to let him out of her sight for a moment. She petted him, oiled him, dressed him in little silk shirts; she would not let him walk without shoes and socks and would not let him play with other children for fear of infection. But he grew into a robust boy who wanted to run out and play robust games. When she tried to stop him, he defied her and they had tremendous quarrels and she frequently lost her temper and beat him mercilessly.

'He will be coming home for his holiday soon,' Khan Sahib said. 'He will be here for two weeks.'

'Two weeks! What is two weeks! When my heart aches for him – my arms are empty –'

'Go now,' said Khan Sahib who had heard all this before.

'You want only one thing: to take everything you can away from me. To leave me with nothing. That is your only happiness and joy in life.'

'Go go go,' said Khan Sahib.

When she went into the other room, Hamida was surprised to see the girl sitting there. She had forgotten all about her. She was sitting very humbly on the edge of Hamida's grand overstuffed blue-and-silver brocade sofa. She was studying the photograph of Sajid, a beautiful colour-tinted studio portrait in a silver frame. When Hamida came in, she quickly replaced it on its little table as if she had done something wrong. And indeed Hamida picked it up again and inspected it for fingermarks and then wiped it carefully with the end of her veil.

'He is coming home soon for his holidays,' she informed the girl.

'Then he will be there for the wedding?'

Hamida frowned. She said, 'It will be the time of the big Music Conference. His father will want him to be here.' She spoke as if the wedding was very much inferior in importance and interest to the Music Conference.

'Look,' she told the girl. She opened her work-basket and took out a fine lawn kurta which she was embroidering. 'It is for him. Sajid.' She spread it out with an air as if it were a great privilege for her niece to be allowed to look at it. And indeed the girl seemed to feel it to be so. She breathed 'Oh!' in soft wonder. Hamida's work was truly exquisite; she was embroidering tiny bright flowers like stars intertwined with delicate leaves and branches.

'Can you do it?' Hamida questioned. 'Is your mother teaching you?'

'She is not very good.'

'No,' Hamida said, smiling as she remembered Roxana's rough untidy work. 'She never worked hard enough. Always impatient to be off somewhere and play. Without hard work no good results are achieved,' she lectured the girl.

'Please teach me, auntie,' the girl begged, looking up at Hamida with her sad childish eyes. Hamida was quite pleased, but she spoke sternly: 'You have to sit for many hours and if I don't like your work I shall unpick it and you will have to start again from the beginning. Well we shall see,' she said as the girl looked willing and humble. Suddenly a thought struck her, and she leaned forward to regard her more closely: 'Why are you so thin?' she demanded.

The girl's cheeks were wan – which was perhaps why her eyes looked so large. Her arms and wrists were as frail as the limbs of a bird. Hamida wondered whether she suffered from some hidden illness; next moment she wondered whether she got enough to eat. Oh that was a dreadful thought – that this child, her own sister's daughter, might not be getting sufficient food! Her father was poor, her mother was a bad manager and careless and thoughtless and not fit to run a household or look after children though she had so many.

Hamida began to question her niece closely. She asked how much milk was taken in the house every day; she asked about butter, biscuits, and fruit. The girl said oh yes, there was a lot of everything always, more than any of them could eat; but when she said it, she lowered her eyes away from her aunt like a person hiding something, and after a time she became quite silent and did not answer any more questions. What was she hiding? What was she covering up? Hamida became irritated with her and she spoke sharply now, but that only made the girl close up further.

The servant came in with a telegram. He gave it to Hamida who held it in one hand while the other flew to her beating heart. Wild thoughts – of Sajid, of accidents and hospitals – rushed around in her head. She went into the bedroom and woke up Khan Sahib. When she said telegram, he at once sat up with a start. His hands also trembled though he said that it was probably something to do with the Music Conference; he said that nowadays everything was done by telegram, modern people no longer wrote letters. She helped him put on his reading-glasses and then he slowly spelled out the telegram which continued to tremble in his hands.

But it was from Hamida's brother, asking her to start as soon as possible. Evidently they needed her help very urgently for the wedding preparations. Khan Sahib tossed the telegram into her lap and lay down to sleep again. Now he was cross to have been woken up. Hamida remained sitting on the edge of the bed. She was full of thoughts which she would have liked very much to share with him, but his huge back was turned to her forbiddingly.

She *had* to go. She could not not go. Her family needed her; she was always the most important person at these family occasions. They all ran around in a dither or sat and wrung their hands till she arrived and began to give orders. She was not the eldest in the family, but she was the one who had the most authority. Although quite tiny, she held herself very erect and her fine-cut features were usually severe. As Khan Sahib's wife, she was also the only one among them to hold an eminent position. The rest of them were as shabby and poor as Roxana and her husband. They were all musicians, but none of them was successful, and they eked out a living by playing at weddings and functions and taking in pupils and whatever else came their way.

'They really want me,' she said to Khan Sahib's sleeping back. Let him pretend not to hear, but her heart was so full – she had to speak. 'Not like you,' she said. 'For you what am I except a servant to keep your house clean and cook for your guests.' She gave him a chance to reply, but of course she knew he wouldn't. 'Just try and get your paid servants to do one half of the work that I do. All they are good for is to eat up your rice and lick up your butter, oh at that they are first-class maestros if I were not there to see and know everything. Well you will find out when I have gone,' she concluded.

To her surprise Khan Sahib stirred; he said, 'Gone where?'

Actually she had meant when I have gone from this earth, but now she took advantage of his mistake: 'Gone to my brother's house for my niece's wedding, where else,' she said promptly.

'You are not going.'

'Who says no? Who is there that has the right to say no!' She shrieked on this last, but then remembered the girl in the next room. She lowered her voice – which however had the effect of making it more intense and passionate: 'There is no work for me here. No place for me at all. Ever since you have snatched away my son from me, I have sat as a stranger in your house with no one to care whether I am alive or what has happened.'

She was really moved by her own words but at the same time remained alert to sounds from the kitchen where the servant was up to God knew what mischief. There was no peace at all – not a moment for private thought or conversation – she had to be on the watch all the time. She got up from the bed and went into the kitchen. She looked at the servant suspiciously, then opened the refrigerator to see if he had been watering the milk. When she saw the jug full of milk, she remembered the underfed girl in the next room. She gave some orders to the servant and became very busy. She made milk-shake and fritters. She enjoyed doing it – she always enjoyed being in her kitchen which was very well equipped with modern gadgets. She loved having these things and did not allow anyone else to touch them but looked after them herself as if they were children.

The girl said she wasn't hungry. She said this several times, but when Hamida had coaxed and scolded her enough, she began to eat. It was a pleasure to watch her, she enjoyed everything so much. Hamida suddenly did an unexpected thing – she leaned forward and tenderly brushed a few strands of hair from the girl's forehead. The girl was surprised (Hamida was not usually demonstrative) and looked up from her plate with a shy, questioning glance.

'You are like my Sajid,' Hamida said as if some explanation were called for. 'He also – how he loved my fritters – how he licks and enjoys. Oh poor boy, God alone knows what rubbish they give him to eat in that school. English food,' she said. 'Boiled – in water.'

She stuck out her tongue in distaste. It was one of her disappointments that Sajid did not complain more about the school food. Of course when he came home he did full justice to her cooking, but when she tried to draw him out on the subject of his school diet, he did not say what she desired to hear. He just shrugged and said it was okay. He always called it 'grub'. 'The grub's okay,' he said. She hated that word the way she hated all the English slang words which he used so abundantly, deliberately, knowing she could not understand them (she had little English). 'Grub,' she mimicked – and translated into Urdu: 'Dog's vomit.' He laughed. She would have liked to cry over his emaciated appearance, but the fact was he didn't look emaciated – his face was plump, and his cheeks full of colour.

Not like this poor girl. She looked at the child's thin neck, her narrow little shoulders; she sighed and said, 'You're seventeen now, you were born the year before father went.' It was certainly time to arrange for her. Hamida thought wistfully how well she herself would be able to do so. She would make many contacts and look over many prospective families and choose the bridegroom very carefully. And then what a trousseau she would get together for her: what materials she would choose, what ornaments! There was nothing like that for a boy. Even now Sajid did her a big favour if he consented to wear one of the kurtas she embroidered for him. He preferred his school blazer and belt with Olympic buckle.

'I was married by seventeen,' she told the girl. 'So was Roxana, so were we all. Look at you – who will marry you –' She lifted the girl's forearm and held it up for show. The girl smiled, blushed, turned aside her face. Hamida began to question her again. 'What does she give you in the morning? And then afterwards? And in between?' When the girl again became stubborn and silent, Hamida scolded her gently: 'You can tell me. Don't I love you as much as she does, aren't you my own little daughter too, my precious jewel? Why hide anything from me?' She took the end of her veil and wiped a rim of milk from her niece's lips. She was deeply moved, so was the girl. They sat closer together, the niece leaned against her aunt shyly. 'You must tell me everything,' Hamida whispered.

'Last Friday –' the girl began.

'Yes?'

'They both cried.' Her lip trembled but at Hamida's urging she went on bravely: 'Baba had an upset stomach and she wanted to cook some special dish for him. But when she asked Papa for the money to buy a little more milk, he didn't have. So they both cried and we all cried too.'

'And I!' Hamida cried with passion. 'Perhaps I'm dead that my own family should sit and cry for a drop of milk!' Then she stopped short, frowning to recollect something; she said, 'She did come last Friday.'

She remembered it clearly because she had got very cross with Roxana who had arrived in a motor-rickshaw for which Hamida had then had to pay. When Hamida had finished scolding, Roxana had asked her for a hundred rupees and then patiently listened to some more scolding. She cried a bit when Hamida finally said she could only have fifty, but when she left she was very cheerful again and knotted the fifty rupees into the end of her veil. Hamida had climbed on the roof to spy on her, and it was as she had suspected – when Roxana thought she was unobserved, she hailed another motor-rickshaw and went rattling off, with her veil fluttering in the wind. Hamida worried that the money might come untied; she almost had a vision of it happening and the notes flying away and Roxana not even noticing because she was enjoying her ride so much.

Khan Sahib was calling. He had woken up from his nap and required attendance. He informed Hamida that visitors were expected and that preparations would have to be made for their entertainment. When she asked when they were expected, he answered impatiently, 'Now, now.' She made no comment or complaint. People were always coming to visit Khan Sahib. She took no interest in who they were but only in what and how much they would eat. She sent in platters of food and refilled them when they came out empty. She rarely bothered to peep into the room and did not try to overhear any of their conversation. Besides food, her only other concern was the clothes in which Khan Sahib would receive them.

She scanned his wardrobe now, the rows and rows of kurtas and shawls. He needed a lot of fine clothes always – for his concerts, receptions, functions, meetings with Ministers and other important people. It was her responsibility to have them made and keep them in order and decide what he was to wear on each occasion. But if he was not pleased with her choice, he would fling the clothes she had taken out for him across the room. Then she would have to take out others, and it was not unlikely that they too would meet with the same fate. Sometimes the floor was strewn with rejected clothes. Hamida did not care much. She let him curse and shout and throw things to his heart's content; afterwards she would call the servant to come in and clear up, while she herself sat in the kitchen and drank a cup of tea to relax herself.

But today his mood was good. He put up his arms like a child to allow her to change his kurta, and stretched out his legs so she could pull off his old churidars and fit on the new ones. He was in such a jolly mood that he even gave her a playful pinch while she was dressing him; when she pushed him away, he cackled and did it again. She pretended to be angry but did not really mind. Actually she was relieved that such childish amusements were all he required of her nowadays. It had not always been so. When they were younger, they had rarely managed to get through his toilette without her having to submit to a great deal more than only pinching. But now Khan Sahib was too heavy and fat to be able to indulge himself in this way.

She began to tell him about Roxana's family. She repeated what the girl had told her. 'What is to become of them?' Hamida asked. She reproached him with not putting enough work in Roxana's husband's way. It was so easy for Khan Sahib to arrange for him to accompany other musicians at concerts (Roxana's husband played the tabla) or help him to get students. Khan Sahib defended himself. He reminded her of the many occasions when he had arranged something for his brother-in-law who had then failed to turn up – either because he had forgotten or because he had become engrossed in some amusement.

Hamida had to admit, 'He is like that.' She sighed, but Khan Sahib laughed: he was fond of his brother-in-law who in return adored, worshipped him. When Khan Sahib sang, his brother-in-law listened in ecstasy – really it was almost like a religious ecstasy, and tears of joy coursed down his face that God should allow human beings to reach so high.

'Brother too is the same,' Hamida said. 'How will they manage? The bridegroom's family will arrive and nothing will be done and we shall be disgraced. I *must* go.'

Khan Sahib did not answer but stretched out one foot. She rubbed talcum powder into the heel to enable her to slip the leg of his tight churidars over it more easily.

'They are like children,' she said. 'Only enjoyment, enjoyment – of serious work they know nothing . . . Have you seen that poor child?' She jerked her head towards the room where the girl sat. 'Seventeen years old, no word of any marriage, and thin as a dry thorn. Come here!' she called through the door. 'In here! Your uncle wants to see you!'

The door opened very slowly. The girl slipped through and stood there, overcome. 'Right in,' Hamida ordered. The girl pressed herself against the wall. Hamida, anxious for her to make a good impression, was irritated to see her standing there trembling and blushing and looking down at her own feet. 'Look up,' Hamida said sharply. 'Show your face.'

'Aie-aie-aie,' Khan Sahib said. He spoke to the girl as if she were some sweet little pet; he also made sounds with his lips as if coaxing a shy pet with a lump of sugar. 'You must eat. Meat. Buttermilk. Rice pudding. Then you will become big and strong like Uncle.' He was the only one to enjoy the joke. 'Bring me these,' he said, pointing to something on his dressing-table.

When the girl didn't know what he meant, Hamida became more irritated with her and cried out impatiently, 'His rings! His rings!'

'Gently, gently,' said Khan Sahib. 'Don't frighten the child. That's right,' he said as the girl took up the rings and brought them to him. He spread out his hands for her. 'Can you put them on? Do you know which one goes where? I'll teach you. The diamond – that's right – on this finger, this big big fat finger – that's very clever, oh very good – and the ruby here on this one – and now the other hand . . . '

He made it a game, and the girl smiled a bit as she fitted the massive rings on to his massive fingers. Hamida watched with pleasure. She loved the way Khan Sahib spoke to the child. He never spoke like that to his wife. His manner with her was always brusque, but with this girl he was infinitely gentle – as if she were a flower he was afraid of breaking, or one of those soft, soft notes that only he knew how to sing.

Later, when his guests had arrived and everything had been prepared and sent in to them where they reclined on carpets in the practice-room, it was Hamida's turn to lie on the bed. She felt very tired and had a headache. Such sudden fits of exhaustion came over her frequently. She was physically a very frail, delicate lady. She lay with the curtains drawn and her eyes shut; her temples throbbed, so did her heart. Sounds of music and conversation came from the front of the house but here, in these back rooms where she lived, it was quite silent. Often at such times she felt very lonely and longed to have someone with her to whom she could say, 'Oh I'm so tired,' or 'My head is aching.' But she was always alone. Even when Sajid was home from school, he usually stayed with the men in the front part of the house, or went out to play cricket with his friends; and when he did stay with her, he clattered about and made so much noise – he was an active, vigorous boy – that her rest was disturbed and she soon lost her temper with him and drove him away.

But today, when she opened her eyes, she saw the girl sitting beside her on the bed. Hamida said, 'My head is aching,' and the girl breathed, 'Ah poor auntie,' and these words, spoken with such gentle pity, passed over Hamida like a cooling sea-breeze on a scorching day. In a weak voice she requested the girl to rub her temples with eau-de-cologne. The girl obeyed so eagerly and performed this task with so much tenderness and love that Hamida's fatigue became a luxury. The noise from the practice-room seemed to come from far away. Here there was no sound except from the fan turning overhead. The silence – the smell of the eau-de-cologne – the touch of the girl's fingers soothing her temples: these gave Hamida a sense of intimacy, of being close to another human being, that was quite new to her.

She put up her hand and touched the girl's cheek. She said, 'You don't look like your mother.' Roxana, though she was scrawny now, had been a hefty girl. Also her skin had been rather coarse, whereas this girl's was smooth as a lotus petal. The girl's features too were much more delicate than Roxana's had ever been.

'Everyone says I look like –'

'Yes?'

'Oh no,' the girl said blushing. 'It's not true. You're much, much more beautiful.'

Hamida was pleased, but she said depreciatingly, 'Nothing left now.'

She sat up on the bed so that she could see herself in the mirror and the girl beside her. Their two faces were reflected in the heart-shaped glass surrounded by a frame carved with leaves and flowers; because it was dim in the room – the curtains were drawn – they looked like a faded portrait of long ago. It was true that there was a resemblance. If Hamida had had a daughter, she might have looked like this girl.

She fingered the girl's kameez. It was of coarse cotton and the pattern was also not very attractive. Hamida clicked her tongue: 'Is this how you are going to attend the wedding?' But when she saw the girl shrinking into herself again, she went on, 'Your mother is to blame. All right, she has no money but she has no taste either. This is not the colour to buy for a young girl. You should wear only pale blue, pink, lilac. Wait, I'll show you.'

She opened her wardrobe. The shelves were as packed and as neatly arranged as Khan Sahib's. She pulled out many silk and satin garments and threw them on the bed. The girl looked on in wonder. Hamida ordered her to take off her clothes and laughed when she was shy. But she respected her modesty, the fact that she turned her back and crossed her little arms over her breasts: Hamida herself had also been very modest always. It was a matter of pride to her that not once in their married life had Khan Sahib seen her naked.

She made the girl try on many of her clothes. They all fitted perfectly – aunt and niece had the same childish body with surprisingly full breasts and hips. Hamida made her turn this way and that. She straightened a neckline here, a collar there, she turned up sleeves and plucked at hems, frowning to hide her enjoyment of all this activity. The girl however made no attempt to hide it – she looked in the mirror and laughed and how her eyes shone! But there was one thing missing still, and Hamida took out her keys and unlocked her safe. The girl cried out when the jewel boxes were opened and their contents revealed.

There were many heavy gold ornaments, but Hamida selected a light and dainty necklace and tiny star-shaped earrings to match. 'Now look,' she said, frowning more than ever and giving the girl a push towards the mirror. The girl looked; she gasped, she said, 'Oh auntie!' and then Hamida could frown no longer but she too laughed out loud and then she was kissing the girl, not once but many times, all over her face and on her neck.

At that moment Roxana came into the room. When she saw her daughter dressed up in her sister's clothes and jewels, she clapped her hands and exclaimed in joyful surprise. Hamida's good mood was gone in a flash, and the first thing she did was shut her jewel boxes and lock them back into her safe. The girl became very quiet and shy again and sat down in a corner and began to take off the earrings and necklace.

'No leave it!' her mother told her. 'It looks pretty.' She held up another kameez from among those on the bed. 'How about this one? The colour would suit her very well.'

'Why did you come?' Hamida asked.

'There has been a telegram. We have to start at once. Brother says our presence is urgently required. This lace veil is very nice. Try it on. Why are you shy? It is your own auntie.'

Hamida began to fold all the clothes back again. She felt terribly sad, there was a weight on her heart. She asked, 'When are you leaving?'

'Tomorrow morning. Husband has gone to the station to buy the tickets. It may be difficult to get seats for all of us together, but let's see.'

'You're *all* going?'

'Of course.' She told the girl, 'You can pack up your old clothes in some paper that auntie will give you.'

'Khan Sahib has called brother-in-law to come for the Music Conference.'

'It is not possible. He-has to attend my niece's wedding. And you?' she asked. 'When are you leaving?'

Hamida didn't answer but was busy putting her clothes back into her wardrobe.

'He says no?' Roxana asked incredulously. Then she cried out in horror: 'Hai! Hai!'

'Naturally, it is not possible for me to go,' Hamida said. 'Do you know what sort of people will be coming for this Conference? Have you any idea? All the biggest musicians in the country and many from abroad also will be travelling all the way to be present.'

Roxana deftly snatched another kameez from among the pile Hamida was putting away. The girl meanwhile had unhooked the earrings and necklace and silently handed them to her aunt. Hamida could see Roxana in the mirror making frantic faces and gestures at the girl; she could also see that the girl refused to look at her mother but turned her back on her and began to take off Hamida's silk kameez.

Roxana said, 'Come quickly now – there is a lot to be done for the journey. You can keep that on,' she said. 'There is no time to change.'

'Yes keep it on,' Hamida said. The girl gave her aunt a swift look, then put the kameez back on again. She did not thank her but looked down at the ground.

Just as they were going, Hamida said, 'Leave her with me.' She said it in a rush like a person who had flung all pride to the wind.

'She can come to you when we return,' Roxana promised. 'She can stay two-three days if you like . . . You want to stay with auntie, don't you? You love to be with her.' She nudged the girl with her elbow, but the girl didn't say anything, didn't look up, and seemed in a hurry to leave.

When she was alone, Hamida lay down on the bed again. Khan Sahib seemed to be having a grand time with his visitors. She could hear them all shout and laugh. Whenever he spoke, everyone else fell silent to listen to him. When he told some anecdote, they all laughed as loud as they could to show their appreciation. He would be stretched out there like a king among them, one blue satin bolster behind his back, another under his elbow; his eyes would be twinkling, and from time to time he would give a twirl to his moustache. Of course he wouldn't have a moment's thought to spare for his wife alone by herself in the back room. He would also have completely forgotten about the wedding and her desire to go to it. What were her desires or other feelings to him?

She shut her eyes. She tried to recall the sensation of the girl's fingers soothing her headache, but she couldn't. The smell of the eau-de-cologne had also disappeared. All she could smell now was the thickly scented incense that came wafting out of the practice-room. She found she was still holding the jewellery the girl had returned to her. She clutched it tightly so that it cut into her hand; the physical pain this gave her seemed to relieve the pressure on her heart. She raised the jewellery to her eyes, and a few tears dropped on it. She felt so sad, so abandoned to herself, without anyone's love or care.

Khan Sahib was singing a romantic song. Usually of course he sang only in the loftiest classical style, but occasionally, when in a relaxed mood, he liked to please people with something in a lighter vein. Although it was not his speciality – others devoted their whole lives to this genre – there was no one who could do it better than he. He drove people mad with joy. He was doing it now – she could hear their cries, their laughter, and it made him sing even more delicately as if he were testing them as to how much ecstasy they could bear. He sang: 'Today by mistake I smiled – but then I remembered, and now where is that smile? Into what empty depths has it disappeared?' He wasn't Khan Sahib, he was a love-sick woman and he suffered, suffered as only a woman can. How did he know all that – how could he look so deep into a woman's feelings – a man like him with many coarse appetites? It was a wonder to Hamida again and again. She was propped on her elbow now, listening to him, and she was smiling: yes, truly smiling with joy. What things he could make her feel, that fat selfish husband of hers. He sang: 'I sink in the ocean of sorrow. Have pity! Have pity! I drown.'

Desecration

It is more than ten years since Sofia committed suicide in the hotel room in Mohabbatpur. At the time, it was a great local scandal, but now almost no one remembers the incident or the people involved in it. The Raja Sahib died shortly afterwards – people said it was of grief and bitterness – and Bakhtawar Singh was transferred to another district. The present Superintendent of Police is a mild-mannered man who likes to spend his evenings at home playing card games with his teenage daughters.

The hotel in Mohabbatpur no longer exists. It was sold a few months after Sofia was found there, changed hands several times, and was recently pulled down to make room for a new cinema. This will back on to the old cinema, which is still there, still playing ancient Bombay talkies. The Raja Sahib's house also no longer exists. It was demolished because the land on which it stood has become very valuable, and has been declared an industrial area. Many factories and workshops have come up in recent years.

When the Raja Sahib had first gone to live there with Sofia, there had been nothing except his own house, with a view over the ruined fort and the barren plain beyond it. In the distance there was a little patch of villagers' fields and, huddled out of sight, the village itself. Inside their big house, the Raja Sahib and Sofia had led very isolated lives. This was by choice – his choice. It was as if he had carried her away to this spot with the express purpose of having her to himself, of feasting on his possession of her.

Although she was much younger than he was – more than thirty years younger – she seemed perfectly happy to live there alone with him. But in any case she was the sort of person who exudes happiness. No one knew where the Raja Sahib had met and married her. No one really knew anything about her, except that she was a Muslim (he, of course, was a Hindu) and that she had had a good convent education in Calcutta – or was it Delhi? She seemed to have no one in the world except the Raja Sahib. It was generally thought that she was partly Afghan, perhaps even with a dash of Russian. She certainly did not look entirely Indian; she had light eyes and broad cheekbones and a broad brow. She was graceful and strong, and at times she laughed a great deal, as if wanting to show off her youth and high spirits, not to mention her magnificent teeth.

Even then, however, during their good years, she suffered from nervous prostrations. At such times the Raja Sahib sat by her bedside in a darkened room. If necessary, he stayed awake all night and held her hand (she clutched his). Sometimes this went on for two or three weeks at a time, but his patience was inexhaustible. It often got very hot in the room; the house stood unprotected on that barren plain, and there was not enough electricity for air-conditioning – hardly even enough for the fan that sluggishly churned the hot air. Her attacks always seemed to occur during the very hot months, especially during the dust storms, when the landscape all around was blotted out by a pall of desert dust and the sky hung down low and yellow.

But when the air cleared, so did her spirits. The heat continued, but she kept all the shutters closed, and sprinkled water and rose essence on the marble floors and on the scented grass mats hung around the verandas. When night fell, the house was opened to allow the cooler air to enter. She and the Raja Sahib would go up on the roof. They lit candles in coloured glass chimneys and read out the Raja Sahib's verse dramas. Around midnight the servants would bring up their dinner, which consisted of many elaborate dishes, and sometimes they would also have a bottle of French wine from the Raja Sahib's cellar. The dark earth below and the sky above were both silver from the reflection of the moon and the incredible number of stars shining up there. It was so silent that the two of them might as well have been alone in the world – which of course was just what the Raja Sahib wanted.

Sitting on the roof of his house, he was certainly monarch of all he surveyed, such as it was. His family had taken possession of this land during a time of great civil strife some hundred and fifty years before. It was only a few barren acres with some impoverished villages thrown in, but the family members had built themselves a little fort and had even assumed a royal title, though they weren't much more than glorified landowners. They lived like all the other landowners, draining what taxes they could out of their tenant villagers. They always needed money for their own living, which became very sophisticated, especially when they began to spend more and more time in the big cities like Bombay, Calcutta, or even London. At the beginning of the century, when the fort became too rough and dilapidated to live in, the house was built. It was in a mixture of Mogul and Gothic styles, with many galleries and high rooms closed in by arched verandas. It had been built at great cost, but until the Raja Sahib moved in with Sofia it had usually remained empty except for the ancestral servants.

On those summer nights on the roof, it was always she who read out the Raja Sahib's plays. He sat and listened and watched her. She wore coloured silks and the family jewellery as an appropriate costume in which to declaim his blank verse (all his plays were in English blank verse). Sometimes she couldn't understand what she was declaiming, and sometimes it was so high-flown that she burst out laughing. He smiled with her and said, 'Go on, go on.' He sat cross-legged smoking his hookah, like any peasant; his clothes were those of a peasant too. Anyone coming up and seeing him would not have thought he was the owner of this house, the husband of Sofia – or indeed the author of all that romantic blank verse. But he was not what he looked or pretended to be. He was a man of considerable education, who had lived for years abroad, had loved the opera and theatre, and had had many cultivated friends. Later – whether through general disgust or a particular disappointment, no one knew – he had turned his back on it all. Now he liked to think of himself as just an ordinary peasant landlord.

The third character in this story, Bakhtawar Singh, really did come from a peasant background. He was an entirely self-made man. Thanks to his efficiency and valour, he had risen rapidly in the service and was now the district Superintendent of Police (known as the S.P.). He had been responsible for the capture of some notorious dacoits. One of these – the uncrowned king of the countryside for almost twenty years – he had himself trapped in a ravine and shot in the head with his revolver, and he had taken the body in his jeep to be displayed outside police headquarters. This deed and others like it had made his name a terror among dacoits and other proscribed criminals. His own men feared him no less, for he was known as a ruthless disciplinarian. But he had a softer side to him. He was terribly fond of women and, wherever he was posted, would find himself a mistress very quickly – usually more than one. He had a wife and family, but they did not play much of a role in his life. All his interests lay elsewhere. His one other interest besides women was Indian classical music, for which he had a very subtle ear.

Once a year the Raja Sahib gave a dinner party for the local gentry. These were officials from the town – the District Magistrate, the Superintendent of Police, the Medical Officer, and the rest – for whom it was the greatest event of the social calendar. The Raja Sahib himself would have gladly dispensed with the occasion, but it was the only company Sofia ever had, apart from himself. For weeks beforehand, she got the servants ready – cajoling rather than commanding them, for she spoke sweetly to everyone always – and had all the china and silver taken out. When the great night came, she sparkled with excitement. The guests were provincial, dreary, unrefined people, but she seemed not to notice that. She made them feel that their presence was a tremendous honour for her. She ran around to serve them and rallied her servants to carry in a succession of dishes and wines. Inspired by her example, the Raja Sahib also rose to the occasion. He was an excellent raconteur and entertained his guests with witty anecdotes and Urdu couplets, and sometimes even with quotations from the English poets. They applauded him not because they always understood what he was saying but because he was the Raja Sahib. They were delighted with the entertainment, and with themselves for having risen high enough in the world to be invited. There were not many women present, for most of the wives were too uneducated to be brought out into society. Those that came sat very still in their best georgette saris and cast furtive glances at their husbands.

After Bakhtawar Singh was posted to the district as the new S.P., he was invited to the Raja Sahib's dinner. He came alone, his wife being unfit for society, and as soon as he entered the house it was obvious that he was a man of superior personality. He had a fine figure, intelligent eyes, and a bristling moustache. He moved with pride, even with some pomp – certainly a man who knew his own value. He was not put out in the least by the grand surroundings but enjoyed everything as if he were entirely accustomed to such entertainment. He also appeared to understand and enjoy his host's anecdotes and poetry. When the Raja Sahib threw in a bit of Shakespeare, he confessed frankly that he could not follow it, but when his host translated and explained, he applauded that too, in real appreciation.

After dinner, there was musical entertainment. The male guests adjourned to the main drawing-room, which was an immensely tall room extending the entire height of the house with a glass rotunda. Here they reclined on Bokhara rugs and leaned against silk bolsters. The ladies had been sent home in motorcars. It would not have been fitting for them to be present, because the musicians were not from a respectable class. Only Sofia was emancipated enough to overlook this restriction. At the first party that Bakhtawar Singh attended, the principal singer was a well-known prostitute from Mohabbatpur. She had a strong, well-trained voice, as well as a handsome presence. Bakhtawar Singh did not take his eyes off her. He sat and swayed his head and exclaimed in rapture at her particularly fine modulations. For his sake, she displayed the most delicate subtleties of her art, laying them out like bait to see if he would respond to them, and he cried out as if in passion or pain. Then she smiled. Sofia was also greatly moved. At one point, she turned to Bakhtawar Singh and said, 'How good she is.' He turned his face to her and nodded, unable to speak for emotion. She was amazed to see tears in his eyes.

Next day she was still thanking about those tears. She told her husband about it, and he said, 'Yes, he liked the music, but he liked the singer, too.'

'What do you mean?' Sofia asked. When the Raja Sahib laughed, she cried, 'Tell me!' and pummelled his chest with her fists.

'I mean,' he said, catching her hands and holding them tight, 'that they will become friends.'

'She will be his mistress?' Sofia asked, opening her eyes wide.

The Raja Sahib laughed with delight. 'Where did you learn such a word? In the convent?'

'How do you know?' she pursued. 'No, you must tell me! Is he that type of man?'

'What type?' he said, teasing her.

The subject intrigued her, and she continued to think about it to herself. As always when she brooded about anything, she became silent and withdrawn and sat for hours on the veranda, staring out over the dusty plain;' Sofia, Sofia, what are you thinking?' the Raja Sahib asked her. She smiled and shook her head. He looked into her strange, light eyes. There was something mysterious about them. Even when she was at her most playful and affectionate, her eyes seemed always to be looking elsewhere, into some different and distant landscape. It was impossible to tell what she was thinking. Perhaps she was not thinking about anything at all, but the distant gaze gave her the appearance of keeping part of herself hidden. This drove the Raja Sahib crazy with love. He wanted to pursue her into the innermost recesses of her nature, and yet at the same time he respected that privacy of hers and left her to herself when she wanted. This happened often; she would sit and brood and also roam around the house and the land in a strange, restless way. In the end, though, she would always come back to him and nestle against his thin, grey-matted chest and seem to be happy there.

For several days after the party, Sofia was in one of these moods. She wandered around the garden, though it was very hot outside. There was practically no shade, because nothing could be made to grow, for lack of water. She idly kicked at pieces of stone, some of which were broken garden statuary. When it got too hot, she did not return to the house but took shelter in the little ruined fort. It was very dark inside there, with narrow underground passages and winding steep stairs, some of which were broken. Sometimes a bat would flit out from some crevice. Sofia was not afraid; the place was familiar to her. But one day, as she sat in one of the narrow stone passages, she heard voices from the roof. She raised her head and listened. Something terrible seemed to be going on up there. Sofia climbed the stairs, steadying herself against the dank wall. Her heart was beating as loudly as those sounds from above. When she got to the top of the stairs and emerged on to the roof, she saw two men. One of them was Bakhtawar Singh. He was beating the other man, who was also a policeman, around the neck and head with his fists. When the man fell, he kicked him and then hauled him up and beat him more. Sofia, gave a cry. Bakhtawar Singh turned his head and saw her. His eyes looked into hers for a moment, and how different they were from that other time when they had been full of tears!

'Get out!' he told the policeman. The man's sobs continued to be heard as he made his way down the stairs. Sofia did not know what to do. Although she wanted to flee, she stood and stared at Bakhtawar Singh. He was quite calm. He put on his khaki bush jacket, careful to adjust the collar and sleeves so as to look smart. He explained that the man had been derelict in his duties and, to escape discipline, had run away and hidden here in the fort. But Bakhtawar Singh had tracked him down. He apologized for trespassing on the Raja Sahib's property and also – here he became courtly and inclined his body towards Sofia – if he had in any way upset and disturbed her. It was not a scene he would have wished a lady to witness.

'There is blood on your hand,' she said.

He looked at it. He made a wry face and then wiped it off. (Was it his own or the other man's?) Again he adjusted his jacket, and he smoothed his hair. 'Do you often come here?' he asked, indicating the stairs and then politely standing aside to let her go first. She started down, and looked back to see if he was following.

'I come every day,' she said.

It was easy for her to go down the dark stairs, which were familiar to her. But he had to grope his way down very carefully, afraid of stumbling. She jumped down the last two steps and waited for him in the open sunlight.

'You come here all alone?' he asked. 'Aren't you afraid?'

'Of what?'

He didn't answer but walked round the back of the fort. Here his horse stood waiting for him, grazing among nettles. He jumped on its back and lightly flicked its flanks, and it cantered off as if joyful to be bearing him.

That night Sofia was very restless, and in the morning her face had the clouded, suffering look that presaged one of her attacks. But when the Raja Sahib wanted to darken the room and make her lie down, she insisted that she was well. She got up, she bathed, she dressed. He was surprised – usually she succumbed very quickly to the first signs of an attack – but now she even said that she wanted to go out. He was very pleased with her and kissed her, as if to reward her for her pluck. But later that day, when she came in again, she did have an attack, and he had to sit by her side and hold her hand and chafe her temples. She wept at his goodness. She kissed the hand that was holding hers. He looked into her strange eyes and said, 'Sofia, Sofia, what are you thinking?' But she quickly covered her eyes, so that he could not look into them. Then he had to soothe her all over again.

Whenever he had tried to make her see a doctor, she had resisted him. She said all she needed was him sitting by her and she would get well by herself, and it did happen that way. But now she told him that she had heard of a very good doctor in Mohabbatpur, who specialized in nervous diseases. The drive was long and wearying, and she insisted that there was no need for the Raja Sahib to go there with her; she could go by herself, with the car and chauffeur. They had a loving quarrel about it, and it was only when she said very well, in that case she would not go at all, would not take medical treatment, that he gave way. So now once a week she was driven to Mohabbatpur by herself.

The Raja Sahib awaited her homecoming impatiently, and the evenings of those days were like celebrations. They sat on the roof, with candles and wine, and she told him about her drive to Mohabbatpur and what the doctor had said. The Raja Sahib usually had a new passage from his latest blank-verse drama for her to read. She would start off well enough, but soon she would be overcome by laughter and have to hide her face behind the pages of his manuscript. And he would smile with her and say, 'Yes, I know, it's all a lot of nonsense.'

'No, no!' she cried. Even though she couldn't understand a good deal of what she was reading, she knew that it expressed his romantic nature and his love for her, which were both as deep as a well. She said, 'It is only I who am stupid and read so badly.' She pulled herself together and went on reading, till made helpless with laughter again.

There was something strange about her laughter. It came bubbling out, as always, as if from an overflow of high spirits, but now her spirits seemed almost too high, almost hysterical. Her husband listened to these new notes and was puzzled by them. He could not make up his mind whether the treatment was doing her good or not.

The Raja Sahib was very kind to his servants, but if any of them did anything to offend him, he was quick to dismiss him. One of his bearers, a man who had been in his employ for twenty years, got drunk one night. This was by no means an unusual occurrence among the servants; the house was in a lonely spot, with no amusements, but there was plenty of cheap liquor available from the village. Usually the servants slept off the effects in their quarters, but this bearer came staggering up on the roof to serve the Raja Sahib and Sofia. There was a scene. He fell and was dragged away by the other servants, but he resisted violently, shouting frightful obscenities, so that Sofia had to put her hands over her ears. The Raja Sahib's face was contorted with fury. The man was dismissed instantly, and when he came back the next day, wretchedly sober, begging pardon and pleading for reinstatement, the Raja Sahib would not hear him. Everyone felt sorry for the man, who had a large family and was, except for these occasional outbreaks, a sober, hardworking person. Sofia felt sorry for him too. He threw himself at her feet, and so did his wife and many children. They all sobbed, and Sofia sobbed with them. She promised to try and prevail upon the Raja Sahib.

She said everything she could – in a rushed, breathless voice, fearing he would not let her finish – and she did not take her eyes off her husband's face as she spoke. She was horrified by what she saw there. The Raja Sahib had very thin lips, and when he was angry he bit them in so tightly that they quite disappeared. He did it now, and he looked so stern and unforgiving that she felt she was not talking to her husband at all but to a gaunt and bitter old man who cared nothing for her. Suddenly she gave a cry, and just as the servant had thrown himself at her feet, so she now prostrated herself at the Raja Sahib's. 'Forgive!' she cried. 'Forgive!' It was as if she were begging forgiveness for everyone who was weak and had sinned. The Raja Sahib tried to make her rise, but she lay flat on the ground, trying over and over again to bring out the word 'Forgive' and not succeeding because of her sobs. At last he managed to help her up; he led her to the bed and waited there till she was calm again. But he was so enraged by the cause of this attack that the servant and his family had to leave immediately.

She always dismissed the car and chauffeur near the doctor's clinic. She gave the chauffeur quite a lot of money – for his food, she said – and told him to meet her in the same place in the evening. She explained that she had to spend the day under observation at the clinic. After the first few times, no explanation was necessary. The chauffeur held out his hand for the money and disappeared until the appointed time. Sofia drew up her sari to veil her face and got into a cycle rickshaw. The place Bakhtawar Singh had chosen for them was a rickety two-storey hotel, with an eating shop downstairs. It was in a very poor, outlying, forgotten part of town, where there was no danger of ever meeting an acquaintance. At first Sofia had been shy about entering the hotel, but as time went on she became bolder. No one ever looked at her or spoke to her. If she was the first to arrive, the key was silently handed to her. She felt secure that the hotel people knew nothing about her, and certainly had never seen her face, which she kept veiled till she was upstairs and the door closed behind her.

In the beginning, he sometimes arrived before her. Then he lay down on the bed, which was the only piece of furniture besides a bucket and a water jug, and was at once asleep. He always slept on his stomach, with one cheek pressed into the pillow. She would come in and stand and look at his dark, muscular, naked back. It had a scar on it, from a knife wound. She lightly ran her finger along this scar, and if that did not wake him, she unwound his loosely tied dhoti, which was all he was wearing. That awakened him immediately.

He was strange to her. That scar on his back was not the only one; there were others on his chest and an ugly long one on his left thigh, sustained during a prison riot. She wanted to know all about his violent encounters, and about his boyhood, his upward struggle, even his low origins. She often asked him about the woman singer at the dinner party. Was it true what the Raja Sahib had said – that he had liked her? Had he sought her out afterwards? He did not deny it, but laughed as at a pleasant memory. Sofia wanted to know more and more. What was it like to be with a woman like that? Had there been others? How many, and what was it like with all of them? He was amused by her curiosity and did not mind satisfying it, often with demonstrations.

Although he had had many women, they had mostly been prostitutes and singers. Sometimes he had had affairs with the wives of other police officers, but these too had been rather coarse, uneducated women. Sofia was his first girl of good family. Her refinement intrigued him. He loved watching her dress, brush her hair, treat her skin with lotions. He liked to watch her eat. But sometimes it seemed as if he deliberately wanted to violate her delicacy. For instance, he knew that she hated the coarse, hot lentils that he loved from his boyhood. He would order great quantities, with coarse bread, and cram the food into his mouth and then into hers, though it burned her palate. As their intimacy progressed, he also made her perform acts that he had learned from prostitutes. It seemed that he could not reach far enough into her, physically and in every other way. Like the Raja Sahib, he was intrigued by the look in her foreign eyes, but he wanted to seek out that mystery and expose it, as all the rest of her was exposed to him.

The fact that she was a Muslim had a strange fascination for him. Here too he differed from the Raja Sahib who, as an educated nobleman, had transcended barriers of caste and community. But for Bakhtawar Singh these were still strong. All sorts of dark superstitions remained embedded in his mind. He questioned her about things he had heard whispered in the narrow Hindu alleys he came from – the rites of circumcision, the eating of unclean flesh, what Muslims did with virgin girls. She laughed, never having heard of such things. But when she assured him that they could not be true, he nodded as if he knew better. He pointed to one of his scars, sustained during a Hindu-Muslim riot that he had suppressed. He had witnessed several such riots and knew the sort of atrocities committed in them. He told her what he had seen Muslim men do to Hindu women. Again she would not believe him. But she begged him not to go on; she put her hands over her ears, pleading with him. But he forced her hands down again and went on telling her, and laughed at her reaction. 'That's what they did,' he assured her. '*Your* brothers. It's all true.' And then he struck her, playfully but quite hard, with the fiat of his hand.

All week, every week, she waited for her day in Mohabbatpur to come round. She was restless and she began to make trips into the near-by town. It was the usual type of district town, with two cinemas, a jail, a church, temples and mosques, with a Civil Lines, where the government officers lived. Sofia now began to come here to visit the officers' wives whom she had been content to see just once a year at her dinner party. Now she sought them out frequently. She played with their children and designed flower patterns for them to embroider. All the time her thoughts were elsewhere; she was waiting for it to be time to leave. Then, with hurried farewells, promises to come again soon, she climbed into her car and sat back. She told the chauffeur – the same man who took her to Mohabbatpur every week – to drive her through the Police Lines. First there were the policemen's barracks – a row of hutments, where men in vests and shorts could be seen oiling their beards and winding their turbans; they looked up in astonishment from these tasks as her saloon car drove past. She leaned back so as not to be seen, but when they had driven beyond the barracks and had reached the Police Headquarters, she looked eagerly out of the window again. Every time she hoped to get a glimpse of him, but it never happened; the car drove through and she did not dare to have it slow down. But there was one further treat in store, for beyond the offices were the residential houses of the police officers – the Assistant Deputy S.P., the Deputy S.P., the S.P.

One day, she leaned forward and said to the chauffeur, 'Turn in.'

'In here?'

'Yes, yes!' she cried, mad with excitement.

It had been a sudden impulse – she had intended simply to drive past his house, as usual – but now she could not turn back, she had to see. She got out. It was an old house, built in the times of the British for their own S.P., and now evidently inhabited by people who did not know how to look after such a place. A cow was tethered to a tree on what had once been a front lawn; the veranda was unswept and empty except for some broken crates. The house too was practically unfurnished. Sofia wandered through the derelict rooms, and it was only when she had penetrated to the inner courtyard that the life of the house began. Here there were children and noise and cooking smells. A woman came out of the kitchen and stared at her. She had a small child riding on her hip; she was perspiring, perhaps from the cooking fire, and a few strands of hair stuck to her forehead.

She wore a plain and rather dirty cotton sari. She might have been his servant rather than his wife. She looked older than he did, tired and worn out. When Sofia asked whether this was the house of the Deputy S.P., she shook her head wearily, without a smile. She told one of her children to point out the right house, and turned back into her kitchen with no further curiosity. A child began to cry.

At their next meeting, Sofia told Bakhtawar Singh what she had done. He was surprised and not angry, as she had feared, but amused. He could not understand her motives, but he did not puzzle himself about them. He was feeling terribly sleepy; he said he had been up all night (he didn't say why). It was stifling in the hotel room, and perspiration ran down his naked chest and back. It was also very noisy, for the room faced on to an inner yard, which was bounded on its opposite side by a cinema. From noon onward the entire courtyard boomed with the ancient sound track – it was a very poor cinema and could afford to play only very old films – filling their room with Bombay dialogue and music. Bakhtawar Singh seemed not to care about the heat or the noise. He slept through both. He always slept when he was tired; nothing could disturb him. It astonished Sofia, and so did his imperviousness to their surroundings – the horribly shabby room and smell of cheap oil frying from the eating shop downstairs. But now, after seeing his home. Sofia understood that he was used to comfortless surroundings; and she felt so sorry for him that she began to kiss him tenderly while he slept, as if wishing to make up to him for all his deprivations. He woke up and looked at her in surprise as she cried out, 'Oh, my poor darling!'

'Why?' he asked, not feeling poor at all.

She began for the first time to question him about his marriage. But he shrugged, bored by the subject. It was a marriage like every other, arranged by their two families when he and his wife were very young. It was all right; they had children – sons as well as daughters. His wife had plenty to do, he presumed she was content – and why shouldn't she be? She had a good house to live in, sufficient money for her household expenses, and respect as the wife of the S.P. He laughed briefly. Yes, indeed, if she had anything to complain of he would like to know what it was. Sofia agreed with him. She even became indignant, thinking of his wife who had all these benefits and did not even care to keep a nice home for him. And not just his home – what about his wife herself? When she thought of that bedraggled figure, more a servant than a wife, Sofia's indignation rose – and with it her tender pity for him, so that again she embraced him and even spilled a few hot tears, which fell on to his naked chest and made him laugh with surprise.

A year passed, and it was again time for the Raja Sahib's annual party. As always, Sofia was terribly excited and began her preparations weeks beforehand. Only this time her excitement reached such a pitch that the Raja Sahib was worried. He tried to joke her out of it; he asked her whom was she expecting, what terribly important guest. Had she invited the President of India, or perhaps the King of Afghanistan 'Yes, yes, the King of Afghanistan!' she cried, laughing but with that note of hysteria he always found so disturbing. Also she lost her temper for the first time with a servant; it was for nothing, for some trifle, and afterwards she was so contrite that she could not do enough to make it up to the man.

The party was, as usual, a great success. The Raja Sahib made everyone laugh with his anecdotes, and Bakhtawar Singh also told some stories, which everyone liked. The same singer from Mohabbatpur had been called, and she entertained with the same skill. And again – Sofia watched him – Bakhtawar Singh wept with emotion, She was deeply touched; he was manly to the point of violence (after all, he *was* a policeman), and yet what softness and delicacy there were in him. She revelled in the richness of his nature. The Raja Sahib must have been watching him too, because later, after the party, he told Sofia, 'Our friend enjoyed the musical entertainment again this year.'

'Of course,' Sofia said gravely. 'She is a very fine singer.'

The Raja Sahib said nothing, but there was something in his silence that told her he was having his own thoughts.

'If not,' she said, as if he had contradicted her, 'then why did you call for her again this year?'

'But of course,' he said. 'She is very fine.' And he chuckled to himself.

Then Sofia lost her temper with him – suddenly, violently, just as she had with the servant. The Raja Sahib was struck dumb with amazement, but the next moment he began to blame himself. He felt he had offended her with his insinuation, and he kissed her hands to beg her forgiveness. Her convent-bred delicacy amused him, but he adored it too.

She felt she could not wait for her day in Mohabbatpur to come round. The next morning, she called the chauffeur and gave him a note to deliver to the S.P. in his office. She had a special expressionless way of giving orders to the chauffeur, and he a special expressionless way of receiving them. She waited in the fort for Bakhtawar Singh to appear in answer to her summons, but the only person who came was the chauffeur, with her note back again. He explained that he had been unable to find the S.P., who had not been in his office. Sofia felt a terrible rage rising inside her, and she had to struggle with herself not to vent it on the chauffeur. When the man had gone, she sank down against the stone wall and hid her face in her hands. She did not know what was happening to her. It was not only that her whole life had changed; she herself had changed and had become a different person, with emotions that were completely unfamiliar to her.

Unfortunately, when their day in Mohabbatpur at last came around, Bakhtawar Singh was late (this happened frequently now). She had to wait for him in the hot little room. The cinema show had started, and the usual dialogue and songs came from the defective sound track, echoing through courtyard and hotel. Tormented by this noise, by the heat, and by her own thoughts, Sofia was now sure that he was with the singer. Probably he was enjoying himself so much that he had forgotten all about her and would not come.

But he did come, though two hours late. He was astonished by the way she clung to him, crying and laughing and trembling all over. He liked it, and kissed her in return. Just then the sound track burst into song. It was an old favourite – a song that had been on the lips of millions; everyone knew it and adored it. Bakhtawar Singh recognized it immediately and began to sing, '*O my heart, all he has left you is a splinter of himself to make you bleed!*' She drew away from him and saw him smiling with pleasure under his moustache as he sang. She cried out, 'Oh, you pig!'

It was like a blow in the face. He stopped singing immediately. The song continued on the sound track. They, looked at each other. She put her hand to her mouth with fear – fear of the depths within her from which that word had arisen (never, never in her life had she uttered or thought such abuse), and fear of the consequences.

But after that moment's stunned silence all he did was laugh. He took off his bush jacket and threw himself on the bed. 'What is the matter with you?' he asked. 'What happened?'

'Oh I don't know. I think it must be the heat.' She paused. 'And waiting for you,' she added, but in a voice so low she was not sure he had heard.

She lay down next to him. He said nothing more. The incident and her word of abuse seemed wiped out of his mind completely. She was so grateful for this that she too said nothing, asked no questions. She was content to forget her suspicions – or at least to keep them to herself and bear with them as best she could.

That night she had a dream. She dreamed everything was as it had been in the first years of her marriage, and she and the Raja Sahib as happy as they had been then. But then one night – they were together on the roof, by candle- and moonlight – he was stung by some insect that came flying out of the food they were eating. At first they took no notice, but the swelling got worse and worse, and by morning he was tossing in agony. His entire body was discoloured; he had become almost unrecognizable. There were several people around his bed, and one of them took Sofia aside and told her that the Raja Sahib would be dead within an hour. Sofia screamed out loud, but the next moment she woke up, for the Raja Sahib had turned on the light and was holding her in his arms. Yes, that very same Raja Sahib about whom she had just been dreaming, only he was not discoloured, not dying, but as he was always – her own husband, with grey-stubbled cheeks and sunken lips. She looked into his face for a moment and, fully awake now, she said, 'It's all right. I had a nightmare.' She tried to laugh it off. When he wanted to comfort her, she said again, 'It's all right,' with the same laugh and trying to keep the irritation out of her voice. 'Go to sleep,' she told him, and pretending to do so herself, she turned on her side away from him.

She continued to be haunted by the thought of the singer. Then she thought, if with one, why not with many? She herself saw him for only those few hours a week. She did not know how he spent the rest of his time, but she was sure he did not spend much of it in his own home. It had had the look of a place whose master was mostly absent. And how could it be otherwise? Sofia thought of his wife – her neglected appearance, her air of utter weariness. Bakhtawar Singh could not be expected to waste himself there. But where did he go? In between their weekly meetings there was much time for him to go to many places, and much time for her to brood.

She got into the habit of summoning the chauffeur more frequently to take her into town. The ladies in the Civil Lines were always pleased to see her, and now she found more to talk about with them, for she had begun to take an interest in local gossip. They were experts on this, and were eager to tell her that the Doctor beat his wife, the Magistrate took bribes, and the Deputy S.P. had venereal disease. And the S.P.? Sofia asked, busy threading an embroidery needle. Here they clapped their hands over their mouths and rolled their eyes around, as if at something too terrible, too scandalous to tell. Was he, Sofia asked – dropping the needle, so that she had to bend down to pick it up again – was he known to be an . . . adventurous person? 'Oh, Oh! Oh!' they cried, and then they laughed because where to start, where to stop, telling of *his* adventures?

Sofia decided that it was her fault. It was his wife's fault first, of course, but now it was hers too. She had to arrange to be with him more often. Her first step was to tell the Raja Sahib that the doctor said she would have to attend the clinic several times a week. The Raja Sahib agreed at once. She felt so grateful that she was ready to give him more details, but he cut her short. He said that of course they must follow the doctor's advice, whatever it was. But the way he spoke – in a flat, resigned voice – disturbed her, so that she looked at him more attentively than she had for some time past. It struck her that he did not look well. Was he ill? Or was it only old age? He did look old, and emaciated too, she noticed, with his skinny, wrinkled neck. She felt very sorry for him and put out her hand to touch his cheek. She was amazed by his response. He seemed to tremble at her touch, and the expression on his face was transformed. She took him in her arms. He *was* trembling. 'Are you well?' she whispered to him anxiously.

'Oh yes!' he said in a joyful voice 'Very, very well.'

She continued to hold him. She said, 'Why aren't you writing any dramas for me these days?'

'I will write,' he said. 'As many as you like.' And then he clung to her, as if afraid to be let go from her embrace.

But when she told Bakhtawar Singh that they could now meet more frequently, he said it would be difficult for him. Of course he wanted to, he said – and how much! Here he turned to her and with sparkling eyes quoted a line of verse which said that if all the drops of water in the sea were hours of the day that he could spend with her, still they would not be sufficient for him. 'But . . . ' he added regretfully.

'Yes?' she asked, in a voice she tried to keep calm.

'Sh-h-h – Listen,' he said, and put his hand over her mouth.

There was an old man saying the Muhammedan prayers in the next room. The hotel had only two rooms, one facing the courtyard and the other the street. This latter was usually empty during the day – though not at night – but today there was someone in it. The wall was very thin, and they could clearly hear the murmur of his prayers and even the sound of his forehead striking the ground.

'What is he saying?' Bakhtawar Singh whispered.

'I don't know,' she said. 'The usual – *la illaha il lallah* . . . I don't know.'

'You don't know your own prayers?' Bakhtawar Singh said, truly shocked.

She said, 'I could come every Monday, Wednesday, and Friday.' She tried to make her voice tempting, but instead it came out shy.

'You do it,' he said suddenly.

'Do what?'

'Like he's doing,' he said, jerking his head towards the other room, where the old man was. 'Why not?' he urged her. He seemed to want it terribly.

She laughed nervously. 'You need a prayer carpet. And you must cover your head.' (They were both stark naked.)

'Do it like that. Go on,' he wheedled. 'Do it.'

She laughed again, pretending it was a joke. She knelt naked on the floor and began to pray the way the old man was praying in the next room, knocking her forehead on the ground. Bakhtawar Singh urged her on, watching her with tremendous pleasure from the bed. Somehow the words came back to her and she said them in chorus with the old man next door. After a while, Bakhtawar Singh got off the bed and joined her on the floor and mounted her from behind. He wouldn't let her stop praying, though. 'Go on,' he said, and how he laughed as she went on. Never had he had such enjoyment out of her as on that day.

But he still wouldn't agree to meet her more than once a week. Later, when she tried ever so gently to insist, he became playful and said she didn't know that he was a very busy policeman. Busy with what, she asked, also trying to be playful. He laughed enormously at that and was very loving, as if to repay her for her good joke. But then after a while he grew more serious and said, 'Listen – it's better not to drive so often through Police Lines.'

'Why not?' Driving past his office after her visits to the ladies in the Civil Lines was still the highlight of her expeditions into town.

He shrugged. 'They are beginning to talk.'

'Who?'

'Everyone.' He shrugged again. It was only her he was warning. People talked enough about him anyway; let them have one more thing. What did he care?

'Oh nonsense,' she said. But she could not help recollecting that the last few times all the policemen outside their hutments seemed to have been waiting for her car. They had cheered her as she drove past. She had wondered at the time what it meant but had soon put it out of her mind. She did that now too; she couldn't waste her few hours with Bakhtawar Singh thinking about trivial matters.

But she remembered his warning the next time she went to visit the ladies in the Civil Lines. She wasn't sure then whether it was her imagination or whether there really was something different in the way they were with her. Sometimes she thought she saw them turn aside, as if to suppress a smile, or exchange looks with each other that she was not supposed to see. And when the gossip turned to the S.P., they made very straight faces, like people who know more than they are prepared to show. Sofia decided that it was her imagination; even if it wasn't, she could not worry about it. Later, when she drove through the Police Lines, her car was cheered again by the men in underwear lounging outside their quarters, but she didn't trouble herself much about that either. There were so many other things on her mind. That day she instructed the chauffeur to take her to the S.P.'s residence again, but at the last moment – he had already turned into the gate and now had to reverse – she changed her mind. She did not want to see his wife again; it was almost as if she were afraid. Besides, there was no need for it. The moment she saw the house, she realized that she had never ceased to think of that sad, bedraggled woman inside. Indeed, as time passed the vision had not dimmed but had become clearer. She found also that her feelings towards this unknown woman had changed completely, so that, far from thinking about her with scorn, she now had such pity for her that her heart ached as sharply as if it were for herself.

Sofia had not known that one's heart could literally, physically ache. But now that it had begun it never stopped; it was something she was learning to live with, the way a patient learns to live with his disease. And moreover, like the patient, she was aware that this was only the beginning and that her disease would get worse and pass through many stages before it was finished with her. From week to week she lived only for her day in Mohabbatpur, as if that were the only time when she could get some temporary relief from pain. She did not notice that, on the contrary, it was on that day that her condition worsened and passed into a more acute stage, especially when he came late, or was absent-minded, or – and this was beginning to happen too – failed to turn up altogether. Then, when she was driven back home, the pain in her heart was so great that she had to hold her hand there. It seemed to her that if only there were someone, one other living soul, she could tell about it, she might get some relief. Gazing at the chauffeur's stolid, impassive back, she realized that he was now the person who was closest to her. It was as if she had confided in him, without words. She only told him where she wanted to go, and he went there. He told her when he needed money, and she gave it to him. She had also arranged for several increments in his salary.

The Raja Sahib had written a new drama for her. Poor Raja Sahib! He was always there, and she was always with him, but she never thought about him. If her eyes fell on him, either she did not see or, if she did, she postponed consideration of it until some other time. She was aware that there was something wrong with him, but he did not speak of it, and she was grateful to him for not obtruding his own troubles. But when he told her about the new drama he wanted her to read aloud, she was glad to oblige him. She ordered a marvellous meal for that night and had a bottle of wine put on ice. She dressed herself in one of his grandmother's saris, of a gold so heavy that it was difficult to carry. The candles in blue glass chimneys were lit on the roof. She read out his drama with all the expression she had been taught at her convent to put into poetry readings. As usual she didn't understand a good deal of what she was reading, but she did notice that there was something different about his verses. There was one line that read 'Oh, if thou didst but know what it is like to live in hell the way I do!' It struck her so much that she had to stop reading. She looked across at the Raja Sahib; his face was rather ghostly in the blue candlelight.

'Go on,' he said, giving her that gentle, self-deprecating smile he always had for her when she was reading his dramas.

But she could not go on. She thought, what does he know about that, about living in hell? But as she went on looking at him and he went on smiling at her, she longed to tell him what it *was* like. 'What is it, Sofia? What are you thinking?'

There had never been anyone in the world who looked into her eyes the way he did, with such love but at the same time with a tender respect that would not reach farther into her than was permissible between two human beings. And it was because she was afraid of changing that look that she did not speak. What if he should turn aside from her, the way he had when she had asked forgiveness for the drunken servant?

'Sofia, Sofia, what are you thinking?'

She smiled and shook her head and, with an effort, went on reading. She saw that she could not tell him but would have to go on bearing it by herself for as long as possible, though she was not sure how much longer that could be.

Plain Tales from the Hills
Rudyard Kipling. Foreword by Griff Rhys Jones
'These stories are the best account of the nature of the Victorian Raj ever written.' Griff Rhys Jones writes of these penetratingly observed stories of not only the British in India but their Indian charges at the high noon of Empire as told by the young reporter Kipling at the outset of his writing career.

The Incredulity of Father Brown
GK Chesterton. Foreword by Ann Widdecombe
Sensation followed the sudden death of Chesterton's priestly sleuth; as well it might, when he sat up in his coffin and applied a little quiet detachment to his situation. But then sensation was never absent from any of the cases Father Brown so self-effacingly tackled.

On Horseback and Other Stories
Guy de Maupassant. Foreword by Anthony Guise
In his stories of Normandy and Brittany in the 1870s de Maupassant found the perfect vehicle for his wondrous gift of inspecting the truth of men (and women), truth made perennial by the infallible sharpness of his observation and his wit.

Tales of Sexual Desire
Leo Tolstoy. *Foreword by Richard Godwin*
Together these three stories – The Kreutzer Sonata, The Devil and Father Sergius – give us a picture of Man caught by the imperiousness of obsessive concupiscence and sexual challenge, such as the sage himself was no stranger to.
Forthcoming